A FAIRER
TOMORROW

Praise for Kathleen Knowles

A Spark of Heavenly Fire

"[T]his thoroughly researched, well-nuanced tale of what happens after happy ever after is unusual, touching, and sweet in its portrayal of a good marriage during a bad time."
—*Publishers Weekly*

Somewhere Along the Way

"This book affected me deeply. For me there were two stories, of course the main one of Max and her life, her choices and her future but also one of AIDS and is awful affect it had on a generation. This is a time in history we should never forget. The rawness will touch you and make you think."—*Rainbow Literary Society*

Trade Secrets

"Fascinating and intense!…Kathleen did a great job of focusing on how corrupt morals can become in professional settings where money is concerned and business is at the heart of the decisions rather than the consumer. An interesting addition to Kathleen's unique catalogue of books, and I look forward to reading more in future."—*LesBiReviewed*

Forsaking All Others

"Jules and Sylvia, although at first it looks as if they'll never make it, do reconnect to see if they can smooth things out. It is more than a delightful journey to watch Jules and Sylvia's relationship take form and handle some extremely niggly issues. I was completely captivated by the journey along with all the history about California, Proposition 8, and marriage equality issues. In addition, I was totally absorbed by this moving, very spirited, but bumpy trek focused around Jules and Sylvia, but involving so many more people and issues. Extremely satisfying."—*Rainbow Book Reviews*

Taking Sides

"I'm not sure I've ever seen a more different set of characters in an opposites attract pairing. And yet, Gail and Trevor very obviously care for each other, even when they think they're only having a fling. The story moves along at a good pace and keeps things interesting even when the characters are in the thick of politics. If you're a fan of romance and politics, you'll want to check out *Taking Sides*."—*Lesbian Review*

Awake Unto Me

"Knowles has a deep familiarity with the history of San Francisco and weaves the events and geography of the place deeply into the story. *Awake Unto Me* does a good job at providing a window into a variety of women's lives in historic San Francisco, for those interested in exploring history through women-centered lives. There's a richness to the setting that goes beyond a straightforward girl-meets-girl story."—*Lesbian Review*

"I really enjoyed the focus on character development, the painstaking historical details, and the slow romantic buildup in *Awake Unto Me*. This debut novel is well-crafted and manages to avoid lesbian romance clichés…This is a sweet historical romance that stays true to a unique setting and interesting time period."—*SmexyBooks*

"*Awake Unto Me* does a good job at providing a window into a variety of women's lives in historic San Francisco, for those interested in exploring history through women-centered lives."—*Alpennia*

By the Author

Awake Unto Me

Forsaking All Others

A Spark of Heavenly Fire

Warm November

Two Souls

Taking Sides

The Last Time I Saw Her

Somewhere Along the Way

Trade Secrets

A Fairer Tomorrow

Visit us at www.boldstrokesbooks.com

A Fairer Tomorrow

by

Kathleen Knowles

2021

A FAIRER TOMORROW

ISBN 13: 978-1-63555-874-6

This Trade Paperback Original Is Published By
Bold Strokes Books, Inc.
P.O. Box 249
Valley Falls, NY 12185

First Edition: December 2021

Credits
Editor: Shelley Thrasher
Production Design: Stacia Seaman
Cover Design by Tammy Seidick

Acknowledgments

I received help from Isaac Felmann at the GLBT Historical Archives, whose collections include all the oral histories collected for Allan Berube's essential book *Coming Out Under Fire*. Nan Boyd's book *Wide Open Town* covers the history of San Francisco's LGBT community from the Gold Rush through the Sixties, and the oral histories she collected are also in the Archives. For background on the African American experience in WWII, I used Gretchen Lemke Santangelo's work *Abiding Courage: African American Migrant Women and the East Bay Community*. The full list of books I consulted for historical background is too long to list here, but I recommend any reader who wants to know more about our history to check out the multiple sources available.

A special thanks goes to BSB author Ann Shade, who graciously gave the manuscript a sensitivity review to ensure I got my characters right.

Thanks as always to my editor Shelley Thrasher and the team at BSB.

For Jeanette

CHAPTER ONE

Treasure Island Naval Station Training and Distribution Center
San Francisco
August 1945

In her camouflage-roof bus, Gerry Stern drove the blue-route commuter circuit on Treasure Island. TI was such an enormous naval base, the size of a middling city, it needed its own bus service. Gerry had been a member of the WAVES, short for Women Accepted for Volunteer Emergency Service, for one and one-half years, and she felt like a veteran. She also loved her job, both the location and the work itself.

As she steered around the curve of the northern end of the island. she could see, in the distance, the almost brand-new Golden Gate Bridge, which guarded the entrance to the San Francisco Bay. Gerry knew, as did all the seamen on Treasure Island, that part of their mission was making sure the Japanese didn't attack the West Coast. Treasure Island was the number-one target.

Treasure Island felt different today. A lot of rumors were in the air saying the Japanese were about to surrender. Gerry would be one of the first to know if this happened because her best friend, Petty Officer Shirley "Woody" Woodward, worked in the communication division. Woody would tell her straight off as soon as she heard any news. That was how Gerry had found out FDR had died a few months before and the new US president would be Harry Truman. She liked knowing things before anyone else.

Gerry returned to the bus depot for a break and decided to call Woody to see if she'd heard any news.

"Hi, Ger. It's a zoo here, but I'm glad you called. The scuttlebutt is the Japs are going to make it official tomorrow. Don't tell anyone else, but we have to start making plans. I heard from Jimmy we're all going to get shore leave, and I want to go to Mona's."

Jimmy was also one of her best pals, and he worked in the base commander's office. He was an administration rating, a secretary low on the totem pole, but he knew everything and gladly told them whatever he knew. The navy tended to shove boys like Jimmy, an "artistic" type, into administrative jobs. Jimmy said with a wink, "I'm not sorry I didn't get shipped off to the South Pacific. I get seasick anyhow."

"Roger," Gerry had said.

Jimmy, Gerry, and Woody stuck together at work, and they went out to San Francisco whenever they could. If it was really going to be the end of the war, there would be a huge party in their favorite night spots.

Back on the bus, Gerry picked up and dropped off sailor boys across the giant base.

They called out to her, "Stern! What do you know? What do you say? Is the war over? I got to go back to my girl in___." Fill in the blank with the name of a city anywhere in the US. Gerry had met sailors from the Bronx in New York to the Arizona desert and everywhere in between.

"Don't know. I'll hear when I hear, just like you will," she replied.

Cleaned up and in the uniform of the day, she went over to the enlisted men's club to kill time before chow. It was a nice place because the brass wanted the troops to stick around base mostly, so it had to provide them with something to do. The club had Ping-Pong tables, a piano and dance floor and a stage, and plenty of cushy sofas and armchairs. It wasn't as fancy as the officers' club, but it was all right.

Gerry found a newspaper and a seat with a table and ashtray, so she could smoke and settle in to wait for Woody. If her folks knew she smoked, they'd have a fit. Never mind what would happen if they ever found out what else she liked to do in her spare time.

Jimmy tapped her shoulder and made her look around, but he was already in front of her. Then he laughed. Gerry got it wrong every time, and Jimmy laughed. Every time.

"Greetings, Seaman Stern."

"Cut it out, Jimmy, you dolt."

"I love calling you Seaman. It's not wrong," Jimmy whispered.

"It's sure as shit wrong, but you're not going to make me mad today." She mock-glared at him.

She added, "Pretty soon, I might not be Seaman Stern anymore. I'll go back to being regular ole Miss Stern. What if the war *does* end, Jimmy? What then?"

He flopped down in the chair catty-corner to hers and lit a cigarette.

"Don't know, don't care. I might stay here." He was from Omaha, Nebraska, as indicated by his flat drawl. Woody was one of the few native San Franciscans Gerry knew. She'd grown up in the Sunset District of San Francisco.

"I don't want to go back to Fresno either." Fresno was an overgrown cow town, and Gerry hated it. She didn't think she could stand it after living in San Francisco for almost two years.

Jimmy squinted through the smoke. "Then what are you going to do?"

"I want to stay in the navy. Right here."

He shook his leg up and down. "You like the uniform, hey?"

"That's not the only reason."

"Hi, kids." It was Woody. She pulled over another chair and flopped down on it.

"What's new?" Gerry asked. Woody arranged herself unhurriedly in her chair. She was on the tall side and enjoyed showing off her legs.

"It's happened, but you can't breathe a word. It's not official until tomorrow. We have to make plans. Jimmy, find out about our shore leave."

"Aye, aye, sir." He saluted, and she glared at him.

More and more people were coming into the club, so they scooted their chairs together for more privacy.

"Gladys is playing at Mona's," Woody said as though no further discussion was needed. She meant Gladys Bentley, the piano player and singer from LA.

"You want to go to the Top of the Mark first? I think George will want to meet me there."

"Yeppers. But we'll still go to Mona's later," Woody said. Gerry didn't mind that Woody made the decisions on what they would do for shore leave.

"Then it's settled."

❖

The next morning, the loudspeaker blared over the entire base. "President Truman has announced the Japanese have unconditionally surrendered. The war is over."

The sailors poured out of their barracks yelling and screaming. Gerry didn't mind that several of them in their exuberance kissed her. It meant nothing; they were just happy. She was happy too, so she even kissed them back.

Woody appeared out of the throng, and they hugged.

"It's over. We made it through, kid," Woody grinned as she stood back.

❖

They stood at the bar of the Mark Hopkins hotel on Nob Hill. When they went out in San Francisco, they often went there first, so Jimmy could discreetly mingle with other single gentlemen. It was a classy joint, and the three of them could speak softly and sip cocktails with an excellent live band in the background. Woody and Gerry would dance with Jimmy, and later with George. It had been just the three of them until he'd met George the year before.

"This beats the dives in the Tenderloin and down on Market Street," Jimmy always said.

Standing by the Mark's elegant bar, Woody made the first toast. "Here's to the war being over. We don't have to worry about the Japs slinking in under the Golden Gate Bridge ever again."

Jimmy said, "Here's to the navy for getting me to San Francisco so I could meet George. And where the heck is he, anyhow?"

Gerry laughed. "I have to thank the Japs."

Her friends looked at her curiously. "But why?"

Gerry twirled her cocktail glass, staring at the liquid. "Well. If it wasn't for them starting the war and the navy recruiting me and sending me here, I'd still be in poky old Fresno, slopping hogs instead of drinking in a classy place like this with my two pals."

Jimmy and Woody laughed, and then they all clinked glasses and tossed back their drinks.

"Here you are," Jimmy said as George walked over to them. He and Jimmy locked gazes and nodded. If Jimmy so much as touched George's arm, the bartender would reprimand him. They had to be discreet so the Top of the Mark wouldn't become another target of the shore patrol.

Gerry and Woody often started out their night at the Top of the Mark with Jimmy and George before they headed a few blocks away to Mona's 440 Club on Broadway in North Beach.

"It's getting kind of lively out here," Woody said to Gerry as they walked down Nob Hill and then across Broadway to Mona's. It was true. Crowds of men in sailor suits and army uniforms wandered up and down the streets. The sailors and soldiers looked as though they didn't know what to do with themselves. Some carried bottles of liquor, and they yelled and slapped each other on the back.

"War's over, and I don't have to go nowhere and get killed," a young guy shouted.

"Oh, you know what?" Woody grabbed Gerry's arm. "These aren't the regulars. They're the recruits. You know—the new guys."

"Yeah. I saw that one guy who just yelled, I think, on the bus yesterday."

"They never even set foot on a ship, never mind going out to one of the theaters. They got lucky." She meant the war had passed them by, and they were celebrating their lucky escapes.

Gerry just shook her head. "I'm glad for them, but I don't want to be around later when they get good and drunk."

"Then let's go. I want us to get a good seat anyway, near the front."

Woody grinned and grabbed Gerry's arm as they walked down the street. They were catcalled by the knots of soldiers and sailors, but they forged on as fast as they could through Chinatown to Mona's.

There were other gay bars they liked to go to, but Mona's 440 was their favorite. The entertainment was the best there. The banner over the door read "Gladys Bentley Appearing Now," and the placard by the door announced, "The Brown Bomber of Sophisticated Song" next to a photo of Gladys in a white tuxedo.

It was already almost filled because Gladys Bentley was popular and only showed up in San Francisco once in a while.

"Gladys draws a crowd, that's a fact," Woody said as they waited in line to get in.

Mona's was a big place, nicely laid out and decorated. The "show room" was huge, and they found a table near the middle, where the stage wasn't too close but not too far. Since, for safety reasons, Woody and Gerry never went out in uniform, they couldn't receive any perks for being service people. No one bought them drinks or showed them to the best tables, but it was worth it. The MPs didn't bother with women, but they would have been targets if they were in uniform. If Jimmy got caught out of uniform or in an off-limits bar, he would be severely punished.

They settled themselves at a table, and one of the boyish waitresses took their orders. Woody was on a rum-and-Coke kick ever since she'd fallen in love with the Andrews Sisters. Gerry liked beer. A couple of beers and she was set for the night.

They spotted a few acquaintances here and there and waved at them. Gerry sighed. She wanted a girlfriend, but it seemed like there were always practical obstacles. She couldn't stomach the idea of necking with someone in the toilet, a method Woody often employed either at the base or in one of the bars.

Their status as WAVES was problematic. They had no homes to speak of, because they lived in barracks. If she got an overnight pass, she could stay in a hotel in the City, but first she had to have a girl to spend the night *with*. And she was picky. Gerry had an idea of who and what she was looking for, but she had standards.

A few tables over, a couple of women seated themselves, but they made Gerry look twice because, one, she'd never seen women like them in Mona's 440, and, two, they were beautiful, three, they were Negroes. She nudged Woody and pointed discreetly.

Woody, ever the jaded sophisticate, yawned. "So? Sometimes Negroes come to see Gladys. What's the big deal?"

"It's not. I didn't mean it was." Gerry was stung. "I'm just saying I've never seen these two. The shorter one, wow."

"Yep. If you go for that kind of thing. I had a friend in boot from New York who used to talk about Harlem and…"

Gerry let Woody's talk drift over her as she tried as discreetly as possible to get a better look at the two strangers.

The taller one seemed to be explaining things to the shorter girl. They both were nicely dressed, wearing patterned dresses with their black hair styled in bobs. Gerry was taken by the smaller girl's expression. She listened attentively to her companion and nodded now and then but said almost nothing. She took in the room, the other patrons of Mona's, and her companion as though she was collecting information like a newspaper reporter. She was small-boned, with a delicate russet skin color. The way she scrutinized her environment, Gerry doubted if much would get by her. She wondered if she was making judgments or simply absorbing what she saw and heard. She wondered if they were gay. That wasn't necessarily a given for all Mona's patrons. Gerry wanted to go over and say "hi" to them and talk to them so she could try to figure out their stories. Were they a couple? Friends? Gerry, mesmerized by the shorter girl of the two, really hoped it was the second.

Then the MC came out on the stage. She was a butch girl in a tailored suit, and the crowd started to clap and yell.

"Welcome to Mona's 440 Club, where girls will be boys." She winked, and the already well-oiled customers whistled and shouted.

"We're honored to present tonight, in her only appearance in San Francisco, straight from the Joaquin Room in Los Angeles, house favorite and America's greatest sepia piano artist—Gladys Bentley."

Out walked Gladys, clad in impeccable white tails, tailored to fit her considerable size. She waved and beamed, then sat herself at the grand piano. Gerry recognized the opening chords of "Worried Blues."

She tried to pay attention to Gladys, but her eyes always were drawn to the two women sitting a couple of tables away.

Woody whispered, "They might be straight, ya know."

"I know." Gerry hoped that wasn't true and longed to find a way to talk to them, especially the smaller one.

Gladys moved on to sing "Red Beans and Rice," then "In the Mood." Her deep voice made the words of the already seductive tune sound even more inviting. She stopped playing to chatter a bit and make eye contact with the audience. She walked off the stage, carrying the microphone with her, and went up to the table nearest the stage. The two seated there looked like Mr. and Mrs. Midwestern Tourist. They were bug-eyed, staring at Gladys like she was some sort of ghost.

"How you doin'?" she asked, and they stuttered out they were fine, thanks. She asked them where they were from, how long they were staying, and how they liked San Francisco. The man acted like he'd been given some sort of challenge, and he grew bolder and answered the last question with a brazen air, "It's…different."

Gladys laughed. "Mister, you don't know the half of it." The audience laughed louder and clapped. Gladys focused on the female half of the couple and batted her eyes. "You having a good night, sister?"

The woman almost couldn't answer, she was so shy, but she nodded.

"Good to hear. This fellow, he's good?"

She nodded again, and Gerry could see, even in the dim light, the woman was blushing. She knew exactly what Gladys meant: was her man good in bed?

Gladys stood up, looked around, and zeroed in on the two Negro girls. She sauntered over and sat down with them as every person in the club watched.

She paused. "Hello there, ladies. How's tricks?"

The taller girl appeared to enjoy the attention, and she grinned and nodded. The other one stayed quiet and blank-faced.

"Are you enjoying the show?"

Gerry couldn't hear the response, but she didn't care. She was concentrating on the girl who wasn't talking to Gladys and trying to figure out how to meet her. She usually relied on Woody to make introductions for her.

Gladys eventually moved on to one or two other tables, chit-chatting expertly. Then she went back to the piano and played a few more tunes and took a break.

"We ought to get going," Woody said, draining her drink. "We need to report back to the Island by midnight."

"Yeah. I guess so," Gerry said glumly. "I'll be right back."

As she stood in line for the can, she happened to turn, and there was the Negro girl she'd been staring at all evening. Gerry had a choice. She could either do nothing, or she could at least try to strike up an acquaintance.

"Hi," she said. And the girl who'd been staring into space turned and met Gerry's eyes.

"Hello," she said, softly.

"I saw Gladys talking to you."

"Yes," the girl said. "That was fun." However, she sounded like it was anything but, and she was apparently not ready to say any more.

"I like the shows here."

"Oh?" the girl said, with a little more verve. "Do you come often?" Gerry watched her face, the garish light in the hallway shining on it. Her skin was the color of an old penny—brown, with the barest hint of red undertones. Gerry had never seen anyone who looked like that.

"No. We can't. We don't get shore leave very much."

"What? Are you in the service?" She sounded disbelieving.

"Yep. I'm a WAVE over on the Treasure Island base." Gerry couldn't keep the pride out of her voice.

"I'll be darned. Oh, it's your turn."

When Gerry came out, she lingered near the door, enduring stares from those in line. Her quarry reappeared and actually smiled at her in a friendly fashion.

"Sorry. I've got to mosey. My sister's waiting."

"Yeah. Me too. Woody wants to leave now."

They walked back together to the showroom. Gerry stared at the girl as she spoke to her sister and put on her coat.

"You're such a dope," Woody said. "Why don't you get her phone number if you're interested?"

"Look. Don't bug me," Gerry replied, irritated with Woody but mostly disappointed at her own lack of nerve. On the stage, another singer was doing a poor imitation of Doris Day.

They were right behind the strangers as they all walked out the front door, and then as they reached the sidewalk, all four of them stopped abruptly. The street was choked with cars blaring their horns and masses of men in uniform. One group was trying to overturn a car that was stuck in traffic. Gerry looked down the street to their right and spotted a group of men, one of them carrying a baseball bat careening toward them.

"We have to go back," she told Woody. She tapped the shoulder of the taller of the two Negro girls.

"Hey. You have to go back inside. It isn't safe."

They evidently saw what she saw since they spun around and followed Woody and Gerry back through Mona's door.

They stopped in a knot just inside as the gang flew past.

"What's going on?" the shorter girl asked Gerry, to her pleasure.

"It's the VJ Day party, I think."

She shook her head. "Crazy White boys."

"Yeah," Gerry said. "Guess so."

Behind her, Woody asked of no one in particular, "What the heck are we going to do?"

Even agitated, Woody never used bad words.

"I don't know, but we've got to get to the Transbay Terminal to catch our train," Gerry said, feeling anxious.

"We have to get the bus on Fourth Street to Hunters Point somehow," the shorter girl said. Her sister just looked worried but didn't speak.

"Look. Do we have enough for a cab?" Gerry asked Woody.

"Just barely. I'll be broke 'til September," Woody said, sadly.

Gerry turned to the other two women. "You ought to come with us. It's not safe to be on the street now. We'll have the cabbie drop you off, and we'll wait until you catch your bus."

"Thank you kindly, but we don't have the money."

"*We* do," Gerry said. "Come with us. It's fine." It had occurred to her that this was her chance finally to talk to the unknown girl, and she better seize it.

The two women drew aside for a whispered talk.

"Okay," the smaller one said. "We'll come with you."

"Stay close. We can find a cab here on Broadway, I'm sure."

The four of them moved out to the curb.

"You look that way and I'll look this way," Woody said.

Around them, the mayhem appeared to increase. As they anxiously scanned the traffic for an available cab, a couple of drunken sailors approached them.

"Come on, beauty. The war's done. Give me a kiss," he said, slurring his words. He seemed to be directing his question to all four of them.

"Nope, not now, swabbie," Gerry said firmly. "On your way." She sharpened up her tone like a drill instructor, and it seemed to work.

He frowned in drunken concentration and then turned to the two Negro girls. "How about one o' you black beauties?"

Woody drew herself up to full height. "Hey, sailor. Be on your way." Even out of uniform, she sounded formidable.

"Okay, okay. I'm going." He staggered away.

"There's one!" Gerry waved vigorously, and the cab stopped, causing all the cars behind it to slam their horns.

"Let's go, hurry." Gerry grabbed the arm of the smaller girl, and the four of them sprinted across the traffic to the other side of Broadway and piled into the cab.

Panting, Woody answered "Fourth and Market" when the cabbie asked where they wanted to go.

They arranged themselves in the back of the taxi with the two strangers on the seat and Gerry and Woody on the jump seats. Gerry was directly across from the girl she'd been talking with by the can. She looked frightened but was controlling her nervousness.

"Might be a while," the cabbie said. "Traffic's backed up." They could see that for themselves.

"We're happy you picked us up."

Sure enough, the faces of two sailors appeared in the windows of the cab, peering in at them with leering menace.

"Hi, girls. Where ya going?" one of them asked.

"Get the hell away from my cab," the cabbie roared and laid on his horn for good measure as the two sailors backed away.

The taxi driver forced his way onto Sansome Street and inched his way down to Market Street, where it was even worse. People were climbing lamp posts, and mobs stood on top of streetcars. Gerry watched the face of the smaller young woman as she gazed out the window. Her expression changed from fear to curiosity to fascination to exhilaration and back again. Gerry felt the same emotions course through her mind.

"Look. There's the shore patrol," Gerry said. "Maybe they could arrest us so we can get back to base safely."

"Don't be a dope," Woody said.

"Then we are taking the train home?" Gerry asked, a tad irritated. Woody just rolled her eyes.

"What are your names," Woody asked their two companions.

"Wilma Grace Weeks," the taller one said.

"Maddie Weeks." *Aha. They're related. Thank God, they're not a couple.*

"I'm Shirley Woodward. Woody for short." Woody said, as calmly as though they were still back at Mona's having a casual drink and not running for their lives.

"I'm Gerry Stern." They shook hands all around.

"Y'all are in the navy?" Maddie asked.

"Aye-aye," Gerry said, then saluted and grinned.

Woody nodded.

"Well, we're kinda connected to the navy, since we work at the shipyard building y'all's ships," Wilma Grace said.

"Oh, you're like Rosie the Riveter." Gerry meant the girl on the recruiting poster whose name was unknown, but the public had christened Rosie the Riveter, and it stuck.

"Oh, yes. That's what we are." Maddie started to giggle and glanced at Wilma, then back to Gerry. Her giggle was girlish, at odds with her mostly serious demeanor.

"Here we are, ladies," the cab driver said as he pulled in at the curb.

Gerry panicked because she couldn't think how to ask how they could keep in touch. She didn't want Maddie to drift out of her life forever.

Wilma said, "Thanks for helping us out of that jam."

"Oh, it was nothing. Was it, Woody? It seemed wrong to leave you to fend for yourselves in that mob."

"You could have. Most people would."

"Well, not us." Gerry said, and she looked at Maddie as she said it.

"Wilma Grace, honey. We ought to properly thank Woody and Gerry," Maddie said and stared at Wilma and raised her eyebrows.

"Well…sure." Wilma looked uncertain.

"How about dinner? We can make you some old-fashioned, home-cooked Southern food," Maddie said.

"Wow. I mean, sure. We'd love to." Gerry looked at Woody, who shrugged. Out of the corner of her eye, she caught Wilma Grace's skeptical expression, but mostly she was focused on Maddie and her broad, but slightly uncertain smile.

"We don't know when we'll get leave again," Woody said, sounding like it wasn't going to happen in this century.

"Well, how 'bout you find out when you can, and we can invite you. How can we get hold of you?"

"Just call Treasure Island and tell the switchboard Geraldine Stern, Company A. They'll send me a message, but how 'bout we call you?"

"Don't have a phone."

"Oh."

"Better we call you. We can do that from the foreman's office at the dock, or maybe the pay phone on H Street," Maddie said and caught Gerry's eye.

"Well, then. Sure," Gerry said.

"We have to get back. Now," Woody said with some urgency.

"Nice to meet you," Maddie said and shook hands formally with Gerry. Wilma Grace nodded politely to Gerry and Woody. Then they turned and walked away to catch their bus. Gerry watched them, but Woody seized her arm and dragged her back into the taxi.

"Transbay Terminal, and step on it."

❖

Wilma Grace was irked at her, and Maddie knew to wait and presently she'd find out why. Wilma Grace couldn't hold back on her feelings for long. It was true that Wilma Grace would be the one mainly cooking the supper that Maddie had spontaneously offered, but Maddie would help her. She was cheesed at something else.

They were safely seated on the bus back to Hunters Point. Maddie was thinking about their evening, especially about Gerry and her sweet, friendly grin.

They'd been so lucky to meet Gerry and Woody. Otherwise, who knew what would have happened to them? Those two didn't have to do what they did. If the same thing had happened back in their hometown, Sawyer, Arkansas, no way would any White women have come to their aid. It really was different in California. Maybe not the perfect paradise they'd hoped for, but Maddie's mother had taught her to be hopeful yet realistic. She jumped when Wilma Grace finally spoke up.

"I just can't make out why you think it was a good idea to invite those two to supper. What could I say? No?"

"Well, what else are we gonna do to thank them for showing us some Christian charity? Give them money? For one, they likely wouldn't take it. Two, that's tacky. And three, we don't *have* any money. What we had, we spent seeing Gladys. You got a better idea?"

"I don't know," Wilma Grace said irritably. "We said thank you."

"Yeah. They saved our butts, and you know it. We coulda ended up raped or killed."

Wilma Grace shifted in her seat and didn't respond right away. "But why? Whatever would make them do such a thing?"

"Wilma Grace, honey, I don't know. You could ask them when they come to supper, if you're so curious." Maddie suspected that back in Sawyer, Wilma Grace had had more than enough bad run-ins with the local White folk and had assumed right off the bat that nothing good would ever come from any encounter with one.

"I don't know what to tell Thom." She meant her husband and Maddie's brother.

"Tell him the truth. I expect that's the easiest."

"He'd be bothered to hear what kind of place we ended up at."

"Well. It *was* your idea," Maddie said. And that was true.

Wilma Grace had showed her some magazine that had a big ad in it for Gladys Bentley. As a teenager, Wilma had visited some family in Harlem in New York, and they all had gone out to a Gladys Bentley show at the Apollo Theater. Wilma talked about it endlessly, as well she might. It was a big deal for a little girl from the sticks in Arkansas to visit New York City. When she found the magazine ad that talked about Gladys, she practically danced, she was so excited.

Thom was a little cranky about them going out without him because he had to work, but one of the things about her brother Maddie loved was how he didn't go around trying to control his women all the time. He shrugged when they told him what they were going to do.

"I didn't know anything about the place. I just wanted to see Gladys."

"And we did. And I thought it was fun, other than the part where the drunk-ass sailors bothered us," Maddie said. She suspected it bugged Wilma Grace that Mona's 440 was so White and made her feel uncomfortable, or maybe it was something else. All the girls in suits, maybe. That was a shocker at first, but in a strange way, Maddie wasn't disturbed by it. They were all, including Gladys, having such a ball. When Gerry had started talking to her at the door of the club, Maddie wanted to keep talking to her. And in spite of the riot being scary, she loved that they all ended up in that taxi.

"Yeah, but I never thought Gladys would be in a place like that."

"She was wearing a tuxedo, Wilma Grace. She fit right in."

As usual, when Wilma Grace couldn't think of thing to say back, she turned away and went silent.

"You noticed nobody said nothin' to us about being in that club and us being Colored and all. We not in Sawyer anymore. We can't be tossed out of places and talked down to just cause people feel like it," Maddie said.

"I know, but still…"

Maddie sat back, closed her eyes, and first she pictured Gladys in her white tuxedo at her piano. Then she thought about Gerry in her twill slacks and starched shirt grinning at her as they rode in the cab. That cab ride had turned out to be as exciting as seeing Gladys perform, maybe more. She thought maybe she'd try to leave Gerry a telephone message later in the week.

CHAPTER TWO

Outside Fresno, California
January 1943

The speech by the WAVE recruiter was electrifying enough, but it was how she looked in uniform that truly caught Gerry's attention. Afterward, Gerry spoke to her, and before they'd finished their conversation, she'd made up her mind to sign up for the navy. The recruiter invited her to come downtown to the armory to complete the paperwork.

"Ma, I'm of age so I can go if I want to," Gerry told her mother firmly. "It's the right thing to do, the patriotic thing to do. They need our help. The farm'll be okay with you and Dad and the boys. The president says we have to sacrifice, so that's your sacrifice—letting me go into the WAVES. You'll have to try to do without me, and I know you can."

Having failed on one argument, Gerry's mom switched to another one. "You'll be far from home, and those women who go into the service, well, they're not the right sort for you to be around. If you come home pregnant, that'll be the end of it, young lady." Gerry's mom was parroting something she'd heard God knows where. Maybe in church.

"I'm not going into the service to run around with men, Mom. Don't worry."

Quite the opposite. Gerry had no interest in men, and she had only needed one kiss from one boy to be convinced of it. To her, being around a lot of women sounded just fine.

Her mother fretted and cried, but Gerry's mind was made up. The patriotism argument softened her a little. Her dad, as usual, said nothing beyond a grunt.

The whole adventure of taking the train across the country to boot camp in New York merged with the actual boot-camp experience itself in a blur of activity. Gerry went to sleep every night with the voices of drill instructors in her ears, always shouting, "Move, move, quick-time. What's your serial number? Ten-hut." If they weren't marching, they were running, and if they weren't running, they were sitting in a classroom hearing endless details about navy rules, navy organization, and navy traditions. Boot camp lasted only six weeks.

When she was asked where she wanted to be stationed, she chose to return to California to be assigned to San Francisco's Treasure Island. She'd gone there once as a little girl on a rare family trip. She retained hazy impressions of hills and water and the clang of cable cars. Having grown up in the landlocked Central Valley, being near the ocean appealed to her.

At Treasure Island, the WAVE commander was, if anything, more impressive than the recruiter. She was of medium height, but her straight-back posture and shrewd eyes behind rimless spectacles impressed Gerry enormously. Other than the recruiter, she was the first bona fide WAVE she'd seen up close. All their boot camp instructors had been men.

"You have some mechanical aptitude, and you can drive, Seaman Stern. That's excellent. We need drivers, and that's where we'll assign you. Report to PO Atkins at 0700 tomorrow at the motor pool. You're in Barracks B. It's PO Woodhouse who'll get you squared away."

Gerry stepped out the front door of the administration building. She'd come from the March cold of New York where, along with all the running, she'd shivered in East Coast temperatures. It was a relief to feel California warmth again, even if it was cut by the chilly ocean breeze. The sun was welcoming, gleaming on all the buildings on Treasure Island.

When she arrived at the WAVE barracks B, there to greet her was a tall drink of water who introduced herself as PO Shirley Woodhouse.

"Greetings, Seaman Stern. Welcome to Treasure Island. Here's your bunk." It amused Gerry that they were all called Seaman. The navy, she was learning, was nothing if not rigidly consistent. It was comfortable to her though. She'd grown up with the routine of farm life. The navy was wonderfully different, but it was still predictable, and that comforted Gerry.

"You can call me Woody," the PO said. She had twinkly brown eyes and a big grin.

"I'm Gerry."

"Yep. Suits you," Woody said and grinned even bigger. "Lunch is at 1300. See you there."

PO Woodhouse didn't so much as sit at her table in the mess hall but preside over it. A couple of other WAVES were present when Gerry sat down. Woody introduced everyone. Gerry had noticed during boot camp that some of the WAVES were more boyish than others, though with everyone in uniform it was hard to tell. Just as Woody had, her lunch companions sized her up in a not unfriendly but a sort of speculative way, as though they were looking for something special.

"Where you from?"

"Out near Fresno. I grew up on a farm."

Woody cocked her eyebrow. "Farm girl, eh? You're not a debutante, I'm guessing."

Gerry snorted. "Not hardly."

Looking at her closely, Seaman Riggs said, "I bet you're pretty strong."

"Yeah, I suppose. Where are you from?"

"Pittsburgh P-A."

To Gerry, Woody said, "Friday night we're all headed into the City. Want to go?"

"Sure. Can I leave the base?"

"I'll see to that. Don't you worry none, sister." She looked at Riggs, and they both laughed. Gerry was happy to be included, but she sensed Riggs and Woody shared a secret she wasn't yet part of.

On Gerry's first day on duty in the motor pool, she stood in a small knot of other newly recruited WAVES and listened to the (male) PO in charge.

He made it clear that he didn't have high expectations of his crew of WAVES. Gerry had to admit their giggles and nervous smiles wouldn't have prompted much confidence in her either. He kept calling them "you girls" as he explained their duties, and he spoke with elaborate clarity, as though they were mentally deficient or young children.

"So, I don't suppose any of you girls know what to do if your old bus gets a flat?" His tone telegraphed his doubt that he'd get a "yes" answer to his question. There were only a few uneasy snickers in response.

"I do," Gerry said. Her bold reply drew a look of surprise and respect from the crusty PO and a chorus of appreciative laughter from her fellow trainees. She then demonstrated her skill by changing a tire on a jeep. It wasn't much of a challenge since she'd grown up around farm vehicles. Her taciturn father always said no mechanics were hiding in the barn to come to their rescue if one of their vehicles broke down. Gerry had learned to drive when she was ten years old and reckoned it wasn't going to be much more difficult to drive a bus than a tractor.

She was assigned to drive whatever vehicle wherever necessary, but she liked the bus-driving best. It was the most relaxed since it was mostly a matter of carrying lots of ordinary bluejackets, as the navy boys were called, to the train or the water taxi into San Francisco. And they were all happy to go on shore leave, so they were in a good mood. It was better than driving the visiting navy brass around, which happened often. Some of the gold-braided officers glared at her as though her very presence in uniform and behind the wheel of a jeep was some sort of insult to them or to the navy itself. She steeled herself not to mind the nasty looks. And if she was spoken to, she responded crisply and cheerfully in the navy style, with lots of "sirs."

The navy had rules for everything, including clothes. Gerry liked wearing a uniform. She just wished it was the nice navy-blue serge all the guys got to wear. They looked so slick in the eight-button pants and the white caps. At least Gerry wore the navy anchor insignia on her sleeve and her lapels like they did. As she dressed, she checked herself in the mirror. It wasn't notable that WAVES often had short hair. Thanks to navy barbers, she could keep her dark-brown, wavy hair short and neat.

❖

Gerry thought she might be staring too much, but she'd never imagined being in such a place and wanted to take everything in, not miss a thing. She struggled to keep up a calm, blasé attitude so she didn't look or act like a hick, even if that was what she was.

They were in a nightclub called Mona's 440, and Riggs and Woody were mostly ignoring her as they smoked and sipped drinks and traded barbed observations of the other customers.

"I hear she threw over Maggie for something better," Woody would say with an all-knowing air.

"Huh. That's a gal who's always looking for the greener grass, but when she gets there, she finds out it's crabgrass," Riggs said, to which Woody howled with laughter.

"Who are you talking about?" Gerry asked. They pointed to a short, dark-haired gal in a pinstripe suit.

"Spike Jones over there."

"Why is she wearing a suit, and why is her name Spike?"

Her two companions laughed harder.

"Oh, my." Woody said, wiping her eyes and regaining her composure. "You *are* a greenhorn."

"Hey. I might be from the country, but I'm not stupid. Just tell me."

The two WAVES shifted uncomfortably in their chairs and glanced at one another.

"You talk," Riggs said.

"I took a chance on bringing you along with us tonight, because the day you walked into the barracks, I got one look at you and thought, 'Good grief. Here's another one.' I told Riggs, and she agreed."

"Another what?"

"Gay gal."

"A what?" Gerry didn't know that term. Riggs and Woody started to laugh all over again. She waited them out.

"A girl who likes girls. Like the girls in this club," Riggs said.

Gerry looked around again silently before saying in a low voice, "I think I might be one of those girls." The inchoate yearnings of her high school years and her utter lack of interest in boys abruptly began to make sense as she talked with Woody and Riggs and looked around at the other customers at Mona's.

Woody nodded sagely. "We thought you might be."

"So if I am, what do I do?"

They started to chuckle again, but Gerry, annoyed, said, "Stop it. Stop making fun of me. I'm serious, and if you want to help, fine. But don't treat me like I'm dumb, because I'm not."

They looked embarrassed, and Woody said, "Okay, kid. You're right. You're not dumb. You're just new. We'll show you the ropes. No more teasing, or at least less teasing and more help."

"Deal. That sounds grand."

So Gerry became a tourist, with Woody as an expert tour guide. Riggs came along at first, but she'd acquired a girlfriend and was less available, her girlfriend discouraging her from joining Woody and Gerry's forays into the night.

She joked, "Right now, Tina"—she meant her girlfriend—"says my shopping days are done," at which she and Woody laughed uproariously. Gerry only dimly understood what they meant, but based on her high school experiences and her memory of boy-girl courtship and all the drama and jealousy, it seemed there might not be much difference between that and what her navy pals did.

As for Woody, in answer to Gerry's question, she shrugged. "I like to play the field. I don't like to be tied down. But that's just me."

With stunning speed Gerry went from knowing nothing whatever about what she wanted, to what she didn't want, to not only knowing what and whom she desired but, with Woody's encouragement, an active pursuer.

What she didn't know was what she would do once she found a girl, but she'd figure that out when the time came.

When they could get free time and shore leave, they'd speed into the City via the commuter train on the Bay Bridge and into a world that Gerry found as compelling and fascinating as she found the navy she'd so recently joined. The navy was order, predictability, neat ranks of marching seaman. Mealtimes, work periods, and orders. Clear directions and expected consequences. They spent their free time, however, in the North Beach area of San Francisco and in certain bars where, according to Woody, the gay girls went. There was the opposite of the navy. Excitement, unpredictability, the eternal possibility of romance.

"It's literally a fairyland" was how Woody put it.

Woody introduced Gerry to Ensign Jimmy Price. "He's a member of the gang."

By now, Gerry understood the gang was the gay gang at Treasure Island, who knew about each other, but no one else knew who they were. It was the same as being a member of a secret club.

Jimmy was a font of information about how to get along in the navy when one was in the gang.

"Everyone knows which places are the ones to go. Even the navy knows, and they helpfully tell us by posting a nice list of off-limits bars."

He laughed. "Disorderly houses, they call them. Meaning we're there. Of course, if I get caught in one of those places out of uniform, then I'm going to be in big trouble."

"But we girls are safe," Woody assured Gerry. "The navy barely acknowledges we're here, so they don't pay much attention to what we do in our free time. *We're* not going to cause them any grief."

The reason for this became obvious the first time Gerry attended a "hygiene" lecture given by a humorless, blank-faced WAVE officer.

"Be extremely careful in your behavior with men while in uniform. Not only do we expect you to comport yourselves with discretion, but we also want you to avoid getting caught in any unfortunate situations."

Woody whispered, "She means getting pregnant," making Gerry giggle and earning a frown from the officer.

After the hygiene lecture, Woody told Gerry that the officer who gave the lecture was a member of the gang.

Gerry was astounded, but she was quickly coming to realize that she enjoyed being part of a secret club with its own lingo and signals.

And off they went every other weekend to North Beach, into the glamour and chaos of gay clubs.

"We have to find you a girlfriend," Woody said.

"What about you?" Gerry asked.

"Oh, not me. I'm a loner. I have my ways." She grinned conspiratorially. "And you, Miss Down on the Farm, want to fall in love, I expect."

"Yep. I guess so." Gerry wasn't sure, but it sounded like what she wanted. She'd never been in love, except possibly with her eleventh-grade history teacher, Miss Farnsworth. She recalled those feelings with a combination of "now I get it" and deep embarrassment. But Woody was showing her a world where those feelings were not only not embarrassing but could possibly be returned by a beautiful woman.

"I still don't understand why some of the girls are in dresses and lipstick, and some are wearing suits," Gerry said.

It was their third foray into Mona's 440, because that was Woody's favorite spot. Riggs was gracing them with her presence this night, along with Tina. This meant Gerry was in the hands of three tour guides instead of two. She wasn't yet sure if that was an improvement.

Seaman Riggs was wearing a gabardine suit, and Tina was more or less draped over her shoulders, much like the suit jacket. Tina wore a cocktail dress, a great deal of makeup, and a slinky smile.

She contemplated Gerry with a practiced eye as she smoothed Riggs's lapels and patted her cheek. "Sweetie, you're so cute. She's so cute, isn't she?"

This was how Tina's remarks ran every time she spoke—a line directed to Riggs, then repeated to Woody and Gerry. After a short while Gerry thought she might find Tina unbearable. Also, it wasn't an answer to her question.

"There's butch and then there's femme. You're either one or other," Riggs said with conviction.

"I guess I'm butch," Gerry said.

"Yes, honey, you are," Tina said, and they all laughed, except Gerry.

"You got to look the part," Woody said. "Like us."

"I see."

"But there's more to it than that." Riggs arched her eyebrow. "Isn't that true, toots?" She and Tina locked eyes.

Tina chuckled, then said, "You have to know what you're doing, like my baby does." She stuck her tongue in Riggs's ear.

Gerry suspected Tina was speaking in some kind of code. She'd ask Woody later. She felt like she was in a foreign country and was still learning to speak the language.

"Don't mind those two," Woody said. "Look around and tell me who you see that catches your eye." She gestured with her drink.

Gerry dutifully gazed around the nightclub. All she saw were couples.

"I don't see anyone," she said, disappointed.

"Look over there," Woody said and subtly pointed.

There at the bar a girl in blue sparkly dress sat by herself, and Gerry took a closer look. She had a beehive hairdo and an air of melancholy. Gerry thought she was attractive but potentially too old, though it was hard to tell her age in the dim light of Mona's. She looked jaded in the manner she smoked her cigarette and gazed off into space. Every so often she'd share a remark with the bartender. All the Mona's bartenders were gay men. Women weren't allowed to tend bar in California, Woody and Jimmy told her.

"I don't think so," she said. Gerry didn't think the woman was the type she'd be attracted to.

"Ger. Don't be so quick to dismiss her. Her name's Pauline, and she's a swell girl when you get to know her."

Gerry rolled her eyes but nodded, and Woody went over to the woman and returned to the table with her. Tina and Riggs said hello. Pauline sat next to Gerry and took out another cigarette. It occurred to Gerry that she was expected to light it for her, and she did.

"Thanks," Pauline said, her tone breathy and confidential.

"You're another one of the girls in blue, Woody told me."

"Yeah," Gerry said, but stopped there. She turned shy as Pauline scrutinized her, really took her in with a practiced up-and-down look and slowly grinned. Her look and her expression made Gerry shiver. She was being judged against some invisible standard, but the process pleased her somehow. Gerry also wondered when Woody had had time to clue Pauline in on her.

Pauline asked Gerry questions about where she was from and how much she liked the navy. As Gerry answered, she began to relax a little more. She forced herself to focus on Pauline, but it was Pauline's focus on *her* that drew her.

"Come on, gals. Let's go someplace where there aren't so many tourists," Riggs said, "I got invited to a party over to someone's flat a few blocks from here. We can go there, relax and let our hair down." She winked.

They all grabbed their coats and, after a few minutes' walk, arrived at an apartment jammed with people. To Gerry's surprise, some men were there.

She asked Woody, "I thought this was for girls."

"Relax, kid. They're gay, like Jimmy. That guy over there, it's his place."

It felt odd but good to be in an actual regular apartment instead of the barracks and the common room. She wandered through the flat. Couples were everywhere, touching, even kissing and dancing in the living room. It made Gerry dizzy. The atmosphere was dense with smoke and sex. Sexual attraction, desire, whatever you called it. It was oozing into her as well.

Woody caught up with her and said, "What do you think?"

"It's nice."

"We can't dance in the bar, or Mona will get busted by the police. The bar's fun, but it's better to go to someone's house if you really want to let down your hair. And I do."

"Where's Pauline?" Gerry asked. "Have you seen her?"

Woody put an arm around her shoulder and led her back toward the front of the apartment. They had to shoulder their way through the packed hall and dining room.

"I'm glad you asked. It would be good for you to get to know Pauline better." Woody looked at her closely.

Gerry scrunched her nose and asked "Why," even though she was beginning to think that might be a very good idea. It wasn't what Pauline had said to Gerry during their brief conversation at the bar, but the tone of Pauline's voice and her eye contact as she asked questions. She had been a bit serious even, as though it was deeply important to her what Gerry said.

They found Pauline huddled on the couch with a few women who looked much like her. They sat smoking and drinking, bare legs crossed. If there were nylons to be had, they'd be wearing them. But the war had caused shortages of a lot of items, including women's stockings.

Pauline looked up and directly at Gerry. Then she turned to the women on the couch and said, "Move over, girls."

The women dutifully scrunched in tighter, and, following Pauline's gesture, Gerry sat down. Woody waved at her and disappeared.

"You made it," Pauline said as though there'd been some doubt, but she also sounded thrilled.

Packed in tight between two women, Gerry was awash in perfume and heat. Her heart began to pound, and she was getting sweaty, though she didn't think that was all due to the crowdedness of the room or the number of women squeezed onto the couch.

"This is nice," Gerry said, though she sounded silly to herself.

"It's marvelous," Pauline said, sounding confidential. "You've never been to a queer party, have you?"

"N-no. Not like this. Do you mean gay?" Gerry wondered if a game of gin with some of the gang in the enlisted men's club counted.

"Yes, I do." Pauline was whispering in her ear. "Do you like it?"

Someone put a record on, and Gerry recognized the opening notes of "Pennsylvania 6500." Male and female couples began to dance.

"Aren't you going to ask me to dance?" Pauline asked, and there seemed to be a trove of meaning behind this question.

"Would you like to dance?" Gerry asked.

"I would."

They squirmed their way into the dancers, and Gerry tried to remember how to lead as Woody had taught her. That, along with the invitation to dance and lighting Pauline's cigarettes, seemed to be what was required of her.

"You're a little baby, aren't you?"

"I'm nineteen," Gerry said, somewhat indignantly.

"Easy. I wasn't trying to insult you. I was just making a comment. Ya got to start somewhere."

Pauline was enveloping her. It seemed as though she was leading Gerry and not the reverse. Other than Woody, Gerry had never danced with a woman. This wasn't anything like dancing with Woody though. Their bodies cleaved together, and Gerry was so warm she thought she might melt. She didn't want to be parted from Pauline, so she stayed where she was.

The music stopped. In the silence, the buzz of conversation rose again.

Pauline didn't move away. She stayed right where she was, holding on tight to Gerry. She nuzzled her cheek, and Gerry's knees got weak.

"Shall we dance some more, or…?" she whispered. "Do you want to go back to my place?"

Almost unable to speak, Gerry managed choke out, "Where do you live?"

"Not far from here."

"I have to be back at the base by six in the morning," Gerry said, stalling, imagining what could happen between now and then. She knew where Pauline was headed, and she wanted to go there with her, but she was also terrified. Yet without the power of conscious thought, she allowed circumstance, fate, and raw feeling to direct her.

"Let's go."

They went out into the night, the cold, fog-tinged air a shock after the smoke and body-heat-filled flat. Gerry concentrated on keeping up with Pauline, who had grabbed her hand and taken off down the street as though the devil was running after them. The lights of North Beach flickered, but Gerry barely noticed them as they trotted by.

Pauline stopped in front of an apartment building on Green Street with a set of steep steps leading up to it. Gerry barely even noticed that they had to climb. She could see off to one side and farther up the hill, the silvery gray illumination on Coit Tower—the summit of Telegraph Hill. That gave her a reference point for her location.

Once inside Pauline's small, neat apartment, Gerry grew anxious again. Pauline moved in a calm, unhurried manner. She turned on a lamp, took Gerry's jacket, and hung it up on a coat tree. She turned on the radio to an almost inaudible volume.

"Drink?" she asked, and it took Gerry a moment to realize she was asking her.

"Um, water," she said and immediately felt foolish. She'd had enough to drink at Mona's and didn't want any more.

"Please sit down and make yourself comfortable," Pauline said as she walked into the small efficiency kitchen.

Gerry obeyed, willing herself to breathe.

Pauline returned with a glass of wine for herself and a glass of water she handed to Gerry.

"It's your first time, isn't it?" Pauline asked, her expression surprisingly serious.

"Yes," Gerry said. No point in lying because it was likely Pauline would know anyhow, once they started to...do whatever they were going to do.

Pauline touched her cheek gently and turned Gerry's face toward her. Gerry was having trouble convincing herself to make eye contact, but she allowed Pauline to help her.

"I want you to try not to worry. This works best when you relax and go along. I promise you, it will be fine."

That was the last thing Gerry expected to hear. She certainly had no idea that Pauline would say anything at all, but especially not that. How did she know so much about Gerry? Was her inexperience that obvious? It must be.

Still palming Gerry's cheek, she kissed her, slowly and gently at first but, as Gerry responded, with increasing urgency. She took Gerry's hand and placed it on her breast. Gerry loved the way it felt, the way Pauline's breathing became faster and faster. She was emboldened to explore further, her hands moving of their own accord over Pauline, her own body heating up.

Pauline stood up and took Gerry's hand and led her to the bedroom that opened off the living room. She turned on another lamp, its shade nearly obliterating the light from the bulb.

"Help me," Pauline said as she turned around. Gerry understood she was to unzip her dress. That act and the sound of the zipper was astonishing. She was barely breathing, but this time not from anxiety. That had faded into the background of her mind, replaced by something else.

She helped Pauline take off her dress and then watched her yank her slip over her head before she turned once again and had Gerry unhook her bra.

"Do you like what you see?" she asked.

Gerry was so overcome she could only nod.

"Good. Then come over here. You're going to show me how much you like me."

Before Gerry realized it, Pauline had gotten Gerry's clothes off and they were in bed.

"I want you. I want you to take me," Pauline whispered.

"I…" Gerry was at a loss for words again. She grasped that she was to be the one to move forward. Woody hadn't explained very much about sex, but she had said that butches were expected to take charge in every way.

It was Pauline, after all, who "took charge." She gently but expertly showed Gerry what to do, how to touch her, how to pleasure her. Gerry felt powerful. The exploration of Pauline's body and the fulfillment of her desire wasn't like anything she'd ever done. As they lay quietly smoking afterward, Pauline asked, "How did that make you feel?"

"Like a million bucks."

"Good. Now I want you to do it again." Pauline stamped out her cigarette and, smiling, turned toward her.

Gerry grinned and put out her own cigarette. All her anxiety was gone in a puff of smoke.

❖

"I'm on top of the world. I don't have the…words," Gerry told Woody the next day.

"Good. Are you going to see her again?"

"Yes. Of course. We have a date next week."

"Oh, a date, is it? Well, enjoy. Be careful though." Woody looked somber as she said this, and it threw Gerry off.

"What makes you say that?" Gerry asked.

"Just be careful."

Being careful was the last thing on Gerry's mind. Her only goal was to see Pauline and get back into bed with her and do everything they'd done all over again. She'd never felt like this She could make a woman ecstatic, make her scream in pleasure and beg her for more. She hadn't known this could be done or that she was someone who could do it. It was a revelation, and she chose to ignore Woody's odd warning.

❖

They forced themselves to get out of bed and went out to eat at Foster's Cafeteria on Geary. It was ridiculously hard to not stare into Pauline's eyes and imagine her as she came. That's what Pauline told her to call what happened when Gerry made love to her.

Pauline stole small looks at her, little grins and glances under her eyelids that practically undid Gerry with longing. They didn't speak much as they ate their blue-plate specials. Gerry hadn't even realized how hungry she was, so absorbed in Pauline.

Over coffee, after they'd eaten, Pauline said, "So. You obviously have never had a girl. Do you know what happens next?"

"I don't know. We keep doing what we're doing?" The question threw Gerry off.

"I wish that were possible," Pauline said, sadly.

"It's not?" Gerry was thoroughly alarmed and confused.

"No. It's time for me to move on. I've turned you out. You're a sweet little butch stud, but it's time for you to go find yourself a real girlfriend."

"Not you?" Gerry was devastated.

"Not me."

❖

"She just dumped me, gave me the kiss-off, just like that," Gerry told Woody, disconsolately.

"I warned you," Woody said.

"You said be careful. Was this what you meant?"

"Not exactly, but close. I didn't want you to fall in love. In practice, that's not so easy to avoid, not with your first."

"I thought we were going to…never mind." Gerry was as despondent as she'd ever been.

"You thought it was forever. Lemme tell you, kid, nothing is forever."

"I guess." Gerry was trying to not be too big of a drag. "I'm done then. There are more girls out there. Mona's is full of them."

"Good plan. Time for you to move on. Pauline was good for you. She's great for a first timer like you. But she's not one to stick around. I wasn't going to tell you that right off the bat, y'see?"

"I guess I see that now. Uh, this is kind of personal, but did you and Pauline…?"

"Yep. That's how I knew she'd be good for you."

"Yeah. Okay. She was. Now I understand what all the fuss is about."

"Good. You'll be fine. Let's go to the Emporium and get you some new clothes."

It was later when she told Jimmy about it that he enlightened her. Woody had *asked* Pauline to seduce her. This galled her, but after she thought about it for a while, it wasn't all that important. That was what Woody did. She made things happen.

CHAPTER THREE

August 1945

Gerry put in another request for shore leave, but it wasn't granted. They'd made it back in time on VJ Day so they hadn't gotten in trouble, but the navy was rattled a bit by the misbehavior of so many of its recruits that night so was wary of letting them loose any time soon. Gerry fretted because she had to wait for Maddie to call, and then she had to try to somehow wangle another night of shore leave.

"I don't think she'll call. Do you really think she will?" Woody asked a few days later.

"Yes. I do. Why wouldn't she?" Gerry was annoyed at Woody's lack of faith.

"Don't know. Just a feeling," Woody said noncommittally.

Gerry didn't know for sure, but she had her fingers crossed. Maddie seemed so real and sincere, which gave her hope. Her confidence was rewarded a few days later, when the switchboard gave her a message.

> *Please come to supper on Thursday, August 23 at six o'clock. Our address is 439 Jerrold Ave. Take the number 15 bus from Market and Fourth Street to Hunters Point depot. Maddie*

She couldn't confirm or decline since there was no phone number with the message. If she didn't show up, Maddie wouldn't know why and likely think badly of her. She *had* to somehow get leave.

"You're going to owe me if I can manage this," Jimmy said after she made her request.

"You're the only one I know who has the right connections," Gerry said. "So yeah, I'll do anything. I'm desperate."

"She must be somebody special," Jimmy said. "You ready to lie through your teeth?" He took out a form and began writing on it, then looked at her solemnly. "Sorry about your grandma, poor thing. She's in the hospital, and she's probably not going to make it." Jimmy slid the form over to her to sign.

"Uh-huh. It's a real about shame about Nana and her bad heart." Gerry smiled and patted Jimmy's shoulder gratefully.

What she wasn't ready to do was accept that Woody refused to go with her.

"You're invited. Why not?"

"Because I'm not comfortable. I don't need to be thanked again for that cab ride. It's over and done with."

Woody had turned away and spoken these words to a corner of their dormitory in the barracks rather than to Gerry. It was obvious there would be no more discussion, but Gerry wasn't ready to let it go.

"Are you gonna tell me the truth, or are you beatin' around the bush?"

"What I told you is the truth."

"Right. Fine."

After she was called in to explain to her commander why she needed a pass, Jimmy handed her the pass two days later. She was so happy, she kissed him.

"I can't thank you enough, and whatever you need, I'll do it."

"I can't think of anything right now, but I'll be sure to let you know. Enjoy yourself. Sounds like this girl is special." Gerry had told him all about Maddie.

She had a sudden thought that she might dress up a little for supper. Something told her Maddie and Wilma Grace would view it as an important occasion. She still had a couple of dresses in her locker. Gerry sensed that slacks and a shirt wouldn't quite be the thing for this meal and finally decided on a gingham print. She put it on and looked in the mirror. She felt like an imposter, but what the heck?

❖

"Come set the table, Maddie, please," Maddie heard Wilma Grace call from the kitchen. Maddie was in her room, critically examining her reflection. She'd cleaned up after work and put on one of the two dresses she owned. This one was blue with a wide collar and oversized buttons. At least it was better than wearing her dungarees and flannel shirt, which also smelled like burning metal because of her welding job.

"Be there in a second." She heard her brother's voice, a low, soft tone, as he talked to Wilma Grace. Though he'd started in the same shipyard as Grace and Maddie, he'd found a better job on the docks, and his salary allowed them to live in a little house instead of in the dormitories. It also meant they had enough food, Maddie realized, to invite her friend to supper. When Thom had heard the story of their VJ Day adventure, he'd grumbled. And when he found out their saviors were coming to dinner, he was dubious but finally agreed that feeding them a meal was the right thing to do.

"Maddie, girl, get in here."

Maddie took one last look at her hair and went to the kitchen, which was all of ten feet away.

She could tell Wilma Grace was nervous, and that made her jumpy too, when she only wanted to look forward to this night and not have to cope with Wilma Grace's attitude. But Wilma Grace was a born worrier, and Maddie caught some of it like it was a cold.

"Thom, go put on a clean shirt," Wilma Grace said.

"This one's fine." he replied but went and did as he was told.

Maddie said, "I got to go meet Gerry at the bus terminal."

The shipyard was too big and too confusing to ask Gerry to find her way on her own to their house, so Maddie had made up her mind to meet the bus.

She waited by the bus stop, nervous but excited, and in due course, the bus arrived, and Gerry stepped down.

Maddie recognized her right off but was startled that she was wearing a dress instead of the clothes she'd worn at the club. She looked fine, but she had an air of masquerading as someone else. She spotted Maddie and waved at her as she walked toward her grinning.

"Hi, there."

"Hello."

No Woody. That made one less person to be nervous about, though only Thom hadn't met Gerry. Wilma Grace's attitude about this supper wasn't that great, but in the end, she'd agreed to it, so Maddie was relieved. Thom was a different problem. Maddie had no idea how he'd react to Gerry.

As they walked down the street together, Maddie watched Gerry taking in the sights of the shipyard.

"I've heard of this place, for sure, but I had no idea how big it is. And it's beautiful."

"We're real lucky. The navy gives us everything—a place to live and a place to work. Every little thing a person might need is right here. We can even go bowling."

Gerry laughed. "That's right. It's wonderful. It's the same at Treasure Island. The navy is the best. I didn't know you were navy."

"I'm not, not exactly. Me and my family, we're civilian workers down at the shipyard." Maddie pointed east, where, in the distance, the enormous graving docks were arranged in a row right by the bay. In a couple of berths were the huge battleships they were currently working on.

"My gosh. What do you do?"

"I'm a welder. My brother's a longshoreman, and Wilma Grace is a fabricator. I guess one way or another, we all work on those big old ships."

"Yes. The navy has all those great big ships. We're not allowed to call them boats." She laughed. Maddie loved the way she laughed. Gerry sounded so happy and relaxed, as though she didn't have a care in the world.

"What do you do?"

"Oh, me? I drive buses and jeeps and sometimes real nice cars, if someone important comes on TI who's got to be driven somewhere. Some admiral or somebody. I like driving the buses better. That's just the sailor boys and girls like me."

"Are there any Colored sailors?" Maddie didn't think too much about this question, but she somehow knew Gerry wouldn't take offense or become uneasy.

Gerry looked at her quizzically. "Yeah, but they only work in the kitchen or digging ditches or something."

"I just wondered." Maddie thought that might have not been a good question to ask, but too late. Gerry's answer wasn't a surprise. Well, it wasn't Gerry's fault that was what it was like. It was something that there *were* Colored sailors anyhow. Like she was still amazed she was an actual real-life shipyard worker alongside White women.

"Here we are," Maddie said, suddenly anxious that their house was shabby and didn't look like much. When they'd moved in, it had almost seemed like a mansion, but Gerry must be used to nice houses wherever she'd come from, even if she lived on a navy base now. Back in Sawyer, their house would be just fine, but here, Maddie didn't know. She couldn't tell if Gerry would see it that way, and though she'd started to relax, she got anxious all over again.

"This is a cute little front porch," Gerry said. It at least was big enough to hold a couple of chairs.

Thom had said, "Well, leastways we got a house, and it's right next to where we work. We're not stuck somewhere way out far away." In Sawyer, none of the Colored people lived near where they worked and had to travel long distances to their jobs on the infrequent buses.

"Come and meet my brother Thom." She put a hand on Gerry's arm to direct her, though there wasn't much mystery where they were headed. They walked through a small living room, and right behind it was the kitchen. Wilma Grace stood at the stove, her back to the door.

Thom stood up and said, formally, "I'm pleased to make your acquaintance." He seemed to be taken aback when Gerry extended her hand, saying, "Good to meet you."

Wilma Grace dried her hands on a towel and shook hands with Gerry. "Welcome to our home."

"Thank you for inviting me."

"Would you all stop being so stiff? She's just a regular person," Maddie said severely. She suspected that Wilma Grace and Thom where a bit intimidated by having a White person come to supper. It was time they got over it. They weren't in Sawyer anymore, and things were different in San Francisco.

The four of them stared at one another in the silence.

"Hey, you can sit here." Maddie indicated a chair opposite her.

"Thanks." Gerry beamed at her, and again Maddie felt it like a physical caress. Maddie was convinced that Gerry was as she seemed, an uncomplicated and friendly, open person. She'd thought it last Thursday night when they met, and seeing her again, she was sure she was right about her first impression.

They settled at the table as Wilma Grace brought over the greens and the barbecued pork and sweet potatoes.

"We couldn't barbecue this pork proper because we can't have an outside fire pit, so I did the best I could."

"I can't wait to taste it," Gerry said. "I love barbecue. We made it at home sometimes."

"Where's home?" Maddie asked as Thom and Wilma Grace looked on with apparent interest.

"Near Fresno, middle of California. I grew up on a farm."

"What crops did y'all grow?" Thom asked.

"All kinds—beans, cabbages, asparagus. We had hogs too. That's why I know barbecue. Where I'm from, the barbecue's cooked and seasoned a little different, but I like how yours tastes too."

"There's nothing like Arkansas barbecue."

Maddie hated that Thom might sound show-offy to Gerry, but she merely laughed and told him, "I'd have to agree."

Maddie didn't care that her brother and sister-in-law took over talking. Somehow because Gerry was from a farming family, it comforted them, like she wasn't some sort of exotic, sophisticated being but a normal person, who also happened to be White.

Gerry praised Wilma Grace's cooking, causing her to look down at her plate but with a shy smile.

After dinner, Maddie drew Gerry out to the tiny front porch, where Gerry smoked a cigarette, and they sat quietly together, partly from shyness but in an easy way as well.

"I'm sorry Woody couldn't come," Maddie said.

"She was busy. She's a noncom so she's got lots to do."

"What's a noncom?"

"Noncommissioned officer. Petty officer. She started as a seaman, like me, but she was promoted."

"Why'd you join the navy?" Maddie asked, really wanting to know.

Gerry took time to answer but turned her head to meet Maddie's eyes and spoke seriously.

"Well, I wanted to get out of the Valley. War seemed like a good way. I met a WAVE recruiter who was really something. She said my country needed me. She said the navy would give me a good job because they had to send all the men off to the war, but that left a bunch of work to do, and women had to rise to the occasion."

"What did your folks say?"

"Not much. They didn't want me to go, but they couldn't exactly stop me. I was eighteen, and I told them I was going and that was that. They had all sorts of weird ideas of what I would turn into if I was in the navy."

"Like turn into a pumpkin? Whatever do you mean by that?" Maddie was mystified.

"Nope. A prostitute," Gerry said, flat and hard.

"What?"

"Mom told me that everyone thought women in the service were whores. I asked them who'd we be whoring with if all the men were gone? That shut them up. Anyway, I'm not what you'd call man-crazy or anything like that."

Gerry fell silent, and Maddie sensed there was something else behind that statement, but all she said was, "Me neither."

Gerry smiled slightly and nodded. They kept on looking at each other, but Gerry broke eye contact first and said, "Sorry, but I got to head back across the bay. I don't have an overnight pass or anything."

Maddie wondered what they would do if Gerry had a pass that would let her stay over. Again, there seemed to be something Gerry wasn't saying.

"I hear you. I've got to be on the job at seven a.m. tomorrow. I have to go to bed early."

They went back in the house, Gerry thanked Wilma Grace and Thom one more time, and they went back outside.

"I'll walk you to the bus stop," Maddie said firmly.

Gerry grinned. "Okay."

What came next, Maddie wondered. She had no idea or even what question to ask. She wanted to see Gerry again, and soon, if possible. She had no idea why this was true, but it felt like it was urgent.

"You wanna meet up again sometime?" Gerry asked, like she'd read Maddie's mind.

"I'd like that. Sure."

"We sometimes go to an ice cream place downtown on Twenty-fourth Street. It'll have to wait for a while because I can't leave the base so soon after I just did tonight. I had to make up a story to get my pass. I'll have to wait 'til my regular leave time comes around again. A couple of weeks."

"I've never had a friend like you," Maddie said suddenly.

"Like me? Like what?" Gerry looked confused.

"Well. In the navy. I just know the people down at the shipyard."

"Oh. Well…" Gerry's voice trailed off. "Say, why don't you give me your address, and I'll write you a letter."

"I don't have anything to write with," Maddie said, upset. "I'll call your base switchboard again and leave a message."

Gerry looked relieved. "Okay."

"I'll do it tomorrow on my break."

The sun was beginning to set as they waited for Gerry's bus. Maddie made a few more comments about the shipyard, little dumb things about what was where and what she liked about her work. Gerry listened and nodded and gave her a big grin and a wave as she boarded her bus, and then she was gone.

Maddie walked home slowly, thinking about the evening and about Gerry. For sure, she'd never have met anyone like her in Sawyer. Like any Colored person, she'd only hoped to not attract any unpleasant notice by a White person. Any little misstep with one of them could bring terrible results.

At the shipyard, the White workers weren't hostile, but they didn't mix much with Colored girls. Maddie wasn't friends with any of them beyond saying hello, and sometimes they had to talk about matters regarding their work. Maddie was fine with that since it saved a lot of trouble trying to figure out how she should behave.

Here she was with a White friend. She smiled to herself, thinking she was happy about it even if she didn't quite understand it. She didn't know if Gerry had some other mysterious motive for wanting to be her friend. It surely didn't seem like she did.

As she helped Wilma Grace finish tidying up the kitchen, she was quiet. Sure enough, Wilma Grace said, "Well she's a decent sort, at least. Polite." There had been a few White folks like that in Sawyer, who treated Colored people like human beings. The postmistress was one, for instance. When Maddie went to pick up their mail, Ruthie was chatty and cheerful with everyone. But there weren't many like her.

"What did you expect? Some kind of upstanding Sawyer citizen with her nose in the air and looking down on us?" Maddie found Wilma Grace's reaction off somehow.

"No. I'm just glad the debt's been paid. It's done."

"I'm going to see her again. Sometime," Maddie said.

"Why? Whatever for?" Wilma Grace's tone was somewhere between confused and angry.

"'Cause I want to. I like her," Maddie said firmly.

"California's finally made you lose your mind, little sister." Wilma Grace shook her head back and forth. "All this good weather's addled you. I don't see anything good coming of you seeing her again."

"Maybe. Maybe not," Maddie said. She hung the dishtowel over a dining-room chair and went into her bedroom to be by herself and think over her evening and about her new friend. She started to remember back to how she'd gotten here and how it felt when they were new to San Francisco and to the shipyard.

❖

Sawyer, Arkansas
July 1943

It was crazy enough that a White man was standing in the back of a pickup truck and talking to a crowd of Colored folk, but what he said was even more astounding. In the crowd, Maddie and Thom listened with increasing excitement.

Thom had come home with a flyer in his hand, so excited he was about to jump out of his skin. He waved the flyer in front of them at supper that evening. Around the table were Maddie, their mama, Edna, and Thom's new wife, Wilma Grace. They stared at him as he talked. Even if she could have gotten a word in, Maddie didn't know what to say because so many thoughts were racing through her head.

"We can go out tomorrow and listen to what they have to say, but look here. It says *GOOD JOBS. Work for Uncle Sam in San Francisco, California. Housing, travel expenses provided.* Look, Mama."

Thom gave the flyer to their mama, who scanned it but said nothing and handed it back to Thom. He continued talking between bites of gumbo.

"I think they want everybody. We can head out West and finally make some money. The man who handed me this said they'll accommodate family members, whatever that means. They'll give us a place to live, I think. He said they need women too."

Maddie looked at her mama. She didn't say anything, but that wasn't surprising. Her mama took her time and thought things over before she said anything. But when she did, you could generally expect her to say something sensible.

The next day, they gathered in a field right outside the Colored section of Sawyer. Next to him stood a Colored man, who was clearly assisting him. This man carried a stack of papers.

"Good morning, folks. Great to see you all here. What I am going to say today you can take on faith. I'm from President Roosevelt's labor department. I'm here to recruit you for the war effort."

His voice was jarringly sharp, and he talked so fast, Maddie had to struggle to follow his words.

"The shipyards, the plane factories, all those places have gone over to making hardware for the war. The president calls it the arsenal of democracy. That's a stirring phrase if I ever heard one. They need to run twenty-four hours a day, seven days a week to meet the demand. As you might have heard, a lot of fellows are being sent off to war. That means they got nobody to work here in the States. You are the answer to that problem. We propose to move you where you are needed and give you jobs and places to live. Think of it. California is one place. Beautiful Seattle, Washington is another. I mainly recruit for the San Francisco Bay Area. There are shipyards out there who need a thousand workers. One of them could be you. California is the land of oranges and sunshine. You heard of the gold rush? This is the second gold rush. See Toby here. He has all the information for you. I encourage you. No, I'm begging you to sign up. Your country needs everyone to help out. You ladies too."

He jumped down to the ground, and people mobbed him and his helper. Thom pushed in and grabbed all the pieces of paper he could.

At supper, he talked nonstop. Wilma Grace watched him but didn't say anything. Maddie decided to stay quiet too and wait to see what Mama would say. Thom finally ran out of words, and there was a huge pause, and the three of them looked at Mama.

"You ought to do it," Edna said. "Get out of this place. Sawyer's got nothing to keep you here. You can earn some money and come back home. Wilma Grace? What do you think?"

Wilma Grace was a pretty, deceptively easygoing young woman. Maddie had observed that she could mostly get Thom worked around to her point of view by sheer persistence, and she usually got her way in everything.

"I don't think it's real. I think they're lying."

Thom's expression fell. "Honey, they're not lying. It's the federal government. Why the heck would they lie about something like this?"

Maddie spoke up. "I wanna go. I want one of them good jobs."

All eyes turned to her.

Thom spoke first. "Don't be silly. For starters, you're too young."

"I'm eighteen next month."

"I don't want to have to look after you."

"I can look after my own self, thanks. You needn't worry yourself."

Maddie was incensed that Thom still considered her a child. He was only three years older.

Wilma Grace cleared her throat. "I don't see where I've agreed to go."

"Well, if I'm going, you're going with me."

They started to argue. Maddie looked at her mother, who tilted her head toward the living room.

"What do you think, Mama?" Maddie asked.

"If Thom can convince his wife, then you can go with them. But I don't want you to go by yourself."

"Really? You'd be okay with me going?"

Edna sighed. "I didn't exactly say that, but you never going to get anywhere here in Sawyer, honey. Best I see for you is working as farm laborer or as a maid. You're smart, and I know you can do better. Thom'll do well too, but he's got Wilma Grace to contend with. If he can get her to go along with him, they'll be fine. It's usually the other way around though." Maddie and her mama shared a chuckle at that.

Maddie hugged her mama and said, "I'm going to go make lots of money, and then I'll come home, and you and I will start a little business. You can sell your knitting and sewing, and I'll help you. I promise you."

"That's fine, honey, if you want to do that. That would be grand."

Maddie hugged her mama again and then went to clean up the supper dishes and listen to Thom and Wilma Grace argue, praying he could convince her to go along with his plan.

❖

In the end, Thom persuaded Wilma Grace that it was the right thing to do, their mama told Thom he was going to take Maddie along, and that was that. They signed themselves up a couple days later, Maddie lying about her age, but she figured it wouldn't matter, and it didn't. She'd be eighteen soon enough.

They made the train ride out West, the three of them in various combinations of excitement and dread. It was something when the train crossed the western border of Oklahoma into New Mexico and, for the first time in her life, Maddie saw train-station restrooms and water fountains that were not marked "White Only." That was almost more exciting than being on a train and going to San Francisco.

They arrived finally at the train station in Oakland. Thom was carrying all their papers with the directions for them. He said they had to board a bus that would take them to the Hunters Point shipyard. California's land of sunshine wasn't clear. It was raining and cold as they rode their bus across the bay to San Francisco.

As chilled as she was, Maddie was thrilled. Everything was so big. The bridge was big, and the bay below them was huge. It dwarfed anything she'd seen in Arkansas. And it was open, wide, and you could see forever. She had no idea what she was looking at, but she loved it all.

Their family was separated when they arrived at Hunters Point because they had to go to dormitories to sleep. Maddie and Wilma Grace shared a room in the women's dorm. Maddie huddled on her cot and listened to Wilma Grace complain. The gist seemed to be that Thom had tricked her into moving west, which wasn't true. Also, it was cold as heck, and there was no heat in the dorm to speak of. Maddie wrapped herself up tightly in her coat and finally fell asleep.

Wilma Grace's problems aside, Maddie was far more concerned about learning the art of welding. They offered a short training, but it seemed as though she mostly had to learn on the job from her coworkers. Fortunately, they were mostly helpful and patient. It was strange to work alongside and talk with White women, but the newness wore off pretty fast. A lot of Colored women were also doing things like welding. It was a dirty, dangerous job, so they seemed to be directed toward it in greater numbers. It didn't bother Maddie. She picked up the knack of it and appreciated the helpful tips of her cohorts.

It took a couple of months, but she, Thom, and Wilma Grace were assigned a small house partway up the hill, one of several that surrounded the shipyard. The navy had essentially created a small city to keep their workers housed, happy, and working hard. They had all kinds of recreations and sports teams and even a movie theater.

It was quickly apparent that California wasn't really sunshine and oranges. They were in a big city, for one thing, so nothing was grown there. And the weather was another thing. It rained all the time in the winter, and they had to work outside in it. Some coverings were rigged up, but they were hardly waterproof. But nothing could interrupt their work on the navy ships. A sense of purpose and urgency infused them every day. Maddie liked it, but it was exhausting.

On her first few days off, Maddie could do nothing but sleep, but six months after they'd arrived, she decided to explore outside of the shipyard. Predictably, Wilma Grace was fearful of her going off on her own, but Maddie dismissed that concern. What she needed the most was distraction from her feelings of disorientation caused by being in a place so radically different from Sawyer. And she missed her mama horribly.

On her day off, Maddie went to downtown San Francisco and looked around. The big city was a little scary but fascinating at the same time. Its energy infused her. At the training school all the new hires were fired up with patriotism and eager to help the war effort. This energy was the same. So many people were swarming the streets, and the traffic was hectic and noisy. Cars and taxis and streetcars were all vying for space, with pedestrians swarming all over the streets.

Maddie boarded a streetcar on Market Street, astonished to see that on the back of the car, collecting nickel fares, was a small, very young-looking Colored girl. This was another thing that told her she wasn't in Dixie anymore.

When the young woman saw Maddie, her face lit up with recognition, and her smile got much bigger. They were the only two Colored people on the streetcar. It was a wonder, though, that no one else seemed to notice. Back in her hometown, such a thing would never occur. The earth would open up and swallow up everyone if a Colored person and a White person did the exact same job. Yet Maddie had seen it. Her first streetcar ride had featured a young Colored boy collecting fares. And here doing the exact same thing was a young woman around Maddie's age, maybe younger.

"Hi, girl. How you doing?" the girl said cheerily.

Though she was startled, Maddie was able to form a reply.

"I'm just fine. Thank you kindly." The girl's voice still carried the lilt of the South, and it thrilled Maddie and made her homesick at the same time. "How are you today?" she added.

"I'm grand. Thank you so much," she said and turned to collect another fare. A White man got on behind her and handed over his nickel and received his ticket just like it was an ordinary, everyday thing.

Maddie sat down still in a mist of wonderment. How in the world could she get a chance to actually talk to this girl? She had a million questions for her.

The streetcar lurched forward, and they had a few moments between stops. She fought her shyness back and approached the young conductor.

"Could we maybe talk? I mean, when you're not at work?"

"Sure. I get off at three, but the streetcar terminal's way out by the ocean. I got one more downtown run before I'm done for the day."

Maddie thought about it. It was already two in the afternoon.

"I'll wait. My name's Maddie."

"Pleased to meet you, Maddie. I'm Marguerite."

At the end of the line, they both marched off the streetcar at the same time.

"My mother's waiting for me. I got to go tell her to wait a little longer." She tilted her head toward an old car idling near the streetcar turn-around.

They sat on a bench along the Great Highway and looked at the ocean.

"I just moved here a couple months ago," Marguerite said.

"Where you from? I know it's not California."

"Stamps, Arkansas."

Maddie was quiet for so long, Marguerite finally said, "What's wrong, girl? Cat got your tongue?"

"I'm from Sawyer, Arkansas."

"Other side of the state, then. What do you know? We a long ways from Arkansas." Marguerite nodded, and Maddie took her meaning that the "long ways" applied to more than just geography.

"I never thought to see someone like you working on the streetcars," Maddie said.

Marguerite laughed. "I liked the uniforms, and my mother told me if I wanted that job, then to go get it."

"How'd you do that?"

"I sat in that office every day all day for two weeks. Them secretaries gave me grief and called me nasty names. You know the ones. But I just ignored them and read my book. One day the manager came out and said, 'You want that job, it's yours.' I learned that if I want something, I have to keep at it and not give up. My mother told me I could do it, and I did it." Marguerite set her jaw, but she grinned.

"Wowee."

"You got a job, Maddie? And how the heck did you end up out here? My mother moved us out a little while back."

"A man came to Sawyer on the back of a pickup truck and said President Roosevelt needed everyone to work. So we—me and my brother and his wife—said yes, and we're all at the shipyard."

Marguerite nodded. "We can work here, even if not everyone's in favor of it. They can't stop us. Not like back in Arkansas." Maddie understood what the "we" meant.

Maddie thought about that. "That's something, isn't it?"

"Yep. It sure is. This war's changed a lot of things, and there'll be more to come, I think."

"My mama didn't want me and Thom to leave Sawyer, but she knew it was a good idea."

"It sure is. Whatever you do down to that shipyard, keep doing it. Don't let anyone try to stop you. You can whatever you want to do. Hey, my mother is waiting, so I have to go. But you take care of yourself. Lovely to meet you."

Maddie went back downtown to catch the bus back home. She'd forgotten to ask how old Marguerite was, but she looked young, and she surely couldn't be older than Maddie. She seemed older though. Maddie's job at the docks was so hard, but she was ready to go back to it. Marguerite had looked at first like a mirage, but she was quite real. *If she can do what she does, then so can I.*

CHAPTER FOUR

September 1945

As far as Gerry was concerned, her visit with Maddie and her family was a success. But how could they meet again? She had Maddie's address so she could write, but that seemed like a crazy thing to have to do when they didn't live that far apart. She wouldn't be able to get another shore leave for a while though, so she might as well make the best of it. But what should she say exactly in a letter? She wasn't that good a letter writer.

> *Dear Maddie,*
> *Tell Wilma Grace thanks again for a great supper. I had fun visiting your house and the shipyard, and I want to come back and see more. We're busy, as usual, over here, and now that they're bringing all the sailors back home, I guess I'll be driving the buses nonstop. No plans for kicking us out of the navy yet. I want to try to stay in since I don't see going back to Fresno. I want to stay in the navy if I can, because I just love it. I don't want to do anything else. Write me back if you can.*

Woody's oddly distant attitude about Maddie and Gerry's friendship made Gerry not want to talk to her about it, though Woody still acted like everything was the same. Instead, she bugged Jimmy both for advice on how and when to get another pass and her feelings about Maddie.

"I don't know what to do, Jimmy. She might be gay, and she might not be. I'm stuck on her. It was love at first sight."

"You're being a silly goose. That's the surest way to heartbreak."

"You're being mean."

"No, dear. I'm being honest. It's going to take time, and I know that's hard to hear, especially since we don't exactly have the freedom to run around with our friends."

Gerry sighed and pouted, but he was right. It was going to be letters or nothing.

Dear Gerry,

I hope you can come back soon. I can show you around the shipyard. We can go visit the cafeteria here. I'd take you on a walk up the hill. It's real pretty, and you can see over the bay.

Sincerely,
Maddie

It wasn't enough, but it would have to do for now. In the meantime, Gerry took extra shifts to occupy herself.

She was startled when, a couple of weeks later, Woody handed her an evening pass.

"The catch is, you're going with me, and we're going out. No Jimmy. I hope no last-minute changes, like last time."

"What do you mean?" Gerry asked.

"I mean, this time we're not going to foot the bill for a cab for a couple of strangers."

"Huh. We woulda had to take a cab anyhow, with that craziness going on."

Woody slid by that logical observation smoothly. "That's not going to happen this time, and we can hoof it down the hill to the terminal just like usual. Come on. I want you to come with me. We'll have a gas."

Gerry shut her mouth. Since the fall of 1943, when she arrived at Treasure Island, fresh from boot camp, she'd been following Woody's lead. She owed her so much because Woody had let her see who and what she really was. More than that, she was her best friend and teacher. Though only a couple of years older than Gerry, she had always seemed way more mature. The Pauline episode rankled her at first, but in the end, she'd accepted that it was a rite of passage, and Woody had only wanted to help her.

Woody always said, "You were such an eager beaver, I was sure you'd be the death of me." But in spite of her teasing, Woody had been loyal, and Gerry had to admit she was always a hell of a good time. So when Woody asked, she went along without question.

Every night at Mona's was party time, but Saturdays were definitely the best. Gerry and Woody hightailed it up to Broadway from the train station as quick as they could.

"Who's playing tonight?" Gerry as they walked.

"Kay Scott."

Kay was a popular singer—not as popular as Gladys Bentley, but pretty close. She sang risqué songs, to the delight of both the tourists and the local girls. And she was little and cute in her sleek tailored suit and wingtip shoes.

Gerry and Woody ordered a couple of drinks and made themselves comfortable.

Woody waved her cigarette in a circle and tipped her head at the straight couple at the next table. "Wait'll they get a load of Kay." She snickered.

"Until she comes on, they can ogle the customers," Gerry said.

As if on cue, the couple's swiveling heads brought their slightly glazed gazes to rest on Gerry and Woody. The female half's mouth was open, and she stared at them openly. Neither Woody nor Gerry went for the heavy butch look. They didn't wear ties, for instance, but they wore slacks and tailored sport-collar shirts. With Woody's help, Gerry picked out her clothes in the boys' department of the Emporium.

The owner of Mona's, Mona Sargent, had told them a long time ago, "I keep a nice joint. Don't worry about the looky-loos. I don't let 'em bother anyone, and it's good business."

"Hey, my fiancé thinks you ain't girls," the woman said in a nasal accent. It sounded like she said, "Goils."

Woody leaned back in her chair and smirked. "Oh, he doesn't? What about you? What do *you* think?" She was issuing a challenge. Gerry watched and waited.

"I think you're a boy," the heavily made-up, slightly tipsy tourist asserted.

"Why don't you come over here and sit next to us and see for yourself."

The woman grinned at her companion and slid into the chair between Gerry and Woody. Her boyfriend looked eager, put his hands behind his head, and leaned back, pretending he was going to casually enjoy whatever was going to happen.

"What's your name, sweetie?" Woody asked genially.

"Stella." The woman was clearly full of alcohol-fueled bravado. "What's yours?" Her screechy voice hurt Gerry's ears.

"Woody. This is Gerry."

"Pleased to make your acquaintance."

Stella made an elaborate show of shaking hands with both of them.

"So, Stella, where you from?" Woody asked.

"We're from New York." *New Yawk.*

"You're far from home. How do you like Frisco?"

"I like it. It's pretty, it's a big city like New York, but it's, you know, different."

Woody and Gerry chuckled.

"Yeah, kind of," Woody said, catching Gerry's eye. Gerry had seen her do this act with tourists before as a kind of game, especially when she was bored.

"How do I know if you're a boy or a girl?" Stella asked.

"Well. How about I kiss you?" Woody asked. "Maybe that will help you decide."

Stella leaned over and kissed her right on the lips. Woody kissed her back, putting some passion into it. Stella started to pull away, but then she came back. Woody captured the back of her neck and kept her in place. Their kiss began to look heated. Over at their table, her companion flushed as he watched them. Gerry hoped it was interest and not anger.

Stella pulled away at last and tossed her head. "I still don't know what you are, but you kiss like crazy." She dove back in, and Woody responded eagerly. She grabbed Stella's hand and put it on her breast, which was almost invisible under her loose shirt. Stella didn't take her hand away.

"Oh, my God, you're a girl."

"Yup."

All of a sudden Stella's swain appeared right at their table. "That's enough, Stella. Come back and sit down."

"Oh, Frank. Don't be a wet blanket. She's a girl."

"Yeah, pal. I'm a girl. I just kissed *your* girl much better than you do. Am I right, Stella?"

"Wait a god damn minute here." Frank was losing his temper. Yes, his flush was an angry one. Gerry wished Woody didn't act so smart at times like this.

"Come on, Frank." Stella pulled his arm. "Don't be a dope."

"Yeah, don't be a dope, Frank," Woody repeated insolently. He made a lunge toward her, but Stella blocked him.

"How you all doing?"

It was Mona, standing right next to Frank. She didn't wait for an answer. "Sir, come sit down and have another drink. On the house. Show's going to start soon."

Frank looked like he might continue, but instead he nodded, and he and Stella went back to their table. As she led them away, Mona patted each of them on the shoulder. "What're you drinking?"

Gerry swiveled to glare at Woody and said, "What the hell were you thinking?"

"Nothing," Woody said. She crossed her leg, took a gulp of her drink, and lit another cigarette.

"Bullshit. You got a bug up your butt about something. You know it's not a good idea to tease the rubes too much, especially the guys."

Mona liked her gay girls to be nice to the tourists. It was part of the club's draw, and it gave the out-of-towners a little thrill. They came to Mona's so they could play being bad in wicked San Francisco. Things could get of hand, though, if one of them got a little too friendly with a female whose boyfriend or husband got jealous, as had just happened.

Gerry wanted Woody to come clean, but it would have to wait, because Kay Scott walked onto the stage. Gerry liked her because she was funny.

Sure enough, she opened with a favorite of Gerry's: Kay was a little girl but sharply dressed in a miniature suit. She winked a lot and played to the crowd.

Gerry wondered what Maddie would make of Kay. She didn't mention Gladys during their visit. *What* did Maddie think about Gladys? What did she think about anything? Gerry longed to know, but she guessed she'd have to wait.

She listened to Kay, but her mind wandered. What did Woody think? She'd said more than once, *Don't try and understand dames. You'll break your brain.* Woody obviously didn't think she and Gerry were dames. They were butches, and that was that. Gerry didn't question Woody about it, like she didn't question anything Woody told her.

Guess I sort of look up to her. But baiting that tourist…

Darn. It might be time to ask. She longed to discuss Maddie with her or, if not, find out *why* Woody was so closemouthed on the subject of Maddie.

When Kay's set was over, Woody went and bought them two more drinks. They would be their last ones. It was eleven p.m., time to head out so they could make it to the eleven-thirty commuter train back to base.

When they were in their seats in the almost empty car, Gerry steeled herself and asked, "How come you didn't go over to supper at Maddie's with me? And why don't you want to talk about Maddie? I like this girl, and I'm going to see her again, just as soon as I can. You're my best pal. *Come on.*" She gave Woody a little dig in the ribs.

Woody sat with her eyes closed, head back. She wrinkled her nose a little. "Kid. Remember what I told you back when we met?"

"You told me a heck of lot of things. What in particular?"

"That part about who you go with and who you don't go with. I said watch out for the dopers and the drunks. And don't go after any other butches. I gave you the lowdown, told you what's what and all."

"Yeah. You did. I appreciate it. But what are you getting at?"

"Well, there's right and there's wrong. Just because the straight people think we're all sick and we're all wrong doesn't mean we don't have rules."

"*What* are you talking about. Spit it out, why don't ya?" Gerry was becoming impatient.

"You can't get together with Maddie."

"Why not? I mean, I don't know if she's one of us or not. I want to find out."

"No. Ger, you don't want to even try."

"Hey. She's no drunk, and I'd bet my life she's no doper." Gerry remembered Maddie and her shyness that went away as they had talked. And her neat home with her brother and sister-in-law.

Gerry added, "And she's not a butch as far as I can tell. So what's the story?"

Woody sighed and put her palm over her eyes. "Look. You're from Hicksville Fresno, and I forgive you for not understanding what's what. But she's a Negro. You can't be around her. You just can't. Okay? There, I told you."

"Oh, cripes. You're kidding me. What's her being a Negro got to do with anything?"

"Everything. I'm telling you. It's not right."

They sat in angry silence.

Finally, Gerry said, "I don't know why you feel that way. She's just a person like you and me. I don't know if she's gay. But she likes me and I like her, and this time, I'm not going to listen to you, Woody. I'm gonna listen to myself. Sorry."

"You'll regret it" was all Woody said. They didn't say another word to each other for the rest of their train ride.

❖

Maddie had the kind of job where, if you didn't pay close attention, you were likely to injure yourself or maybe hurt someone else. She'd seen it happen to a couple of women. Being a welder didn't leave much time for her to think about anything else, which was both good and bad. Good because the workday went fast, and she was so worried about staying safe and doing a good job that she didn't have extra time to wonder where Gerry was and why she hadn't written. *Busy, I expect.* It was bad because she *wanted* to think about Gerry and relive the night they met and Gerry's visit for supper.

She liked thinking about Gerry and how she looked and how she talked and how she moved and her happy grin. Even the calm and easy way she treated Thom and Wilma Grace. And the way Gerry acted with her, all kind and attentive and asking her questions. All she basically had was a little time to think before she fell asleep at night. When she wasn't working, she was expected to help Wilma Grace keep house. And that was sort of a nonstop stream of chores because Wilma Grace would die if she missed some little thing. It wasn't because of Maddie or even Thom. He wasn't demanding. He worked long hours, and then he wanted to eat and go to sleep. Wilma Grace had her standards, Maddie guessed.

She could at least write to Gerry, but even when she wrote she felt she had to be careful.

One night after dinner, Maddie sat at their kitchen table with a pad of paper and composed a letter to Gerry.

Wilma Grace came by and looked over her shoulder. "What are you doing?"

"I'm writing a letter." Maddie hoped that would be enough to shut her up, but no.

"To who? Mama?"

"Nope."

"Well, who then?"

"Goodness, Wilma Grace. Leave me be." She knew she sounded short-tempered, but really, Wilma Grace needed to mind her own business.

"Is it a letter to that girl, Gerry, who was over here?"

Maddie curled her arm around the paper tablet. "Yes. If you must know."

"Hmph." Wilma Grace snorted but walked away and went back to sit on the porch with Thom. Maddie was grateful she'd let it drop but sure she hadn't heard the last of Wilma Grace's opinions.

> *Dear Gerry,*
>
> *I hope you're doing okay. I'm doing fine. We had to work overtime yesterday to finish something. I don't know why the big hurry, since the war is over. Ha, ha. But we still got to build these ships. I would like you to see them sometime. I know you see them out there where you are, but I mean see how we build them. It's really something, how it all fits together and how many of us work on the ship and how long it takes.*

She stopped and tapped her pencil on the table. She wanted to go on and on but didn't want to bore Gerry silly. Yet it was good to be able to tell her stuff. She wanted to say more but didn't know what was proper or not. They'd only known each other a short time.

> *I'm going to try and work some more shifts. I'm saving money. I send some back home to Mama, but I want to have a pile so when the war's completely done I can go back to Sawyer and start a little business that me and my mama can work at.*
> *Yours truly,*
> *Maddie Weeks*

Maddie folded the letter and put it in an envelope. She went to the kitchen and ran herself a glass of water and returned to the kitchen table and looked at the writing tablet. It was time for her weekly letter to her mama, but all the things she normally wrote about, mainly her job and the doings at the church, seemed less relevant than her new friend Gerry. She wondered what her mama would say if she told her about Gerry and said she was White. Her mama wasn't like some others Maddie knew from Sawyer, who were so anxiously attentive about every single little thing about their daughter's life that their love came to seem a kind of burden their daughters carried. Wilma Grace's mama was like that, and Maddie thought that was exactly why Wilma Grace was how she was.

No. Maddie's mama was easy-going about almost everything. She was nothing like the women Maddie was thinking of. But she hadn't had, in Maddie's memory, *any* good interaction with any White people except the postmistress and maybe crazy old Mrs. Tate, and she always cautioned Maddie about letting her guard down. She might consider Maddie making friends with Gerry a prime example of that. Yet Maddie had always been honest with her mama because she had never had any reason not to be. This time, however, she decided she was going to commit a small sin of omission and not mention Gerry.

When Gerry read the letter from Maddie, she was ecstatic and despondent at the same time. Maddie was planning to leave when the war ended. That meant she didn't have much time to get to know her, and they'd just met. She could get exactly one day of shore leave every two weeks, and once a month she could stay out overnight until seven the next morning. The idea of staying out "overnight" gave her a shiver. What would that mean? She had no idea what Maddie even felt about her because they'd barely talked. Was Maddie a gay girl? Did she even like Gerry that way? Given her attitude, Gerry couldn't even ask Woody anything about what she thought about Maddie. Maybe Jimmy could help her, but she doubted it. She was on her own. One thing was certain, though. She had to see Maddie soon. She rolled her pencil on the desk and thought hard. She had a night off coming the following week and an idea. Then she went back to writing her letter to Maddie.

I hope you can get away to meet me. Six o clock at the St Francis ice cream shop on 24th street.

When Maddie was a little girl, her mama had taught her where she was *not* to go in Sawyer. Certainly not by herself and not even with her brother. She didn't explain, but when she was older, getting toward her teens, Edna told her why.

It's the White parts of Sawyer. We'll either get asked what we're doing there and then told to leave. Or if we meet the wrong person, someone in a bad mood or someone nasty, we could get beat up or even killed. You get it?

It was years later, and she'd never seen or heard of any reason why she couldn't go to this particular part of San Francisco. But she still felt unsure. Of course, the only place she'd ever been besides the shipyard and downtown was to the club with Wilma Grace, and that had been as daring a thing as she'd ever done. When she went to downtown San Francisco, she merely looked around the streets. It was with old Wilma Grace, but still, they'd gone off to another neighborhood to a bar and had even survived a riot. Her mama would have been alarmed by that.

Still. Maddie was full of random anxiety about finding this St. Francis Ice Cream Fountain. Even the thought of seeing Gerry couldn't quite quell her fear. Nonetheless, go she would. No way was she going to miss a chance to see Gerry.

"You're doing what?" Wilma Grace asked.

Maddie repeated herself patiently. "I'm going to meet Gerry at 24th and Potrero Ave. for ice cream. I won't be out long."

"Are you sure that's a good idea?"

"Yes. I'm sure."

"Is this a safe place to go?"

"Well. You probably thought Mona's 440 Club was a safe place, and look what happened there." That was most likely unfair, but Maddie didn't want to get into a whole argument about it, and sure enough, Wilma Grace clammed up.

The soda fountain wasn't that hard to find, and when she arrived at the corner of 24th and Potrero, Gerry was there already, leaning against the window with her hands in the pockets of her trousers. She grinned and waved when she saw Maddie.

"Hey. Glad you could come."

"I was thinking about vanilla ice cream."

"Oh? Is that a fact? I was thinking about chocolate. Oh, hey. That's funny." Gerry started to laugh.

"Why is that funny?" Maddie asked.

"Don't you think it ought to be the other way around?" Gerry said, still giggling.

"Oh," Maddie said, finally understanding what Gerry meant. "Right. I ought to like chocolate, and you ought to like vanilla. Ha-ha."

They went in and took seats at the counter. A tiny corner of Maddie's mind went on alert. *They may not want me here.*

But nothing like that happened. The soda jerk came over and took their orders. Gerry opted for a chocolate milkshake.

They decided to move to sit in a booth where they could examine the juke-box choices.

It helped them get talking. Gerry turned the pages of the juke box so fast, Maddie could hardly read the song titles, but she stopped finally and said, "How about Tommy Dorsey?"

Maddie grabbed the metal tab and flipped the pages forward again. Gerry didn't react. "How about Nat King Cole instead?" She raised her eyebrows in a question.

Gerry grinned. "Sure. I like a gal who knows what she wants." She put in a nickel and pressed the button. Nat's mellow voice filled the diner. They were the only customers, probably because it was a Wednesday at six p.m., and everyone was home eating supper, Maddie reckoned. She grabbed a piece of bread before she left the house, not having time to wait for Wilma Grace to cook their evening meal.

"I want to hear about your work at the shipyard. That's something, isn't it? That we get to have jobs, and not just any jobs? It's real work like men do."

"I guess so. I never thought of it that way. I only know if I was back home, I'd be working in a laundry or picking cotton or being a maid."

"That's it?"

"Yeah. They don't let Colored people in Sawyer work at most stuff. I couldn't go to college, so I couldn't be a teacher or something."

"I never wanted to be a farmer myself, but that's what I thought I'd be doing my whole life—or be a farmer's wife. My people were all farmers."

"Did they have their own farm or work it for someone else?" Maddie thought about the Colored tenant farmers around Sawyer. That didn't seem to her like an ideal life. The war had come along and changed everything for everybody.

Gerry drew invisible lines on the Formica table. Then their ice creams arrived, and she stayed quiet until the soda jerk left.

"It was my dad's farm, but it wasn't big. He had a couple of hands for help at harvest, but mostly me, my two brothers, and my mom did all the work. I'm glad to be gone."

Gerry's mood had changed, and Maddie wondered why, but she didn't ask. Her long experience with Wilma Grace's nosy questions made her wary. If Gerry wanted her to know something, she'd tell her, Maddie reasoned. She *did* want to know more about Gerry, but she could wait.

"Never mind me. I want to know about you," Gerry said, and her friendly grin came back.

"I got a chance, and I took it," Maddie said. "Wasn't ever going to happen again. Me and my brother listened when the federal man told us we could work in San Francisco for the government."

"You wanted to leave your hometown and come all the way out here?" Gerry asked, curious.

"If you was a Colored girl in Sawyer, you would have too," Maddie said, nodding for emphasis. No way Gerry would understand how difficult a decision that was—or how necessary. She was nice, but she wouldn't know anything about what Maddie's life was like.

"I needed to leave where I was too. And the navy gave me a way to do it. Guess we're alike in some ways."

Not too damn many.

But Maddie smiled and said, "Yeah. In a little bit of a way."

They both took more sips of their milkshakes, and Maddie said, softly, "You still want to come out to the shipyard?"

Gerry had become thoughtful and quiet but said brightly, "Yeah. I sure do." Then she slumped down, looking sad. "But I can't right now. Maybe next month."

"I don't expect we're going to stop building them ships anytime quick. I'll be there."

They lingered outside the ice cream shop, both reluctant to leave. Finally, Gerry said, "I'll write you again. Will you write me?"

And Maddie said, "'Course I will."

They parted, walking off in opposite directions.

It wasn't like her brother Thom didn't care about her. Wilma Grace did too, in her own busybody way, but Gerry seemed to care about her a great deal in a real personal and specific way, like Maddie meant something special. It was good to be cared about like this, not watched for making a mistake like at work or, God forbid, like she was watched in Sawyer to make sure she didn't do something wrong. But to be seen as a person who was interesting and fun—that was something.

❖

Woody wasn't talking to her, but she wasn't *not* talking to her. It was confusing and hurtful, but since their last conversation, Gerry had come to accept her attitude. She and Woody talked every day, but they didn't really talk like they used to, at least about anything important. It was sad, but Gerry wasn't at all ready to give up on Maddie because Woody thought it wasn't right. She had no idea what was going to happen for the two of them, but she intended to find out.

The problem with trying to make plans to see Maddie was that Treasure Island had been thrown into a new level of frenzied activity since the war ended. All the US troops were coming home, and they were being brought home by the navy to Treasure Island. That was thousands of men. The war had entailed a huge amount of work itself while it was going on, but the ending of it seemed to rise to a whole other level. They called it demobilization, or de mob for short.

Gerry didn't mind the incessant bus trips or the crowds of exuberant seamen she had to transport, but she *did* mind not seeing Maddie. They exchanged letters every week, but it wasn't good enough. Three weeks had passed since they'd met at St. Francis soda fountain. Her navy stint was going to be up soon, and she thought about leaving, but what then? She didn't know what she would do if she wasn't in the navy. She sure as heck wasn't going to back to the farm.

She asked Jimmy about possibilities.

"You could go overseas—work in Japan or something. Or you could be a recruiter, travel all over."

Neither of those things were what Gerry had in mind. She didn't want to be farther away from Maddie, and she craved more time for herself.

"Become a civilian" was Jimmy's advice. "In another year that's what I'm going to do. I'll stick with it until my tour of duty is up. Then I'll do something else, I guess."

It was no good. She wasn't ready to leave it. Quite the opposite.

The navy was the best thing that had ever happened to her. Aside from Maddie, of course.

She hadn't wanted to go into a lot of detail about her life as a kid when Maddie asked. As far as she was concerned, she never wanted to think about it again. It was a lot of hard work, not much love, and truly something she hoped she'd left far behind her.

CHAPTER FIVE

October 1945

Gerry liked ice cream as much as the next girl, but she wasn't going to make any romantic progress sipping on milkshakes like a pair of teenagers. She wanted to take Maddie to Mona's on a real date. It was a good sign that Maddie had come to Mona's the night of Gladys's show. But she was there with Wilma Grace, and they'd come to see Gladys perform, so it wasn't at all clear what or who Maddie really was.

Woody once admitted she took Gerry to Mona's 440 Club to watch her reactions.

"Like I said, I was pretty sure, but it's still a good way to find out about someone. How does she act around the women? Is she afraid? Disgusted? Curious? What's the story?" Woody had told her. "I couldn't come right out and ask you."

Jimmy added, "It's called dropping hairpins. You say little things, make little hints, and see if the person reacts. If she's not that way, she won't notice. Taking someone to a gay bar is gutsy, but that's our Woody."

Fortunately, Maddie wrote back that she'd love to go to Mona's for a drink, and they made a date.

"You going to make your play this time?" Jimmy asked. "I would. You better find out for sure before you waste any more time or money."

"I'm not making my play, as you call it. That's crass."

Jimmy sniffed. "It's none of my business, I suppose, but I'd hate to see you barking up the wrong tree."

"Just can it, will ya?" Gerry was already nervous enough. She had no idea what Maddie's true feelings were, but she hoped she'd be able to find out.

She couldn't pick up Maddie from her house like she wanted to, so they had to meet at the club. She recalled that during one of Woody's many talks with her on how to treat femmes, she stressed the need for "taking care of your girl." Gerry assumed that meant always escorting her from one place to another. So she was already failing at that part of being a butch. She supposed she'd be more confident if she'd already had at least one girlfriend. Pauline didn't really count.

Gerry waited anxiously at Mona's front door, shifting from one foot to the other and smoking too much. Maddie showed up wearing a pretty dress and lipstick and had styled her hair with victory rolls over her ears.

Gerry swallowed, thrilled that Maddie took such trouble to look pretty. She put on her best smile and made a show of leading Maddie to a table.

"I'm sorry there's no singer tonight. I hoped we could talk."

"I'd like that."

One of the "waiters," a short girl with slicked blond hair, came over to them. "What can I get you?"

"I'll have a dry martini," Gerry said with as much confidence as she could summon. She looked at Maddie.

"Ginger ale, please."

"She'll have a ginger ale," Gerry said to the waitress as though she was deaf. The waitress smirked and wrote down their orders. Somehow, the whole act made Gerry feel foolish. Maddie, however, appeared unconcerned.

When the waiter left, she said, "I'm not much of a drinker."

"That's okay. I'm not either." In spite of her choice of drink, that was true. She only ordered a martini to impress Maddie. She usually drank beer.

"So you've only been here once, and that was to see Gladys?"

"Oh, yes. Wilma Grace kind of dragged me along. She really wanted to go, but not alone. She'd seen Gladys with her cousin in Harlem."

"Did you like it?" Gerry asked.

"Oh, my, yes. I loved Gladys."

"I meant did you like the place? In general." Gerry couldn't come right out and ask her if she liked girls in suits and ties, so she tried to find out in a roundabout way.

Maddie looked puzzled, her neat eyebrows scrunched up.

"Yes. I wouldn't come back here if I didn't."

"Oh. Yes, of course. That's true." Gerry immediately felt silly. She had to pull herself together and stop saying dumb stuff.

"I come here a lot. The music's fine and"—and she was about to say—"and the company's good," but she didn't want come right out and say that.

As if on cue, the band filed onto the stage, sat down, picked up their instruments, and began warming up. Maddie watched them without much expression.

"I thought you said there was no singer tonight?"

"Uh." Gerry paused, trying to form a sentence. "No. I don't think so."

"Then what are they doing?"

"Eh. I don't know," she finally said, lamely. So much for her hope to appear sophisticated. This wasn't going well at all.

The band leader raised her baton, and Gerry heard the familiar notes of "In the Mood."

"How come no one's dancing?" Maddie looked around curiously.

"Uh, this isn't a dancing place."

She looked around again. "Men aren't any part of this, are they?" she asked. "But I saw a few when we came in."

A few gay boys were there, which wasn't unusual. They were drinking at the bar, having a gay old time.

"They're friends of the bartender," Gerry replied, thinking it best to not try to explain.

"Well. I, for one, am real glad there aren't any men around to bother us." She grinned.

"Yep. Me too." Gerry was attempting to appear nonchalant.

All of a sudden, Maddie focused on Gerry and asked her, "How come half the women here are wearing pants and the other half dresses?"

Gerry was at a loss. She knew the answer, but she didn't want to try to explain it to Maddie.

"Uh. I don't know. I guess it's just how they like to dress."

"What about you?"

"Oh, you know. I like wearing pants. I'm not so good in a dress."

"Hmph. Why?" Maddie wasn't being nosy exactly. She seemed to genuinely want to know.

Gerry shifted in her chair and took another gulp of her drink to stall. "I'm more comfortable this way."

"That's it? That's all?"

"Yep. That's all." Gerry affected unconcern.

"Hmph." There was that skeptical sound again. Gerry didn't know if Maddie was dissatisfied with her explanation, irritated by it, or exactly what she was thinking. Gerry and Maddie sat through two songs by Kay Scott. Gerry kept throwing glances at Maddie to try to gauge what she was thinking, but she couldn't tell.

The singer took a break, and Maddie drained her ginger ale, stood up, and said, "I think I'm going to go."

"So soon? Why?" This was a genuinely startling and unwelcome development.

"I'm tired. I have to work in the morning."

"But we just got here." Gerry was aghast.

"I'm sorry. Thanks for the invitation. I appreciate it."

"How are you going to get home?"

Maddie looked at her, and this time her expression clearly said, *Are you dumb or what?*

"Same way I got here. On the bus."

Gerry looked at her watch. What she was about to suggest would be a risk and could make her late reporting back to base.

"I can go with you, see you home."

"I been going places by myself since I was eight. Don't think I need any help now."

Maddie closed her mouth with a snap, then added, "But thanks anyhow."

"Are you sure?" Gerry right away felt silly, but she was desperate to somehow prolong their time together.

"Yeah. I'm sure." Maddie stood up, gathered her purse and her coat, and stuck her hand out.

Gerry shook it numbly.

"Thanks for a nice evening."

"Wait. Can we get together again?" Gerry asked, unable to keep the pleading tone out of her voice.

"Yeah, we can. Look, I'm going to miss my bus. Bye."

And she was gone.

Gerry sat back down, staring at the empty chair across from her. She could dimly hear the band playing and the laughter and ice rattling in glasses, but it was all in the background. In her mind, the questions fired. *What happened? Why she'd change?*

❖

The downtown streets were so dark, Maddie wondered if there was still a wartime blackout on. Only one other person rode the bus with her, but it was just as well. She wanted to be by herself for a bit, because when she got home, she most certainly would not be alone. Her brother would be sound asleep, most likely snoring away. But not Wilma Grace, who stayed up late doing God knows what, and she'd be there with her questions for Maddie. Maddie didn't want to answer anyone else's questions. She had too many of her own.

Maddie's thoughts were a mess, bouncing around in her head. She replayed the evening like she was watching a movie. The bar, Gerry's shiftiness. And, above all, Maddie thought she'd been brought to Mona's for a purpose Gerry had failed to explain. It all made her mad. It seemed she was being courted, but that didn't seem possible.

It must have something to do with all the women in the bar. Maddie had noticed them the first time she and Wilma Grace had gone to see Gladys Bentley. It was also sad but true that Maddie wondered about Gerry's motives. It wasn't normal for someone White to pay so much attention to her. Not that anyone at all had ever been so interested in her, other than her mama. Finally, and most disturbing, she didn't know why she liked Gerry's attention so much.

She wasn't proud she'd seemed so cold and distant when she left Mona's. She was sorry she acted that way and wondered what Gerry must be thinking of her.

❖

Jimmy sat in an easy chair, swinging his leg over the armrest, his head wreathed in cigarette smoke. Gerry had admitted to him that she was sweet on Maddie and didn't know what to do. Now her level of frustration and mystification over Maddie's actions had prompted her to seek him out. She also told him that Woody's reaction made her ineligible as a confidante.

He snorted. "So she's not in favor of you going for the chocolate flavor."

Gerry didn't like the sound of that phrase, but she was willing to put up with Jimmy's wisecracks if he could help her.

He said, "I don't know about you girls, but I do know if you've got a virgin, you're going to have to be a lot more patient. You say she doesn't seem to know about the gay life? What was she doing in Mona's in the first place anyhow?

"They just came to see the show. She and her sister-in-law."

"But aren't they wise to Gladys?"

"I don't think so."

Jimmy waved his cigarette. "I'll be darned. People are plain blind."

"Yeah, maybe, but what am I going to do?"

"Keep doing what you're doing, but sometime you're going to have to figure her out."

"No other words of wisdom? Nothing to help me?"

"Nah. But please feel free to talk to me anytime."

Gerry slumped in her chair and exhaled.

Jimmy reassured her. "You'll be fine. Sometimes it just takes persistence to nab your target."

"Yeah. Say, what do you know about the brass's plan for the end of the war?"

"We'll be bringing the boys back home, so we're gainfully employed for the time being. But otherwise, I don't know."

That was a relief but still no help to Gerry in solving her Maddie dilemma. She couldn't do anything else but write Maddie another letter and pray she'd answer.

❖

Dear Maddie,

I'm sorry about the other night. I don't know what I did wrong, but whatever it was, I'd like to make it up to you if you'll say you'll see me again.

We can go back to the St. Francis ice cream fountain or anywhere you want.

Yours truly,

Gerry

Maddie held the letter. It was written on a funny sort of folded paper that was its own envelope, with the navy symbol embedded in the paper. It was official US government stationery. She turned it over, thinking hard. She'd sensed Gerry was holding back something, and it bothered her. She was so confused about her feelings and guilty about the way she'd treated Gerry. She ought to write back and say "no thank you" and leave it there. Then she wondered what Marguerite would say about this situation. She bet Marguerite would say "yes" to Gerry, and then she would go back to see where it would it lead, no matter what her doubts. Maddie had many of those, and even more questions, but she sure as heck wasn't going to get any answers if she didn't ask. The only person she had to ask was Gerry herself. It hit her that they ought to go somewhere where they would have some privacy to talk. Her house wouldn't be good, with Wilma Grace and Thom around. Maddie wasn't even sure how she could actually get to Treasure Island, but she remembered riding the streetcar all the way out to the end to the ocean so she could talk with Marguerite.

She was lying in bed, staring at the ceiling as though somehow the answers she wanted were written there. The picture of Gerry sitting in Mona's grinning at her floated into her mind. Despite her misgivings, she wanted to see her again, and she wanted to know everything.

It took some time to get the same day off, but they met again where San Francisco ended and the ocean began. In the wind and the blowing sand, they sat on the same bench where Maddie had had her talk with Marguerite, the streetcar conductor. She knew it was silly to think it, but she hoped the location would somehow help.

Gerry smiled at her shyly and asked, "Can you start?"

Maddie was dreading that question because she would have to figure out what exactly it was that was bothering her and explain it to Gerry.

She looked at her shoes then, and although she was scared, she forced herself to make eye contact.

Once when she was about ten, back in Sawyer, she was in town with her mama, and she'd been bored waiting for her mama to finish what she was doing and started skipping around and ran smack into some White lady, who got mad and began to fuss at her. She had dared to look the lady in the face, and that made the woman even angrier. Maddie's mama rushed over and apologized to the woman and dragged Maddie away.

"Never look at a White person like that. They might think you're being uppity. Keep your eyes down, make your apologies quick, and leave as soon as you can."

This was not the same situation, but somehow Maddie was remembering that day.

"I'm sorry I acted so off-kilter the other day when we was out."

"That's okay. I want to know what I've done to make you feel that way. I want to tell you I'm sorry and that I'll be better."

Maddie was floored. Gerry was apologizing to *her*.

"Thank you for saying that. I left because I didn't know what to think about you. It seemed like you wanted to be my friend when we were having ice cream. Then it seemed like something else when we were in the bar. It's like you've got something in your mind, but you haven't told me yet."

Gerry swallowed and looked embarrassed.

"You're right." She stopped. "Have you ever heard of girls that like other girls?"

Maddie thought hard. There was one woman in Sawyer the others used to whisper about. They said she was "off." She lived by herself, and she wasn't married. Another woman had lived with her at one time, but she was gone. People talked about her being lonely, but she apparently wasn't going to try to find a man. Maddie didn't know why exactly, but she understood that the lonely woman, though not disliked, was somehow not part of the community. It was what people said, and when they talked about her, they rolled their eyes and tutted. But they never said exactly why she was "off."

"I might have."

Gerry perked up a bit and said, "Well, that's me. I'm one of them." She said it with a sort of defiance, like she was proud of it in some way.

"I see" was all Maddie could reply, but something shifted in her heart.

"I wondered if you are too. I, um, like you very much," Gerry said softly. "Since you were at Mona's to see Gladys and all, I wanted to take you back there. To see."

Maddie looked over to her. "I like you too, but I don't know if I am. I never had any interest in boys. Some tried, and I just told them to go away and don't bother me."

Gerry laughed at that. She seemed in a better mood since she'd said what she said, as though it was weighing on her.

"All those girls in pants at the club—they like other girls?" Maddie asked, knowing the answer.

"Yeah, they do." Gerry kept her eyes fixed on Maddie. She was unnerved by Gerry looking at her but liked it all the same. It gave her a shiver of pleasure.

"I like spending time with you," Gerry said. "Very much."

Maddie was looking out to sea, thinking. She could sense that Gerry was still looking at her, waiting for her answer.

Now would be a time to be completely honest with Gerry, and that was what she wanted to do, but it was an alien thought. Her mama's voice in her head counseled extreme caution. Her mama had told her over and over how to act around White people.

Be polite, but they don't have to know what you're thinking. Whatever it is—good, bad, or indifferent—your thoughts are your own, and you don't owe no one else to tell them. You don't know what will happen if you do.

But it wasn't like that here and now with Gerry.

Gerry wasn't some random White citizen on the street in Sawyer questioning Maddie on who she was and what she was doing. She had done Maddie and Wilma Grace a huge favor that night by helping them get away from the riot. She was sweet and friendly, and they had shared ice cream. There was something else too. Maddie didn't know what it was, and she couldn't put it into words. She'd never wanted so much to trust someone. Gerry looked at her with such affection and spoke so sincerely, Maddie's heart hurt, but in a good way. No one but her family had ever looked at her and spoken to her like that.

"I'm not used to talking to people I don't know."

Gerry's eyebrows furrowed. "But you know me. I'm not a stranger."

"It's hard to explain," Maddie said. "But where I come from, Colored folks don't talk to White folks unless they have a real good reason to. I don't have White *friends.*" That came out way more harshly than she meant it, but Gerry just kept looking at her and said nothing.

"You're different," Maddie said. "I know you're real different, and I see why. Back when we went to Mona's 440, I had a good time, truly, but I got scared. I didn't know if I could trust you."

"You can," Gerry said, very quietly. "I wouldn't ever hurt you. But maybe you have to spend more time with me to believe that. And time is hard for us to find."

"Yes. It is. I want to trust you. I like you."

"I like you too." Gerry took her hand.

"And that's the other thing I don't know about. Like how?"

"Like a boy would like you," Gerry said quietly, with some effort.

"Yeah. That's kinda what I thought, but I thank you for saying it out loud."

Gerry took her hand away. She sat, seeming to wait for Maddie to say more.

"I think we ought to keep going like we're going. I'm not going to act dingy around you no more," Maddie said with finality.

"That's a relief." And Gerry let out a big breath. To her surprise, it made Maddie very happy to be the person who could change Gerry's mood for the better. What was going to come next, she hadn't a clue, but at least they'd cleared the air, and no one's feelings were sore.

They boarded the streetcar and rode back downtown. As Maddie left, they hugged briefly.

"I'll see you when we can," Gerry said. "Whenever that is."

"Yes, when we can. You take care. Bye." When she was on the street, Maddie turned around and waved. From the door of the streetcar, Gerry waved back, beaming. Thrilled, Maddie waited for her bus back to Hunters Point.

❖

"Are you sure this is okay?" Gerry asked, sounding nervous.

"Yeah. We get visitors all the time. I'll tell you to stay back when it's time."

Maddie had recently switched to the swing shift at the dry dock. It wasn't as busy as the day shift, but it was still busy. The end of the war hadn't stopped the need to repair the navy ships, and working swing shift paid a little more. She was always thinking of the day when she had saved enough money and could quit and return to Sawyer.

"I like your clothes. You look like you mean business." She grinned, and Maddie mirrored her.

"Have to wear this. You can't weld in no dress," Maddie said. "First, I need to find out what I got to get done tonight."

She stopped at a little wooden shelf and picked up the notebook that rested on it. Then she flipped through to the last shift notes.

To Gerry she said, "I have to find out where to pick up the welds. The last shift wrote down what they did and where."

She wore dungarees with leather pants over them, a flannel shirt, and a leather apron. Plus, she had a bandana on her head to keep her hair out of the way. She walked down the side of the dry dock, using a flashlight to see her way, and she carried her welding helmet, plus a coiled electric cable.

It was early December now, and the night was chilly. Maddie didn't mind because she would get sweaty in her thick gear if the temperature got above seventy. She shuddered to think what welding would feel like if she had had to do it in Sawyer in the middle of summer.

"What's this?" Gerry asked. She pointed to the rod at the end of the cable.

"That's how I weld. This here thing is an electrode. I plug in this cord, and the stinger on the end melts the metal. Tonight, I have to weld the two plates together. It's the side of the ship, and it's got to be perfect. Elsewise she'll leak and sink the ship."

Gerry looked alarmed and Maddie laughed.

"Don't worry. I know what I'm doing. I had to go to welding school, and man, they were hard on us. I made so many mistakes at first, I wasn't sure I'd be able to do it, but I got the hang of it, finally."

Scaffolding was clinging to the side of the huge ship.

"I've got some vertical welds to do. Up there." She pointed as Gerry craned her neck to see in the dark. "You can come up to two levels below, and stay off to the side so's you can be out of the way. I'll point to you where to stand. You need to keep back, or them sparks'll burn you."

Maddie plugged her cord in to an extension and started to climb up the scaffold, and Gerry followed her.

"Stay right here," Maddie ordered her and kept climbing.

She stopped near the top of the scaffold. She'd unwound her cord as she climbed, and now she found the area of the seam she had to start with. She turned on the rod and lowered her shield, and as she started to run the probe smoothly downward between the plates, the sparks cascaded. She needed no light to see where she was going. The arc of the current hitting metal gave her enough to see, even through the dark glass plate on the front of her helmet. She completed one seam and moved down to the next level. Then she motioned Gerry to move farther down.

A couple of plates later, Maddie climbed off the scaffold, and

Gerry followed her. She led them off to the side, where they could sit on a railing.

"Give me that thermos," she said after she raised her shield. Gerry handed the thermos to her, and she drank thirstily.

"You're sweating," Gerry said quietly. "That looks like hot work."

Maddie took out her other bandana and wiped her face. Gerry was looking at her intently.

"Yep. It's hot and it's dangerous. Back at the beginning, one of girls who was an old hand told me to stop welding every time I could to get away from them fumes. Welding is burning metal, so it kicks up some nasty-smelling gas. Sometimes one of the girls'll pass out if she gets too much. I don't want that mess in my face. The shield keeps the sparks off me, but I can still smell it. So after every big seam, I take a little break."

"Does your boss mind?"

"Nah. I can throw a seam together faster than almost anyone. I get all my welds done real fast. He's got no reason to complain about my work."

"That's good."

Because she had an audience and the audience was Gerry, whom she wanted to impress, she couldn't help but brag a little more.

"Welding's like sewing. You need a steady hand and a good eye. My seams are all perfectly straight. Once you start, you can't stop or the electrode'll stick, and that's a pain. I learned how not to let the electrode get stuck."

"What's this?" Gerry asked, pointing to a burned hole on the shoulder of her flannel shirt.

"That's the slag flying on me," Maddie said. "I got another shirt underneath." She took another drink. "I have to keep going. You're not bored, are you?"

"Nope. I like to watch you. I used to go different places at Treasure Island and watch different guys do their jobs, especially the signal men and the radio men and the gunners. I even used to watch the seamen polish the metal on the ship fittings. I love to watch folks do their jobs who do them well. I like watching *you*."

"I'll let you come up and see when I'm done," Maddie said, charmed and gratified by the attention from Gerry. She put the lid back on her thermos and handed it back to Gerry.

It took a few hours for Maddie to finish her welds, but Gerry wasn't bored. She watched Maddie climb around the scaffold, trailing the cord. Then the sparks would fly as she laid her seams. She was, as she said, an expert. Gerry thought that her driving, while enjoyable, didn't take the same level of skill as Maddie welding the giant plates on the side of a battleship. There was no comparison. This was clearly meant to be a man's job, yet Maddie was able to handle it. Her slight appearance was deceiving. She had to be as strong as a man, with a lot of muscle underneath her leather and thick clothes.

When Maddie was done, it was after midnight, but lights were on everywhere, blinking off the bay. The dark shapes of the ships in dry dock loomed, outlined by the random lights.

Maddie took off her welding leathers and came back out onto the porch carrying two bottles of beer. She sat next to Gerry and tipped her drink back.

In the dark, Gerry could see the lights glance off Maddie's dark irises, surrounded by slivers of the whites of her eyes. Even her hair, disordered from the welding helmet, seemed to glow. There was no moon, but there was light enough from the buildings in the shipyard to illuminate them.

"We have to be quiet and not wake up Thom and Wilma Grace," she whispered.

"Right," Gerry whispered back.

"Do you think they'll keep you on now that war's over? The navy probably still needs their ships fixed."

"I hope so. I'd like to stick around for a bit, make some more money, and then I'll go back to Sawyer."

Gerry's heart froze. She remembered what Maddie had said in one of her notes. But it hadn't happened yet. It was too soon to worry about that. Gerry was way too happy in that moment, and she let Maddie's statement about leaving float into and right out of her mind.

Here they were sitting together in the dark, with no one around. Maddie's profile was in shadow, and she looked out toward the bay solemnly. She was beautiful even being dirty and rumpled. Gerry thought about how she'd look dressed up to go to Mona's and compared it to how she looked now. It was scarcely possible to believe she was the same person, yet she was, and she desired both versions of Maddie. Gerry cleared her throat, trying to calm her nerves.

She scooted her chair closer to Maddie's. Maddie had been thinking apparently, and she hadn't been paying close attention, but then she turned to face Gerry. Their gazes met. Maddie said nothing, and before Gerry could think too much, she leaned over the arm of the chair and kissed her. Her lips were sculpted, full, and wonderfully soft. The faint odor of burnt metal emanated from her hair and her shirt, but Gerry didn't mind. It was the smell of hard work.

As Gerry moved her lips gently over Maddie's, Maddie kissed her back, not enthusiastically exactly but attentively, sweetly, as though she wanted to memorize the shape and feel of Gerry's lips. Gerry stayed where she was as long as she dared, then drew back.

Maddie's eyes were closed, but then she opened them, and they looked at each other silently. Then, to Gerry's surprise, Maddie leaned forward and started to kiss her again, this time with some force. Gerry happily responded and put a hand out to feel Maddie's hair. They both started to be a little out of breath. The feelings were too much, and Gerry had to stop, though she didn't want to.

"I have to go," she said, finally.

"That's too bad."

"I know. I want to stay, but if I can get back to the barracks before reveille, this won't count as an overnight pass. I can catch the last train at one thirty in the morning."

"You ought to get going, then. I don't know when the last bus leaves to go back downtown."

"Soon. I have the schedule."

Their mundane discussion of the bus schedule let Gerry back away from her strong feelings a bit. Maddie leaned into her as much as she could as they sat on the porch. She was happier than she'd ever been, but she hated that they would be cut off from each other for who knew how long. It was as if she were on the other side of the world, much like what happened to the sailors who were sent off to fight the Japanese. Maddie was just across the bay, but it felt as far away as she imagined Japan was.

Once again, Maddie walked her to the bus stop. In the dark, late-night gloom, they were still free to touch. The neighborhood on the hill above the dry docks was so empty they could have been on the moon.

"I'll come back. Soon, I promise," Gerry swore.

They stood, arms around each other.

"I hope you will," Maddie whispered.

"I'm going to write you. I promise."

Maddie giggled. "Stop making all these promises. You don't know for sure what's going to happen."

"Well, I know what I want," Gerry said, burying her nose in Maddie's hair.

She got on her bus, giving Maddie a last long look. Maddie waved again.

Gerry dozed on and off—first on the bus, then on the train back to Treasure Island—but in between, she relived their evening together. *She does like me. Maybe we can be together somehow.*

Jimmy had told her the brass was going to ask for all sailors in non-combat ratings, including WAVES, to stick around until the next January. Gerry's first thought was that was what she wanted to do. For the first time, though, she wondered if she ought to leave the navy. If she wasn't in it, she could get some other kind of work. Maybe she could work in the city, and she and Maddie could see each other more often. She didn't *want* to leave San Francisco. She loved it. But now there was Maddie.

Jimmy said, "It's called Operation Magic Carpet. Don't you love their names for these things?" He rolled his eyes.

"Are you staying?" she asked him.

"Hell, yes. I'm not going anywhere."

Gerry thought about seeing Maddie more often, and she thought about Maddie and doing a lot more than just kissing. She wanted to try all the things Pauline had taught her. She wanted Maddie to be her girl.

CHAPTER SIX

December 1945

"What were you doing out on the front porch in the middle of the night in December?" This was Wilma Grace's abrupt question at breakfast the next morning after Gerry's visit with her at the dry dock. Maddie had to tear herself away from reliving the night with Gerry in order to focus on Wilma Grace's question. It didn't help that it took a long time for her to fall asleep after Gerry left. She was tired but stirred up and restless. Maybe she could sneak in a nap before she had to go back on shift at two in the afternoon.

"I asked you a question." Wilma Grace's voice grated on her. Maddie had to say *something.* It seemed like the basic truth was likely the best road, but not all the details.

"We came back here for a drink after I got off work. If you remember, I don't get off 'til twelve."

"You ought not be fooling around at all hours then."

Maddie started to reply sharply, but then she figured Wilma Grace must mean staying up too late, not the type of fooling around Maddie had been doing with Gerry.

She was off balance though, as well as sleepy, and she answered back with more heat than she intended.

"You can let me live my own life and not worry about how late I stay up. Thank you kindly."

"Well, I only looking after you, and besides, you're going to make pies this morning with me for the church social tomorrow. So, if you thought you was going to get a chance to make up for not going to bed on time, you got another think coming."

Oops. Maddie had forgotten about that. No way she would be able to manage to take a nap before her shift started. Once Wilma Grace was set on a path, no way would she change her mind. Thom had already gone to work. He was on the first shift and wouldn't help bake pies anyhow, even if he was at home. Wilma had the day off, lucky for her. Somehow, Maddie was going to have to cope.

She sighed. "When you want to start?"

"Right away, 'cause, sister, we got a slew of pies to make. Finish your breakfast."

Maddie wondered if Wilma Grace had noticed anything else going on besides the fact that she and Gerry were sitting out on the porch. But she wasn't going to ask.

Breakfast was the old navy favorite, SOS, otherwise known as shit on a shingle. Gerry was so tired and distracted by her thoughts of Maddie, she didn't care. She barely looked up when Woody sat down across from her.

"Where were you last night?" Woody asked abruptly.

The first answer that popped into Gerry's head was "none of your business." But she decided to be generous about Woody's motives for asking. At one time, Woody asked this sort of nosy question because she actually cared about Gerry.

"I had a twelve-hour pass and went into town."

Woody took a bite of her SOS and said, "To do what?"

"To see a friend."

"At Mona's?"

Gerry was becoming annoyed. "No. And why are you bothering me about it?"

"I'm concerned. Was the friend that Colored girl?"

"Yeah. It was. So?" She was feeling defiant.

"Well, you might want to be discreet."

"Why?"

"I heard the shore patrol was getting ready to start looking for girls in the bars. They're going after the boys first, but they might get to us."

"How do you know that? And I wasn't *at* Mona's."

"I hear things. In case you haven't noticed, the war's over. Pretty soon they're not going to need WAVES anymore, after all the boys are

back home. We've got to help with all the demobilizations but after…"
Woody waved her hand in a sweeping motion.

"Of course, they still need us, until January next year I heard they
want people to re-up, and they never cared that much before where we
go when we have shore leave, so long as we stay out of trouble."

"That could change."

"What are you talking about?" Gerry asked.

"I said, I hear things. I'm telling you as a friend."

"It's nice to know you're still my friend."

Woody looked pained. "I never stopped. I've always tried to steer
you right, haven't I?"

"You have, I know, and I'm real grateful, but since I met Maddie,
you aren't the same."

Woody sighed. "Dames. They'll be death of you. I'm only trying
to make sure you don't get hurt."

"What makes you think I'll get hurt?" Gerry became annoyed all
over again.

"Number one, you can't see a Colored girl. It's just not done.
Number two, if you're in love, you're so lame-brained you're going to
stop looking out for yourself and do something dumb and get caught by
the shore patrol, and there'll be hell to pay."

"First, I'm not going to stop seeing Maddie because she's Colored.
That doesn't matter to me. Two, I'll be careful just like you taught me,
and I won't get caught. She doesn't *like* going to the bar anyhow."

Woody shook her head. "Gerry, I hope to God you know what
you're doing."

❖

It had been that recruiter in her crisp navy uniform that first sparked
Gerry's interest in the navy. Her talk of patriotism was compelling. Her
assurance that everyone was needed and everyone would have a role in
the war effort had lit Gerry's imagination. It was the uniform, though,
with the gold anchors on the lapels and the neat little cap with the navy
insignia that had made up Gerry's mind.

As she put on her dress blues, she thought of that recruiter and
wondered again if she was a gay girl and where she was. She'd likely
never know.

"But PO Shrader, it's you I have to thank for being here," Gerry
said aloud. She was brushing her hair one more time before putting on

her cap and her white gloves. Good thing she had the type of hair—short and springy—that tolerated wearing a cap well. The other girls complained a lot about messing their hairdos up.

About two weeks after her kiss with Maddie, it was time to spruce up because they were going on review for a new commander's arrival on Treasure Island to kick off Operation Magic Carpet. Gerry loved marching almost as much as she loved her uniform. In fact, the only thing wrong with the world at that moment was she didn't know when she would be able to see Maddie again.

She'd heard from Jimmy what the men's barracks were like, and she was glad the navy had made some changes for WAVES. The toilets had doors and showers had curtains, and there were more mirrors. That morning, Gerry had awakened before anyone else and was enjoying the peace and quiet and the chance to prepare herself in privacy. The rest of them would be crowding into the bathroom when reveille was sounded. Until then, no one could hear her talk to herself.

"You look good, Seaman First Class Stern," she said to her image in the mirror.

She crept back into the dormitory and sat on her cot to polish her dress pumps and her brass buttons. That didn't take too long, and as she always did when she had time, she thought about what Maddie would be doing and visualized her. It was seven thirty in the morning, so Maddie might only now be waking up. That was a thought: Maddie in bed, sleepy and a little messy, but beautiful anyhow. She was going to be able to see her that way someday. Somehow.

The reveille call went off, and her fellow seamen stirred and started waking up. They would be at breakfast in a half hour, and then it would be parade time. Gerry dashed outside to get out of the way of the hordes of women who needed to start their day.

It was December and the morning was bright. Gerry looked west toward San Francisco and didn't see any fog on Twin Peaks, the sun shining. The blue and white of Treasure Island was the blue and white of the navy and the blue and white of San Francisco and the bay. It felt great to be alive. She turned around and walked back into the barracks to wait for her bunkmates to be ready to head to breakfast.

❖

"Eyes right!" their drill captain shouted. Thirty pairs of eyes swiveled, and thirty hands flew up to thirty foreheads in the required salute. They marched past the reviewing stand where the officers stood, returning their salutes.

The new commander for Operation Magic Carpet had arrived, which had occasioned their all-troops review. Gerry snapped her head back around to center and concentrated on following the back of the head of the girl in front of her. They turned right and then left, their corners sharp and neat.

In the afternoon, the transportation officer called a meeting. Gerry sat at attention in the front row, hands folded. The officer gave out the assignments and posted a schedule for everyone's turn at bus driving. None of it was startling, but Gerry noted transportation was going to be hopping, and there was always a chance of bus breakdowns.

"We expect the start of re-entry next week, with two ships bearing upward of one thousand men to be demobbed from each transport. Then it could go up to four ships a day. In anticipation of that, I'm posting a list later this afternoon for drivers, the more senior ones who will be given a three-day pass Friday, Saturday, and Sunday."

When Gerry looked at the list, her name was on it. *Three days!* How could she best put that time to use? Maybe she could see Maddie, and if she could, what would they do?

She dashed off a letter and managed to get it into the afternoon out-going post. She fervently wished Maddie had a telephone, because it would make things so much easier. Ah, well, that wasn't the case.

At the enlisted men's club before dinner, Gerry looked for Jimmy and found him playing the piano in a distracted manner.

"What's wrong with you?" she asked. He wasn't usually moody and he looked so sad, she added, "You look like you lost your best friend."

"Not yet, but it might be coming. Willy over in the map department told me he was nabbed by the shore patrol in a Tenderloin dive last weekend. He doesn't care that they might punish him, but they're looking to discharge him as dishonorable."

"Really? That's awful," Gerry said.

"Worse, they're leaning on him and wanting him to name other guys, and then maybe they'll let him off."

"Oh, no. Is he going to do it?" Gerry asked.

Jimmy looked into space. "Who knows? If he does, I might get named. Might not. Who knows how many names they want? There's probably a quota." Jimmy's last sentence was bitter and sarcastic.

"But why now? Willy's been in the service since early 'forty-two."

"And his reviews were perfect, but that doesn't matter. They know he's queer, but he never hid it very well anyhow. Then he was in the wrong place at the wrong time. Now that the war's over, they don't need us anymore. We're expendable. Some big kahuna probably got a bug up his butt and told the personnel office to get busy finding all the queers so they can get rid of us, and they're sending the SP out all over the place."

"Woody said something about that the other day," Gerry said, musing.

"If I were you, I wouldn't worry about it. They don't even think girls do anything, so they don't care about you."

"I suppose. I've got a three-day, and I'm not going to any of the bars."

"Are you seeing your girl?"

"I hope so."

"Well, have fun." He went back to noodling on the piano.

Gerry, unsettled by what Jimmy said, decided to take a walk around the base in order to think. She had only one day to decide if she wanted to use her pass that weekend or try to persuade her superior to let her use it later. It all depended on when she could see Maddie.

❖

Yawning, Maddie helped Wilma Grace bake her pies, then went to her shift. She was happy that she needed to concentrate so she could keep her seams straight and avoid being burned because it kept her awake.

On Sunday morning, she and Thom helped carry the finished pies over to their church. All church members stayed after church for socializing since it gave them a bit of back-home familiarity that comforted them amidst the strangeness of California and the demands of their work. Almost everyone at church worked in the shipyard, sometimes two shifts a day. And like Maddie, they were all dog tired most of the time, but they still came to church and to social hour after.

Maddie walked around the church hall, greeting people she knew from the dry dock and those, like her, who were from Sawyer. This reminded her of her mama too, and that was sweet in a sad way. She longed to return home with some money and get started on what she and her mama had talked about. Her mama was good at sewing, crocheting, embroidering, all that stuff.

Then Maddie thought about Gerry, and she was sad, happy, and confused all at once. She wanted to be with Gerry in whatever ways that might mean. She'd never been in love before, but she thought being with Gerry might be what love was supposed to feel like. She liked being seen. Gerry concentrated on her like she focused on welding her seams. It was wonderful and unnerving.

She watched her brother and sister-in-law. Thom was friendly and talkative with everyone. Wilma Grace ran around making sure all the folks had enough to eat, being a bit of a pest, but people still appreciated her care as much as they liked her baking. Maddie felt close to Thom and Wilma Grace but far away at the same time. She didn't want to tell them about Gerry. At least she didn't want to tell them everything. She was protective of her thoughts anyhow, and somehow, she knew it was best to be closed-mouthed about the subject of Gerry.

As for the conflict between going home to her mama and staying here with Gerry, she didn't have anything to decide at the moment. She'd go right on working at the shipyard until they told her to leave, and they hadn't yet. There was always a backlog of repair jobs to do, even if the navy wasn't looking to build anything new. Besides, the longer she stayed, the more money she'd take back to Sawyer when this was over.

She wished she could talk to Marguerite again. She tried to think what Marguerite would say about Gerry. Marguerite was the sort of woman who would not let anything or anyone stop her from going after what she wanted. At least the story of how she got her streetcar conductor job said so. Maddie wanted to be like that, but first she had to figure out *what* she wanted. It had always seemed clear that she would go home to Sawyer, but that didn't seem as obvious now. Gerry hadn't been around when she made those plans two and a half years ago.

She was still not mentioning Gerry in her letters home. *If Mama wouldn't want me to be friends with a White girl, she surely would have something to say if she found out I kissed her.* Not talking to her mama about it made her heart ache, and when she thought about it, she started worrying what would happen when it was time at last to return to Sawyer. So she dismissed the subject from her mind.

❖

"Hey, Maddie. Foreman wants you in his office," one of her friends said right after her shift started. A jolt of anxiety shot through her. Travis didn't call someone in to give her good news. He was a taskmaster, and sometimes Maddie visualized him as a plantation manager with a whip like her grandmother, who'd been a slave, had told her about. He didn't beat people, but his attitude wasn't much different than someone like that. Disdain oozed out of his pores whenever he talked to any of the Colored girls. Maddie walked over to his office with her stomach doing backflips.

"Weeks." That's how he talked. Not "Hi, Maddie. How are you doing?" Just a terse "Weeks" by way of greeting.

He shoved a piece of paper across his desk toward her, and on it was a phone number.

"I'm not in the business of taking messages for you girls. But this girl pleaded with me. She gave her name as Seaman Stern. She wants you to call her." He sat back and picked his teeth as he glared at her.

"Thank you, sir. May I use your phone?"

"You may, but remember, I'm doing you a favor, and don't let it happen again." He stared at her. Maddie was aware that he allowed many White workers who didn't have home phones to make calls on his office phone, and it didn't seem to matter much to him. Oh, well. She needed to call Gerry back. It must be something important.

She waited until he belatedly realized she couldn't reach his phone and moved it closer to her. He obviously wasn't going to give her any privacy, so she went ahead and dialed the number.

Before the first ring was done, she heard the phone line open and Gerry's voice. "Hello? Maddie?"

"Yes. This is Maddie."

"Oh, thank God. I wasn't sure you'd call me back. I'm so sorry I had to call you at the dock. It's kind of urgent."

"I see." Maddie didn't want to show any reaction while Travis was staring at her.

"It's just that I have a three-day pass, and I can be in the city Friday, Saturday, and Sunday. I'm going to get a hotel room so I can stay in town. And I, er, wondered if I could see you."

"Yes. That's fine." A rush of happiness had surged through her, overriding her anxiety, but she made sure to keep her face straight and her voice calm. The first problem was her work schedule. She could go on nights. That would make it possible to go into town to see Gerry. That is, if Travis would okay it.

"Can I call you back?"

"Uh. Sure. When?"

"Tomorrow. This time." Maddie thought quickly. She could go to the one pay phone on the shipyard property and pray no one was using it. She would spend the money required to be able to talk to Gerry in private.

Gerry gave her the phone number.

Maddie hung up the phone. She clasped her hands.

"Thanks, Mr. Travis, for letting me use your phone."

"Everything all right?"

None of your damn business.

"Yes. Thanks. Say, Mr. Travis. I'd like to switch to graveyard shift, if that's okay with you." Maddie was aware that he was always looking for workers to switch. Most people didn't want to work nights so they could have a family life.

"Yeah." He narrowed his eyes as though she was trying to put something over on him. Typical White boss. He made a note on a paper in front of him.

"Thanks very much. I'll start tomorrow."

She went back to the dry dock and picked up her equipment. One obstacle to seeing Gerry was overcome. The next problem was Wilma Grace and her nosy ways.

❖

Gerry put the phone receiver back in its cradle and blew out a breath. She'd have to finagle her driving schedule tomorrow in order to be able to call Maddie. She hoped she could scrape together enough money for two nights at a hotel that wasn't too shabby. She wanted them to be comfortable, with their surroundings at least. Also, Gerry decided beer wasn't going to be good enough for this occasion. She wanted to have champagne. That seemed nicer than a bottle of whiskey, anyhow. She'd seen movies where the lovers drank champagne. *Lovers.* That had a lovely sound. Gerry recalled her encounter with Pauline. She was relieved she knew what to do, but she still didn't know how to get started since Pauline had taken care of that part. It was important that Gerry appeared to be experienced to Maddie, even if she wasn't, not really.

There was also still the problem of exactly what else they would do and where they could go for fun, if it wasn't Mona's or to the hotel right away, and she wished she could talk to Woody. Damn it. Why, of all things to get stuck in Woody's craw, did it have to be Maddie's skin color? She couldn't ask Jimmy's advice because he would be no help, and that was way too embarrassing to consider anyway. He'd probably just make a bad joke of it. It was going to be up to her to find her way.

The next day, she took up her post by the common-room phone and prayed Maddie would call when she said she would.

The phone rang, and Gerry snatched it.

"Hello?"

"Gerry?" It was her.

"Hi. Yes. It's me." She was so relieved she almost fainted.

"I can get into town around seven thirty tomorrow morning. Where do we meet?"

"We can have breakfast at Foster's on Ellis Street." Merely saying those words sent a thrill through Gerry. They could have fun like normal people and eat out at a diner.

"I'll see you then. I can't wait," Maddie whispered. "I got to go. Someone's waiting to use the phone."

"I'll be seeing you. Bye." Gerry put the phone back and grinned to herself. This was all going to be okay. More than okay, it was going to be great.

❖

Gerry got a letter from her mother in the afternoon mail. Somehow, her mom knew exactly the wrong time to send a letter. When Gerry wanted to think only about Maddie and what they would be doing in a few days' time, she had to cope with her mother and her questions. She loved her mom, but ever since she'd figured out she was gay, there was an invisible wall between them, one only she was aware of.

Now the war's done, we are looking forward to having you home for good. Daddy says he wants you back in time for harvest. When do you think you can come home?

Gerry tamped down her guilt. She'd gone back to Fresno only once in three years. Fresno no longer felt remotely like home. She considered Treasure Island her home. Her parents talked as though exactly the opposite was true, and she supposed that was to be expected. How was she going to explain that she planned to stay in San Francisco? It wasn't only being gay and knowing she would never be able to explain that to her mom and dad. It was everything. She didn't want to be a farmer's wife. She didn't know what she wanted, but whatever it was going to be, it would be in San Francisco, and she hoped it would be with Maddie.

She knew it wouldn't be hard to find a hotel room, but she fretted about what else they would they do and where would they go and, most of all, how she was going to approach Maddie.

Their kiss had convinced her she wasn't imagining things. Maddie felt something too, of that she was sure. As she walked back to the motor pool after their phone call, she decided she would ask Woody some questions. If she was willing to help, Gerry wanted her advice even if she wasn't one hundred percent in favor of Gerry choosing Maddie as a girlfriend.

After she parked her bus in the motor pool, Gerry went in search of Woody in her office on the other side of the base. As she walked over, she rehearsed her questions.

"Oh. Hi, Ger," Woody said coolly when Gerry stood in front of her desk "What can I do for you?"

"Buy you a cup of coffee?" Gerry asked. In reality there was nothing to buy. A coffee pot was always on in the enlisted-men's social club.

Woody squinted. "Yeah. I suppose. Sure."

Gerry led them to a quiet corner of the room, near the currently empty stage.

Woody, as usual, struck a pose of casual unconcern. She lit a cigarette and fixed Gerry with a smirk.

"Didn't think you were still talking to me." She may have sounded a bit regretful, but Gerry could also be imagining it.

"Well, I'm sore that you can't be happy for me, but I still want to be your friend, and I still need you to be my friend, if you can."

"That's affirmative." Woody used the language of the navy with a certain irony. "What is it you need, kiddo?"

"Some advice, and you're the only one I can ask."

"You don't say. Lucky me. Shoot." She blew out a cloud of smoke and then looked at the filter on her cigarette, where the imprint of her lipstick showed bright red. *Even a butch has to dress up*, she'd said more than once. It had to do with blending in. The Woody who introduced Gerry to Mona's and what she called the "life" co-existed with the sleek, coiffed, lipsticked Woody who fit in nicely with all the rest of the WAVES. A uniform made everyone look alike, at least on the surface. Add a little makeup and styled hair, and no one could tell you were gay. Woody lectured Gerry about not looking like a butch.

Gerry sighed and looked at the ceiling, where a huge fan whirled slowly.

"I've got three days of liberty at the end of the week, and I want to take Maddie to a hotel."

"Ah." Woody fell silent for a moment. "You need to romance her. Don't try anything right away. Wine and dine her first."

"Well, I think I know about *that*. But when we get to, you know, the moment…she'll want me to know what I'm doing."

Woody held up her hand and waggled her fingers. "Go slow and do lots of kissing, loads of kissing. Women are like clothes irons. They need to heat up. It takes time and lots of—you know—touching."

Gerry didn't find this advice especially helpful. She understood the mechanics of it. Pauline had had been helpful for that. She was really asking how she would know if Maddie would be receptive.

"Seaman Stern," Woody said. "When I met you two years ago, you didn't have the foggiest idea who or what you are. Now you know, and I've been watching and waiting for you to actually make the next step. It's not the nitty-gritty that's your problem. It's your head."

"My head?" Gerry was furious.

"Why do you think you haven't had a girlfriend yet?"

What was the reason for that question?

"I don't know. I haven't found the right woman yet. Until now."

Woody lit another cigarette and frowned. "We'll leave that be for the moment, and that's not the reason. I've read Freud. I know your problem."

"Oh, yeah. If you're so smart, what's my problem?" Gerry instantly regretted asking that question. Woody had always been such know-it-all, but up to this point, that hadn't bothered Gerry. It did now because she knew what Woody thought about her choice of girlfriend, and it rankled her.

"You're repressed. That's what's wrong with you. Well, we all are, or were. You have to loosen up. You have to let whatever will be will be. Freud wasn't wild about gay people, but at least he knew we existed, even if he thought we were stuck at the stage of infantile underdevelopment."

"You're talking crazy, Woody." Gerry suspected she might be right but wasn't ready to admit it.

"I recommend a little booze, a little moonlight, and some sexy music. You and that Negro girl will find your way. Remember what Pauline showed you." She winked. "Also how do you know she's not in the know already? That sort matures fast."

"Oh, geez, Woody. You're talking crap again. Stop. She's not like that."

Woody shook her head in an infuriatingly superior way. "Don't get your back up. Look. Don't be scared. You'll know what to do when the time comes."

"Okey-dokey. Well, thanks. I guess."

Gerry went for a walk. Woody was such a snot sometimes, it made hard to remember how kind she could be. Woody's suggestion of romance made sense. Gerry would have to make the lights of downtown substitute for moonlight. Also, the only sights in San Francisco she knew were the bars and clubs up in North Beach. This time she wanted to do something else with Maddie. She wanted their time together to be super special. It wasn't only about the hanky-panky.

CHAPTER SEVEN

January 1946

Gerry leaned against the fence surrounding Lotta's Fountain. She'd picked it as a place to hang around until she went up to Fourth Street to wait for Maddie's bus. She had left Treasure Island at dawn in a fever of anticipation and worry. She checked into a hotel on Geary Street. On one of their nights out, Jimmy had taken Woody and Gerry up to George's room there so he could show it off to them. This hotel room wasn't terrible, but it wasn't nice like the St. Francis Hotel was.

Gerry didn't want to spend all her money on a room, so she'd found one that wasn't too expensive but also not cheap. When she checked in, she'd pulled the bedspread and sheet back. No bugs. That was good enough for her, and she hoped it would be good enough for Maddie.

Her anxiety and the gray morning couldn't dampen her mood though. She was going to spend the day with Maddie, and maybe the night, but she didn't want to presume anything. She leaned and smoked and looked around as the City woke up. Even at this early hour, it was busy. If she was home in Fresno, she would be milking cows. In fact, she would have already been at that task for some time. She surely didn't miss Fresno. Her watch said six forty-five. It was still too early to go to the bus stop, but she was too excited to wait and strolled up Market Street to Fourth. She looked at the buildings around that intersection and wondered what went on inside them. She thought about working in an office, but it didn't seem appealing. But working in an office won out, in her mind over, say, cleaning out the stable back at the farm. Yet driving a bus sounded much better. Yes, if she couldn't stay in the navy, maybe she could do that.

Finally, the Hunters Point bus pulled up, and Gerry craned her neck trying to see the exiting passengers. There she was. Maddie walked down the steps and toward her. Gerry's exuberant mood plummeted because Maddie didn't hold a suitcase in her hand. She wasn't going to be spending the night. Gerry swallowed her disappointment.

Suddenly they were face to face.

"Hi, "Gerry said.

"Hi, yourself," Maddie replied.

"How long can you stay?" That seemed like an innocuous way to ask Maddie what she was prepared to do. The answer wasn't welcome though.

"A few hours. I have to get back home and sleep a while."

"Sleep?" Gerry asked, stupefied.

"Yeah, girl. I been working all night and have to go back to work at eleven tonight. I'm on graveyard."

"Oh. Yeah. Of course. You told me you were going to do that."

Maddie nodded slowly. "I changed to graveyard shift so I can actually spend some time with you. I couldn't do that if I was on day or swing shift."

"I see." Gerry absorbed this information and thought about her plans, which were all of a sudden upended.

"So, what are we gonna do?" Maddie asked, a perfectly reasonable question.

Gerry looped her arm through Maddie's. "Let's go eat breakfast."

Maddie slowly started to smile. Her expression at the beginning of their conversation had been skeptical, to say the least.

"That sounds good. I'm starving."

Gerry led Maddie back up Geary Boulevard a short way, and they arrived at Foster's Cafeteria. It was busy this hour of the morning as downtown San Francisco awakened and prepared for its workday.

They went through the serving line and managed to find a table.

"You can tell me what else you got in mind. I'm a person who likes to know what I'm getting into." Maddie said it in a good-humored way, though it struck Gerry that she might have meant it as more than simply what they would be doing that day.

"I've never done tourist things in San Francisco. Have you?"

Maddie looked surprised. "You've been here, what, three years, and you haven't seen that much?"

"No. When we have leave, we go to the clubs in North Beach."

"Oh. I don't want to do that, at least not now. I want to be a regular person and look at regular things," Maddie said.

"I see." Gerry laughed.

"Well, what have you seen before?"

Maddie grinned. "Nothing. Except downtown a little bit."

Gerry grasped that this encounter was deeply meaningful to Maddie, though she understood only imperfectly what its exact meaning was. Gerry pulled a brochure out of her pocket, something she'd picked up at her hotel. She spread it out on the table, and the two of them bent their heads over it. "See what takes your fancy."

Maddie dutifully scanned the glossy document. "I want to do that." She pointed at a cable car climbing a steep hill.

"Okay," Gerry said. "You know it's kind of a wonder that we've both been here a few years and don't know a darn thing about the place."

"True. We only know our little corners, and you know them bars in North Beach."

"Yep. I know those clubs and other places where we, our crowd, I mean, can have a good time."

"Before I started work, I went downtown and rode the streetcar, and I met someone. Marguerite. She was a Colored girl, and she was a conductor, and I'd never seen nothing like that. Where I came from, I mean, no Colored person would be able to do that. She told me she was the first one to do it."

"Huh." Gerry didn't know what to say.

"But after that I never went nowhere else. I just stuck around home and the shipyard. There's plenty to do there. But now I want to see more. I like it that I'm with you, though I thought you'd have seen more of San Francisco already."

"Well, then we both get to find out."

Maddie beamed and Gerry wanted to kiss her right then, but she couldn't do that in the middle of a cafeteria during the breakfast rush.

The sun was breaking through the morning gloom as they walked up Market Street toward the Powell Street cable-car stop.

They had to wait a few minutes as the cable-car workers turned the car around. They did this by actually leaning on the back of it and using themselves as weights. The man in the back rang a bell, and they got on. The driver in the front threw one of his levers forward, and the cable car lurched. Gerry heard a sort of metallic grinding noise underneath the car.

The cable car rolled up the hill on Powell Street, its chain chattering, and stopped at the level part of the intersection, blocking traffic on the cross street. More folks boarded, some got off, and away they went. They sat on the side in the open air, and Maddie edged closer to Gerry.

"Do you want to go inside?" Gerry asked.

"No. I want to sit outside and see everything."

A young sailor hung onto the pole at the corner and swung himself out, showing off to his girlfriend, who squealed and told him to stop, but he didn't listen.

Maddie craned her neck, trying to see as much as she could. As they climbed an even steeper hill, Maddie said, "Lord, I don't how they do this. Seems like this thing ought to go sliding down the hill, though I'm sure glad it don't."

"I know, but it's fun, isn't it?" Gerry wanted Maddie to have a good time.

"I think so, but I'm not sure."

They stopped talking again and looked around. Gerry thought she ought to try to converse with Maddie, but Maddie was focused not on her, but on watching the scenery go by.

They rounded a corner onto Jackson Street, and Gerry was glad she was seated instead of hanging off the side off the cable car, like so many other people. After they turned an even sharper corner on to Hyde Street, they started to climb another hill. They reached the crest of it hill, and all at once, the San Francisco Bay was spread out below. The cable car dropped down, and Gerry's insides floated up, giving her a physical thrill much like she had when she rode a roller coaster at the county fair back in Fresno.

Maddie let out a little gasp. Whether it was from the view or the same sensation that Gerry felt or both, Gerry wasn't sure, but Maddie sounded the way she felt: thrilled. The cable car descended toward the bottom of the hill, and they finally came to rest not far from the water's edge.

"End of the line," the conductor shouted.

Without a word, Gerry and Maddie both stepped off the cable car and turned to look at each other.

"What do we do now?" Maddie asked.

"I don't know. Look around, I guess."

"What's that?" Maddie asked, pointing to a forbidding-looking white building on an island in the bay.

"I don't know," Gerry replied. She was less interested in what they were looking at and more concerned about what Maddie was thinking and feeling, and she almost asked her but decided not to.

They ambled down the street toward the fishing docks without another word.

CHAPTER EIGHT

January 1946

Maddie had started her trip downtown from Hunters Point in good spirits. She was looking forward to being with Gerry and seeing parts of San Francisco she knew nothing about, but her good mood was sliding away.

After they had breakfast, Maddie began to notice how tired she was. She'd started out determined to ignore the fact she'd been up all night and try to enjoy herself. That had worked for a short while. But, after they got off the cable car, all she wanted to do was sit down or, better yet, lie down.

Worse, Gerry seemed ill at ease and anxious, though on the surface she was as she usually was—good-natured and happy. She was hiding something. Again. Maddie debated about asking Gerry directly but decided not to for the time being.

They simply walked along the waterfront, and Maddie was content with that. If someone had asked her when she was back in Sawyer if she liked the ocean, she would have said "no" without ever having seen it. In her imagination it was huge and scary, and merely walking beside it she'd get swallowed up. Then she arrived in San Francisco and found that she would be living within a few blocks of it. After that, she quickly came to like it and admired the view every day when she left her home to walk down the hill to the graving dock to head to work.

In San Francisco, it was as though she was breathing a different air. Sawyer was closed in and stifling with its hot, muggy summers. The atmosphere there was heavy. In San Francisco, it was easier to breathe somehow. The coolness made her feel more alive. The sun wasn't glaring. It was soft, especially in the morning when it a wash of fog filtered the light. As the fog cleared, she could see far away across the bay to hills and buildings.

Here, down by the wharf, there was even a greater expanse of sea and sky because it was nearer the Golden Gate Bridge. They found a bench and sat down, quietly looking at the scenery.

"Do you ever want to go on a boat?" Gerry asked, startling her.

"Nah. I'd get scared or maybe seasick, I expect."

"I went out on the ocean, but just once."

"You from a part of California that's nowheres near the ocean, right?"

"That's right. It's called the Central Valley."

"Where the farms are. You said you grew up on one."

"Uh-huh." Gerry was peering at her, probably wanting to know what she was getting at.

"We both didn't know a thing about the ocean 'til we moved here."

"Right. I couldn't imagine it until I got to the naval base. My basic training was in New York City, and suddenly, there I was on Treasure Island, with the ocean on all four sides of me." Gerry chuckled, clearly remembering how she felt.

"I couldn't either while I was still in Arkansas, but here we are."

"So we're alike in that way," Gerry said. "We come from places that are far away, and there's no Pacific Ocean anywhere close by."

They looked at each other for a few moments, and then Gerry said, "I'm hungry again. How about you?"

"I could eat." Maddie thought maybe more food could stave off her increasing sleepiness. She'd have to go get some shut-eye sometime, but she wanted to stay with Gerry as long as possible.

There were some food stands along waterfront, where the fishermen were selling their catch. Maddie liked fried fish very much, but she doubted the fish here would be the trout or catfish from her home in Arkansas.

"What about this?" Gerry had walked ahead to a different fisherman and stood pointing at a tray of ice full of some odd-looking creature.

"This is the best thing you'll ever eat. Dungeness crab. Fresh as can be," said the young man. "My uncle and I caught them this morning in the bay."

"How do you eat it?" Gerry asked, dubiously.

Maddie had the same question as they stared into the tank full of crabs. They had flat shells and eight legs, some of them still moving sluggishly. They were, she realized with horror, still alive.

The fisherman said, "I'll boil one and crack it for you. Comes with sourdough bread."

"Okay. We'll take one," Gerry said. Maddie breathed deeply, remembering that she happily ate freshly caught fish, breaded and fried, crispy and golden. This crab thing was nothing like that, other than it came from water.

They waited while the fisherman prepared their crab.

"This isn't like nothing I ever ate. Except maybe crayfish," Maddie said, making conversation mostly to distract herself from her own dismay at what she was about to put in her mouth.

"I know. Me too. But I'm game." Gerry's smile was encouraging.

When the crab was cooked, they walked away to find another bench to sit on.

"You first," Maddie said firmly.

Gerry picked up a hunk of bread and put some butter on it and bit into it.

"Mmm. You'll like this." She handed a piece to Maddie.

The taste was odd, like no bread she'd ever eaten. It was slightly bitter, like the name implied, but it was bitter in a pleasant way.

Gerry was gingerly scooping the crab's pink tinged flesh out of the shells the fisherman had cracked for them. She popped a morsel into her mouth as Maddie watched anxiously.

Gerry's eyes widened as she chewed. She scooped out another piece and put it on top of the bread and ate that.

"You're going to really like this," Gerry assured her and prepared a piece of bread with crab meat for her.

The crab smelled briny, but again, it was nice rather than nasty. Maddie avoided thinking about what the whole crab had looked like and closed her eyes as she took a bite. She was determined to impress Gerry, if nothing else. She wanted to be adventurous like her.

The crab flesh almost melted in her mouth—soft, better than any fish she'd ever eaten. Its flavor was also light. It tasted salty like the ocean or like something else Maddie couldn't describe, but it was, as Gerry had implied, delicious.

"Give me another piece," she said, and Gerry laughed as she did.

"That's something," Maddie said finally. "I wasn't too sure about it, but I'm sold."

"Me too. That's about the best thing I ever tasted." Gerry had a dreamy look on her face.

Maddie sat back on the bench and closed her eyes. She wasn't more awake after eating the crab, she was less awake, and she had to get home and get some sleep real quick, though she didn't want to leave Gerry.

"Can we go back down to Market so I can catch the bus home? I have to get me some shut-eye before work."

Gerry's expression, blissful after consuming the crab, clouded up. Her forehead furrowed, and she narrowed her eyes. "Do you have to, really?" You could take a nap in my hotel room."

Maddie hesitated, then said, "Nope. I got to get home."

Gerry slumped over. "Okay. Let's go." She sounded put out.

They arrived back on Market Street, and when the bus got there, Maddie gave Gerry, who stood glumly with her hands in her pockets, a quick hug.

Maddie felt bad. "Come on. Cheer up. I had a wonderful time."

"I'm glad. I'd hoped you'd stick around, cause I'm off tonight, tomorrow, and tomorrow night, and then I have to report back the next day at seven a.m." Gerry smiled sadly.

"I know, baby. But I'm on-shift at midnight. I'll come back in tomorrow morning and meet you—same time, same place. Okay?"

Gerry perked up a little. "Sure. That's great."

Maddie gave her another quick little hug before she boarded her bus.

❖

Gerry wandered the downtown streets, at a loss as to what to do with herself. She'd wanted to beg Maddie to stay, but she sensed Maddie, once set on her path, wouldn't alter her plans. Only tomorrow evening was left if they were to sleep together, and now that didn't seem like a sure thing either. It was good that Maddie could be with her during the day, but that wasn't enough. She wanted more, although she was uncertain if Maddie would welcome the "more" she was thinking off. She couldn't tell.

She went back to Foster's Cafeteria and ate some roast beef for dinner and, not knowing what else to do, walked over to Mona's 440 Club for a drink. It was a Saturday night, and it was crowded. Gerry sat the bar, ordered a beer, and scanned the crowd as she sipped it, trying to make it last. She didn't want to waste money on anything that didn't involve Maddie.

The couples in the club were almost all the same. A butch in men's clothes had her arm draped around a garishly made-up femme, who flipped her eyelashes as her butch brought her drinks and lit her smokes with elaborate courtesy. That was the way things went, Gerry knew, and she hadn't questioned it. It made it easy to know who was who, as Woody had instructed her a long time ago. Gerry had no idea if Maddie would go along with something like that with her. She seemed too independent, and besides, she was oddly not either butch or femme. She was just…Maddie.

Gerry longed for Maddie to be there with her, but more than that, she wanted to be alone with her in the hotel room, where they didn't have to worry what anyone thought of them or answer to anyone, but where they could at last find out about love. Gerry fell asleep later in her room with her arms around her pillow, thinking of holding Maddie close.

Maddie couldn't sleep. She flip-flopped like one of the dying fish the boys used to catch out of the creek back in Sawyer. This was maddening and a little scary. She had to be up at eleven thirty and back on the dry dock at midnight sharp, or she'd have to answer to the night supervisor, who would surely tell Travis if she was late.

Her damn mind wouldn't stop thinking. She hadn't had this problem before she met Gerry. Gerry got her all stirred up, mostly in a good way. She'd hated to leave her in the afternoon to come home, but both her sense of duty and her exhaustion demanded it. Yet she might as well have just stayed with Gerry. She got up, went to the kitchen, and brewed a cup of tea finally. That helped her go to sleep, but when the alarm went off, it was a shock. She was dragging by the time eleven p.m. rolled around. She consoled herself, thinking about the money she was earning by working graveyard and that she'd be seeing Gerry again in a short time. What would they do today? Would they go to another part of San Francisco to sightsee?

Gerry was at the bus stop waiting for her, a big grin on her face and her hands in her pockets. They embraced, and Maddie stepped back to make eye contact. She thought about what it would be like to kiss Gerry as they had that night on the porch.

"Oh, girl. I'm so tired. Last night just about did me in."

"Didn't you sleep yesterday afternoon?"

"Some, but not near enough. Never mind. Let's talk about something else, like what are we going to do today?"

"I think I want to go to the park." Gerry pulled something out of her pocket and showed it to Maddie. *Visit Golden Gate Park.*

"Let's do it," Maddie said. A park would at least be restful. Maybe that could take the place of the sleep she was missing.

They took another bus after breakfast, and in twenty minutes they arrived at what the bus driver told them was the eastern end of the park.

"It's good to see trees and grass," Gerry said as they walked into it. "I don't miss much about home, but I do miss that. In the summertime when it's real hot, I'd go into the woods, where it was cooler, or maybe I didn't mind the heat so much."

"Down in Hunters Point," Maddie said, "there's nothing but concrete everywhere. There's a little bitty park, and the bay and all, but that's it. Where I grew up, it was all woods and fields except for the town of Sawyer."

"How big is Sawyer?" Gerry asked.

"About two thousand folks, I think."

"Fresno was way bigger. But I lived on a farm, and we only went into town sometimes."

"Were there any Colored people there?"

"I don't know."

"So you never met any when you were growing up?"

"Maybe one." They were quiet for a few minutes. Maddie wasn't sure what she wanted to know. Could it be that Gerry never knew any Colored people, and therefore she hadn't any reason to be prejudiced?

"You know who my folks were always talking about?"

"No. Who?"

"Japanese people. They had them in a camp outside of Fresno."

"Why?"

"I don't know for sure, but I think because the Japanese bombed Pearl Harbor, they were, you know, somehow, enemies. My mom and dad argued about it. My dad thought they were all traitors. My mother asked how that could be since no one ever looked into that to be able to say for sure. A lot of them were already US citizens. But they were sent away anyhow."

"Huh," Maddie said, contemplating what Gerry said. But she was getting real tired and didn't want to think anymore. "Hey. Can we go back to your hotel room so I can lay down for a while?"

Gerry's eyes lit up, and she said, "Sure. If you want to."

❖

What if she doesn't want to do anything? I don't think I could take it if she doesn't want to do it or she's not that way. But we kissed that time. OR maybe she's really tired from working nights and just wants to sleep. What am I going to do?

They sat quietly during their ride back downtown. Maddie actually dozed off for a couple of minutes. Gerry dared to put an arm around her. It was sweet, but she was so anxious she couldn't really enjoy it. She whispered, "Here's our stop," and squeezed Maddie's shoulder gently.

As they took the elevator up to the third floor, Gerry's heart pounded between nervous uncertainty and definite desire. She opened the door to her room and let Maddie walk in before her.

Maddie was awake, but her eyes were drooping, and Gerry's main thought was that Maddie really ought to lie down before she fell down. Gerry seated her on the creaky single bed and took off her shoes, and Maddie made no move to stop her. Gerry got her to lie down and then tucked herself in around her but belatedly realized they needed a cover. With a lot of effort, she maneuvered them underneath the ratty chenille bedspread. Getting in bed in their clothes didn't seem right and wasn't what she wanted, but she couldn't think of a way around it. Gerry put her arm under Maddie's neck and marveled at their closeness, the scent of her hair and the unbelievable tenderness she felt. Tenderness mixed with lust. Their body heat rose and combined. Maddie drifted off to sleep, and, after a few moments, so did Gerry.

❖

Gerry woke up to the room washed in gray light. Maddie was still asleep, and they were cuddled together in the narrow bed, in their clothes with the bedspread covering them. Gerry reached a tentative hand to pat Maddie's shoulder. Maddie murmured something unintelligible and seemed to settle more deeply into sleep. Gerry debated with herself what to do. Maddie was clearly tired, or otherwise Gerry couldn't imagine how she'd be able to sleep so soundly in the tiny, uncomfortable hotel bed. *I ought to let her sleep. But...*

She wanted to make love to Maddie, that was the truth, but she was scared. She didn't know how Maddie would respond. Their one shared kiss said Maddie was receptive, but Gerry wasn't positive she ought to go further. *Stop being such a scaredy cat.*

Gerry gripped Maddie's shoulder, scooted back as far as she could, and turned Maddie over to face her. She kissed her gently, first on the forehead and then on her cheek. Maddie stirred and opened her eyes. In the low light of the room, Gerry could see the sparkle in her dark irises from the light coming through the window.

"Hi. Sorry to wake you up but..." She didn't know what to say and wasn't sure talking would be a good idea. Instead, she kissed Maddie a third time, this time on her lips. She kissed her for a fair amount of time, and Maddie kissed her back. Feeling brave, Gerry reached under her blouse and managed to get her bra unhooked. Maddie's back was so warm and smooth that Gerry almost wanted to stay there, but she also wanted more. She moved her hands around, and Maddie's breaths quickened. She wasn't at all resistant. Emboldened, Gerry moved her hands lower. It was sweet and gratifying as Maddie yielded to Gerry's touch. It seemed quite easy to get their clothes off and to move under the covers.

❖

Something was wrong. Maddie forced her eyes open as she struggled to wake up. She was aware that she wasn't alone. *Gerry.* They were naked and crammed together, and Gerry was deeply asleep. Maddie's legs and arms felt too heavy to move, but she managed to crane her neck. Next to her was a window, but it was black outside except for a streetlight nearby. A tiny amount of light was coming in. *Oh.* Slivers of memory burst behind her eyes. *They'd...* Maddie couldn't think of the word. That wasn't what sent a stab of anxiety through her. *Work? What time is it?* Immediate anxiety brought her fully awake.

"Gerry, I got to go." She shook Gerry's bare shoulder. Gerry groaned and turned over.

"Where's your clock?" Maddie asked frantically.

"Huh?" Gerry couldn't seem to wake up, and Maddie became irritable.

"I need to go to work. Can you help me?"

"Yeah. All right. What can I do?"

"Turn on a light and help me find my clothes."

"Okay." Gerry struggled out of bed, located the one small lamp in the room, picked up her alarm clock, and peered at it. "It's one in the morning."

"Sweet Jesus, I'm two hours late. What am I going to do?"

"Don't worry. I can help you get ready. You can use my toothbrush if you want."

"Thanks," Maddie said, hauling herself out of bed and stumbling into the bathroom.

She had no time for a bath, so she grabbed a washcloth and tried to clean up the sticky residue on her thighs. She blushed, remembering how it got there, but she had no time to think about that. She tried to pat her hair into some kind of order but gave up. It looked like a fright wig, but she could wrap it in a bandana, and it wouldn't be visible.

She threw on her clothes and shoes and tried to remember the bus schedule, but she couldn't.

"How can I get back to Hunters Point at this time of night?" she asked aloud, on the edge of panic. Gerry was slowly pulling her clothes on.

"I don't know. Cab, I guess."

"I don't have money for a cab."

"I'll give you some. I think I have enough."

"I'll pay you back."

"Don't worry about it."

They walked to the corner of Geary and Market, and Gerry waved her arm. A cab pulled up, and Gerry said, "I'll write you soon. I…I— last night—I…Oh, here's some money." She pressed a few bills into Maddie's hand. Maddie squeezed her hand as she took the money and looked into Gerry's face, wanting so much to kiss her, but all she could do was nod and climb into the back seat of the taxi.

She told the driver where she wanted to go, and as he pulled away from the curb, she turned and saw Gerry waving good-bye.

She gave herself a moment to breathe, then began to formulate a reason for being late to give to the night-shift foreman that wouldn't sound like too big a lie, especially if she could frame it with many sincere apologies. It was the first time she'd ever been late, which she hoped would work in her favor. It was hard to tell how he'd take it or if he'd tell Travis.

Overslept. I overslept is all. That's the truth. It *was* the truth on one level, but of course there was so much more to it than that.

She had been asleep, but not soundly, and she had felt the weight of Gerry's hand on her shoulder, first merely stroking her arm and then turning her over on her back. Then Gerry's lips on her, testing and teasing. After that…well, a lot had happened. It was not dream-like exactly because their two bodies were quite solid and real in a kind of dance, awkward at first, but then slowly and steadily finding a rhythm and a pace. In the back seat of the cab, Maddie shivered, her crotch throbbed, and she got wet all over again. Damn. She'd have to spend the rest of her shift like this. In her mind, her worry about being late mixed with marvel at what had just happened to her.

She arrived at the dry dock and went to the locker room to retrieve her gear. Then it occurred to her that she didn't remember the last time she'd eaten. She recalled lunch with Gerry, which was ages ago. She had to eat and soon. She was hollowed out, her stomach turned over. She pawed through her locker frantically but couldn't find a crumb. She wouldn't store food there because of mice. What to do? Other women hid food in their lockers in spite of the mice. Sally would have something. She opened Sally's locker. Sure enough, she found half of a baloney sandwich with tiny bite marks in the crust. And around it was a small collection of mouse turds. Maddie brushed away the mouse turds, closed her eyes, and wolfed it down. She'd have to apologize to Sally later, though Sally had likely forgotten all about it.

She put on her welding leathers and went outside. The foreman was standing on the dock and staring up at the hull of the ship.

"I'm sorry. I overslept. Where should I go?"

He spun around. "Weeks. Finally. You're late." He seemed irritated but not really angry.

"I'm sorry," she said again.

"Never mind. Get up to level two and tell Cindy to come down. Pick up where she left off."

She was so relieved she didn't say another word. She had forgotten her electrical lead, so she guessed she'd have to take over Cindy's, and Cindy wouldn't like that, but too bad.

Maddie climbed up the scaffold. Good thing they had floodlights to help her find her way, as well as the sparks showering down.

"Cindy!" she shouted. The sparks stopped and she yelled, "It's me, Maddie. Kurt said for me to take over for you. You got to give me your rod and lead."

Cindy had raised her helmet so she could see, and her face screwed up. "What about me?"

"I don't know. Ask Kurt. I need to get on, girl. I'm late."

"You sure are. What happened?"

"Not now."

Cindy shrugged and climbed over to the ladder and down to the dock.

What happened? Gerry made love to me is what. I never in a million years thought something like that would happen to me. Maddie put her welding helmet on and checked her lead. She thought about how Gerry had touched her—with such gentleness, reverence even. But then her touch had become something different, something primal. And so had Maddie's response to Gerry. She went to a place she hadn't known existed in herself. But she wouldn't be able to tell anyone.

The girls at the dry dock were always gossiping about themselves and their boyfriends. It was entertainment while they worked and had an undercurrent of competition. Maddie wouldn't be sharing anything. She couldn't feature what she would say. *I found out how a girl can make me feel the best I ever felt in my whole life. I found out what two bodies are able to do together. It's like a miracle. It's the human version of the welding sparks.* Maddie shook her head and tried to get rid the thoughts. She had to get to work, and she needed to concentrate.

She wanted to, but her head was fuzzy, and she felt slow and heavy all over. Neither her mind or her body was as quick and alert as usual. She found the seam she was to work on and adjusted her helmet. She struck the arc and began to direct the weld from top to bottom. Suddenly, the arc went out. She cursed silently and gently tugged on the lead, which was loose. Somehow her power source had become unplugged. Maddie muttered in irritation and started to climb down the scaffold, but her foot slipped off the scaffold rung, she lost her balance, and before she could do a thing, she fell hard onto the deck. Her helmet jolted her head to one side, and the metal dug into her neck. Pain burst in her left arm. She'd fallen awkwardly with her arm caught underneath her. The pain was terrible, and when she tried, she couldn't move.

Kurt's face appeared above her. "Weeks? Are you all right? Say something."

Maddie could only groan. She heard him say to someone, "Get the stretcher and call the ambulance." Then she blacked out.

CHAPTER NINE

February 1946

Gerry woke up by herself. The night before didn't seem to be real. She patted the sheet as though somehow that would conjure up Maddie in the flesh. *In the flesh.* That phrase had a new meaning. Gerry put her head back on the pillow and closed her eyes and remembered. It hadn't been as scary to do as she feared. It had actually been easy. They had come together as though they had done it in a past life and merely had to remember the moves.

She hauled herself out of bed, cleaned up, and went to Foster's to have breakfast. Because of Maddie's abrupt departure in the middle of the night, they'd made no promises to meet the next morning, and Gerry had no idea whether Maddie would return at the same time she had the day before. She longed to see Maddie and talk to her and find out how she felt about what had happened.

She went to the bus stop and watched Maddie's bus arrive and leave without Maddie appearing. She didn't know what to make of it and spent the rest of the day wandering around downtown San Francisco in a fog, though the weather was clear. It was a hell of a disappointment for her last day of leave, not to mention a gross waste of time. She had to report back to base at midnight and decided she might as well go back early. She checked the desk of the hotel a couple of times but didn't receive any messages.

As she sat in the day room of the WAVES' barracks trying and failing to read a newspaper, a few women she knew walked by and asked her why she was back on base so soon.

"Just couldn't stay away, could you?" one joked. Gerry managed a weak smile, but she was worried. It seemed so unlike Maddie not to at least leave a message, especially after they had…but Gerry shook her head. She didn't want to think about that now. Maybe she could reach Maddie tonight, but that seemed impossible. If the foreman was around, he might or might not answer the office phone. At least it was worth a try. She had to talk to Maddie.

She went to the club and played a game of cribbage, then had dinner. Woody tried to talk to her, but she pled exhaustion and left.

Not knowing what else to do, Gerry lay on her bunk, tossing and turning. She was tired enough to doze off, but she wanted to be up at midnight to call the shipyard, so she set her alarm.

The phone rang and rang and rang. She didn't know how long she waited, but the hollow ringing seemed to go on forever. By then she was terrified. What had happened to Maddie? And how could she find out?

❖

Maddie couldn't open her eyes fully, but through the slits of her eyelids, she could tell she wasn't at home in bed. Nor was she in the hotel with Gerry. With an effort, she managed to get her eyes mostly open. Her mouth was so dry it seemed like her tongue was stuck to the roof, but it felt like she was nailed to the bed. Her right arm was jacked up somehow, and she couldn't move even if she'd wanted to try.

"Where…am I?" Her voice was a croak.

Then she saw a figure in white and felt a cool palm on her forehead.

"Good to see you awake."

"Water?" She was surprised she could say that loud enough for the person to hear.

The same figure left, then came back and raised her head enough so she could drink from a straw. It tasted so good.

"What happened?" Maddie was revived enough to move a bit more. "My arm hurts, and I can't remember anything at all." *Flashes of Gerry's hands on her.*

"Easy there. You've broken your arm. You can't move because you're in traction, and you're muddleheaded because we gave you some morphine."

It was hard to understand all of it. She remembered being on the scaffold trying to finish a weld. Before that, she'd been with Gerry in the Rutherford Arms hotel. In bed.

Maddie understood that the person hovering over her was a nurse, but that was as much as her mind could handle. She shook her head, trying to get some kind of clarity. The nurse fussed around with her and propped her head and shoulders up, adjusted her traction, and gave her more water.

"But where am I?"

"St. Luke's Hospital. You fell at work, I believe they said. Can you eat something?"

"Yeah. I think so. Has anyone been to see me?" Maddie's first thought was of Gerry, but she wouldn't have any idea what happened or where she was.

"Your brother and sister-in-law were here earlier because your boss let them know about you. They left as soon as they were sure you were being cared for. You were out for the count, anyway, and couldn't talk." The nurse chuckled as though this was funny, but Maddie wasn't amused.

"I need to get a message to someone."

"To your family?" The nurse raised her eyebrow.

"No. Someone else."

The nurse looked at her closely but only said, "We can't do that. We can call your family for you if you want."

"They don't have a phone." Thom or Wilma Grace would come by when they were able. Maddie needed to talk to Gerry and couldn't see how to do that.

"I only need a few hours," Gerry said, and she didn't disguise the pleading note in her voice. She was begging Jimmy to help her get a pass. Only one day was left before Operation Magic Carpet would be bringing the first batches of sailors returning home. When that started, Gerry had no idea when she'd be able to leave Treasure Island.

"You have a lot of nerve asking me for the same thing so soon. I could get in trouble, and Ralph could too." He meant the clerk in the commander's office who generated the shore-leave passes.

"I know, but this is really important. It's Maddie. I have to find her."

"I told you that you owe me big-time for the last favor. This means you owe me more."

"I know, I know, but I have to get a pass for tomorrow or the next day while I still can go and not be missed. Come on, Jimmy."

"Okay. This is only because you're a great gal and I love you, Ger."

"You're truly the best, Jimmy. I swear I'll make it up to you somehow."

❖

She knew in general where Maddie's house was located, but she hadn't memorized her address. When she reached the bus terminal at Hunters Point, she looked around carefully to orient herself and remember the way she'd walked to Maddie's house when Maddie was with her, and she set off in that direction.

She recognized the two little cheap dining-room chairs on the front porch. Then when she turned to look toward the San Francisco Bay, the perspective looked like the one she remembered. Maddie's house seemed like the best place to try since she had no idea how to find the ship Maddie had been working on a few weeks before when she'd visited the dry dock.

She knocked on the door but got no answer, so she sat down in one of the chairs to wait. Maddie's family members were likely at work, and she couldn't go looking for them since she didn't have a clue where they were.

When Gerry was a kid, she'd helped her father with the birth of calves, and that meant a lot of waiting. She grew to love those times with her father. He was kinder than he normally was, since the birth of a calf was a happy occasion. Another cow for their herd was good news. He and she sat on the floor of the stall with the heifer, talking quietly and patting and encouraging her.

Gerry hoped her wait on Maddie's front porch would lead to a joyous conclusion as well.

She'd dozed off but woke up with a start to Wilma Grace standing directly in front of her.

"Can I help you?" she asked, her tone neither friendly nor unfriendly.

"Oh, hi. I'm Gerry. Don't know if you remember me." She stood up, feeling self-conscious.

"I remember you." Wilma Grace sounded like she'd rather have forgotten her.

"Ah, good. Well, sorry to bother you. I came by to find out where Maddie is. She was supposed to meet me yesterday downtown, but she didn't show."

Wilma Grace shot Gerry a surprised, skeptical look. "She's broke her arm, and she's in the hospital," she said after a pause.

Desperate to go see Maddie right away, she asked, "Which hospital?"

Wilma Grace didn't answer right away, seeming hesitant to tell Gerry where Maddie was. This annoyed her, but she struggled to be patient.

Finally, Wilma Grace said, "It's St. Luke's over on Army Street. She's hurt bad, and I don't know if she can take visitors."

"I won't stay long. Can you tell me how to get there?"

Again, there was a long pause.

"The number 29 bus. You got to go back downtown and pick it up on Fourth Street."

"Thanks so much. I really appreciate your help." It *was* true.

"Uh-huh. You're welcome." It sounded as though Wilma Grace considered Gerry's interest in Maddie anything *but* welcome and her expression of gratitude suspect.

She dashed back to the bus terminal and went back to Fourth and Market Street, where she waited for the 29 bus. She had to be back to Treasure Island by dinnertime, and it was going to be a close shave.

Gerry considered how much Wilma Grace might suspect about the nature of her relationship with Maddie and how that could account for her not-well-hidden hostility. Or was it simple distrust of a White stranger? The things Maddie had told her made that seem quite possible. Well, she couldn't worry about Wilma Grace's feelings at that moment because she had to find Maddie.

After asking around and running the gauntlet of nurses at St. Luke's, she finally found Maddie, who was sound asleep, her arm suspended from a scary-looking set of straps and pulleys and encased in a cast. She sat down to wait for her to wake up. Meanwhile, it was pleasant to watch her sleep.

"What? Who?" Maddie asked in hoarse voice.

Gerry leaned close and whispered, "It's me." Taking advantage of the curtain around them, she kissed Maddie lightly on the cheek.

"Oh, Lord. Gerry. How'd you get here?"

"I went to your house and asked Wilma Grace, and she told me."

Maddie turned over restlessly and raised her good arm, then dropped it on the bed.

"I hope you didn't say nothing about nothing else."

Gerry sat back in the folding chair, feeling a bit put upon. "Well, no, of course not. I only wanted to find you and make sure you were okay. I was worried."

To her relief, Maddie's face softened, and she took her hand. "Oh. I know. I'm sorry for saying that. I'm not myself."

"I can see that. What happened?"

Maddie described what she remembered, which wasn't much. "I'm in the hospital for two weeks, but then I'll be off work 'cause I can't work with a broke arm."

"No, you can't, but you have to get better. I have to leave now, but I'll come see you again. I promise. I miss you." She squeezed Maddie's hand, thinking of their night in the hotel. She wanted to climb in bed with her right there in the hospital ward, but that would never do.

"I miss you too." They hazarded a quick kiss, but then Gerry tore herself away to start back to Treasure Island.

❖

Gerry went back to her bus-driving duties, interspersed with driving guest officers around. It was almost busier now than it was during the war. She wrote Maddie letters, but she couldn't get any more leaves, either sanctioned or unsanctioned. And she wasn't going to be getting any letters back, either, from a woman who'd broken her right arm. She doubted Maddie would try to get someone else to write a letter for her. It was odd how much the change in their relationship affected Gerry, and she wanted to talk to Maddie about it so much, which was another source of frustration.

Years before, when she'd met Woody, and Woody had explained everything to her, she'd said, above anything else, she couldn't let anyone who wasn't one of their crowd or a close friend in the know find out if you managed to find a girlfriend. Gerry understood that need for silence and caution clearly, but her experience with Maddie that night made her want to stand on the bow of a big navy destroyer and loudly shout her happiness to the entire world.

She talked to Jimmy a little, but he was distracted and not too interested in the details, and she supposed she understood. Yet he seemed unusually quiet and distant, and he didn't make a single joke or quip. She still avoided Woody. Her other friends were, well, just not the sort of people she could confide in. It was a surprise then when Woody asked her to come have a drink at the club Saturday night.

On the one hand, Woody was also oddly quiet. Usually, one drink loosened her up so she was even more talkative than usual. Gerry thought it might be due to their recent estrangement, but why would Woody specifically ask her to join her for a drink?

They settled down in a couple of chairs in a corner, as they used to when they had confidences to share. Now Gerry was even more mystified.

Woody chattered some about the usual base gossip. In this case it was a rumor about the pregnancy of some girl they both knew, though she was in another unit. Woody lit a cigarette and took a big gulp of her drink—a Rusty Nail.

She blew out a cloud of smoke, wrinkled her nose, and looked at the tip of her cigarette.

Gerry had had enough. Her patience with Woody was already worn thin. "So what did you want to say to me?"

Woody smirked. "There isn't a lot I can say to you, because apparently you don't listen to me anymore."

"I'm not that wet-behind-the-ears, naive young recruit I was when we met. And you haven't gotten used to me not hanging on your every word is what I think."

"Yeah. You would say that, but oh, I think I got over you growing up. But I'm hoping you'll see your way to pay attention to what I have to say one last time, because it's important."

Woody's hints were even more annoying than her usual ever-present attitude of superiority.

"Will you stop beating around the bush and say what you have to say, already?"

"You have to start being more careful about who you talk to, how you get shore leave, and where you go."

"What the heck do you mean?"

Woody stubbed out her smoke and leaned close. "You got Jimmy to jigger you another emergency leave, didn't you?"

"Yeah. So?" What business of Woody's could that possibly be?

"So, the company commander heard about it."

The company commander, Marty, was one of their crowd, but she wasn't a close friend. She was so butch she looked like a man in drag, and Woody told Gerry early on that they needed to avoid her like the plague, else they would be tainted by association with someone like her.

"And again, so what?"

"Ger." Woody's voice was, for once, gentle. "We have to start being careful. More discreet. I heard they're going to start looking for reasons to get rid of us. War's over. They don't need us anymore." Gerry understood the "we" Woody meant was the gay guys and gals.

"I wouldn't put it past Marty to turn you in to steer attention away from herself. She's a target, a big one, and if I know her, at first sign of trouble, she'll be looking to save her own hide. And Jimmy, he's not one to keep his mouth shut, and that's how Marty heard about you getting leave, though he didn't say it was to see your girlfriend."

Gerry was silent. At least Woody seemed sincere. Maybe there was something to it. She wouldn't be racing off to see Maddie anytime soon anyway. This caused an ache in her heart, but she accepted it because she had to.

"What about you?"

"What about me? I keep my nose clean and my business to myself. I'm not worried about me. I *am* worried about you."

There was that patronizing tone again.

"Don't worry about me."

"Just watch out is all I'm telling you."

❖

Wilma Grace came by to visit Maddie, which was a mixed blessing, to say the least. Being in the hospital was so boring, almost any change was welcome, but Wilma Grace was doing her usual routine of chilly silence, which meant she had something on her mind but wanted to torture Maddie by withholding it. She sat in the guest chair by Maddie's bed, clutching her purse and barely saying a word.

"I'm fine. At least as much as I can be. You really didn't have to come visit. I know you're busy," Maddie said. She had, in fact, started playing cards with the other patients on her ward, and that helped pass the time. The rest of the time she spent thinking about Gerry and how they could see each other again.

"I'm happy to visit. It's the least I can do when family's in the hospital." She spoke with such exasperation and smugness, Maddie wanted to smack her.

She would be going home pretty soon, which was a welcome thought, even if home did include Wilma Grace.

"Wilma Grace, something's bothering you, and you might as well let me know. I'm not going to let you pout about it."

Wilma Grace's face said she knew she'd been caught out.

"That Gerry person came around looking for you, and I had to tell her where you were. What's she after?"

"She's not after a thing. She's a friend, and she was worried about me 'cause I'm in the hospital with a broken arm. That's easy enough to understand, I think." Maddie said this, hoping Wilma Grace would get the message that Maddie thought she was acting like an idiot and to drop it. Maddie felt uncomfortable even talking about Gerry because she was much more than a friend, and she surely didn't want to get into *that* with Wilma Grace. Maddie wasn't one to hide stuff, not that she'd ever had anything to hide much and she'd never been able to outright lie. Her mama could always tell if she was fibbing. But her mama wasn't here, and she didn't owe Wilma Grace any explanations about her business.

"Well, all right. You know it's hard to tell folks' motives sometime." She meant White folks.

"Yeah, I hear that, but, really, she's my friend, and she cares about me, and she wanted to make sure I was okay. That's the truth of it." That at least *was* true.

"Okay, then." Wilma Grace actually seemed to accept Maddie's explanation, but Maddie wasn't sure her acceptance was any more than temporary.

When she arrived back home a couple days later and settled in, one of her first thoughts was how to engineer a visit from Gerry. If she could come during the day while Thom and Wilma Grace were at work, they could have some privacy and pick up where they left off a couple weeks before in that hotel. Maddie was fairly sure they could make out how to maneuver around her broken arm. The thing was not to reinjure it. Gerry would know what to do. She was clever and gentle anyhow. And with that thought, Maddie's fantasies took off.

Silently thanking God she was left-handed, she lounged on her bed and wrote a letter to Gerry, mentioning how she'd tried to set a time they could talk on the phone. Maddie saw no reason she couldn't manage to walk to the pay phone. This being home alone had a lot of advantages. She mailed her letter at the corner post box, then returned to the house and took a nap.

❖

Woody's warnings made Gerry pause, but she didn't have any serious concerns about them. As far as she could tell, the return of sailors from the Pacific Theater to Treasure Island kept on going, and she was needed to drive the buses that ferried them around as they went through their demobilization routine. It made her happy to transport the gangs of relieved, soon-to-be-civilian sailors. Really, her only problem was how to find a way to see Maddie and spend some more time with her, preferably in bed, but that required a place and privacy. She thought about what that would mean and shivered. She would get another evening pass in two weeks but…her head ached trying to work something out so she could see Maddie more often. Meanwhile, she hadn't heard from her.

The letter arrived the next day and instructed her to stand by the phone at a certain time the following day. She was just able to manage it between bus runs.

"How are you feeling?" she asked Maddie, deeply relieved they could talk again.

"Eh, not bad. I get the cast taken off next week. I can start back to work in about a month, which is good, because I'm about out of my mind with boredom. But I'm home by myself during the day, so that's good too."

Gerry longed to be able to visit Maddie at home, which certainly contained her bed. That would be perfect. But home also contained her brother and sister-in-law. And she'd have to wait to be invited.

"During the day no one's around. It's just me. Would you be able to come see me?" Maddie asked.

Something in the way she asked that question told Gerry Maddie was as eager as she was to get back to bed.

"Not 'til next week, when I can get a pass, but it won't be overnight. Just the evening. I can't come during the day 'cause I'll be at work."

"Shoot. What are we going to do?"

"I don't know. You could come to the base, but I'd have to get you a visitor pass. And I don't know where we'd go to be…alone. This place is like a beehive. It's always buzzing, and there's nowhere to get privacy."

"What if I get rid of Wilma Grace and Thom?"

"You could do that?"

"I think so. I have two weeks to figure it out."

Maddie had an idea, but she didn't know if it would work. There was a covered-dish supper at the church on Wednesday nights. The suppers began at five p.m. and lasted until eight or nine, which would give them a few hours alone in the house.

A covered-dish supper meant that Wilma Grace would drag Thom along, and she would normally insist that Maddie go too, and she mostly would, but she had a handy excuse this time: her broken arm.

At supper that night, she asked in as casual a tone as she could, "What are y'all taking to next week?"

Wilma Grace looked puzzled. "Lord. I don't know. Why do you ask?" *Damn, she could be so suspicious.*

"Just curious."

"Sweet-potato pie, I suppose. I think I'm on the list for dessert."

"Sounds good," Maddie said cheerfully.

❖

"You're not coming? Why not?"

"My arm's acting up. The therapist did some stuff with it today, and she went at too hard, I guess. Hurts a lot." Maddie was surprised at how easily she could lie. It was an unexpected talent.

She added, "I'm try to get well so's I can go back to work." Maddie grinned winningly. Her arm, in fact, was not hurting much except for occasional twinges. She planned to put it around Gerry, along with her left arm and both her legs, and hold on tight.

"Hmph. You don't have to do anything but sit around and eat and talk. I didn't even ask you to help make pies."

"Yeah. I know. Thanks, but I want to rest."

Wilma Grace shrugged, and it seemed that all was well. As soon as they left, Maddie ran around and tidied up the house, especially her bedroom. They might be in the light. Again. She'd felt shy last time with the curtains closed, and it had been dark enough in the hotel room. But not this time. She didn't know what she was feeling—jangly nerves or happy anticipation. Both.

When Maddie heard a knock on the door, she ran and wrenched it open. They stared at each other for a fraction of a second, then flung themselves together, hugging tight. They leaned back at the same time, and Gerry began to kiss her urgently. Maddie responded, and as they warmed up, Maddie guided them toward her bedroom, where they fell on the bed.

Between kisses, Gerry spoke in a rush of words. "I didn't know how you would feel after the first time. You were late to work, and then you fell and broke your arm. Am I hurting you? Does your arm hurt?"

Maddie put her palms on either side of Gerry's face to hold her steady and make her stop talking for a second.

"I'm all right. I can't do very much yet with my arm, but just don't put your weight on it, and I'll be fine."

Gerry's expression changed to relief, and her dark eyes became darker.

"Good. I haven't stopped thinking about you and us this whole time. I know we made you late to work, and you got hurt, and you ended up in the hospital, and—"

"Please don't talk anymore. We don't have a lot of time. I want more of what we did in that hotel. Right now."

Gerry grinned, then kissed her again as they both took off their clothes. Under the covers, being pressed together felt like the most normal thing in the world. Gerry made love to her as she'd done before. The day faded as they lay together wrapped up. Maddie reflected that she never thought much before about how wonderfully solid bodies were.

Gerry traced her eyebrows and cheeks and kissed her gently. "You are the most beautiful woman I've ever seen."

Maddie put her hand on Gerry's neck and looked at her hard. "How many women is that exactly?"

Gerry's face fell at her tone. "Like this? Just one other. I was thinking of the girls in Mona's, and girls in general."

"In general?"

"Yeah. But I—"

Maddie put a finger on her lips to shush her. "I'm messing with you. What I really want is for you to show me how to do to you what you do to me."

Gerry fell back on the bed and put an arm over her eyes. She was silent so long, Maddie began to worry.

"What's wrong? We don't got much time, honey. We got to be up and dressed and look all neat and normal for when the folks get home. We only got about another hour."

"I know." Gerry didn't move or say anything more.

"So let's go," Maddie said with some sharpness.

"You—uh—don't do anything. That's not how it goes. I'm the one who takes care of you. Not the other way around."

"Huh? What kind of nonsense is that?" Maddie was confused and irritated.

"It's how it is."

Maddie absorbed that statement, and her need for Gerry's touch won out. "Okay. I don't have time for this argument. Let's go."

Gerry beamed and started all over again, with lots more kisses and much more touching in Maddie's sensitive spots. Maddie thought she might melt into a big puddle of goo before the end of it.

"We need to get presentable," she said, out of breath, wanting to do it again. And again. She'd never in her life felt so much joy, and it was both physical and feeling, and it was amazing.

In the fading light, they lay side by side looking at each other.

"Why is your hair so soft?" Gerry whispered, stroking it.

"Don't know. It's the process, I guess."

"What process?"

"Never mind. I don't have the time to explain that now."

"Look," Gerry said, and she put her forearm next to Maddie's. "We're the opposite color. Black and White. Like piano keys."

Maddie couldn't help but smile. Gerry was so sweet, but then reality of time passing came flooding in. "Uh-huh. Put your clothes on, honey. We got to be out of bed and sitting at the table like proper, polite friends."

"Ugh," Gerry said. "That's not enough time."

"I know, but come on." Maddie was visualizing Wilma Grace's face if she walked in at that exact moment.

They were quietly drinking coffee, a foot of space between them but connected by their intense eye contact, when Maddie heard the steps and voices on the front porch.

"Hi, y'all. How was it?" Maddie asked as brightly as she was able as Thom and Wilma Grace appeared in the kitchen.

"Fine. Whatcha doin'?" Wilma Grace glanced back and forth between Gerry and Maddie.

"Hey, Wilma Grace. Hey, Thom," Gerry said, and Maddie appreciated and was amazed by her calm, friendly tone. They really could have been regular friends talking and enjoying a routine cup of coffee instead of nearly devouring each other barely ten minutes ago.

Thom mumbled a greeting and then fled to their bedroom.

Wilma Grace stood there, seemingly waiting for Maddie to say more on what Maddie hoped was clear: Gerry had come for a simple, friendly visit.

"Who was at supper?" Maddie asked, trying to deflect Wilma Grace's obvious suspicion.

"Oh, I don't know. The usual folks. Minnie Lee and Rhoda Green Bush are still trying to outdo each other cooking fried chicken. Their constant back-and-forth makes me tired."

Maddie laughed dutifully.

"I better be going," Gerry said. "Have a good evening, Wilma Grace. You too, Thom," she called toward the bedroom.

"I'll walk you to the bus stop," Maddie said, hating to see Gerry leave. It was like an invisible but strong string was tying them together.

They walked slowly down the hill to the bus terminal. It was full dark, and the lights of Hunters Point glittered.

Maddie took a careful look around and then kissed Gerry. She pulled herself away by sheer force of will. "Write me?"

Gerry looked near tears as she nodded. "As soon as I can. Soon. I swear."

Then the bus came, and Maddie watched her get on, feeling about as lonely as she ever had in her life, and she'd been plenty lonely growing up. Funny, it seemed to take having someone special in her life to make their separation hurt worse than her broken arm.

"You might want to let us know if you're going to be having company," Wilma Grace said when she walked in the door.

"It didn't seem important, seeing as you were going to be out."

"It's just a courtesy," Wilma Grace said. "Seein' as how you were well enough for company."

"She stopped by to see how I was doing. I pay rent here too. I can have anyone I like over for a visit." Maddie was struggling to keep her voice neutral, but she couldn't help being a little angry. She knew Wilma Grace too well.

"Well, I'm just saying. If you're going to be bringing her around on a regular basis…"

"What's eatin' you, sister? You might as well tell me."

"There's something funny about her is all."

"Funny like what? Like 'cause she's White. Is that it?"

Maddie was feeling put out, mainly because she was angry about Wilma Grace's attitude and her nosiness and also guilty because of what she and Gerry were up to and that they had to keep it secret.

She somehow knew that if they were discovered it could be very bad. Wilma Grace would blab to her mama right off. She didn't know what Thom would do. He tended to not want to be part of any drama. But she didn't want to hear what he would say if he found out about them.

"Well, yeah, that's not a way to endear herself to me."

"Oh, for Lord's sake. That's not her fault, and why do you even care?"

"Considering where you met her, I'd say I've got cause to question her."

"What the heck do you mean?"

"I don't think I want to talk about this right now. I'm going to bed."

This abrupt change of direction threw Maddie for a loop, but she decided it was just as well. She had challenged Wilma Grace, but she wasn't sure if she actually *wanted* to have the conversation that she suspected they might have to have. Wilma Grace thought she knew something 'cause she'd been to New York City and all. She thought she knew what was what. But Maddie was sure if she was careful enough, she could keep her secret about Gerry.

She put on her nightgown and crawled into her creaky single bed. The sheets and the pillow smelled like Gerry and like the two of them together. It comforted Maddie, and in spite of her aching arm, she fell asleep.

CHAPTER TEN

March 1946

"They told you to do what?" Gerry asked Woody, shocked.

"I told you. I have to go in and talk to some officers from somewhere or another. They didn't tell me why. Guess I'll find out later," Woody said, acting nonchalant but not fooling Gerry.

She wouldn't meet Gerry's gaze and fell silent and smoked with a distracted air. She wasn't telling the whole truth.

Around the base, a lot of people had started whispering in corners, and a lot of conversations stopped all of a sudden when she walked by. Everyone seemed on edge, and Gerry had no idea why. She didn't want to try to puzzle it out anyhow. Her main goal in life was figuring out when and where she could see Maddie again.

Well, the *when* wasn't too hard, but she couldn't quite solve the *where*. Not back at Maddie's house. That was out, according to Maddie's last letter. Gerry couldn't afford to book a hotel room. She was broke until her next payday. Maddie couldn't help with money because she didn't have a cent either. She wouldn't be paid until she returned to work, and that wouldn't be for another couple of weeks. She and Maddie were separated, stuck, and they couldn't find a solution.

The doctor moved Maddie's arm all around and ran his fingers along where the break had been.

"How's your pain?"

"It's okay." Maddie didn't want to give the doctor any reason not to clear her to go back to work.

"Might linger. The break has healed cleanly, though."

"So can I go back?" Maddie asked eagerly.

"Yes. Two weeks. I'll see you again before you go back. You still need to take it easy, though, so I'll write a note to your foreman. You won't be fully well for a few more weeks."

Maddie went back home, brooding because she couldn't go to work and she couldn't see Gerry.

When she showed up back at the graving dock, Maddie was gratified by all the hugs and the good wishes and *welcome back*s she received. Even Travis was halfway nice. He shook her hand and sort of smiled. She took up her welding rod and electrical lead and scrambled up the scaffold to get started. She had agreed with the doctor to stay on day shift for a while to make sure her arm was doing okay.

Gerry had warned her that her mail was sometimes opened and read for some security thing, so they stuck to facts and harmless generic wishes for one another's health in their letters. They couldn't risk saying what they felt and thought.

> *Dear Gerry,*
>
> *I'm back on shift and so far, so good. My arm is working pretty well, and I can do my welding almost like I could before the accident. I'm on limited hours. Can't go on night shift for another two weeks. Once I can do that, I'll let you know. Hope all is well with you. If you can talk, I'll call you at the non-com club number at four p.m. next Thursday.*
>
> *Best wishes,*
> *Maddie*

"Hi, you. How's it going? How's the dry dock?" Gerry sounded down, glum, not like she usually did.

"It's okay. My arm's still a little weak, but I'm coping. How about you?"

"I don't know. All right, I guess. There's still a ton of boys coming home from the Pacific Theater. I drive them around to where they have to go. It's okay, but I can't see you, so I don't feel all that great."

Gerry lowered her voice. "If we could be alone right now, guess what I'd do?"

Maddie felt the butterflies in her stomach dancing around, and they danced lower down. Her privates tingled and throbbed like Gerry's hands were on her right then.

"I can't say it out loud, but I can think about it," she whispered, looking around to make sure no one was listening. The pay phone was in a busy area.

Maddie said, "I want to come see you in a week. Where can we meet?

"Well, I have to work, so I can't spend much time with you. Can we get a room?"

They both fell quiet, and then Gerry asked, "Are Wilma Grace and Thom going to another covered-dish supper anytime soon?"

Maddie laughed without humor. "Yeah, next week, but I can't use my arm for an excuse. Besides, I have to work so I wouldn't be home."

"I guess that means we have to telephone or write another letter," Gerry said, and her tone made it clear that she didn't like either of these acts.

"No, but that's how it is, baby." Maddie was somewhat put off by Gerry's focus on the negative. She obviously hadn't had much hardship in her life, at least not the same as Maddie and her family endured, so she ought to get over her disappointment pretty quick and start looking for the silver lining in what was going on.

"Yeah. That's how it is."

"Look. On your day off, come over to the house, and we'll leave and go somewhere until I have to work. Be there at, say, four, and I'll be awake. Thom and Wilma Grace won't be home for two hours."

"Okey dokey." Gerry had recovered some of her good humor.

As Maddie walked home back up the hill, she felt her spirits lifted at the thought of seeing Gerry, but underneath there was a worm of unease. The guilt about hiding and, well, lying to those closest to her gnawed at her.

❖

It was a half hour or so until dinner, so Gerry returned to her barracks and lay down on her bunk so she could replay her conversation with Maddie and think about their plans for the following week. On impulse she opened the trunk at the foot of her bed and found all of

Maddie's letters. She began to reread them in order, grinning to herself at Maddie's tentative expressions of affection and the homely details of her work.

"Seaman Stern."

She looked up, startled. She was so absorbed in reading she didn't notice at first that two shore-patrol officers were standing in the aisle between the rows of bunks, staring at her stone-faced.

"Yes?" Fear rushed in, and her throat became tight.

"Come with us, please."

She was so rattled it was all she could do was to stand up, mindlessly obeying the order and leaving Maddie's letters on her cot.

Stiff with fear, she walked out of the barracks between the two officers. "Where are we going?" she asked, trying to keep her voice steady.

They didn't answer but walked her silently to a distant corner of the Treasure Island base, to a small building behind a bunch of warehouses. As she walked, Gerry remembered Woody's vague warnings to be careful. She was sure she *had* been careful. The only people who knew about Maddie were Jimmy and Woody. She noticed that one of the SP men had, clutched in his hand, the little pile of Maddie's letters. She felt like she might throw up.

They ushered her into a bare room with a table where three naval officers sat, one of them a WAVE captain. A single chair stood in front of them, and as one of her shore-patrol escorts sat her down, the other SP officer handed the letters to the officer in the center.

She knew she had to keep her head and not voluntarily say anything. She breathed deeply, inhaling through her nose, trying to calm down.

"Seaman Stern. I'm Commander Reynolds. This is Lieutenant Commander Frank." He indicated the WAVE officer. "And Lieutenant Commander Terry."

Suppressing her impulse to either start crying or screaming questions, Gerry waited. They stared back at Commander Reynolds as he read through her letters. He didn't hurry, but he glanced up at her now and then.

"We have some questions for you."

"Why am I here?" Gerry blurted out. She couldn't help it.

"You're part of an investigation."

He went on to ask Gerry a bunch of questions about where she was from, where she trained, how long she'd been in the WAVES.

She patiently answered them, wondering why they didn't know this information already.

"Seaman Stern, are you a homosexual?"

"N-no." The lie came surprisingly easy, but she hated that her voice shook.

"Do you know Maddie Weeks, welder at Hunters Point Shipyard?"

"Yes." It didn't seem like something she ought to deny.

"And is she your girlfriend?"

"No," Gerry said as firmly as she was able.

"Do you like girls?"

Gerry made a lightning-fast decision. "Yes. I like girls."

The three interrogators looked at each other, and Gerry thought, oh ho. They think they got me.

"In a romantic way?"

"I don't know what you mean."

"Do you like to touch them?"

"I don't know what you mean."

They shifted around, and finally they had a whispered conversation, and Reynolds cleared his throat.

"We are going to make this easier for you," he said, "and turn the questioning over to Lieutenant Commander Frank."

"Why am I here? What is it you want to know?" Gerry was happy her voice was steady. She sensed her questioners were a bit taken aback at her lack of complete surrender.

"Eh. We'll explain later. Commander Frank?" The two male officers stood up and left, as did the shore patrol officers.

Gerry was left staring at the WAVE officer who was clearly pretending she was not uncomfortable with her task. Gerry had gained a little more confidence and was determined to not let this process break her. She thought about Woody's warnings and realized this must be what Woody was talking about. There was nothing bad in her letters from Maddie. They were all about making arrangements to meet or call. And she had been discreet at all times. Woody herself had taught her how to do that.

"Seaman Stern…may I call you Geraldine?"

"If you like." Gerry hated her given name. but that didn't matter in this instance.

"You volunteered for the WAVES in 1943. Correct?"

"Yes. That's true."

"And why did you join the WAVES?"

Gerry drew herself to a seated attention position. "I wanted to serve my country. We were at war, and a recruiter said I was needed, and I wanted to help."

"You were comfortable doing a man's job?"

"Sure. I grew up on a farm. I learned how to drive when I was eleven."

"That's the only reason?" Commander Frank adopted an air of gentle curiosity. "It wasn't because you wanted to be around women?"

Gerry favored the officer with a skeptical smirk. "I believe the WAVES are women. I knew I wasn't joining the regular navy."

"But you knew what your environment would be, and isn't that why you joined?"

"No, it isn't. I told you why."

"Do you like touching girls?" the commander asked suddenly.

"I do. Why do you ask?" Gerry had a strategy in mind.

"Do you like to kiss girls?"

"I have kissed some. What do you mean?"

"Did you like it?"

"I don't know what you mean by like it. I sometimes kiss my friends."

"Young lady, you are trying to evade my questions?"

"Sorry, ma'am. I'm trying to be cooperative."

"Have you ever kissed Shirley Woodward?" *Woody. They know something.*

"I might have sometime. I don't know."

"Did you or didn't you?" Frank demanded, clearly irritated, and she glared at Gerry.

Gerry weighed the pros and cons of telling the truth. They clearly knew things about her already. "Sometimes we kissed hello or good-bye."

The commander grinned unpleasantly. "Now we're getting somewhere. Did you enjoy it?"

Gerry scrunched up her face to look thoughtful. "I didn't think about it."

"Come on. You must have felt something."

"No. I didn't feel anything."

"Do you date men?" Frank demanded, catching Gerry off guard.

"I, uh. I do. sometimes." It was another lie, but Gerry thought it worthwhile. She understood what Frank was trying to get at.

"Who?"

"James Price." Frank wrote the name down.

"Anyone else?"

"No."

Frank closed the tablet she was writing on and left the room.

She left Gerry sitting there for quite some time, and Gerry's mind spun out in all sorts of directions. *They are trying to find out if I'm queer and if I'll admit it. They know something, but not much.*

Frank returned with the other two officers.

"Seaman Stern, your answers are not satisfactory. But we are going to give you a chance to improve your situation. We want you to provide us with names of other WAVE seamen you know who are like you."

"I don't know what you mean, 'like me.'" Gerry thought she might know, but she wasn't going to give them the satisfaction. They clearly knew something about her, and they just wanted her to admit it out loud. She wouldn't do that. Nor would she name anybody else, though, besides Woody, she knew a few women.

"Seaman Stern, don't be insubordinate."

"Sorry, but I don't know who you're talking about."

They whispered among themselves for several minutes.

Commander Reynolds spoke in official tone. "We are going to recommend you be discharged from the navy as an undesirable under the Uniform Code of Military Justice, section 8, article 615-360. Until such time as we can complete your discharge, you will be confined to barracks. You are dismissed."

The shore-patrol officers appeared and escorted her back to the B barracks, where she sat on her bunk and stared into space. She couldn't quite make her mind accept what had just happened. She was being kicked out of the navy, for being homosexual, she assumed.

One of her barracks mates, Tina, walked in. "Hi, Gerry. What's with the goons outside?"

Gerry lay on her back staring at the ceiling. "They're here to make sure I don't go anywhere. I've been confined to barracks. I'm going to be discharged."

Tina's face said it all. "Gee, that's crazy. Why?"

"I can't talk about it."

Tina said, "I'm sorry. Hope you're going to be okay."

Gerry nodded, realizing not only that she wasn't okay, but she wouldn't be able to talk to Maddie to let her know what had happened.

She also wanted to talk to Jimmy and to Woody, but she didn't see any way to do either. If she was going to be kicked out of the navy, she had no idea what she could do except go back to Fresno to her folks. She needed to find Woody and Jimmy and discuss this with them. Somehow. She also had to get word to Maddie. Her head ached with the number of and the intensity of her thoughts racing through it. She couldn't see any solutions to any of her problems. She was stuck in the barracks until the powers that be made their move. And when they did, what then?

The phone rang and rang. Then it rang a few more times. Maddie wondered if Gerry had been delayed somewhere. She hoped *someone* would answer. And she could maybe leave a message. After a long wait, she gave up and replaced the phone in its cradle. Maybe she could call the main base number and leave a message like she had before. She awkwardly picked up the phone book dangling below the phone and found a number for Treasure Island.

A cheerful female voice answered. "How can I direct your call?"

"I'd like to leave a message for Seaman Gerry Stern."

"Just a moment."

The wait couldn't have been long, but it seemed to last forever.

Finally, the operator returned. "I'm sorry, ma'am. There's no one here by that name."

"WAVES. She's in transportation." Maddie began to feel panic rising and fought to tamp it down.

"Yes, ma'am." There was another long silence.

"Ma'am, I'm sorry. Seaman Stern was stationed here until yesterday. She was discharged."

"I see," Maddie replied, numbly. "Thanks." She hung up and stood there a long time. Why would Gerry not tell her she was leaving? Why *did* she leave? She loved the navy. It made no sense. Maddie had no idea what to do. She could go out to Treasure Island and try to find someone to give her some answers. But she imagined that would be really hard, if not impossible. What was Gerry's friend's name, the one she was with the night they'd met? Shirley Woodward. That was it. She called the base back and gave the name to the operator.

"I can ring her for you."

Maddie's mood jumped. She was hopeful but still worried.

"Treasure Island Communication Command, Petty Officer Woodward."

"Uh. Hi. I'm Maddie Weeks. I don't know if you remember me? You and Gerry Stern gave my sister and me a ride from Mona's the night of VJ Day?"

There was a long pause. Then the voice, noticeably chillier, said, "Yes. I remember."

"Look, I'm sorry to bother you, but I'm trying to find Gerry. They told me she was gone."

"I'm sorry but that's true." Woody sounded even more distant.

"Well, do you know where she is?" Maddie struggled to not sound desperate.

"No. I don't."

"Well. Is there someone who might know?"

"Jimmy Price, maybe, but he was discharged too."

"Where can I find him?"

"I don't know. Look, I'm sorry, but I can't help you."

"Okay. Thanks. Sorry to bother you." Maddie slid down the wall of the building where the pay phone was and sat on the ground, her legs suddenly unable to hold her up. She had to go home get ready to go to work, but she needed time to think.

She had to have faith that Gerry would get in touch eventually. Gerry had, after all, come to find her when she was in the hospital. She'd come over to the house and asked Wilma Grace where Maddie was.

Something must have happened. Gerry wouldn't just leave without a word. With this slim hope, Maddie picked herself up and walked back to her little house.

❖

Gerry was in the Transbay Terminal holding a suitcase with her few belongings. She had her last payroll cash in her pocket, and she didn't know what exactly she would do or where she would go. Again, she thought about heading back to her family in Fresno, but she couldn't fathom returning to that life. Not now. Not ever. How would she ever explain any of this to her family? When she had the time, she'd write her mother a letter with some sort of explanation. Like after she found a job.

Right now, she had two priorities—finding a place to stay and getting word to Maddie. Also, she'd have to find a job pretty soon. She was kicked out of the navy, and she needed to earn a living. The paper that stated that was in her pocket, but it still didn't seem real. Gerry told herself she wasn't going to cry about it. No way would she shed a single tear. She put it out of her mind and thought about where she might go.

When she had been sightseeing around downtown San Francisco with Maddie, she'd seen signs on some of the buildings on streets north of Market. "Rooms for rent by the week." She walked up Fourth Street, past Foster's Cafeteria, and saw one of those signs on the door of an oldish building. Its archway entrance said "Rutherford Arms."

The woman at the desk looked her up and down, not in a way someone would at Mona's, but as though she could tell Gerry's character.

"Help you?"

"I need a room."

"How long?" the woman asked, impersonally.

"A week, I guess, to start."

"Okay. Five dollars, payable in advance. Bathroom's down the hall to the left. Absolutely no cooking." She glared at Gerry. "And no men."

If she'd not been in a sad mood, that would have made her smile. Instead, she nodded numbly, handed over the money, and was given a key. The lobby was shabby, as though no one cared much to make it neat. Gerry couldn't help but compare this to the naval base, where everything was shipshape and squared away, as they used to say. And that made her sad all over again. She walked up the stairs, reminding herself she wasn't in the navy anymore.

She let herself into her room. It wasn't much: just a single bed with an indifferent bedspread. There was a window that overlooked an airshaft where a dim column of light shown. A scarred table. She'd need to find a dresser or else keep her clothes in her suitcase. Suitcase for now.

She sat down on the bed and looked into space.

Well, two things were true. She was no longer subject to the constant scrutiny of navy life, and no one could tell her what to do and when to do it. Or where to go. Or who to see.

And, secondly, she had her own room with a bed. The sooner she could get in touch with Maddie, the better, because she could invite her over, and they could make good use of that bed. Gerry's mood brightened since she had something to look forward to. She'd better get started on finding a job, though, because her small pile of money would go quick.

The other burning question was how to *find* Maddie. The only way she knew to do that was to go out to Hunters Point once more and visit her. And that was one more thing to brighten her day. She assumed that Maddie was still working the night shift, so she'd probably be home during the day, without her family around. On that happy thought, Gerry unpacked a few toilet articles and arranged them on the table. Then she set off for Maddie's house.

❖

Maddie lay in bed staring at the ceiling. She ought to be asleep, but the more she tried to fall asleep, the less likely it seemed she would. The house was quiet, thank goodness. She'd drawn the curtains, but light was still coming in. She was comfortable, warm, and snug, but she wasn't sleepy though she'd worked all night.

She couldn't stop thinking about Gerry and wondering what had happened to her and why she hadn't been by the phone to answer her call. When she'd come home that morning, Wilma Grace had mentioned that she seemed hangdog and too quiet, but Maddie put her off. She didn't want to get into a discussion with Wilma Grace about Gerry, and she didn't want to lie to her and make excuses. She was grateful when Thom had, surprisingly, told his wife to let up and leave Maddie be.

She flopped over onto her side. She had to be at work in ten hours, and once Thom and Wilma Grace came home at six, she wouldn't be able to sleep.

She went to the kitchen and filled a glass with water and drank some. Then she went back to bed. She folded her hands over the top of the blankets and sighed. A knock at the door made her jump. She leaped out of bed and put on her bathrobe, walked through the kitchen to the living room, and listened at the door. There was another knock.

"Who is it?" she asked, injecting a tough note into her voice in case she might need that sort of attitude.

"It's Gerry."

A surge of happiness and relief ripped through Maddie, and she threw open the door. They clung together, and both of them cried a bit.

"You're here," Maddie said. "I can't believe it."

Their lips met, and they kissed for a long moment.

"Come in." Maddie took Gerry's hand and led her over to sit on the little couch.

Gerry was smiling, but something was wrong with her smile. It didn't look like her at all. It was a tight smile, not the open, happy grin Maddie was familiar with. She squeezed Gerry's hand to encourage her to talk.

"The navy discharged me for being 'undesirable,'" Gerry said.

"Oh no, and what the heck does that mean?"

"It's because I'm gay." Gerry hung her head.

"How do they know that?" Maddie was mystified.

"I'm not sure. Someone must have said something. If I could talk to Jimmy or Woody, they might be able to tell me..." Her lips trembled, and Maddie hugged her.

In fits and starts, Gerry told Maddie the whole story. She ended it by saying, "That's why I missed your call. I was confined to barracks and couldn't be by the phone. I hope you're not mad."

Maddie wrapped her up a big hug. "Silly. "Of course, I'm not mad. I was worried."

They began to kiss again, a little desperately.

"Maddie, oh my God, I didn't know if I would ever see you again." Gerry kissed her from her cheek down her neck.

"I'd never thought I'd see *you* again."

Gerry pressed her backward onto the couch. Maddie was more wide-awake than ever and didn't want Gerry to stop. She'd started out relieved and was quickly getting aroused. Gerry slid her hand up Maddie's pajama top to reach her breast.

Maddie moaned, then whispered, "We can get in bed."

Gerry leapt up to her feet as though a bomb had gone off underneath her, grabbed Maddie's hand, and they skipped into Maddie's small bedroom. In a jiffy, they were naked and under the covers.

"Don't stop," Maddie whispered urgently. She'd thought about this moment so often since their last time, she had practically memorized every step and how each touch felt. Gerry clearly had had the same memories. They moved together, trying to get as close as possible.

Breathless from kissing, Maddie boldly grabbed Gerry's hand and stuck it between her legs. Her eyes tightly closed, she surrendered to the sensations, aware of nothing but Gerry and her own rush of feelings.

"Oh, my Lord," Maddie heard Wilma Grace say. She opened her

eyes, and Wilma Grace was standing in the doorway with her hand clapped over her mouth and her eyes so wide, Maddie could see the whites all the way around her dark-brown irises.

"Ger." She pushed Gerry's shoulder rather roughly, but Gerry was so intent on what she was doing, she didn't notice, and she didn't stop. Maddie pushed her again, harder, and this time she fell backward out of bed and onto the floor.

"Maddie, what's wrong. Why—?" She must have read Maddie's horror in her face, and she turned around.

She stared back at Maddie, looking shocked and terrified.

No one said a thing for one long moment.

"What in the world…?" Wilma Grace was almost speechless. That would normally have made Maddie burst out laughing, but not this time.

"You better go," she said to Gerry, who nodded dumbly.

Gerry picked up her scattered clothes and began to dress, staying mercifully silent. Maddie didn't say a thing either. What, after all, was there to say?

Gerry finished getting her clothes on and kissed her cheek, saying, "You can call me at the Rutherford Arms Hotel and leave a message."

As she walked by, she said, "Bye, Wilma Grace."

Wilma Grace, naturally, didn't say a word but moved away from her to give her plenty of room as she walked past.

❖

Gerry tried to get her breath as she walked down the hill toward the Hunters Point bus terminal. When she got there, she flopped down on the bench. It didn't even matter to her when the bus was supposed to arrive. She was a mass of feelings ricocheting every which way in her head. She shook with adrenaline and thwarted arousal. She was afraid for Maddie and what might be happening to her, horrified at their discovery, and heartsick she couldn't stay around to comfort and support her. She finally calmed a little. The bus pulled up, and she slipped into a seat, trying to think clearly but failing. Her stomach hurt and her head ached. The dizzying switch from seeing Maddie again, to making love, to being discovered by Wilma Grace, to finally sitting, shaken and unhinged in a bus, was too much handle.

She went back up to her dump of a room at the Rutherford, lay down on her lumpy bed, lit a cigarette, and tried to think clearly. It was about six in the evening, and downtown San Francisco was moving from daytime bustle to nighttime revelry. It was Friday night, and that, Gerry suddenly recalled, had once meant shore leave and carousing at Mona's. That would be just the thing to take her mind off her troubles.

She knew she ought not to drink so she could conserve her meager pile of cash, but she could get a free glass of ginger ale and sit at the bar. She couldn't bear the idea of staying alone in her room. She didn't even have a radio to keep her company, let alone Maddie. If only she'd waited and invited Maddie to come to visit her, then she could have avoided what happened. She couldn't wait, though, and she'd had no idea when Maddie would be able to come downtown. So they'd been discovered. She hoped it wasn't too bad for Maddie, but she had no idea what would happen with Maddie's family and, frustratingly, no way to find out.

Gerry stubbed out her smoke and jumped up to pace her small room. She didn't want to spend the evening lying on her bed, smoking, fretting about Maddie and waiting to go to sleep.

She went to Foster's Cafeteria, asked for a cup of coffee, told the waitress she would order in a moment, and she was brought some bread, which she tore into small pieces to consume as slowly as she could. She was determined to spend as little money as possible on food. She left a dime for her coffee and, feeling guilty, swiftly left the restaurant.

She walked around the downtown streets for a couple of hours, noting businesses where she might apply for a job. Once such place, Stemple's Bakery, had a "Help Wanted" sign in the window. She decided to return the next day to apply.

She ought to go visit her family, since they were a few hours' train ride away. But she had no idea what she would say to them and didn't want to ask them for money. Her mom would ask her a million questions that she didn't want to try to answer. They were proud of her for joining the WAVES, but once they discovered she'd been kicked out, they'd want to know the whole story. Then they'd want her to come back to the farm right away. No matter how poor she was, she wasn't doing that. She couldn't have them find out about her or about the blue discharge or about Maddie. She'd find a way to survive. Somehow.

When it became late enough, she walked up Nob Hill to the Mark Hopkins Hotel, praying Jimmy would be there. She thought he might be because he loved that bar and was like a homing pigeon always returning to its base.

She peered into the gloom, and slowly her vision adjusted. There he was, standing at the bar with George, a drink in front of him and waving a cigarette.

She walked up behind him and tapped him on the shoulder. He spun around and said, "Gerry." She couldn't interpret his expression. Was he happy to see her or not? George looked concerned.

"Hi, Jimmy. I'm glad I found you."

"Yeah. It's good to see you too. I guess you heard."

"I don't know. Heard what?"

"I got the boot. Section Eight." He took a big gulp of his drink. He favored Manhattans and generally drank several of them each night.

"Yeah. Me too," she said. "They kept me confined to quarters while it was going on. I couldn't see anyone or use the phone."

"That's right. Once they decide you're going, you might as well be nonexistent. It doesn't matter how hard you worked before, how many good performance evals, nothing. They were just waiting 'til the war ended before making their move. Funny how much they needed us while the war was going on. Once it was done, poof! You're undesirable, so we're going to survey you and kick you out. You know what that means, don't you, Ger?"

"No. What does it mean besides the obvious?" Gerry asked.

Jimmy snorted and took a pull on his cigarette, then blew out the smoke before he answered.

"No GI benefits. I asked. We get nothing. Zilch. Zip, zero. We can't even apply for jobs as veterans because no one's going to hire a blue-discharge vet. We're screwed." He pointed to his glass, and the bartender mixed him another drink.

Gerry let his words sink in without saying anything else.

"Lucky for me, I have old George here to tide me over." He looked fondly at his boyfriend, who grinned back at him sadly.

"I'm going to look for work tomorrow. Wish me luck," Gerry said.

"Lots of luck, kid. It's tough out there."

"What about Woody? Where's she?" Gerry asked.

"Woody, eh. How come you want to talk to Woody?" Jimmy looked and sounded evasive.

"Cause, she'd started dropping hints to me about this a couple of weeks ago. I wanted to tell her she was right after all. I should have listened to her, though I'm not sure I'd have done anything different. *I* didn't think I did anything that would make me get caught."

"Oh, she was more than right. In fact, she's still happily at work, sitting right there in the comms office, in the catbird seat, you might say." He took a vicious draw on his cigarette and blew the smoke out.

"Oh, that's good. So she wasn't discharged like us?"

Jimmy looked at Gerry with a dumbfounded expression and shook his head. "You didn't know?"

"Know what?" she asked.

He shook his head again and laughed without humor.

"Come on, Jimmy. Stop beating around the bush."

"She saved her own skin by telling on everyone, including you."

"What?"

"You heard me. She and I went out for drinks, and she spilled the beans about how she spilled the beans. They gave her a deal that if she'd give up a few names, she could stay. One of those names was yours."

Gerry stepped back, her knees weak. So that was what happened. Woody ratted her out. So much for friendship.

"You too?" Gerry asked in a strangled voice.

"Nah. They had their eye on me already. I always mouthed off too much, and I liked camping it up, so they had my number. I got 'surveyed,' as they say. They told me I could take a quiet exit because of how hard I'd worked. A lot of guys weren't so lucky. They got thrown in the queer brig. Some closet queens way high up in the navy brass decided the best way they could protect themselves was going after everyone else."

"There's nothing we can do?"

"Nope. That's all she wrote. Welcome to civilian life. Let me buy you a drink, and we can toast the glorious US Navy. Or, rather, George can buy you a drink, won't you, George? What's your poison?" Jimmy looked at George, who shrugged and waved the bartender over.

Gerry left shortly thereafter and walked over to North Beach to Mona's. She half hoped she'd see Woody there and began to rehearse what she might say. Her one drink, courtesy of George at the Top of the Mark, was a strong one, and she was feeling feisty. She pushed thoughts of Maddie to the back of her mind.

CHAPTER ELEVEN

March 1946

Maddie crossed her arms and listened to Wilma Grace's flood of words. After a short time, it became a meaningless drone. The gist of it was Maddie was going to hell, and she'd be lucky if Thom let her stay with them, and she had half a mind to tell Maddie's mama herself, but she'd leave that to Thom or to Maddie, if she had the gumption to come clean with her mama, and she better do that if she knew what was good for her. And so forth.

"I knew that Gerry was trouble when I saw her."

"We met her at Mona's, I might remind you, Wilma Grace. While we were hearing Gladys Bentley. You picked the place, so you can't say you didn't understand what was what and who was what. You knew very well what kind of place it was. And Gerry helped us out that night, and she didn't have to do that, but she did."

Wilma Grace tossed her head. "Well, I didn't know what kind of place it was, and no one cares what women like Gladys Bentley do in their spare time. It's different for normal, God-fearing folks like you, Maddie Weeks. And you know it. Wait until I tell your brother, and I have a good mind to write your mama. We'll see what *she* has to say about your shenanigans. I cannot believe you're doing what you're doing, and furthermore—"

Maddie had heard enough. "I have to get to sleep, if you don't mind, Wilma Grace. I have to be at work in about five hours. If you have more to say, it'll have to wait 'til tomorrow."

Wilma Grace looked like she was about to explode, she was so mad, but, with a snap of her jaw, she at least stopped talking. Maddie could go into her room, close the door, get some quiet—and relive the time she'd spent with Gerry up to the point when old Wilma Grace waltzed in and interrupted them.

Maddie dozed a bit, but the sound of the alarm clock jolted her awake all too soon. It was going to be another long night at work. But behind her shock about Wilma Grace's sudden appearance, she was actually calm. Her brother wasn't about to kick her out of her home because he wasn't like that. Wilma Grace would fuss and fume and threaten, but it was all noise. Maddie refused to allow herself to be upset. Her life was her own, and now her life had Gerry in it, and she wouldn't let anything disrupt that. They'd have their challenges and troubles, but so be it. That was another thing her mama had drilled into her. Life *was* a vale of tears, just like the Bible said, but she, Maddie, was still able to choose for herself, and she could find happiness if she worked on it. And Marguerite had said if she wanted something, she had to put her mind to it, work on it, and not stop until she got what she wanted.

Maddie went about her work, drinking coffee on breaks to keep sharp. She liked Wilma Grace for the most part, and though to be caught was embarrassing, after all, it might be a good thing. She was tired of hiding. In the end, what difference did it make what Wilma Grace thought? She focused on Gerry and when they could see one another again. She would call her at the hotel the first chance she had, and they'd work out how to get together.

Gerry slid onto a barstool at Mona's and ordered a beer. She was glad she'd had one drink already with Jimmy. She could make this second one last a long time. She wanted to people-watch for a bit. If Woody showed up at Mona's, as she half wanted her to and half didn't, she didn't know what she'd say to her. *Thanks a lot, pal, for ruining my life.* Then she pushed that thought out of her mind. She didn't want to be sad; she wanted to be happy. She'd be happier if Maddie was with her, for sure. She put aside the fact that she'd been booted out of the navy and didn't know what she was going to do next. She took the tiniest sip of her drink and glanced around.

There at the other end of the bar sat a woman in a red dress. Idly, Gerry wondered who she was. If she was a femme, as she certainly appeared to be, her butch was nowhere to be seen. She also looked like she was feeling a bit uneasy and out of place but trying to hide it, smoking with elaborate unconcern.

She looked toward Gerry finally, and their eyes met. Gerry threw her a devil-may-care grin and raised her glass in salute. The strange woman nodded. Gerry had dressed in her best butch clothes, mainly to make herself feel better. She wore gabardine slacks, a wide-collared blue shirt, and a tweed jacket, but she wasn't looking to pick anyone up. Maddie was her girl, and that wouldn't change. She was at Mona's for diversion, and diversion was looking at her right now, sitting at the other end of the bar in a tight cocktail dress. It certainly would do no harm to talk to her, if she was unattached. If she was attached, Gerry would find out soon enough.

She walked over to the unknown woman and said, "Hiya. You look like you're all by yourself, and that sure doesn't seem right." She lit a cigarette for the strange woman.

"Oh, yes. I broke up with my guy last week and needed to do something to cheer myself up. So I says to myself, why don't I take a trip somewhere? I heard about the Golden Gate Bridge and ended up here."

"I'm Gerry. What's your name and where you from?"

"Indiana. Muncie. Name's Gertie."

"Nice to meet you, Gertie from Muncie."

Gertie offered her fingers, and Gerry took them, grinning like crazy.

"Pleased to meet you, I'm sure, Gerry with no last name."

"What made you want to visit Mona's?" Gerry was curious.

Gertie opened her purse and took out a pamphlet. "It talks about it in here." She handed it to Gerry.

Sure enough, it was a tourist guide, inviting those who wanted to "take a walk on the wild side" to visit North Beach and see Mona's, "where girls will be boys," and Finocchio's, "where boys will be girls."

That was something. *We really are a tourist attraction. I'll be damned.* Woody had told that her a long time ago, and here they were in an actual tourist brochure. She handed the pamphlet back to Gertie.

"You're one of them, right?" Gertie asked. "The girls who'll be boys." She quoted the ad and giggled.

Feeling bold, Gerry said, "Sure am."

Gertie's eyes widened and she beamed. "I can't wait to tell 'em back in Muncie that I went to this place they talk about here." She guffawed.

Gerry was astonished Gertie knew the term. "That's what I am," she said with an air of pride. There seemed no good reason to deny it.

"I'll be darned. The folks back home will be so impressed they hear I met the real thing." And Gertie batted her eyelashes so hard, Gerry thought they'd fall off. No irate butch was going to show up, and it struck her that Gertie was flirting with her.

Gerry was flattered, but she wasn't so sure about being called the "real thing," as though she was a monkey in a cage. But she had nothing better to do than go back to her dreary room at the Rutherford Arms and think and wonder about Maddie and how she was going to find a job, so she decided to keep talking to Gertie.

Gertie asked, "How come you don't have a last name?"

"We don't use them much." Gerry leaned against the bar and smoked.

"Is that a fact? You like to be mysterious, huh?" Gertie giggled and tapped Gerry's hand with her fingernail.

"Yes, we do. We're like a secret club." *That was true.*

"Don't seem so secret to me." Gertie's head swiveled around from one side to the other.

Gerry didn't feel like now was the time to try to explain the gay life to the likes of Gertie. "Looks can be deceiving," she said in a bantering tone.

"They sure as heck can. I'd swear that half the people here were guys and it was a regular-type club, but when I get up close and personal-like, I see that ain't the case. You're a girl for sure, though you're in pants and a jacket." This time Gertie gave her an even more intimate look, eyelids lowered, her gaze traveling from Gerry's face down to her shoes.

But as gratifying as Gertie's come-on was, Gerry wasn't about to follow through. She had Maddie to think about. Her drink was about empty, and she didn't want to spend any more money for another.

"Buy you a drink?" Gertie asked, shyly.

Gerry hesitated for a second. That wasn't the way it was supposed to go, but since she had so little money, she said, "Sure. Thanks." *Just this once. She's a tourist. I hope word doesn't get around that I let a femme buy me a drink.*

After their fresh drinks arrived, Gertie chugged hers down.

"Jeez-Louise. I never seen any place like this. Or anyone like you." She put a warm hand on Gerry's thigh, and Gerry froze. At that moment, it struck Gerry that she could take this strange lady tourist from Muncie to bed if she wanted to. If not for Maddie, she'd be tempted. It would a be a gas. *No.*

"You're a swell girl, Gertie, but I have to scram." She stayed long enough to drink her second drink.

"Oh, so soon? We're just getting to know each other."

"I know, it's sad, but there's a whole bar full of people you can get to know." She winked and slid off her barstool. "Bye, Gertie-from-Muncie."

Gerry walked back to the Rutherford Arms, half drunk and despondent. She wondered how Maddie had handled matters with Wilma Grace after she left. Part of her felt cowardly for deserting her, but Maddie had asked her to leave. When would they be able to see each other, and what the hell she was going to do with her life?

In the morning when Maddie returned home from work, Thom sat on the front porch. His hands were on his knees, his face unreadable.

"Don't start," Maddie said by way of greeting. "I'm not in the mood. I want to go to sleep."

"I know, but can you give me a few minutes? Wilma Grace went to work, so we got some time to talk."

Because she loved her brother, Maddie sat down in the other front porch chair. "She told you."

"Yep. She told me." Then he didn't say anything else.

That was the bad part of having a brother who never said much about anything. He was damned hard to get words out of when it was necessary.

"Look, you got something to say, say it. You asked me to talk."

"I love my wife, and I love my sister. I want you to get along. This house isn't near big enough for feuds."

"I'm not about to have any feuds. I have my own my life to live, and I'm not asking for Wilma Grace to like it. Or you either, for that matter." There she was, getting all defensive. She didn't want to, but she thought she knew what was coming.

"But you were in the house with someone, messing around."

"Yeah. I was. So? Would you rather it was a guy?"

"No. Now don't be a smart-ass, sis. It's not nice."

"I'm not being a smart-ass. It's a question."

"I don't want anything like that going on." He paused. "I knew when you was thirteen that you had no use for boys."

"You did? How?" Maddie was truly surprised.

"Because I got asked by so and so could he call on you, and you always said no. No *if*s, *and*s, or *but*s. Just no. Happened more than once. Same since we moved out here to California. I don't give a rat's ass who you want to be with. I truly don't, though Mama might have a thought or two. But, as you might have noticed, Wilma's got a whole lot of stake in everything looking perfect. She wouldn't want the neighbors to talk. So just don't bring the girl around here, okay? I got to have peace here in my home."

"All right. I can agree to that. But tell Wilma Grace to leave me be."

"I will. Let's hope when she's calmed down, she'll agree."

"I need some sleep, brother." She kissed him on the cheek and patted his shoulder.

She fell asleep with an easier mind. It was better that she didn't have to sneak around anyhow. The secrecy had been wearing on her. She supposed Wilma Grace could still write her mama, but Maddie would handle it when and if it happened.

❖

The message said, "I have a day off next Tuesday. I'll meet you at the fountain at six in the evening."

Gerry read it again, folded it neatly, and put it in her pocket, smiling. Three days from now, she'd see Maddie. That thought gave her a great boost, something she really needed. Along with her new job at the bakery, she was feeling fine. Next was to find a cheap place to live.

She'd been hired as a baker. It was a good thing that, of all the domestic skills her mother had failed to instill in her, baking was one thing she *could* do. She merely bent the truth a little to expand her experience on whipping up a cake or some cookies at home to being able to bake at higher volume. The problem was she had to show up at four a.m. That was earlier than reveille at Treasure Island. But she got off at three in the afternoon, and that gave her some time for herself.

What she didn't want to do was dwell on her dismissal from the navy. She didn't even mention her discharge to the bakery manager. She lied and said she'd resigned, and they didn't check her story because they were desperate for a baker.

When she saw Maddie alight from the bus, all smiles, she was relieved. After their last meeting, she wasn't sure what would happen next with them.

They hugged lightly on the street, then dashed over to the cafeteria for something to eat. Gerry told Maddie all about her new job.

"What happened after I left the other week?" she asked, aching to hold Maddie's hand but not daring to. Their eye contact said it all. They both wanted to get back to bed, but they observed a sense of propriety.

"Oh, you know Wilma Grace wanted to make a fuss over it, but Thom took care of her. He said just don't bring you around."

"I see. Well, that's the way it goes, I guess."

"It could have been worse. Wilma Grace might have tried to kick me out, but she can't do that as long as my brother wants me there. He's not going to change, and *I'm* not about to change, so she just has to cope. Though I wonder if she has something else in mind, like telling my mama. But I won't know until I know." Maddie shrugged.

"Meanwhile I guess we can see each other on your day off. Don't know when I'll get one, but it don't matter."

Back at the Rutherford Arms, after they made love and Gerry was enjoying a smoke, Maddie asked, "How you doing about your trouble with the navy?"

"Trying not to think about it."

"Doesn't it hurt?" Maddie asked, and she sounded concerned and patted Gerry's shoulder "Yes, but I don't want to think about it, and I don't have to. How about we talk about something else."

Maddie dragged her fingers along Gerry's arm, raising goose bumps. "Okay. How about we talk about what else we want to do while I'm here. And not just this." Maddie responded to Gerry's lusty grin.

"Okay. How about we go to Mona's for a drink. I got some money coming in again, so I can afford it."

Maddie turned over on her back and sighed.

"What's wrong?" Gerry asked.

"Nothing. I'm not so keen on hanging around there."

Gerry was confused. "Why not?"

"I don't know. It's not my favorite way to spend an evening. That last time we went, I felt out of place. I felt like folks were looking at me. At you and me."

"I don't think that's true," Gerry said.

"Well, maybe you didn't notice it."

"Well, why don't we go, and you can show me if it happens," Gerry said, and she couldn't keep a challenging edge from her words.

"Um. Not today, okay? I didn't bring anything to change into."

Gerry grinned. "That's fine. Some other time." She rolled over on top of Maddie and kissed her, pressing her into the lumpy mattress. Truly, nothing else and nobody else mattered in the world. There was nothing but the two of them together at that moment.

Two weeks later, Maddie showed up in a blue dress and agreed they could go to Mona's. Secretly, Gerry had been deeply amused and also proud that Maddie thought it so important that she look good when they went out on the town. In Gerry's view, they looked good together. Maddie was the same height as she was, but with her deceptively slender build and in a nice dress, they achieved the required contrast between them. In reality, Maddie was one solid body of muscle from all her welding. The other effect of the welding work were the tiny burn scars dotting her shoulders and neck.

"What are these?" Gerry asked, touching one with her finger.

"Scraps of slag—the burned metal bits from the welds. I told you a little about them when you went to watch me weld that first time."

"Do they hurt?" Gerry wanted to make them go away.

"Nah. Just a little sting at first. Mostly they just poke holes in all my work shirts."

As they walked into Mona's they made a very good-looking couple, and she couldn't imagine why anyone would feel anything other than envy and admiration looking at the two of them. There had been Woody's reaction, but Gerry considered it a goofy form of jealousy. She and Woody had been best friends, but suddenly Gerry had turned her attention to someone else, and Woody was sore. That also might have played a part in her decision to give Gerry's name to the navy investigators. But having the woman she considered her best buddy betray her still stung.

The very first person Gerry saw when they arrived at Mona's was Jimmy. He sat at the bar with two other guys.

She walked over, Maddie in tow, and tapped him on the shoulder. He was, as usual, in mid-laugh. He turned, and when he saw who it was, he grinned and clapped her on the shoulder.

"Well, I'll be a monkey's uncle. I wanted to see you, and here you are."

"Hi, Jimmy. Good to see you. This is Maddie."

She stepped back so Jimmy could see Maddie, who was standing behind her.

"Maddie, this is Jimmy, one of my pals from Treasure Island."

She shook hands with him and nodded. That guarded look Gerry was familiar with was back.

"Nice to make your acquaintance. Finally," Jimmy said.

Gerry couldn't tell from his tone what he was thinking. All of his remarks about Maddie flooded through her mind, and she prayed silently that he wouldn't say anything directly to her.

"It's good to meet one of Gerry's navy friends," Maddie said in an even, pleasant voice.

He smirked, nodded quickly, and turned his focus right back on Gerry.

"I'm sure glad I ran into you, 'cause I have something real important to tell you."

"Oh? Before you start with that, have you seen Woody?"

"Briefly, a couple of weeks ago. Why?" Jimmy looked pained. "I don't want to be in the middle of your tiff with her."

"I don't want you to be. I'm just asking. How is she?"

"She's okay. Truthfully, I don't think she quite thought of how lonely she'd be after the navy went and kicked us all out. She's the only one left on the Island from our gang." He named a few others who had either left the navy or been discharged.

"I see. Well. Thanks." She patted his shoulder.

He nodded, his expression sad. It sounded like Woody was sorry for what she'd done. Kind of.

Then he perked up. "So let me tell you about what I'm doing."

Once Jimmy started talking about something he was enthused about, he was unstoppable. He'd been put in touch with the local San Francisco navy veterans' group, and they were going to help him try to get his undesirable discharge upgraded, and he'd decided to pursue it. The idea came from another Treasure Island sailor, Toby, who'd also been given a blue discharge.

"I can let George support me for the rest of my life, or I can get that undesirable discharge changed to general discharge so I can get a decent job." He waved his cigarette. "I want to work. I need to work. I need to have some self-respect. They can say we're deviants, we're sick, we're vile human beings, but God damn it, I'm still worth *something*. I served in the navy, and I fought in a war. That counts for something. I deserve to be able to work. You do too." Jimmy took a drag on his smoke and eyed Gerry.

She didn't know what to say so she stayed silent.

Jimmy continued. "Toby told me other guys are appealing their discharges. Get this: he told me the Congress of the US of A is talking about it. There are actual politicians who are saying out loud that the navy and the army too don't have a right to mistreat us because we were drafted, and we served honorably."

"Huh." That was all Gerry could think of to say. She thought about her lie to the bakery manager. Lying had felt terrible, but she come up with any other way. And it was a surprise to hear Jimmy speak so passionately about something. He'd mostly always been interested in a good time, and that was about it.

"Give me your phone number. If I see Woody, I'll tell her you're asking about her. Let's keep in touch."

Gerry gave him the number for the front desk at the Rutherford, said good-bye, and she and Maddie found a table and sat down.

"What did you think of what Jimmy said. Are you going to do the same thing?"

Startled, Gerry stared at her. "No. I don't want anything to do anymore with the navy. It's over."

Maddie put a hand over hers, the most physically expressive they could be in Mona's.

"I'm not trying to upset you, Ger, but if they done you wrong and there might be a way to fix that, well…" She widened her big brown eyes and raised her eyebrows. It made Gerry giggle, as it was surely meant to.

"Maybe, maybe. Anyhow, let's have a drink."

❖

Wilma Grace was decidedly more silent around Maddie. Thom must have said something to her. She didn't act very gracious, but Maddie was willing to accept that in exchange not having to listen to her complain about Gerry all the time. Wilma Grace clearly thought if you've been told to not say mean and bossy stuff, don't say anything at all.

Maddie wanted to spend every spare second she could with Gerry, but there was still a community at Hunters she was a part of that she did happen to like very much. When she was invited to the wedding of one of her coworkers down at the docks, Hilma Mae, she decided to attend. As usual, Wilma Grace was tapped to make a bunch of desserts for the reception.

"I can help you," Maddie told her. She didn't bear any ill will toward Wilma Grace, truly. She was family, and Maddie expected they'd be friendly, if not exactly close. She only wanted to not have to listen to Wilma Grace judge her and Gerry. That was all.

Unfortunately, Wilma Grace didn't seem to see any middle ground between being able to run her mouth about what she saw as Maddie's sinfulness, lack of good sense, and general bad behavior and maintaining a cordial sister-in-law relationship.

"No need. I can take care of it."

"Since when? You got thirty pies to bake, and you've always needed my help before."

"I can handle it. You go your own way. That's what you're going to do anyhow."

Maddie opened her mouth and closed it again. "Wilma Grace. There's no reason you and I can't get along. I want to do the things I normally do. My friend's getting married. I'd like to help you."

She looked as though she was about to say no, but then she said, "Fine. You can help."

Maddie helped Wilma Grace produce the required number of pies, and on the day of the wedding, she and Thom and Wilma Grace arrived at the Baptist church and carried them all into the kitchen, where a small army of church ladies was preparing for the reception.

Just as fast as he could, Thom escaped the female horde and went outside. Maddie knew the bride was anxious and a bit crazy-acting and was content to stay in the kitchen and try to be useful until it was time to go to the sanctuary for the wedding.

The thought of Gerry being with her for an occasion such as this entered her mind. That wouldn't work very well. Not only would Gerry be out of place due to her color, but she would also stick out because of the way she dressed. Maddie remembered she had worn a dress when she came to dinner, but that was the first and last time Maddie had ever seen her in one. Maddie tried to imagine what would have happened if she'd brought Gerry along to this wedding for company, but she couldn't. There was clearly a vast difference between the time she spent with Gerry and her routine life. Never could the two meet, as far as she could tell. Wilma Grace and Thom had made it clear they didn't want Gerry around, and it was probably just as well.

When Maddie and her family had made the move from Arkansas to Hunters Point, they were relieved to find out that, aside from the obvious differences of a new city and the novelty of working at the docks for real money, it wasn't that different from Sawyer. Their social life was connected to the church, and from there, they had made friends and took advantage of the recreation the navy offered its civilian workers. It was a comfort, and even though Maddie missed her mama, her life looked very much like it had back in Sawyer. She was surrounded by folks either literally *from* Sawyer or from some place a lot like it, just another part of the South. The familiar parts of her new life had eased her homesickness and helped her miss her mama a bit less.

Then she met Gerry, and everything had changed. She looked around the church kitchen. Women were talking and laughing together as they worked, but she didn't quite feel a part of it anymore. She knew she still looked the same, but she felt different. The church ladies who had always been so kind and protective of her would likely not take well to hearing she was "different." It saddened her to realize this.

Maddie busied herself cutting up Wilma Grace's pies in nice, neat wedges. She spoke pleasantly to a few of the other ladies helping out. When she sat down in a pew with Thom and Wilma Grace for the wedding ceremony, she wondered what Gerry was doing and what she was thinking. It was kind of like she was being split in two. She was both Maddie Weeks, Edna Weeks's younger child from Sawyer, and she was Maddie who was with Gerry. She hadn't been thinking about that much, but being at the wedding reminded her. She wondered how much longer she'd be working at the dry dock. At the end of the work at Hunters Point, she would return to Sawyer to take up life with her mama. And that would mean leaving Gerry. She dismissed this thought from her mind, since it was not something she had to deal with exactly at that moment.

❖

It didn't pay to dwell on her abrupt exit from the navy. It was way too painful to remember, and Gerry was busy enough learning her job at the bakery. It didn't take as much concentration as driving a bus and negotiating traffic on the Treasure Island base, so it left her with far too much time to think, and it was tough to not remember what happened.

She also missed Maddie. She had thought somehow, since she was out of the navy, they'd have more time to spend together, but that wasn't the case. Maddie was working more than ever, and it was still a struggle to meet. She tentatively suggested to Maddie that she could take a day off.

"I have to work to save money," Maddie said firmly.

"Well, that's good—saving money, I mean." They were down by the wharf sitting on a bench looking out at the bay. Gerry slyly stroked Maddie's hair. "Is it for anything special?"

"No. Not really. I never had any money, and it's a treat to actually earn it and get to keep it." She seemed uncomfortable talking about the subject.

"Hmm. Yeah. It is." Gerry brushed her hand over Maddie's shoulder, then reluctantly returned it to her lap.

Maddie asked, "You going to do that thing your friend Jimmy talked about? Talk to someone about your blue discharge?"

"I don't know. It seems like a whole lot of trouble I don't need. I can't imagine talking to some stranger about what happened to me and being judged. I want to pretend it never happened."

"Yeah, but it *did* happen. You loved the navy, but you're not a navy girl anymore. And it wasn't your choice, not what you wanted, but that's how it is."

"I did love the navy, but it's over now. I have to be something else now."

Maddie surprisingly put her hand on Gerry's leg.

"Nothing's ever *really* over. Stuff like what happened to you? That stays in your head."

"Stuff like what?" Gerry was confused.

"The navy did you wrong. You know they did. You're not going to be able to forget that."

"Yes, they did, but…" Gerry shrugged.

"When I was back in Sawyer, we had all these rules about where we could go, what we could do. It was all rules made by White people to control us Colored folk. If anyone made a mistake, just a little one, you were in big trouble. Sometimes a person in the wrong part of town got hit just for being there."

"Really? You could get in trouble for being in the White part of town?"

"Yup. My mama made sure I knew the rules, but it wasn't hard to slip up. Thom and I were on a bus one time that broke down in the

White area, and we all had to get off and walk. It wasn't too bad. We got yelled nasty things at, but that was all. I was so scared. I thought about that for a long time after. That's what I mean. You think something is done, it's done with you, but it's not really. It stays around."

Gerry turned to look at Maddie, and her face had changed. She looked serious and thoughtful.

"I do think about what happened. I remember every detail of when they took me and how they asked me tons of questions and treated me like I was dirt."

"So that might give you an idea how it feels every single day of your life to be a Colored person in Sawyer, Arkansas."

"Yeah. I see what you're saying. I might look like other people. I don't have skin color that makes me stand out, but I'm not the same as everyone else, and I have to hide that. They still found out anyway, and here I am."

"So here we are. I don't fit in too well anymore either, except down at the dry dock when I'm working."

Maddie told Gerry about being at the wedding, but she still said nothing definite about her future plans of returning to Sawyer and back to her mama. She knew she ought to, but she couldn't bear to think about leaving Gerry, let alone say it out loud.

❖

When Gerry wasn't working at the bakery and didn't have plans to see Maddie, she was left with a lot of time on her hands. She walked the streets or went to Mona's, where she learned to make one ten-cent beer last a couple of hours.

She wasn't totally surprised to see Jimmy show up one day about three months after she last talked to him. George was with him, and he was in a gleeful mood.

"Whaddya know, whaddya say, Ger," he said, clapping her on her back.

"I dunno. Maybe you better answer that question." Gerry was down in the dumps since she hadn't seen Maddie for a few weeks.

"I'm glad you asked. Remember I told you I was going to contest my discharge?"

"Uh-huh."

"Well. It worked. I won. The navy is going to issue me a new general discharge."

"That's nice." Gerry couldn't summon up much enthusiasm for this news.

"'That's nice'? That's all you got to say?"

"Congrats," she said, dully. She was happy for him, sort of. But she was too down in the dumps about Maddie and worried about her job at the bakery as well. She was getting suspicious that she was going to be let go soon. The subject of her discharge had come up, and she'd mumbled some excuse about not bringing the paper in.

"Thanks," Jimmy said, but then he became serious. "Gerry, you can do it too."

"I don't think they'll treat me like they treated you. I'm just a WAVE." She shrugged. "Or I used to be."

"You're a veteran just like me. Like anyone else. Yeah. They'll help you."

"Well, what do I have to do?" Gerry was still suspicious.

"You have to go to the SF Naval Veterans office and apply. Then you're going to have to tell one of them your story. After that they help you file an appeal to the US Navy Review Board."

The idea of doing all that made Gerry's stomach turn flips.

"No way I'm going to talk about that. They'll know I'm queer, and I don't want to relive that whole thing. It was the worst moment of my life. I don't want to talk about it. No." She shook her head. She wouldn't meet Jimmy's eyes and stared into her beer.

To her surprise, Jimmy took her arm and turned her around. The bar stool she was on made it easy. She slowly raised her eyes to look at him. He wasn't smiling, but he looked sympathetic.

"Gerry. It's hard, but I'm glad I did it. If you get your discharge reclassified, you'll be treated like any other veteran. You'll get your GI benefits. You could even go to college if you want to. You can get a decent job. They'll help you with all that. I'm telling you it's worth it. You sacrificed for Uncle Sam. We all did. We deserve to be treated decently by the government."

"I don't know." Gerry still wasn't convinced. It seemed like a minefield to have to talk to someone other than Maddie about what happened, and she was terrified.

"Think about it. Here's the veterans' organization phone number. They did a great job of explaining the whole shebang to me. The guy I talked to? He's straight, but he knows our blue discharges were wrong and a hell of a way for the navy to treat veterans who weren't charged with crimes. He told me the whole point was to get rid of people they decided they didn't need without having to court-martial them. If they had to court-martial us, we'd have more rights. A court martial is what it says. It's like a court. He told me a lot of other stuff as well. He said it's a question of fairness."

Jimmy gripped Gerry's arm and made her look at him. "Can you imagine it? These people at the SF Naval Veterans *want* to help us. I got a real job, I cut way back on drinking, and I'm so much happier. It could be that way for you."

"Okay. I'll think about it."

CHAPTER TWELVE

May 1946

"You smell like a doughnut." Maddie said.

"Yeah. I guess so," Gerry replied. "Is that bad?"

Maddie rubbed her shoulder, then her breast, then burrowed in under her arm.

"Nope. Makes me want to eat a chocolate-covered doughnut right this second though." She giggled, which made Gerry giggle too, momentarily lifting her spirits.

"Why are you so quiet?" Maddie had propped herself up on her elbow to look Gerry in the eye.

"Sorry. Thinking too much, I guess."

After a pause, "Maddie asked, "Well? What are you thinking about?" It wasn't quite a demand, but Gerry had come to recognize it as her "I mean business" tone.

Gerry reluctantly told her about Jimmy's story and his urging her to get in touch with the veterans' people who had helped him.

Maddie listened without comment until Gerry stopped talking.

"Well, what do you think?" Gerry asked.

"Hmph. Why wouldn't you do it?"

Gerry moved restlessly and didn't answer right away. After Jimmy had talked to her and she thought about what it might be like to tell someone the story, she got cold from terror. The hard, pitiless gazes of her navy interrogators filled her memory. She had felt lower than a worm, which was clearly how they wanted to her to feel.

"I want to forget about it, go live my life. I don't want to tell the story to some stranger and have to remember what happened. They acted like I wasn't even human."

"So you said." Maddie fell silent once more.

"Well. What do *you* think? Should I talk to them and ask them for help to get my discharge upgraded?"

"Doesn't matter what I think. It only matters what you want."

Maddie had turned over to lie on her back and gaze at the ceiling. Gerry admired the way she looked in the late-afternoon light, which brought out the red highlights under the warm brown color of her skin. Gerry wanted to make love to her again and not talk anymore, especially not about this subject. Maddie would have to leave soon to go home and get some sleep to be ready for her shift.

She'd said, "I can't sleep when I'm with you. I've got to be by myself, at home alone in my own bed."

In all these months they'd never spent an entire night together, making love, going to sleep, then waking up together and eating breakfast. Gerry wondered if they ever would.

Maddie abruptly turned back over and looked at her. "Since you asked, the way I see it, those people took something away from you, and like you said, they tried to make you feel bad about yourself. You've got a chance to get back what they took away. Maybe you can get your own back, even if them people who were so mean to you won't ever know that you did."

Gerry didn't understand what that meant.

"It's revenge. Someone does something bad to you, and you get back at them."

"Maybe I deserved it," Gerry said morosely, voicing a notion that had haunted her since the day she'd walked away from Treasure Island.

"What? How come you think that?"

"I'm queer, and that's what happens to you when you're queer, and you get caught."

This time Maddie grabbed Gerry's shoulder and forced her to make eye contact.

"You may be queer, but you're still a good person. Your so-called friend Woody was to blame more than you. You did your part to help win the war, just like I did, and just like a whole slew of other people. You don't deserve to be cheated out of what the government owes you. It ought to make you real mad. I know something about being mistreated and being mad about it and not being able to do something about it. *You* can do something."

Gerry sighed deeply. Maddie was right. When she wasn't feeling like horseshit or being terrified of talking about her experience, she was actually mad. Hopping mad, in fact. Jimmy's line about what the man at the veterans' office said popped into her head. *He said it's a question of fairness.*

She hugged Maddie close, and the feel of her was comforting.

After a moment, she released her, and Maddie stretched and sat on the side of the bed.

"I'm going to get ready to leave. It's getting late."

Gerry didn't move. She watched Maddie go about the familiar task of getting dressed. It didn't matter what she did—Gerry loved to watch her move around, so graceful and limber.

When she finished cleaning up and putting on her clothes, she came back to sit next to Gerry, and Gerry stroked Maddie's cheek, kissed her tenderly.

"I'll go see the veteran people," Gerry said. "You're right. Jimmy's right. This is something I can do. For myself."

Maddie beamed and kissed her. "That's wonderful. Don't worry. It'll be all right. My mama always told me I need to do what I know is right, and the Lord'll take care of the rest."

"Right." Gerry laughed. They kissed one more time, and then Maddie was gone.

Still Gerry delayed making her appointment with the San Francisco Navy Veterans. She carried their number around in her pocket but didn't call them. At work, she had to show her navy discharge paper, hoping they wouldn't notice what it actually said, but they did. She was fired from her crappy doughnut-making job and then denied unemployment when she went to apply for it. She asked why and was told it was because of her blue discharge. She sat looking at the letter of denial from the State of California. She had enough money for maybe a month's rent and a little money for food, but nothing more.

She couldn't think of doing anything else, so she called the number Jimmy had given her. The voice on the other end was sympathetic and gave her an appointment two days away.

It so happened that she and Maddie were seeing each other the next day, and Gerry told Maddie her tale of woe. Maddie immediately wanted to give her money.

"You can't. You're saving," Gerry said, upset.

"Never you mind about me. Take it. You can pay me back when you can, when you get a new job."

"I'll think about it," she said finally.

This situation threw her into a swirl of confusion. It seemed completely wrong to accept money from Maddie. How could that possibly fit in with her prescribed role as a butch, as defined originally by Woody? She had no one to discuss the situation with, no friends aside from Jimmy. She couldn't turn to anyone for help...except Maddie. How in the world had she ended up in this fix? Her parents had preached self-reliance, so she refused to ask them for anything. If she did, that could prompt a lot of sticky questions about all sorts of things, along with renewed pleas for her to come back home to the farm. She wasn't going to involve them or Maddie. She was going to handle this herself.

❖

If Maddie didn't have enough to worry about with Gerry's troubles, she heard the gossipy rumblings at the dry dock: they were going to start letting people go. *War's over. They don't need us to be building and fixing all these big old ships at top speed. Men are coming home, and they're going to need whatever jobs are left.*

Maddie tended to not pay any mind to whatever was the current talk because it was usually mindless trivia about boys and dates. This time she even asked her coworkers a few questions, but everything was still undefined and uncertain. Nothing changed outwardly in their day-to-day work. Her mama would say don't start worrying about something that hadn't happened yet.

Her home life was the same. She had no outward conflict with Wilma Grace, which she was grateful for. But she missed what closeness they'd had before Gerry showed up. Before Gerry and after Gerry was how Maddie thought of it. And now, though seeing Gerry had used to be a source of joy and anticipation, it had turned into frustration and heartache. Gerry was sore and sad. She wouldn't say anything much about what had happened to her with the navy people, and on top of it, she'd lost her job at the bakery. Maddie wanted to help, but it didn't look like Gerry was going to accept her help. Gerry likely had some cockamamie idea that Maddie wasn't *supposed* to help her. That would fit with her general attitude that she was "like a man." She wasn't like a man at all, except for sex, and even there, Maddie was pretty darn sure she wasn't in any way like a man would really be.

Underneath all this was the reality that Maddie was going to someday leave. She didn't talk about that, but it was there all the same. Her biggest wish was to return to Sawyer and help her mama, but when she thought about leaving San Francisco and Gerry, she was devastated. But if she stayed, she couldn't see what their future would be like. It was a blank, a cipher. What would they do? Where would they live? And besides, what would Maddie's mama have to say about her and Gerry? Or the idea that Maddie wasn't going to come home? Maddie dreaded even having to ask those questions, let alone hear their answers. She wished she could talk to Marguerite. She'd likely have some idea of what Maddie ought to do. But there was no Marguerite. Maddie would have to figure it out for herself.

It wasn't quite the same feeling Gerry had when the shore patrol had come to take her in for questioning, but it was similar. She dreaded answering the questions she was pretty sure the veteran guy would ask. She would again be helpless and exposed. In her high school biology class, they'd had to dissect a fetal pig. She'd felt like the pig getting its innards picked over and ripped out and examined when the navy had questioned her. She was afraid this experience would be the same. She sternly told herself that whatever happened, it was to give her a better future. Jimmy's story had convinced her, along with some prodding from Maddie, that however hard it would be, it would still be worth it. This idea helped convince her to take action, but it didn't help make her feel better.

The office of the San Francisco Navy Veterans Benevolent Association was housed in a nondescript building on Market Street. As she walked from her flat on Bush Street down Fourth Street and across Market Street, her dread increased. By the time she made into the elevator, she was nearly ready to give up and turn around and run back home. Her fear was that huge. But she forced herself to walk down the hall and into the office, and give her name to the receptionist. The receptionist gave her a form to fill out, and that distracted her for a few minutes. She came to the space on the form for the reason for her request for help and hesitated. Then she took a breath and wrote "contest blue discharge."

The man behind the desk stood up and shook her hand quite cordially. He wore a tie and a white shirt but no jacket. Was he a navy veteran? She was glad he was dressed as a civilian. If he'd been in uniform, she might have turned and run out of the office.

He gave his name as Bob Smiley and told her to have a seat and asked her if she wanted coffee, all in a pleasant, friendly tone. Gerry didn't know what she'd expected, but this wasn't it.

He smoothed her form on the desk in front of him and read it swiftly. Then he looked up.

"Why don't you tell me about your discharge and how we can help you?"

In spite of taking a few sips of coffee, Gerry's mouth went dry, and she had difficulty making her tongue work. Bob didn't seem to mind. He smiled gently and said, "Take your time."

Halting and with lots of pauses, Gerry relayed the details of what led up to her discharge.

When she finished, he shook his head. "It's a real shame that happened to you. I'm sorry."

And with those two words, Gerry relaxed a tiny bit. So simple but so profound. Okay, he wasn't exactly "the navy," but he was close enough. She never thought she'd hear anything like that expressed by anyone associated with it.

"This type of discharge, the blue or 'undesirable,' is an attempt by the navy to escape responsibility. You see, if you haven't committed a crime, which I assume you haven't, they can't start court-martial proceedings. And that, as bad as it sounds, would mean you would have to be formally charged with a crime, given a defense lawyer, and essentially, they would have to prove you were guilty. It's just like a civilian court." She remembered what Jimmy had said to her about the court-martial. She was reassured.

Bob continued. "But the navy can't charge you with a crime because you haven't committed one, so they had to come up with some other way to get rid of you. Hence the undesirable discharge. Now they could have given you a general discharge, which would have preserved your GI benefits, but for certain kinds of sailors, they have to be punitive, because that is how some in the navy brass feel about people like you."

Gerry froze at the phrase "people like you." She knew what it meant. One of the navy interrogators had used the term too.

But Bob didn't say it in a mean way. He said it softly, and his expression wasn't one of distaste or dislike. He simply stated a fact.

"You might not be surprised at this, but they use the blue paper on homosexuals, Colored people, and basically anyone they don't want around anymore, now that they have no use for them. The war's done, so out you go." He mimed kicking something with his foot. "But as far as we're concerned, you are still a veteran like anyone else, and you didn't deserve this treatment."

Thinking about Jimmy, Gerry ventured a question. "So there are others…like me."

"Yep," Bob said. "I get ten applications a week like yours. From the sort of veterans I just told you about."

"What do I have to do?" she asked. She wasn't afraid anymore. Bob's straightforward manner and kindness had eased her anxiety.

"I'm glad you asked that question." He grinned. "Not that it'll be easy. It won't. It'll take a while. The navy, after all, is a bureaucracy. We have to petition for review to a review board. They'll hold a hearing and decide. You don't have to go to Washington DC or anything, but you have to wait. We'll help you file the request for review and follow up with them. This process can be intimidating."

"You're not kidding," Gerry said. "I wasn't even sure I wanted to come here at all."

Bob nodded. "I know. You've been treated horribly, and you don't want to go through that again. But it's good that you mustered up the courage to come see us."

He leaned back in his chair. "You likely don't know this, but the question of these discharges has been discussed in a congressional committee. That committee recommended abolishing the blue discharge. Now the service branches often have a lot of internal conflicts over this issue. We were told a while back to petition the review board of the service branch in question. So that's what we do. The policy of kicking the so-called 'undesirables' out is probably here to stay, but we can try to change it on a case-by-case basis. Maybe, eventually, the sheer weight of numbers of all you folks appealing will make them change their minds."

Gerry was silent. She was relieved, but now she had an entirely new set of anxieties about going through with the request for review. This would mean the navy would look at her life again—at least on paper.

"Does the...petition for review actually work?" she asked.

"Yes. But not always. It's not guaranteed, but we have a pretty good success rate."

"Jimmy Price won his case," she said. "Jimmy was at Treasure Island with me, and he got the blue paper."

"I think I remember him." Bob grinned again. She was truly starting to like him and didn't distrust him like she had at first.

"So, Miss Stern. What do you think? Do you want to give it a shot?"

Did she? She was afraid, but the navy had treated her so unfairly. She couldn't get a decent job or any of her GI benefits unless she had her discharge changed. Really. The navy could say no, but they might say yes, according to Bob.

Bob looked her up and down. "You can think about it. You don't have to decide right now. Have you talked to your parents about anything?"

This question took her off guard, and she stuttered, "No-no. I don't...I can't."

"Okay. I wondered. Having someone in your corner is helpful in these situations."

Gerry flashed on Maddie. Maddie would, she was sure, tell her to go ahead.

"Before you leave, I want to show you something." He reached into a drawer and brought out a magazine titled *Yank*. He pushed it across the desk to her.

"This is the army's publication. But you can see on the cover that plenty of army members were targeted the same way you were, and they aren't happy about it. This magazine reached the desk of someone on that congressional committee."

Bob paused, and then he said, "You probably feel like you're all alone except maybe for your friend Jimmy, but that isn't so."

Gerry opened the magazine and started reading at random. She focused on one letter, because though the writer was an army vet, she was a gay girl. The letter described her experience, which was much like Gerry's. The last line of the letter said, "Many army medical doctors believe strongly concerning the injustice of this situation. If only people would realize this and help us with understanding rather than cast us out with condemnation."

Gerry gave the magazine back to Bob. "Thanks for showing me this. I'll be sure and call you back when I decide."

He nodded in a friendly way and shook hands with her again.

❖

It could be worse. *I could still be in Sawyer, broke, having to deal with the horrible White people and without Gerry.*

These thoughts helped Maddie cope with her daily life. She was always tired, and she and Gerry still barely had time to see one another. Plus, Wilma Grace was still acting like a cold fish. Also, what little time they were able to spend together was usually in Gerry's bed. They never went out anywhere. But with Gerry in a state about appealing her discharge, it didn't seem like a good time to start an argument about anything, including how Gerry still wouldn't let Maddie touch her.

She hated having to dash off from Gerry's every time, but it was better to get home and get to sleep so she could be sharp for work. The talk around possible firings was getting louder, and she wanted stay out of trouble for sure and possibly stand out for good behavior.

And then there was the question of leaving San Francisco and going back to Sawyer.

In one of her letters, Mama asked if she was fixing to come home soon. She'd written back that she wanted to stay around as long as she had a job to make more money. That was true, but it was also true that she didn't want to think about leaving Gerry, even if it meant not seeing her mama again. And she didn't want to think about that either.

"I'm going to have to wait while Uncle Sam makes up his mind if I'm worthy," Gerry said.

"And…are you glad you did it?" They were lying in bed, and Maddie was going to have to go home soon. Gerry would try to get her to stay longer, and she was very good at that, but Maddie would struggle to resist.

"Yeah. The guy at the veterans' office was real nice and explained everything to me and told me there was a decent chance I'd win."

Maddie hugged and kissed Gerry. "Oh my, that's so good to hear."

Usually talkative, Gerry was quiet. She dragged her fingers down Maddie's arm from her shoulder to her hand, but she spoke almost to herself.

"I was so scared before I went in there. I was shaking, and I was a little sick to my stomach. I was thinking about getting dragged in front of those officers and that this was going to be like that. It wasn't. Like I said, Bob was nice and helpful. He didn't say anything mean to me.

In fact, he acted exactly as if I was a regular person who'd gotten a raw deal and who had the right to ask for it to be fixed."

"I'll be darned. That's something, isn't it?"

"Yeah. It sure is. When I first met Jimmy and Woody, and I knew I was a gay girl, they told me over and over how important it was to never let anyone know about me except those in the know, like them and a few others. 'Cause if the wrong person got wind of it, there'd be bad consequences. And there was. I never thought the wrong person would be Woody."

A memory popped into Maddie's mind. "You know, there was this one old White lady in Sawyer. She was kind of, you know, considered crazy by other folks. She lived all by herself in an old house and was widowed or something. But she would hire boys to do chores around her house—mow the lawn, paint, clean the gutters, that stuff. She always hired Colored boys, and she not only paid them decent, but she'd have them in her house and give them Cokes or sweet tea when they were done with her chores and sit them at her kitchen table and talk to them like they were White boys. Thom told me about her. He was one of the boys who worked for her a couple times. It was the darndest thing, he said, to have a White woman who was kind and decent and respectful toward him. He said it almost made him stop being angry at all the other White people and their hateful ways."

"She was the exception."

"She was, and she was the only the second one ever I knew about. The other was the town postmistress."

"That's kind of the same as Bob. Is that what you're saying?"

Maddie grinned. "Yep. Kind of restores your faith in the human race."

"My faith in the human race will be improved if I get my discharge upgraded."

"Oh, sure, honey. That reminds me. Do you need money?"

Gerry stiffened. "No. I'm fine."

"Are you telling me the truth?" Maddie asked with a slight edge. She bet Gerry *wasn't* fine. She looked thinner, as though she hadn't been eating much. She'd always looked and felt healthy and strong, but it hadn't felt that way the last couple times they'd been together. The girl was going to let pride starve her if she didn't let go of it.

"Honey, why won't you let me help you? Lend you some money? Not give it you, though I would, but I know you're not ready for that.

Lend it to you." Maddie propped herself up on one elbow and stared at Gerry.

Gerry moved restlessly and wouldn't meet her eye for a moment but finally did. "It's not right," she said.

"Why?" Maddie knew she sounded demanding, but she didn't care. This nonsense had gone on long enough. "'Cause you wear the pants and I don't?"

"Something like that," Gerry said, sounding grumpy.

"Well, you best get over it, cause I'm not about to let you starve to death. You been paying your rent?"

"Yeah. I put in a couple months ahead with what I had, and now I don't have hardly any money left."

"Can you ask your folks for help?"

Gerry moved around again. Maddie almost laughed aloud at her efforts to get away from uncomfortable questions.

"Nope. I can't. They would try to force me to move back home. They won't give me money. I don't want to ask anyhow."

Maddie suspected she knew why. Gerry wanted to keep her business to herself. Maddie understood because she was keeping her own secrets from her mama and felt bad about it, didn't want to think about it, and still didn't know what she was going to do when the time came to make a decision to go back to Arkansas.

"Well, I'm here. I got the money, and I want you to have some. I want you to buy food. If I could, I'd take you back home and feed you up, but I can't." Right then and there she resolved to *bring* Gerry some food next time she came to visit.

Gerry was quiet a long time as she stared at the ceiling, closed her eyes, and then opened them again. She sighed, and Maddie said no more but waited her out.

"Okay. But I only want a little bit. And I'll pay you back."

"Agreed."

CHAPTER THIRTEEN

September 1946

Gerry had to read the letter twice before what it said sank in. Her appeal had worked.

The navy wrote,

> *After due consideration, the United States Navy Board of Review has concluded that the discharge of "undesirable" was issued in error, and your discharge is hereby upgraded to "general." You are eligible for all rights and privileges adhering to this discharge classification.*

They enclosed a brand-new discharge, and Gerry stared at it for a long time. She hadn't been this happy since she met Maddie. She wanted to tell her right away but couldn't until Maddie's day off, a week away. They would celebrate, at least in some way. But the real celebration would come when she was able to get a new job.

She'd had so much time on her hands, she'd been able to consider what she really wanted, which was to become a mechanic. Bob had told her to come back to talk to the SF veterans when she needed help, so she'd do just that after her discharge upgrade came through.

The navy actually came through for me. I don't hate them anymore.

When Maddie came to her flat Friday morning, Gerry grabbed, kissed her, lifted her up, and danced them around.

"What's gotten into you?" Maddie asked, laughing.

"This," Gerry said and showed her the letter.

Maddie beamed, threw the letter down, and said, "Praise God. That's the best."

"I want us to celebrate, but, ahem, you'll have to buy."

"Honey, whatever you want. This is amazing."

"I'll be able to get a good job. I want to try to do that before I apply for unemployment."

"Sure. Where do you want to go?"

"Mona's."

"I'm not dressed up, and it's the middle of the afternoon," Maddie said. She was wearing capri pants and a striped blouse and looked quite fetching.

"I don't care. I haven't been there in months or even had a drop of booze, and I feel like celebrating."

As they walked the blocks between Gerry's flat and North Beach, she noticed the liveliness of the streets. It might be due only to her mood, but it seemed like the City was celebrating. She longed to hold Maddie's hand, but they had to content themselves with happy glances.

Chinatown gave way in an abrupt fashion to North Beach. The look of the buildings changed, the businesses changed, and the people changed. In the daylight, the difference was more obvious than it was at night. It was funny in spooky sort of way.

They were in front of Mona's door, but Gerry stopped suddenly under the sign.

Maddie asked, "What's the matter?"

"Well. For one thing, I've never been here in the middle of the day. For another, what if it's not the same?" Gerry had never given much thought to the concept of change. Her experience with the navy, however, made her uneasy, suspicious. What if Mona's was no longer a gay bar? There were, of course, other bars in North Beach, but Gerry only knew Mona's with any familiarity. It was the first gay bar—outside the Top of the Mark, which didn't really count—that Woody and Jimmy had taken her to, saying to her, "This is where our people are. This is a safe place to let down your hair. And it's fun too." And all of it was true. The straight tourists didn't even bother Gerry. They were harmless, and it was a kick to try to shock them.

And it was where she'd met Maddie.

"I'm all right. Let's go in," Gerry said. She squared her shoulders, took a breath, and pushed the door open.

The very first person Gerry saw was Woody, sitting at the bar. She stopped suddenly, causing Maddie to stumble a bit and ask her, "What's wrong?"

Unable to speak, Gerry cocked her head toward Woody, and Maddie followed her gaze.

"Oh, good Lord," she said, "You want to leave before she sees you?"

"Uh-uh. I'm not the one with a reason to be ashamed. She is. Let's go."

They walked straight up the bar, and Gerry stood right next to Woody, who was speaking to the woman beside her and didn't notice Gerry until she spoke.

"Two beers."

Woody's head swiveled around, and Gerry turned from facing the bartender to facing Woody. "Hello, Woody," she said, pleased her voice sounded even, though her heart was pounding. "How's tricks?"

Woody slowly smirked. "Not bad. How are you?"

She slowly shook a cigarette out of the pack on the bar, put it between her lips, lit it, and blew out a stream of smoke. "Terrific. Cooking with gas." Gerry threw her a smirk of her own.

"That a fact?" Woody asked, taking another drag. Her nonchalance annoyed the heck out of Gerry.

"Yeah. No thanks to you."

Woody's smirk faded, and she looked pained. "Yeah. I'm sorry, Ger, but I had no choice. They were going to kick me out unless I named names." Her tone was halfway between sorrowful and whiny.

"So, you did it to save yourself." It was not a question.

"They had me. I had gotten caught. You probably would have ended up being discharged anyway. Someone else would have given your name."

"I wouldn't have done that to you," Gerry said, forcing Woody to look at her.

"Maybe, maybe not."

"No. But I'd like to think I wouldn't have."

Woody put her cigarette out and signaled for another drink. "Why are you here in the middle of the day?" she asked Gerry. "Hi, by the way." She looked toward Maddie.

"Hello." Maddie had been quiet since they'd encountered Woody, but Gerry could sense the fury radiating from her.

"I could ask you the same question. I don't have a job, but I think I will have one soon. I got my blue discharge changed."

Woody looked genuinely happy. "You did? Wowsa. That's great."

"So? What's your story?"

"Most of the WAVES were discharged over the past couple weeks. Mine was honorable though. The navy's done with us. You knew that was going to happen. I think they might be keeping a few of the gals around. Not me, though. I don't care anyhow." She sounded as though she did care. Very much.

Woody shrugged and went silent. Gerry waited.

"I'm sorry, Ger. I really am. I didn't want to do what I did. I was scared, and they were putting the screws to me. I panicked and I talked."

Gerry didn't say anything for a long time. She'd thought about this moment ever since she'd learned the truth from Jimmy. She wanted to hate Woody, but she couldn't. Gerry had been put in the same position, and she hadn't caved. And she'd been booted, but she was all right now. All squared away, as they used to say back in the WAVES.

"Yeah. I know. It was really scary for me too. It's okay now. Here." She stuck her hand out, and Woody stared at it, studied her face, and at last took it.

They took their drinks over to a table and sat down. Woody and Gerry talked nonstop for an hour.

"Well, we're civilians now," Gerry said. "What do you think?"

"I think I like it. No more reveille, no more marching around. We can go to the bar when we want, just like this."

Gerry grinned. "I wasn't myself at first, but I think the way I was made to leave the navy had something to do with that. I'm going to a training program and learn to be a mechanic, and I'm going to get paid to do it. What do you think of that?"

"Fantastic. That's perfect for you."

Gerry sipped her drink. "What about you?"

"I'm going to be a manager for a stockbrokers' office downtown. Starting next week, I'll have to be there at six thirty in the morning. Stock market opens at six a.m. East Coast time and all. Being in the navy definitely was good training for that." Woody laughed.

"Well, here's to us then. Ex-navy gals, newly minted civilians." They clicked glasses.

Later, as Gerry walked Maddie back to the bus stop, Maddie was unusually silent.

"Something wrong? Why are you so quiet?"

"Nothing. I just don't have nothing to say right now."

"Are you mad 'cause we didn't go to bed today?"

Maddie gave her an "are you crazy?" look, which stung.

"Are you going to tell me what's going on or what?"

Maddie finally turned to face her. "If you don't know, it's not my job to teach you. Why don't you think about it a little bit. It might come to you." Those last two sentences were biting.

Gerry watched the bus drive away and then walked home in a stew. She remembered another occasion when Maddie had gotten upset and wouldn't tell her why. She hoped this time wouldn't be the same. Then it hit her. The whole time they'd been drinking in Mona's, she and Woody all happy and relieved at their reunion, not one time had either she or Woody so much as looked at Maddie, let alone addressed a single sentence to her. She might as well not have been there at all. *It might come to you.*

Gerry's face heated up. God, was she ever a dope. She was going to have to make it up to Maddie somehow. She was the worst girlfriend in the world. Not only had she allowed Maddie to semi-support her, but she had gone out with her and ended up focused completely on Woody and not paying any attention to Maddie.

Why do I even bother?

Gerry didn't mean to totally ignore her. She was caught up in the moment. She hadn't talked to Woody in a long time, and they had been at odds, and they had made up. She used to be Gerry's best friend, so it was understandable or…Gerry didn't really care about her. Or she was tired of her. Or *she* didn't need to have to make excuses for her White girlfriend. That would be likely what Marguerite would say. Or even what her mama would say. No. Scratch that. Mama would have strongly advised against such an idea as Gerry in the first place. She wouldn't have approved of her having a friend like Gerry. If she knew.

No. Maddie didn't want to think about *that* secret. What the heck was she going to do? She cared about Gerry, maybe even loved her, though they'd never talked in those terms or said the word. Maddie was scared to think about that and what it might mean. She grimaced. First things first—try to get Gerry to understand how flat-out rude she'd been to her.

When she was home in her little room in the little yellow house, it didn't feel like home anymore. Nowhere actually felt like home. Not in bed with Gerry in her flat and certainly not at Mona's. She was merely existing in the same house as Thom and Wilma Grace, going through the motions of being part of a family. Ever since that day Wilma Grace had caught them, it seemed like an invisible wall existed, with Maddie on one side and Thom and Wilma on the other.

She walked up the street toward to the house, grateful it would be empty this time of day, but her family would be home soon. She went to her bedroom and undressed and got into bed, hoping to relax enough to sleep for a few hours. But it wasn't happening. She wasn't mad at Gerry anymore. She was, honestly, just tired of having to explain why she felt the way she did. She wanted Gerry to know what to do about their situation and go ahead and fix it, but that likely wasn't realistic. *She'd* have to be the one to spell out the problem. Maddie went to sleep at last with the relief of having made up her mind.

❖

To Maddie's surprise, when they next met, Gerry didn't take her back to the Bush Street flat right away but said, "Let's go have coffee." They went to Foster's Cafeteria and sat at a quiet corner booth.

"You know, I'm sorry about the other day with Woody. I never told you, but she wasn't keen on my seeing you right from the beginning."

That statement drilled right into Maddie's mind and made her mad, but it wasn't a surprise. She kept quiet, though, and let Gerry keep talking. Gerry repeated what Woody had had to say when they started seeing each other.

"I mostly tried to ignore what she said because I'm crazy about you."

Maddie couldn't stop herself. "You wouldn't have thought that by the way you treated me. You didn't say one word to me. Neither did your friend. I think I know why. She's a typical White girl."

"Well, not exactly typical," Gerry said with a ghost of her old grin.

"Okay, so not one hundred percent," Maddie said, grudgingly.

"Anyhow. It doesn't matter what she thinks. It matters that I never act that way again—like you don't exist. I'm really, really sorry."

Maddie believed her. She looked so woebegone, but how many more times was this type of thing going to happen? It was always going to be true that Maddie was Colored and Gerry was White, and there would never be a shortage of folks who had a problem with her and with Gerry. What would Marguerite have to say about any of it? Maddie didn't know, but she didn't think Marguerite would let anything or anybody's stupid opinions slow her down.

"We don't ever have to spend time with Woody."

"Okay. That's something, but who would we spend time with? And why do we have to go to Mona's?" Maddie asked.

Gerry looked thoughtful. "No. We don't *have* to go to Mona's. There are other places, but none quite as nice. Why don't you like it? You and Wilma Grace came to see Gladys's show."

"That was a special occasion. Like I've already told you, I didn't know what sort of place it was 'til after. I suppose it depends on how people are going to treat me."

"If anyone looks at you cross ways, I'll tell 'em off," Gerry said, fiercely. Maddie wanted to reach across the table and pat her hand.

"You don't have to do that," Maddie said and giggled.

"Yes. I do." Gerry's mind was obviously made up. "It's just that I'd like to have some more friends. All my friends were in the navy, and that's no more. So I'd like to get to know some more people."

"Well, since you like Mona's so much, I'll go along." This time Maddie dared to touch her hand and grinned. "You'll protect me."

Gerry smiled back.

Later, back at Gerry's flat, everything seemed easier, more relaxed. Maddie didn't need to rush out to catch a bus because she was able to stay overnight. They snuggled together in Gerry's single bed, whispering and giggling. Maddie reached over tentatively to touch Gerry's thigh, slowly running her hand from Gerry's knee to her crotch, but Gerry grabbed her hand and moved it away. "No," she said, firmly.

Maddie started to object but held her tongue.

"Hi, you," Gerry said when they woke up the next morning.

"Hi there. You hungry?" Maddie asked.

Gerry nodded.

"Good, 'cause I'm going to make you breakfast. Biscuits and gravy and ham."

While Gerry went out and bought what they needed, Maddie searched around the kitchen for the right cooking equipment. There wasn't much but she managed, congratulating herself on her success. She silently thanked her mama once again for teaching her how to cook and, most of all, how to "make do" with whatever was at hand.

When she sat a plate of steaming food in front of Gerry and Gerry looked at her with genuine gratitude, she was thrilled.

"Wow, look at this," Gerry said. "We didn't have to go out and buy anything already cooked."

Maddie sat down at the battered Formica kitchen table with her own plate. "Helps that you live somewhere now besides the navy base," Maddie said drily.

"Yes, it does."

In between bites, Gerry said, "What would you think if we could do this every day? If we had our own place?"

This thought had flitted through Maddie's mind as she'd cooked breakfast, but she dismissed it. She didn't know how long she'd be staying in San Francisco. If the rumors she'd heard at the dock were true, it wouldn't be long before they started laying folks off there.

Stalling, she took another bite of ham and, as she was chewing it, said, slowly, "I haven't thought about it. I don't know if I'd be able to manage to get back and forth between here and Hunters Point."

"Oh, I'm sure you could. Or we could move closer to Hunters Point, though I like this area a lot. It's convenient."

Convenient to your favorite bar.

"I don't know. I guess so." Maddie wanted to stay noncommittal, but Gerry looked disappointed and fell quiet. Maddie tried to soothe her with a cheek pat and a kiss.

Gerry was the only girl in her mechanics class at the trade school. Again, she ran up against men who couldn't believe she could do the job, and this time, there were more of them. As she'd done before in the WAVES, she proved herself through sheer competence.

A couple of classes went by, and Gerry had quieted the skeptics, including the instructors, and even made a couple of friends. Things were looking up. At the end of one day, as the students were cleaning up and preparing to leave, one of her classmates approached her.

He was a quiet guy named Ed, who was neither a class star or, like a couple of the other men, actually not in possession of any mechanical aptitude.

"What kind of job do you think you're going to get after we're finished here?" The trade school helped place their graduates once they completed their six-month course.

Gerry was focused on wiping down her tools and putting them away neatly and didn't really want to be interrupted, but she turned to Ed anyhow. It was best she act friendly, even if the guys sometimes weren't friendly to her. It had worked in the navy with the other bus drivers. And just like the navy, after a period of adjustment, they simply forgot she was a girl, which was fine with Gerry.

"I don't know. I'm thinking I'd like to work on trucks or buses, so maybe a company that makes them. But a regular repair garage for passenger cars would be okay too."

Ed stood next to her, twisting his jacket in his hands. He obviously wanted to say something, or he wouldn't have sought her out. He was having a hard time getting out what he wanted to say.

"I just want to know how come you're here when there's a lot of guys who'd kill to get a spot in a school like this? You're taking something away maybe from some veteran who has to support a family." He asked this question in a somewhat plaintive manner, but it burned up Gerry anyhow.

"Look, Ed. *I'm* a veteran too. I'm here because the VA folks helped me get into this school just the same as they help everyone. You got a problem with that?"

"Oh." He had to think a minute, something he obviously didn't do a lot of.

"Yeah, but you're going get married and all. Your husband won't want you working."

That struck Gerry as funny in a certain way. She began to laugh and shook her head. Ed looked confused.

"No, Ed. I'm not going to get married, so I'm going to have to support myself. No one else is going to take care of me. You don't have the faintest idea what you're talking about. Well, I'm done for the day, and I'm heading home. See you tomorrow." She left him standing there still speechless.

❖

It was Saturday night. Gerry and Maddie stepped through the doors of Mona's 440 Club, and Gerry was feeling great. She wore a new pin-striped, spear-point dress shirt and a jaunty striped tie. Maddie was looking fine as well. Her blue rayon dress fit close to her curves. Her mood, however, left something to be desired.

"Anything wrong?" Gerry asked her.

She shook her head and smiled.

They had timed their entrance so it wasn't too early and it wasn't too late, basically between the first and second shows. Kay Scott was the night's performer, and since she was a local favorite, the place was packed. If anything, the end of the war had brought more people out on the town.

The first person they saw was Woody, standing at the bar and talking to the bartender.

"Hiya," Gerry said as she tapped Woody on the shoulder.

Woody turned and said, "Hi yourself." She didn't sound too happy.

She turned back to the bartender, Roddy.

Gerry listened to their conversation.

"So like I said, watch who you're talking to, and most of all, don't make any funny moves with a gal. That'll get you busted and maybe get us shut down for being a disorderly house."

"Thanks, Roddy."

Woody turned to Maddie and Gerry. "Hey, you two. Good to see you."

"Great to see you too," Gerry said. She glanced at Maddie, who nodded in Woody's general direction, but her expression was unreadable.

They hadn't argued about coming out to the bar that night, but Gerry sensed that Maddie wasn't enthusiastic. She had wondered what to do about that and decided that she needed to pay a lot of attention to her and not to Woody. First, though, she was curious about what Woody and the bartender had been discussing.

"What were you and Roddy talking about?"

"Let's go sit down, and I'll tell you." They found a table near the back of the showroom.

"Roddy said he thinks undercover policemen have been coming around the club, and we need to be alert. *I* do, anyhow," Woody said.

Woody eyed Gerry up and down and smirked. "Maybe you do too."

"Why's that?" It was Woody in her know-it-all but cryptic mode, and it was more irritating than it used to be after her betrayal of Gerry to the navy investigators. Gerry might have forgiven her for that, but she was done trusting her.

"What are you talking about?"

"Are you wearing your one item of women's clothing?"

"Huh?"

Woody leaned back on the bar. "If you're not, and the cops come in and scoop us up and haul us off to jail, you'll be arrested for cross-dressing, which is illegal. But if you're wearing, say, women's underwear, you'll be fine."

"I'm safe," Gerry said. "What about you?"

Woody was wearing a sport jacket, casual shirt, and wing-tip shoes and in fact looked very sharp.

"I've got it covered. Not going to show you though."

Gerry laughed sarcastically. "Never mind. I believe you. But we've never had any trouble with cops before. Why now?"

"Oh. Roddy was telling me it happens in cycles. Sometimes it's because of elections. Some politicians vow to clean up the city and get rid of all the 'deviants.' That's us, you know."

She laughed. "This time he said it's because Mona and Sam haven't paid off the cops."

Mona and her husband Sam owned the club.

Woody continued. "So there we are. We have a couple of places we can go to meet, drink, and have fun. But we're only here by permission of the cops and 'cause we help the tourist trade. Like we were tolerated by the navy as long as there was a war on. Once that was over..." Woody hooked a thumb and gestured.

"Not you," Gerry reminded her, her tone sharp.

"Hey. They would have done the same to me as they did to you if I hadn't given up the names they wanted. You said you forgave me." She looked so woebegone, Gerry was slightly sorry, but not too much. She was still steamed about Woody's attitude and decided she had to speak up.

"Yeah. I said that. I can forgive you because I was able to get my discharge upgraded, and that made me feel a little better about the whole thing and about you. But remember, friend. I had to work for that. I had to make the navy change its mind about me, and they just let you go, no sweat. You were free and clear. I can deal with what you did, but remember that it almost ruined my life. It all worked out for me, but you might be a little sorrier."

Woody looked ashamed. and was silent for a few moments. "I'm sorry. I won't make light of it again. You're right. But, hey, here we are, and it's a new day. Let me buy you and Maddie a drink."

Woody asked Maddie questions and generally exerted herself to be pleasant, and Gerry appreciated that effort. It reminded her what she'd liked about Woody in the first place as she chattered and made snide comments about the Mona's patrons she knew, even getting Maddie to crack a smile.

Gerry looked at Maddie, and they exchanged a look with slightly raised eyebrows.

"Well, we're going home. Have fun, but be careful. We'll see you around." Gerry figured Woody would stick around and flirt and find some company for the night.

"Have fun, but don't do anything I wouldn't do." Woody winked.

❖

They walked back Gerry's flat, not saying anything for a couple of blocks.

Maddie wasn't sure what to say, but finally she said, "I guess going to Mona's is better now. Woody wasn't acting like I was invisible. And you gave her a little piece of your mind, which was long overdue. I'm proud of you, honey. No one's going to treat my girl bad and get away with it."

Gerry beamed but then frowned. "Are you sure? I want you to have a good time and feel okay and all."

"I'm fine," Maddie said pleasantly, and she meant it. She wanted *Gerry* to be okay. And that, Maddie reflected, was what love came down to. *I must love her.* That was a shock. It had been teasing around the edges of her thoughts for a while.

When they got in bed, Gerry was tender and sweet, and for a second Maddie wondered what would happen if she didn't ask but went ahead and rolled Gerry on her back and took over. What would Gerry do then? Considering what had happened before, she decided against it.

"What are you thinking about?" Gerry asked. "You've got an evil little grin on your mug."

"Do I? You can tell?" Maddie stalled for a second.

"Yup." She reached for and lit a cigarette, lay back down, and pulled Maddie onto her arm.

Maddie traced an abstract line across her chest, forward and back. "Ger?"

"Uh-huh?"

Maddie propped herself up on her elbow, looked down at Gerry, and before she could think about it too much, she said, "I love you."

Gerry looked startled, then thoughtful. She stubbed out her cigarette and, beginning with an ardent kiss, started making love to her all over again.

❖

It would be wonderful if someone was at home other than Wilma Grace and all her sighs and eye-rolling or Thom with his air of resignation. Maddie was now spending all her spare time with Gerry, so that meant if she wasn't at work, she wasn't at home. She memorized the bus schedule and kept an overnight bag at the ready. When she could have any time off, she vanished.

Honestly, she felt bad about not being around her family, but not bad enough to change. It had happened gradually, but Maddie had come to feel more at home and more comfortable with Gerry than she did with her own kin. She still wrote to her mama every week, but even that was feeling a bit false since she couldn't share the most important fact of her life, just the usual bunch of trivia. She deposited money into her savings account, and it was wildly gratifying to see it grow. But its balance was a weekly reminder that sometime, she was going to head back to Arkansas.

Though she longed to live with Gerry, she didn't want to move out of the little house on Jerrold Street, mainly because of work. As long as that lasted, she wanted to be close by. The rumors of firings still circulated all around the graving docks, but nothing had happened yet. And when it did, well, Maddie would deal with it then. In the meantime, she commuted into downtown San Francisco and Gerry's arms whenever she could.

They spent the weekend evenings at Mona's, sometimes drinking with Woody, sometimes with others. Maddie would be uneasy every time they met someone new. There was occasionally an awkward remark or an uncomfortable pause, and she knew it was related to her being Colored, but it was rarer than she expected it would be. Maddie even got to like a few women they got to know. They were all, without exception, in butch and femme couples. Maddie stopped going the full-dress-and-makeup route because it didn't feel natural to her. Nor did Gerry demand that she imitate some of their acquaintances. She settled into an easy middle ground. It was possible to buy stylish feminine slacks. With a blouse and usually a scarf, plus a little makeup and styled hair, Maddie held up her end of the deal as a femme.

Maddie thought some of the butch girls pushed their supposed manliness a little too far, and their femmes sometimes seemed liked they were acting, but they were nice people, and although she was the only Colored girl around, they all assumed a stance of outsiders together with an "us against the world" attitude.

Saturday night was the biggest night in the bar. One of the singers, Kay Scott or someone else, always performed, and they had a sing-along or two.

Gerry and Maddie sat with a few other couples to take in the show, and even Jimmy and George showed up for a drink. Woody was there with a striking blonde on her arm, whom she introduced as Sandy.

Maddie listened as Gerry told Jimmy all about trade school.

Jimmy said, "Sounds like you've found your métier."

"If that means what I think it means, then yes, I have."

He grinned. "It means your trade. It's just French."

"What about you?"

"For right now, George is okay with me not working." Although Jimmy was mostly nice to her, she still felt he was rude at times. But she didn't mind as much anymore. It was the same with their gay girl pals. They'd been awkward at first, but in time, they'd gotten used to one another. Maddie was willing to give folks the benefit of the doubt. White people were still much better in San Francisco than they were back in Sawyer.

"What about you girls?" he asked.

"What about us?" Gerry said.

"Well, when are you two going to start playing house?"

Maddie glanced at Gerry, who shrugged. It was a sore point because, every so often, Gerry asked her to move in, but Maddie put her off. She still worked nights at the shipyard, and it would be too inconvenient for her to get to work. Truthfully, in spite of her distant relationship with Wilma Grace and Thom, they were still her folks, and it was sometimes more familiar and comfortable to be around them. And she'd be leaving sometime to go back to Arkansas. She resigned herself to being in split into two Maddies. one that was Gerry's girlfriend and the other one part of her family.

"Well. We're off to the Starlight Room. If only we could dance together." Jimmy looked at George, who shook his head.

"Someday. Maybe." Jimmy sighed. He kissed both Maddie and Gerry on the cheek. "Ta-ta, girls."

They settled in for the floor show, and the lights dimmed.

Kay Scott walked onto the stage. She wore a tuxedo and shaded her eyes as she pretended to survey the room. "Looks like a gay crowd."

This got a big laugh.

Kay said, "This is a tribute to our favorite place, right here in San Francisco. Where we know who's who and what's what. Mona's 440 Club. This is also dedicated to our good friends. I know you're out there. Our honored guests from elsewhere." She winked, and the audience laughed.

The house lights were dimmed for the show, but they suddenly came on, blinked twice, and then were fully lit and on. Kay Scott stood silently holding her microphone. The orchestra had stopped playing.

An unfamiliar man in a suit and a fedora jumped onstage and took the microphone from Kay. "Ladies and gentlemen." He said those two words with an oddly sarcastic tone.

"Please excuse the interruption of the show. The SFPD and the SBE are here to conduct a random check of IDs. This will only take a moment."

The customers sat mostly in shocked silence, but a few jumped out of their seats and ran for the exits, which were blocked by bulky policemen.

One policeman came around to their table and said, "IDs please." They produced their driver's licenses and ID cards. The policeman looked at Maddie's ID and at her and then at her card again. He handed it back to her without a word.

He did the same with Gerry but, with an unpleasant smile, said, "You need to come with us."

"Why," she asked, sharply.

Maddie wished Gerry would tone down her anger. It could make things worse. She thought, briefly, of encounters in Sawyer.

"Because I say so, girlie or bucko or whatever you are." Gerry paled and said no more. The policeman grabbed her shoulder, hauled her to her feet along with Woody and another of their butch friends, Jake, and hustled them out the door. It was all over so fast, Maddie was left sitting in her chair, stunned.

"What do we do now?" she asked no one in particular. She and the two girlfriends of the three women who were hauled off sat at a table looking at each other.

Jake's girl Trixie spoke up. "We have to go bail them out, and then we are going to need a lawyer. We're going to need some cash. Whadda we got? Come on, girls. Cough it up." The three of them took out what money they had, but it didn't amount to much. It was up to their butches to pay for everything.

"We don't have enough," Trixie said. "I've stashed some mad money away at home. I'll go get it. We may as well walk to the Hall of Justice and save the cab fare. Since it's going to take the fuzz some time to do what they do, there's no hurry. Wait here, and I'll be back soon."

The third woman, Sandy, Woody's girl of the moment, said, "No. We'll go with you, and *then* we can head to the Hall of Justice."

Chapter Fourteen

September 1946

The three of them walked over to Trixie and Jake's apartment near the Chinatown border, fetched her money, and took off toward Brannan Street, several blocks away.

"How d'you know what to do?" Maddie asked.

Trixie favored her with a sour smile. "'Cause I been busted before. Soliciting."

Her astonishment at what Trixie said almost stopped Maddie in her forward motion, but she soldiered on as she absorbed the meaning of that statement: Trixie was a hooker, and Jake must know that. What was that like for her? Maddie fought off her distaste. It wasn't her business.

"What are the cops gonna do to them?"

Trixie said grimly, "They're going to strip-search 'em. Rough 'em up a little. I hope to God Gerry's got her little girl pants on tonight."

"I think she does." Maddie remembered Woody's warning from a while back. But she truly didn't recall what kind of underwear Gerry was wearing. They'd been in a hurry, and Gerry always spent more time perfecting her hair than anything else. She used a lot of hair gel to make sure it was just so. Maddie actually enjoyed watching her style her hair. She spent almost as much time with it as Maddie did using her hair relaxer. The thought made her smile, a small pause in her overwhelming anxiety.

"Good. Then she can't be charged with impersonation," Trixie said, grimly.

The three of them arrived at the hulking Hall of Justice, a truly forbidding looking building, and Maddie was happy to let Trixie do the talking. She didn't want to draw any sort of attention to herself. Once they got to the jail, who knew what the San Francisco police might take it in their heads to do with a Colored girl. Back home, they all lived in fear of the police.

They paid the bail money, and, the desk sergeant, in not very friendly terms, told them to take a seat. At least, Maddie reflected, her being Colored didn't seem to have anything to do with the policeman's unfriendliness, which helped her relax just a tiny bit. In due course, Gerry, Jake, and Woody walked out.

They were reserved in their greetings in case the cops busted all of them for something or another, like showing affection. Jake had been caught for male impersonation, and Woody and Gerry hadn't, but they'd still been charged with disorderly behavior, whatever that meant.

As they walked home, Maddie asked Gerry anxiously, "What happened?"

"Well, a female cop made me take off my clothes. Then she searched my private parts. It was horrible. It didn't hurt, but it was awful anyhow. I almost asked her if she enjoyed it. I'm pretty sure she was a gay girl, but I didn't say that. She had a funny expression on her face while she was searching me."

Maddie had nothing to say to this, so she patted Gerry's arm. "What do we do now?"

"We have to talk to Mona and see if she's going to get charged and if she's going to get a lawyer."

"Do you *have* to be part of this?"

"If I want to get legal help, I do."

"Oh, baby. Is the school going to find out?"

"I don't know." Gerry looked at her, upset. "I hope not."

They settled down in bed, and for once, Maddie cradled Gerry and petted and comforted her, and she made no protest.

"It's funny, isn't it?" Gerry said thoughtfully. "When I first joined the navy, I never in a million years thought I was queer, but there it was, like I was just waiting to find out, and Woody showed me. After that, though, all I really wanted was to be left alone and be a WAVE and have fun on my shore leave with my friends. But they just won't leave us alone. First, I'm booted out of the navy with a bad discharge. Last night they just came in and hauled us away like we were trash. From our own bar. Why did they have to do that? We're not hurting anyone.

We're there for a few drinks and a few laughs with our friends. What's the harm?"

She seemed like she was only thinking out loud and wasn't looking for any answers, and Maddie had none anyway.

Maddie stayed quiet and stroked Gerry's hair, thinking she was naive, but they were good questions. Maddie had asked those same kinds of questions back in Arkansas when her mama told her some story of a Colored person getting bothered or beat up or even lynched. None of this was fair or right, but how anyone could stop it from happening was always the question. The only path seemed to be to stay out of the way of the people who wanted to harm you for merely existing. But that wasn't possible all the time. They had to live in the world. They had to work and support themselves. *Don't we deserve respect like anyone else?* She held Gerry until she fell asleep. Maddie drifted off soon after, but her last thought was, *I love her, but I can't protect her any more than she can protect me, and I might soon have to go back to Arkansas anyhow.*

❖

Mona and her husband hired a lawyer to defend themselves, and they generously included Woody, Shorty, Gerry, and a few other women who'd been arrested. Luckily the lawyer managed to get Gerry's disorderly behavior charges dropped, and she didn't have to show up in court. Her name, however, appeared in a newspaper article about the raid. She anxiously waited to be dragged into the office of the director of the trade school and kicked out, but it didn't happen. Maybe he didn't read the papers.

Mona's lawyer told them a bit of the story behind the raid. The State Board of Equalization, who had power over liquor licenses, had been on the receiving end of pressure from some politician who was running for office and claiming he would "clean up" San Francisco's wicked vice trade.

Gerry told Maddie, "He said it happened every so often. When someone complains, the politician sics the cops on North Beach's gay bars. And then the raids happen. But they never get very far because we're part of the tourist trade. The tourist businesses sometimes pay the cops to leave them alone. Maybe Mona didn't pay enough or didn't want to, or it was some cop who decided to teach her a lesson. The lawyer said it could be any reason."

Maddie said, "But here you and Jake and Woody are right in the middle of something that's got nothing to do with any of you."

Gerry shook her head in disgust. "Well, yeah, and I want to forget all about it. I hope the school doesn't find out. I haven't heard anything so far. I'm three months from graduation. Then I can find a real job and start making some real money. And I'll get a better apartment. A bigger one."

She looked at Maddie and raised her eyebrows in question, but Maddie didn't answer. Gerry knew why, but she still hoped she'd get an answer, the right answer, when the time came. It wasn't as though Gerry hadn't asked Maddie already to move in with her, but Maddie put her off with excuses. Well, soon Maddie would have to make her up mind. As much as Gerry loved Maddie, she would wait only so long. If they were going to be together, Maddie had to make a move. She ought to tell Maddie she loved her, but something stopped her.

❖

Thom received his notice first.

"It's the government, the foreman said. We're told we have to lay people off. I noticed all the Colored guys got their pink slips first." He grimaced. "I got two weeks' pay, and that was all she wrote. Wilma Grace, you still got your job. Guess you'll be wearing the pants in this family until I find something else." He was feigning unconcern as he tilted his kitchen chair backward with his hands behind his head.

"Thomas Weeks, I've had a job as long as you have, even if I don't make as much as you. Ever since we came to San Fran, we don't make a good living unless I work too. So save your remarks about wearing pants. We're partners, and don't you forget it."

This statement surprised Maddie no end. She'd never heard Wilma Grace say such a thing, and it impressed her. But then, both she and Wilma Grace received their layoff notices three weeks later.

This time, the three of them sat at the kitchen table as they talked about their common dilemma. Maddie hadn't had an extended conversation with her family for a real long time. When she heard she was being laid off, the first thing she thought of was Gerry and Gerry's wish for them to live together. Gerry had finished school and was hired at a car dealership downtown, exactly as she'd wanted, and she was looking for a new apartment. Maddie's excuse of not wanting to travel back and forth across town to Hunters Point wasn't usable anymore.

Would she return to Sawyer and to her mama with her savings as they had planned? The question hammered in her mind furiously.

"Well, I don't know. Do *you* want to leave?" Wilma Grace asked Thom. It was the same question he'd asked her two seconds before.

"What are we going to do here, darling? The war's over, and they don't have jobs for us no more."

Wilma Grace snorted. "Do you think Hunters Point is the only place we can work in the whole damn city? I don't know about you, but I'm not ready to go back to Sawyer and to shit wages and all the bull with the White folks. They may not always be real friendly here, but it's a damn sight better than home." She stood, hands on her hips and glaring at Thom.

Maddie was washing dishes and listening them talk. *Whoa, girl. Wilma Grace isn't ready to go back to Sawyer. What?*

Thom cracked his knuckles, a sure sign of his turmoil. "I'm not seeing San Francisco as any paradise for us. I ought to have been promoted to foreman, but I wasn't, and y'all know why."

"Well, I'm not saying it's a paradise. It isn't. I'm just saying it's better than where we came from. You're in the union, aren't you? Go find another longshoreman job. Them great big ships are still coming into the docks, and someone's got to unload 'em."

"Well…" Thom started to say something, and then he trailed off. Holy smoke. Wilma Grace and her fussy self might just be making sense. If past experience held, Thom would presently come around to her way of thinking, and they'd stay in San Francisco.

"Furthermore, Tillie told me to go down to City Hall and take the civil-service test. I asked, 'Why would I do that?' She says because the test is scored blind so they can't tell the race of the person who's taking it. You pass it, then you can be hired by the city and county or even take the federal government's test and work there. Tillie did it herself a couple of months ago."

Yep, Wilma Grace's mind was clearly made up. And once that had happened, there'd be no budging her. Thom would have to eventually come around.

Maddie finished putting the last plate in the dish drainer. She didn't know what she was going to do. She hadn't written her mama about being laid off. She was going to see Gerry the day after tomorrow and would have to tell her what happened. She knew what Gerry would say, and she wanted so much to say yes, but there was her promise to Mama, who she needed to write. Hell, she ought to talk to her. But a phone call with her mama would be harder to organize than a phone call with Gerry when she was still in the navy. Did her mama even know anyone with a telephone?

"I think you ought to see about staying, brother. Wilma Grace is right. No sense in going back to Sawyer."

They stared at her as though she'd suddenly grown another head. Wilma Grace nodded and said, "You listen to your little sister. She's talking sense."

"What about Mama?" Thom asked.

"I'm going to be headed back there, so Mama be all right. You know she'll want you to try to find another good job."

She left them and went to her bedroom and wrote the letter.

Dear Mama,

Well, it happened like we thought it would. The navy has laid us off. I have two more weeks' pay, and then that's it. Same with Thom and Wilma Grace, as I expect he'll tell you pretty soon. I've saved almost all my pay, like we agreed. It has been in a bank and has been collecting interest for the past few years. I can start making plans to come back home. I like San Francisco pretty good, but there's no place like the home. I'm still homesick.

She put down her pencil. That wasn't quite true anymore. Since she met Gerry, she'd thought of Sawyer and Mama way less frequently. She really ought to tell her mama about Gerry because they'd never held important facts back from each other, and Gerry was damn sure an important fact. Probably the most important fact of all. Still, she'd promised her mama she'd come back home, and she couldn't break her word. She was going to have to tell Gerry the truth and not hint at it anymore. She dreaded that conversation, not just because of how much it would hurt Gerry, but how much it would hurt *her* to say it, because then it would be real, and she would really have to make up her mind to leave. To leave San Francisco and leave Gerry. But in the meantime, it probably wouldn't hurt to take the civil-service exam. Just to see.

Back in the kitchen, Thom and Wilma Grace were still talking, but they were sitting at the table with coffee cups. No one was yelling. As usual, Thom was nodding while Wilma Grace talked.

"Hey, Wilma Grace. When you go to take that test for civil service, I'll go with you."

Wilma Grace stopped mid-sentence, her eyes wide. "Okay. Sure. Next week."

"That's all I got to say right now. Go back to what you were talking about. Sorry to interrupt."

She went back to her bedroom, reread her letter and thought for a long time, and then she picked up her pencil.

> *If you can find a phone to use, I want to talk to you for real. What I got to tell you, I can't say in a letter.*
> *Love,*
> *Maddie*

Mama would surely approve of her taking the civil-service test. It wasn't a commitment to do or not do something. It was just in case she stayed in San Francisco. It was possible that Mama would even urge her to stay. She was ashamed she even had that thought in her head, but still, it might happen. *What would Marguerite say?* She truly didn't know what to do. She ought to go back to Sawyer like she promised her mama, but she wanted to stay with Gerry.

❖

Mona's defense lawyer met with Gerry, Jake, and Woody in the bar while it was closed. Gerry and her two friends had conferred and decided they'd have to trust this guy to do right by them. The police had ordered Mona to shut down her place until matters could be resolved.

"Mona wants to stay in business, and she needs us to stick with her," Jake said.

The lawyer, Ted Ames, caught them up on where the case was. "The City wanted to scare Mona a little, and the three of you were collateral damage. These types of raids come up now and then whenever somebody wants to make an example of an upstanding business owner like Mona. I'm sorry to say SF's finest got a little carried away with enthusiasm during the raid and snagged you."

He turned to Mona and winked. She wasn't amused, however, and continued to smoke silently.

"We've got a deal with the DA. All the charges against you three are going to be dropped. Mona's gonna pay a fine and promise she'll keep an orderly house. She'll be able to go back to being one of North Beach's tourist hotspots."

Ames said, "It's over for now, but it could happen again, just so you know."

Finally, Mona said, "I'm sorry you girls got caught in this mess. I don't like to see my customers mistreated."

Jake said, "Don't worry. We're not going to stop coming around."

Gerry added, "Your place is like our home. We *like* to be there."

Mona patted her hand. "I know, dear. This type of thing is the cost of doing business. We'll fix it."

When the attorney left, Mona brought the three of them some beers and left them alone.

Looking at Gerry and Jake, Woody said, "Here's to Mona and the 440 Club. Our home away from home."

"You know, all we want is the freedom to socialize and have a few drinks. Even if we can't dance together, we can meet, talk, flirt, what all. Mona makes that possible. Why is that so wrong?" Gerry asked, mostly to herself, but she wondered what her two friends would say.

"They don't want queers to even exist, let alone have a little fun every Saturday or Friday night," Jake said, sounding fed up.

"Well. We *do* exist, and we're not going anywhere. The navy tried to destroy my life for no good reason, but I fought back, and they lost. What do you think we can do about these bar raids?"

Jake took a gulp of beer. "Nothing, Ger. It's over and done with, so best to forget about it. You got lucky with the navy thing. But there's mostly nothing we can do about anything, and it won't help if we get mad. We can keep coming around to Mona's, and she'll treat us right. Same with the other bars in North Beach. At least we have places we can go. Back where I came from, I was the only one like me." Jake was from some Podunk town up north, and her real name was Jane.

Thinking of Fresno, Gerry shrugged, finished her beer, and didn't say anything else.

When she saw Maddie later in the day, she told her about the meeting. Maddie didn't say much, seeming unusually distracted. Normally, she'd ask a lot of questions and want to know details. Instead, she picked at the fried-chicken special she'd ordered at Foster's and mostly wouldn't look at Gerry.

"What's wrong, baby? You're so quiet."

Maddie put her fork down and tilted her chair back, sighing deeply. "The shipyard laid me off with two weeks' pay. Thom and Wilma Grace too."

"Oh, man. That's bad. What are you going to do?" She meant, "Are you going to leave San Francisco," but she didn't want to ask directly.

"Don't know yet," Maddie said. "I have to talk to my mama, for sure."

"Right." Gerry ached to know what Maddie was thinking, but she held back from asking. They walked around downtown and went to the bar as usual later that night, where Maddie stayed to herself. Gerry, Jake, and Woody toasted their escape from the law, and Gerry got a little drunker than usual.

In bed, she reached for Maddie.

"Not now. I'm too tired," Maddie mumbled.

She'd never said such a thing before, and Gerry was upset. "Are you okay? What can I do?"

"Nothing. Just leave me be." Maddie turned over and went to sleep.

Gerry lay awake for a long time. *She's going back home to Sawyer.*

"I'd hoped you stick around awhile, since you don't have to go to work or nothing," Gerry said, hopefully.

Gerry was lying in bed watching Maddie put on her clothes. It was usually an enjoyable exercise, but not this morning. She was unhappy and wanted Maddie to talk and tell her the truth without having to ask her.

Maddie sat on the side of the bed to put on her socks and shoes. She had tiny feet, which Gerry had always considered adorable.

"Maddie?"

"Uh-huh?"

"Are you planning to go back to Sawyer like you talked about before?"

Maddie wouldn't look at her and didn't say anything right away. She finished tying her shoes and came around to Gerry's side of the bed, sat down, and took her hand. "I made a promise to my mama. I got to honor that."

"I know. But that was before we met."

"Yeah, and what difference does that make? A promise is a promise." Maddie sounded angry.

"I don't want you to go," Gerry said, tears starting up though she didn't want to cry.

"I don't want to neither, but, well, it's how it is." She touched Gerry's hand gently.

Gerry repeated, "I don't want you to go." Then finally she couldn't keep from crying.

Maddie had been rubbing her back gently but stopped. "You don't understand. I'm sorry. It's not like I want this, but I have to."

"Do you? Really?"

Maddie put her head in her hands and groaned. "Yes. I do."

She stood up and put on her coat. "I'll come around before I leave. It won't be for weeks."

With that, she walked out of the bedroom, and Gerry heard the front door shut. She turned her face into the pillow and cried for real.

They caught the bus downtown, and it felt both normal and strange. Wilma Grace was again unnaturally quiet, but Maddie pretended not to notice and chattered away about stores and people and how nice it was to have a real break from work however unwanted it was. In due time, they arrived at City Hall, found the right office, and in few minutes were seated and looking at their civil-service exams.

The questions didn't faze Maddie at all. They wanted to know if she could read and write and do basic arithmetic. There was also a couple of civics questions she could answer easily.

She turned in her test paper and then waited for Wilma Grace outside the room, looking at a list of open jobs the city and county were recruiting for: clerks, postal workers, some work involving physical labor. One, for a mechanic, made Maddie think of Gerry, and that was a little painful. She debated if she wanted another welding job or, instead, something indoors and less dangerous.

"I'm ready," Wilma Grace said when she appeared in front of Maddie.

"Let's go get a cup of coffee," Maddie said, causing a look of surprise from Wilma Grace.

They took their coffees and found a spot out on the plaza in front of City Hall that had a view of its large, glimmering dome.

"So what kind of work do you think you want?" Maddie asked.

"Oh, I'd love to be able to sit in some office somewhere and answer a phone. That'd be a sight better than fabricating sheet-metal panels on them old ships."

Maddie nodded. "Me too. I'm done with welding, I think."

"You staying here?" Wilma Grace looked genuinely curious.

"I'm supposed to go back and help Mama start up selling her sewing. You and Thom made up your minds yet?"

"Yep. I told him there was no reason to go back there and just be poor and abused by White people. He wasn't sure, but I talked him into it. He agreed better didn't have to be perfect."

When Maddie and Wilma Grace had come to City Hall to take the test, they were a bit quiet and awkward together on the bus. Maddie hadn't been alone with her or had a private conversation since that day she'd come home and found her with Gerry.

"Where you spending your free time, sister?" Wilma Grace asked. "I never see you no more."

You ought not ask questions you don't want answered. "I'm usually with Gerry," Maddie said matter-of-factly. That wouldn't likely be a shock to Wilma Grace.

"Uh-huh. I expected that. You're a grown woman." Wilma Grace paused, then said, "Thom told me I had to let you be. As long as you weren't putting stuff in our faces, you were free to do what you want."

She didn't sound as snotty as she usually did, and Maddie was grateful. *I'll be darned, Wilma Grace. You're acting a little bit more sensible about this than I ever thought you could.*

Maddie laughed. "Mighty generous of y'all. But I'm all right with that. I'm not about trying to annoy you. I'm certainly happy you noticed that I'm an adult and I can do what I want with whomever I want." She kept her tone light, and Wilma Grace grinned back.

She added, "It's just me and you used to get along okay, and I kind of miss that."

Wilma Grace looked at her a second, nodded with a slight smile, and they went to catch their bus home.

After that day, Maddie was much relieved to feel like her family life was back to normal She wondered what had prompted Wilma Grace's change of heart but concluded it was better to accept it and not ask too many questions. Her mama would say to leave well enough alone.

But then Wilma Grace surprised her some more.

Out of the blue a couple of days later, while they were shopping, she said, "It was a pure shock to me to see you and your friend. It's against the Bible too. I heard the church ladies talking about someone else. Some fella. They were vicious."

"I expect they were. But you're my family, and I think a little live-and-let-live is called for. I think the Bible says that too." Maddie grinned.

"Yeah. You're right. You told Mama anything yet?"

"No. I haven't, but I'm going to talk to her soon. She's going to use Lily Roman's phone."

"Maddie, I'm sorry I said those mean things to you. But darned if you just seem to have passed them right over. You're right. We're family, and we got to stick together," Wilma Grace said suddenly.

Maddie waved her hand. "It's fine. Thank you for saying you're sorry. I accept your apology. Now let's head home so we can make something good for Thom for dinner."

In the end, Maddie couldn't stay away from Gerry. It was sure funny that finally they could spend more time together at the point when Maddie was contemplating leaving her and San Francisco forever.

"I've come to go out with you," Maddie said when she showed up at Gerry's place early one Saturday evening. "Can I come in?" She took a chance and showed up unannounced.

Gerry left the door open as she walked away, and Maddie slipped inside Gerry's apartment.

"Are you mad at me?" she asked.

Gerry stood at the window staring outside for a moment. Then she turned to face Maddie. "Kind of, but not really. I just don't want you to go." She walked over to Maddie and put her arms around her.

Maddie settled inside her embrace, thinking how good and natural and comforting it was.

She whispered, "I don't want to leave, but I have to. I'm talking to Mama late tomorrow afternoon. Can I stay with you tonight?"

Gerry responded by tilting her head and kissing her urgently.

Maddie said between kisses, "I'm thinking that's a yes."

"Yes. I want you to stay, and I don't even care about going to the 440 Club. I want to stay here with you."

Their togetherness was so sweet, it was almost unbearable, and part of Maddie wanted to be able to accept and not long for more, such as being able to touch Gerry. It seemed a bad time again to try to approach her, what with Maddie basically fixing to leave forever, a thought that was becoming more and more painful. That expectation hovering in the background lent a bittersweet taste to all their time together.

The next morning, they ate breakfast out and headed to Ocean Beach to go to Playland at the Beach.

At the top of the roller coaster, they could see far out into the ocean, until its surface met the sky. "There are the Farallone Islands way out there." Gerry pointed to the almost mirage-like sight. Rocks in the middle of nowhere, they were hovering at the horizon of the ocean like a vision.

"Did you ever go out there when you were at the naval base?" Maddie asked.

"Yeah. Once. One of the new Liberty ships took us out for a cruise, and that's where we went. Half of us got seasick. Not me though. Then they never did it again. Couldn't stand to see us having too much fun."

"Do you miss the navy?" Maddie asked, detecting a sad note Gerry talked.

"Yes and no. I miss the other WAVES and the sailor boys who were our friends. Jimmy's moved in with George, and they don't come out anymore. Do you miss the dry dock? I know it hasn't been that long."

"I don't miss the graveyard shift. But yes, I miss the girls I worked with. It was like we were family. Sometimes it felt better than my own family."

Gerry nodded.

They rotated back to earth and decide to cap off the trip with some It's-It ice-cream sandwiches. Maddie told Gerry about her talk with Wilma Grace and the civil service tests as they walked back to the streetcar stop.

"So you might stay?" Gerry asked hopefully.

"I'm not saying I will or I won't, but I thought I might as well take the test. I can apply for a job up to a year from the date of the test. But I have to talk to Mama. I expect she'll want me to come home."

Gerry scuffed her shoes on the sand, glumly. "I expect she will. But Maddie…"

Maddie stopped and they looked at one another.

"I need you too."

"I know, honey. I *will* miss you like crazy."

Gerry looked around briefly. No one was paying any attention to them. She put her finger under Maddie's chin and tilted her face up. "I love you."

"Now you tell me, girl. It's a little late." Maddie felt peeved but happy all at the same time.

"Does that make a difference to you?" Gerry dropped her hand back to her side and clenched her fist.

"Of course, it makes a difference to me," Maddie said quietly. "It makes all the difference in the world."

"But is it enough? Does it make you want to stay? That's the thing."

"Haven't you been listening to me? I want to stay, but I can't. I was always going to have to go. I know that you know that. Don't pester me no more about it."

Maddie was upset and Gerry backed off. What was there, really, left to say?

❖

"Mama, is that you?" Maddie asked.

"Maddie, dear. It's me. Is that you?"

This silly exchange made Maddie smile. It was going to be the only amusing thing about this phone call.

"Course it's me, Mama. After all the trouble we went through to have this call, who else could it be?"

"I just wanted to be sure. You sound good, honey. Why didn't we talk on the phone before now? I love hearing your voice."

Her mama sounded tired.

"I don't know. I guess 'cause it was so hard. Lily didn't have a phone until a little while ago. We don't have one, so…Maddie. I heard from Thom. He told me what happened to him. So it happened to you too?"

"That's right, Mama. The naval shipyard's done finished with us."

"Well, that's too bad, but we always knew it was coming. War didn't last, thank the Lord. So, you fixing to come back home?"

"Yep. I'm fixing to do that." Maddie had to smile at using that phrase because it reminded her so much of Sawyer.

"Honey, I'm so glad. Thom and Wilma Grace don't think they coming back. Thom thinks he can get a new job, and so does Wilma Grace, so they want to stay. What about you, honey?"

Her mama sounded worried.

"I just said so, Mama. Is your hearing okay?" Saying out loud to

Mama she was going to return to Sawyer made it all too real. It made her think of Gerry and how down she looked the last time they were together. Maddie swallowed, not wanting to start crying on the phone with Mama.

"My hearing's fine, girl. I wanted to make sure I understood."

"Yes, Mama. It's exactly like we talked about. I'm coming home, and I'm bringing a pile of money, and we going to start your business, and it'll be grand. Make sure you tidy up that corner of the dining room so that can be your work area. You gonna need some space. Okay?"

"I sure will. And Maddie, I'm so happy. I missed you like crazy. I missed Thom, too, but you're my baby. I don't know what I'd do if you weren't coming home."

"Well. You don't have to worry, Mama. I'll get on that train as soon as I can."

"That's wonderful, baby. You write me, will you? This phone-call business is too hard."

"Yes, Mama. I'll write you with the details when I know."

She hung up the pay phone, sat down on the ground, and cried. *My butt's going to be dusty.*

This thought brought Maddie back to the here and now. She stood up and dusted off her pants. Then she looked eastward, as usual, and at the hills across the bay from Hunters Point. *I'm going to miss the ocean almost as much as I'll miss Gerry.* But there wasn't a thing she could do to change any of it. *Blood is blood, family is family.*

Then she asked herself a very inconvenient question—two of them, to be specific. First, why didn't she bring up Gerry to her mama? She hadn't so far because there hadn't been a good time. *In the year and a half since you've been with her, you've never had a chance?* She snorted out loud. *Right.* The second: was she ashamed? *Maybe.*

She'd always told her mama everything. They'd had no secrets and were almost like best friends since Maddie's daddy Walter had died when she was eight and Thom was eleven. That was the other reason that made it so hard to think of not returning to Sawyer. Mama *was* the closest person in the world to her, and she couldn't abandon her.

But then there was Gerry. What *was* Gerry? She wasn't nothing or nobody, that's for sure. She was somebody. No one in Maddie's world left home until she was married. It was a big deal. No, it was a huge deal for her to come out West to work in the shipyard.

But that had happened with her mama's blessing. She wouldn't give her permission for Maddie to *not* return to Sawyer. That type of thinking wasn't in Mama's universe, just like taking up with a woman, a White one, to boot, wasn't ever going to be part of Mama's thinking.

Maddie dragged herself back up the hill to her soon-to-be former home: the little yellow house with chairs on the porch. She half hoped Wilma Grace or Thom was home, but the other half prayed they wouldn't be so she could be alone with her grief.

She walked into the living room and heard their voices in the kitchen. *Too bad.* She stood in the doorway, but they were so deep in discussion they evidently hadn't heard her come in.

"Hey, there."

Wilma Grace and Thom's heads spun around, and they didn't say anything for a moment.

"Thom's got a new job. He's going to be working down on the Embarcadero on the piers. Same thing as the navy. He's going to be a longshoreman," Wilma Grace said, her voice charged with relief and happiness.

Maddie walked to him and hugged him. "That's wonderful. I'm happy for you."

"You don't sound happy, Maddie girl. What's eating you?" Thom asked.

It wasn't something she could explain since it involved Gerry. And it seemed clear that Wilma Grace and Thom would be staying in San Francisco.

"I'm sad about losing my place at the dock." Thom and Wilma Grace exchanged some sort of a look Maddie couldn't interpret.

"Well, pretty soon, you could be working at the post office, same as me."

"You got the job?" Maddie asked, surprised.

"That's right. We're both set, and we're staying here. No more Sawyer, no more looking over our shoulders all the time to make sure we're not doing something to make somebody mad There'll be no one to notice whether we're coming or going."

"That's terrific," Maddie said without enthusiasm.

"Maddie, what's wrong?" Wilma Grace's sincerity was astonishing.

Maddie sat down at the kitchen table, stretched out her legs, and put her head down.

"Mama's expecting me home in a few weeks, and I'm not as hopped up to go as I thought I would be. I like it here."

Again, her family members looked at each other. "Is it Gerry?" Wilma Grace asked.

Maddie snapped her head up. She'd sounded like she actually cared about what Maddie was feeling. She thought about their talk waiting for the bus home from City Hall.

"Yeah," Maddie said defensively.

Thom asked, "Did you tell Mama?"

"No. Of course not. That's a dumb idea."

"Hmm. Might not be," Thom said. "Mama hasn't been living under a rock, even though she's in Sawyer. She might know more than you think."

"Why don't you try?" Wilma Grace said.

"What's with you two? How come you're acting so nice about Gerry?" Maddie was having a hard time understanding their change of heart.

"We been talking," Thom said. "We figured it didn't make no difference to us. It's not like you're different from what you was like before. We met Gerry and all. She's okay."

Maddie was so surprised she couldn't say a word.

"We want you to stay here in San Fran with us. And if you want to stay, then we may as well just get Mama to move out here. No reason for her to stay in Sawyer then. We'll get us a bigger house. You need to talk to her, though, and make her see the reason for it, which would mainly be 'cause her whole family is here." Wilma Grace stopped talking, and she looked satisfied.

Heaven help me, she's making too much sense. Maddie was dumbfounded. Had somebody come along and replaced Thom and Wilma Grace with different folks but the same bodies?

"Um, okay," Maddie said. "I'll talk to Mama."

❖

When the day came for the planned phone call with Mama, Maddie was a wreck. No way Mama would go along with the big change after all this time. She just wasn't built that way. It wasn't lost on her that Wilma Grace and Thom had left the hard part of dealing with their mama to her. But at the same time, she was hopeful. Their new plan *did* make sense, and it solved part of her problem with Gerry, the part that didn't involve telling Mama about her.

She hadn't seen Gerry for two weeks. She missed her but she couldn't face her knowing how much pain she was causing. She wanted to tell Gerry what she and her siblings were cooking up, but she didn't want to say anything until she'd got it all arranged and was sure it was going to work out. Imagining how happy Gerry would be gave her courage to go forward with her talk with Mama.

CHAPTER FIFTEEN

November 1946

Gerry couldn't imagine Maddie would actually leave town without saying anything to her, but it sure looked that way. They'd hadn't seen or talked to each other for weeks. Gerry had started to take the bus over to Hunters Point about five times but backed off each time. She had *some* pride after all. She wanted to believe Maddie would find her way back to her eventually.

In the meantime, she was about to be finished with her mechanics training, and she'd be in line to get a job placement somewhere. She didn't have any reason not to spend time at Mona's, and she was there almost every night. Since she had some money, and it made her feel better to drink, she drank some. She found out after the first few sips of say, a vodka and tonic, she couldn't taste anything, and it was a matter of effect. Vodka worked way better and faster than beer.

As she looked around, she thought she noticed a lot more good-looking femmes than she ever had before: she'd once had eyes only for Maddie. And that thought both made her feel guilty and alarmed. It was just going to be a flirtation, nothing more. She was lonely and wanted to talk to a pretty woman because she missed Maddie and resented her absence. *She might leave and go back to Arkansas. Probably that's what she'll do since that's what she said she was going to do. Or she might not. But whichever way it is, she isn't talking to me about it. The way this is going, she'll come by to say "so long," and that will be that. I told her I loved her, and I thought that would make a difference. She said she loved me too.*

The woman wasn't sitting at the bar. Instead, she sat boldly alone at a table, smoking and looking around coolly.

Gerry sauntered over and said, "Hi. Is this seat taken?"

"It is not," the strange woman said neutrally as she looked her over. Gerry had bought some new clothes recently: a striped, pointy-collared shirt and gray, high-waisted slacks. She'd had the pants hemmed to the correct length so that her wingtips, also new and brightly polished, were visible.

Gerry beamed and sat down. "Do you come here often?"

The unknown woman tweaked her eyebrow. "That's original."

Gerry was taken aback, but she laughed. "All right. Let me start over. Hello, there. Can I buy you a drink?"

"Good evening, and, yes, you may." The strange woman's oddly formal manner of speaking struck her.

"What would you like?"

"A gin and tonic."

Gerry returned with two drinks and handed her new friend's glass to her.

"Cheers." The unknown woman raised her glass.

"Are you English or something?" Gerry asked. She'd seen movies with English people in them.

"Why, yes, I am. Thanks. I work at the British consulate up in Pacific Heights."

"Wow. Color me impressed. What's your name? I'm Gerry."

"Pamela. Pleased to meet you, Gerry. That was what we used to call the Germans—Jerries. But I won't hold that against you."

"Please don't. I was given the name Geraldine by my folks, and I shortened it to Gerry."

"Indeed. Suitably boyish."

"I'm glad you think so." Pamela's accent and refined manner intrigued her. She was the opposite of most of the girls she'd met in Mona's. She was also very attractive. She had reddish-brown hair cut in a pageboy and a sharp nose and chin. Her blue eyes met Gerry's gaze steadily.

She'd never met anyone English, though their status as staunch allies of the US of A was often talked about during the war.

"Oh, here's to the end of the war." Gerry raised her glass.

"Here's to world peace."

"Have you been in San Francisco long?"

The English girl's wry smile was inviting and, well, charming.

"Depends on what you mean by 'long.'"

Gerry lit herself a cigarette as she made eye contact. "I don't know what I mean. Before the war?"

"No. I was in London, but after the war ended, I took an opportunity I was offered. The conditions in London were almost worse than during the war. They had a changeover of staff in the Foreign Service, and a spot in San Francisco became open. So here I am."

"What do you do there? What's a consulate?"

Pamela laughed gently. "It's like a little piece of our country here in San Francisco. We help British citizens who need things, and we communicate with the US government. I'm a secretary to the assistant consul, but I'm more like his assistant."

"Wow." Gerry gaped at Pamela. "You must be important."

Pamela looked away modestly. "Hardly, but I like to think I am effective."

She was an incredible combination of the familiar and the foreign. Gerry decided she loved Pamela's accent. Even if she sounded hoity-toity, it suited her.

"What do you do?" Pamela asked.

"I'm in trade school, learning to be a mechanic."

"How very practical. If I had car problems, I could call on you. If I had a car, that is."

Pamela said this in a deadpan tone. She didn't even smile, and Gerry paused, then started to laugh when she at last got the joke.

"Ready for another drink?"

"I believe I am. Thank you."

"Hello, Mama," Maddie said, struggling to keep her voice from shaking.

"Hello, honey. So good to hear your voice."

"Good to hear you too." Maddie paused. She had no idea how to frame what she wanted to say. Well, she'd ended up talking about it with Wilma Grace, who thought it wouldn't be easy to convince her mama to leave Sawyer and that her feelings would be hurt that her entire family wanted to stay in San Francisco. That was probably a pretty accurate prediction.

"I tried to get Thom to bring up the subject with her, but no way was he going to be the one to raise the idea. I told him he was a coward, but he wouldn't budge. He's depending on you to convince her."

"My brother isn't the bravest guy when it comes to talking about hard things. He's a chicken, especially when it comes to our mama. Okay. How am I going to do this?"

"I think start with that we're all staying here, then work around to you."

In the silence after their greetings, Mama said, "Girl, you're quiet as a mouse. Have you got some news for me or what? Do you have your train ticket? Time you expect to arrive?"

"Mama, Wilma Grace and Thom are going to stay here in San Francisco."

There was a longish silence.

"I suppose they couldn't tell me that themselves and made you be the bringer of the news."

"Well. They thought it would be easier since I'd already made a plan for us to talk."

"Hmph. Well, Thom's prone to making snap decisions, so I guess I'm not surprised. He's a man, and he can do what he wants when he wants."

"He's going to have a job on the docks, union and everything. Wilma Grace is going to work for the post office."

"That's good. They got things all arranged. I'm happy to hear that. Now what about you? When you coming home?"

Here was the moment of truth. Once she had made a decision, Mama was unlikely to go back on it, and Maddie dreaded telling her of a change in plans. It was all very well for Thom and Wilma Grace to decide to stay in California, but it wouldn't be for her. She and Mama had had their plan for almost three years, and she was about to throw a grenade and blow it all up.

"That's the thing, Mama. Well, Thom and Wilma Grace, me too, we want you to come out here to live."

This time the pause was really long. Maddie closed her eyes and prayed.

"So, you're not coming home?"

She was hurt. Maddie could hear it in her voice. She hated hurting her mama.

"Well, that's not exactly what I meant. I *can*, but Mama, we thought you could come live out here? We'd be all together. You can still have your sewing business. I've got the money saved for you just like we talked about. There's a lot of Colored folks here now. There's the church and all. It's nice, much nicer than Sawyer. I told you the White folks leave us be. They may not be real friendly, but they're not awful. We can live our lives and take care of ourselves."

More silence.

Finally, her mama said, "I've never been more than thirty miles away from home. I don't have any idea how I'd be able to do that, honey." She didn't seem angry, just regretful.

Maddie stayed quiet to let her mama say what she wanted to say.

"You're my baby, but I let you go way out there to California for these last couple years 'cause I knew it would be good for you and for us. I never thought you wouldn't want to come back to me, to come home. I know now you've been living in a better place, and old Sawyer won't mean much to you. I just can't stand the idea of you not being with me."

Maddie heard the tears in her voice and felt horrible. This was exactly what she didn't want to confront. Gerry versus her mama. She wanted to have both of them, in the same city.

"Mama, that's why I want you to come out here. We'll be together, our whole family."

"Have you got yourself a new job?" Mama asked abruptly, throwing Maddie off track.

Then the operator cut in. "Please deposit twenty-five cents to continue this call."

Maddie fumbled in her pocket for a quarter and plugged it in the slot. "Mama?"

"I'm here." She sounded real unhappy.

Maddie sucked in some air and blew out a breath. "Mama. I don't have a job, but I can get one. I took the government's test like Wilma Grace, and I did fine. I can apply if I want one."

"Sounds like you got it all figured."

Now Mama sounded angry, and Maddie was more distressed than ever. She didn't blame her mama one bit since she'd gone and changed everything they had decided on.

"Mama, I'm sorry. I didn't want to upset you. I know this is all a big surprise, all this stuff about Thom's job and you moving out here. I wished I could see you and tell you all this in person, but I can't, so here we are on this stupid long-distance phone call."

There was another pause. "Yes, honey. I know. I'm just in shock. You have to give me a moment."

"Should we make another time to call? Would that help?"

"Well, maybe, but it's sure a fair amount of trouble to have a simple phone call, so no. I want to settle this now. I can't stay here in Sawyer with both my children all the way out in California. Maybe if it was only Thom, I could stand it. But not you. Not you, baby."

Maddie closed her eyes. "Mama, I love you so much, and I want you and me to be together."

"So do I, baby. So what's made you not want to come home?"

This time, it was Maddie who stayed silent. It was so long a silence, she thought of it as a giant hole she'd fallen into.

Mama asked, "You there, honey?"

"Yes, Mama. I'm here. I met someone."

"Well, why didn't you say so? Lordy. No wonder you gone and changed your mind about coming back to Sawyer. Now I understand. Tell me about him."

Maddie's throat closed. She swallowed but still nearly choked when she said, "It's not him. It's her."

Mama's silence this time was not only long, but it was scarily, painfully long.

"Oh" was the only word Mama could come up with, and that wasn't very encouraging.

"I wished I could have told you before, but I was scared to."

"I'm sorry you were scared to be honest with me." Mama's tone had turned pretty frosty.

Maddie finally started to cry from anguish and fear. "I didn't want to be dishonest. I wanted to tell you in person, but I couldn't. So it has to be this way. I'm so sorry. But I'm being honest now. Her name is Gerry, and I love her, and I want to stay here, and I want *you* to come out here to live." She sobbed and couldn't say anymore, though what else there was to say she didn't know. It was all up to what Mama would say. There was still more silence. There was never in time in Maddie's life when she'd known her mama be at a loss for words.

"I suppose I should have expected this. I never should have let you go to California."

"Mama—"

"Don't you 'mama' me, Maddie Weeks." Then *she* started crying. Oops. Now she was going to be angry. Well, that would be expected. *I can just let her be how she's going to be and hope she'll come around in the end.*

"Mama? Let's get off the phone now. Can you get back to Lily's tomorrow at this time, and I'll call you back. Let's us leave this be for the night. You can think about it, pray about it. Remember. I love you more than anything."

In a strangled, tear-choked voice, Mama said, "Yes. I'll be at Lily's, like you said."

"Bye, Mama. I love you." Maddie replaced the phone and again sank down to the ground as her knees gave out. It was sunset now, and she was dimly aware of the glow from the west.

Gerry. We haven't talked in so long. She must be beside herself with worry. I wanted to go to her with the thing settled, with good news, but it looks like I can't. I ought to go anyway and tell her what I want to do. Mama'll come around in time. She'll see the sense of moving here. Meanwhile I really ought to talk to Gerry and not keep all this to myself. I love her, and I ought to tell her what's going on.

Back at the house, Maddie reported to Thom and Wilma Grace as they ate their supper.

"You just dropped that mess on her all of a sudden?" Wilma Grace said, back to her demanding, judgmental self. As if *she* wasn't the one who encouraged Maddie to talk to Mama.

"Well. I thought it might help her understand why I don't want to leave. She'll be fine. She's going to get out here with us and realize this is where she's supposed to be."

"I hope you know what you're doing," Thom said.

"Uh-huh," Wilma Grace said.

"I've got a right to be happy, you know," Maddie said with sudden heat. "I can be with the person I love like y'all can. I deserve that. So I want Mama to be here? So I want to be with Gerry? What's wrong with wanting both?"

"Well, nothing, I guess," Thom said with a note of recognition as though he hadn't thought of such a thing as love in connection with Gerry.

"Anyhow, speaking of Gerry, I need to go over and tell her what's going on with me. I likely won't be home tonight."

Wilma Grace rolled her eyes. "Oh, sure."

But then she softened a little. "I hope you're right about your mama and all. It would be sure nice to have her around just like we used to be back in Sawyer."

"See y'all later." Maddie grabbed her coat and flew out the door so she wouldn't miss the downtown bus.

She rang Gerry's buzzer a bunch of times, but there was no answer. She was likely at Mona's. Maddie tamped down her irritation. She was probably passing the time and drinking a little. Maddie had to admit that if she wasn't around, Gerry had the right to spend time with her friends. She might as well go over to the bar, and then they could come back to Gerry's flat and talk and do other stuff. Thinking about it made her grin. She really had to tell Gerry what was happening. She was pretty certain Mama would come around. The prospect of being back with her family would convince her and get rid of some of her misgivings. Maddie felt better and became excited, thinking of breaking the news to Gerry. As she walked, she rehearsed the nice speech she would give and imagined how Gerry would react. How happy she would be when she heard that Maddie was going to stay and they would be together.

Then she spotted Gerry about half a block away on Broadway, but she wasn't alone. Someone had an arm around her and was half carrying her as they walked. Maddie watched in horror as Gerry's companion came into focus. She was tall, and she was laughing as she jollied Gerry along. Gerry was clearly so drunk she could barely walk, but her friend was holding her upright. To Maddie's further dismay, Gerry, her arm around the stranger's waist, leaned in and clumsily kissed her on the neck. The woman laughed but didn't respond to the kiss.

"Gerry?" They were suddenly face to face, only a few feet apart.

"Maddie. What are you doing here?" Gerry's voice was slow and slurry.

"I came to find you, but it looks like I came at the wrong time."

Gerry's companion appeared worried and surprised. "I'm seeing her home because she's drunk. I'm nobody special. We only just met."

The woman's sincerity didn't make any difference to Maddie. She was also unreasonably furious with the woman's clipped manner of speaking. She thought of the phrase "see red," and that was exactly what she was doing. She was so mad she couldn't say another thing. She turned around and quickly walked away back the way she had come.

❖

"Here you go. Let me pull off your shoes. Here's the wastebasket if you need it."

"What happened? Where's Maddie?"

Gerry's mind refused to work. She could see the table light was on, outlining Pamela's pageboy. Pamela was saying something, but Gerry couldn't understand what it was.

She woke or, more precisely, came to, and the first thing she was aware of was that her head hurt. The second was that she was by herself. She was in bed in her apartment, but no one was there. That, at least, was good news.

Slowly she maneuvered out of bed. Then the memories flooded in. She'd been drinking with Pamela, but then Maddie showed up. But Maddie wasn't here. Where had she gone?

Everything was extremely fuzzy. She wished she felt better, but so be it. She took a shower with some difficulty. In her pants pocket was a scrap of paper with a phone number and a name: *Pamela.* Gerry wished to hell she had installed a telephone in her apartment. *As soon as possible.* She dragged on some clothes and went to the corner to use the pay phone.

"Hello, you. Are you in one piece?" She heard Pamela's cool British voice.

"I'll live. What the hell happened? I remember seeing Maddie, but then she disappeared."

"I was attempting to get you safely home, and your Maddie showed up. She was angry, I think, because you were with me and she didn't understand why, and she left before I could explain that I was only looking after you and wasn't intending to get into bed with you."

"I was way too drunk to have been any good."

"That is likely true, and I wouldn't have wanted to do anything with you last night. That would be quite wrong with the state you were in, and besides, you already have a girlfriend, so it would be doubly wrong."

The slight censure Gerry heard in Pamela's voice made her head hurt worse because she was right. *Why the hell did I drink so much? That's not like me.*

"Gerry? Are you there?"

"Yeah," Gerry said. She pinched the bridge of her nose, trying to make her headache go away.

"Let me pull myself together a bit, and I'll come over to your flat with some aspirin and some food and coffee, and we will try to repair you. Why don't you start with drinking as much water as you can and taking a hot shower?"

"Right. Already took a shower. Here's my address." Gerry managed to respond, though she said it through a wave of nausea. She closed her eyes and tried to breathe.

"See you soon, love."

Gerry went home and lay down on her bed, and by the time Pamela arrived at her flat bearing coffee and a Danish, she was feeling slightly more human.

They sat on the couch, and Gerry realized being cared for even in this basic way was both unusual and deeply gratifying. It also reminded her, painfully, of Maddie.

"I can't thank you enough for doing this."

Pamela waved her hand airily in dismissal. "Oh, my dear. I've had many an occasion to play nursemaid to a hungover gay girl. Now that you've imbibed some coffee and some food, and taken a couple of pills, how are you doing?"

"Better, except for how lousy I feel, and I don't mean my headache. *That*'s almost gone."

"Ah. Of course. The question of Maddie and what you are to do about her."

In the daylight, Pamela was more attractive than she'd been the night before, which Gerry knew wasn't always the case with pickups, and that made her smile as she looked at her. She was dressed in tailored loose slacks, her legs primly crossed, and she was smoking. She looked composed and knowing, but her smile was kind.

"What are you smiling at?" she asked.

"You."

"Well, your appreciation is welcome, but I advise you to nip whatever feelings you may be entertaining in the bud, if you want to win your Maddie back," Pamela said sternly.

"I love the way you talk, but yeah, you're right. What the hell am I going to do?"

"I would wait for a few days before you do *anything*."

"Wait?" Gerry was so displeased that her voice went high and almost sounded like a wail. That was not good butch behavior.

"I can hear your pain, but I strongly advise you to let things lie for a bit. Allow Maddie to calm down and reconsider what you know of her feelings."

Gerry put her head in her hands. "You don't understand. She was getting ready to leave the Bay Area and go back to Arkansas, where she's from. I think she came downtown to tell me...something. Maybe that she was going to stay. But I don't know. If she was as mad as I think she was, she'll leave forever."

"My dear, if she is determined to leave, you can't stop her, but if not, then you have a chance to convince her to stay, but you must approach her carefully. I'd say her showing up last night was a sign of...something."

"Okay. How?"

Pamela patted her arm. "Listen to me closely."

❖

"Well, you're a sorry sight."

This was Wilma Grace's way of comforting her, Maddie supposed. Her bedside manner could use some work, but at least she could actually tell Wilma Grace what had happened with both Mama and with Gerry.

"Hmph." She grunted. Not especially helpful.

"I don't know what to do," Maddie said.

"Well. First you got to decide if Gerry's going to be worth the trouble of a long, drawn-out thing with Mama."

"I don't know what to think about her, for starters, and I don't know what Mama's going to say about anything."

"Your mama is the most sensible woman I ever met, so I'm not worried about her. Thom and I wish she *would* move out here."

"Will you or Thom talk to her and say so?"

"Yeah. I'll have to do it, because Thom won't."

"So when I call her back tomorrow, you'll be there?"

Wilma Grace rolled her eyes. "Yeah. I suppose."

❖

Maddie took a deep breath and slotted a bunch of change into the telephone and dialed Lily Roman's phone number. She didn't know what was worse, her encounter with Gerry on Broadway or her dread at what her mama was going to say.

She kept her eye fixed on Wilma Grace as she waited.

"Hello?" It was Mama.

"Hi, Mama. It's me. Wilma Grace is here too."

"Well, I'll be. I been wanting to talk to her."

"I'll put her on." She handed the phone receiver to Wilma Grace, who rolled her eyes.

"Hey, Mama. How you doin'?" Maddie put her head next to the phone so she could hear what Mama said.

"I'm fair to middlin'. You?"

"I'm good. Thom's doing real well. He's at work and told me tell you he loves you and he really hopes you're going to come live with us."

"Well, that's why Maddie and I are speaking today."

"Yeah. I know that. We're all praying you'll see your way to get on out here so we can keep our family together."

"I'd love that more than anything. Lily thinks it's the craziest thing she ever heard of, but I told her I want to be with my children." Lily was one of Mama's oldest friends.

Maddie and Wilma Grace made eye contact with identical expressions of hope.

"It's only that it terrifies the you-know-what out of me. I've lived in Sawyer my whole life. It's not the greatest town on earth, but it's what I know. I about had a fit when Maddie said she wanted to stay in Frisco and the other thing she told me."

Their expressions fell. Maddie whispered that Wilma Grace should keep talking to Mama.

"Well, Mama. San Fran isn't at all like Sawyer. That's a fact. We all three of us have changed, but we haven't changed how we feel about you."

Impatient, Maddie changed her mind and motioned Wilma Grace to hand over the phone.

"Mama? I hope you've thought hard about this."

"I have, honey, and I've asked God for help."

Maddie closed her eyes and silently pleaded for her mama to make the right decision. If God was involved, that was good, but it could go any which way.

But Mama didn't say anything else.

"Mama, what are you thinking? How are you feeling?"

Mama started sobbing. "I don't know. You've changed so much, honey. I don't know you anymore."

Maddie's patience started to slip, destroying her pledge to let her mama come to terms with the news about herself and Gerry.

"What I told you last time we talked about me and Gerry—is that what's bothering you? Not just moving to San Francisco?"

"Yes."

It wasn't as though this was a surprise. "What can I do? What can I say?"

"I don't know." Mama cried even more.

Wilma Grace grabbed the phone away from Maddie and said, "Mama, if you're concerned about Maddie, don't you think the best thing to do is get on out here and straighten her out? She'll do a lot better if you're around. We all could use your help, really."

In spite of her dismay, Maddie was amused by Wilma Grace's unconscious joke about "straightening" her out.

There was silence again on Mama's end of the call so at least she'd stopped crying.

"I never thought of that. I've only been thinking about how afraid I am to leave Sawyer."

Maddie took the phone back. "Mama, I need you here. We all need you. Sawyer's never done nothing in particular that's good for you."

"That's the truth. It's what I know is all."

"You know us—me, Thom, and Wilma Grace," Maddie said, softly.

"Well, I used to think I did, but I'm not sure anymore." Mama stopped talking, and Maddie waited fearfully.

Then her mama said, "But I sure am not going to find out anything 'bout you if you're there and I'm here. I suppose I got to get myself pulled together and make my way out West."

And just like that, Maddie's first dilemma was solved. Maddie and Wilma Grace exchanged triumphant grins. Maddie talked a while more with Mama, avoiding the subject of herself. No sense in complicating things. They'd have plenty of time to deal with that later.

After they hung up, Wilma Grace wanted to talk some more, but Maddie said, "I'm kinda wrung out. I want to be by myself for bit."

She went up the hill to Jerrold Street and sat down to look at the bay. What to do about Gerry? It was all funny in a sick sort of way. Mama had made her decision to move out to San Francisco, and Maddie wasn't going to return to Sawyer. But now her reason for staying no longer seemed to exist. She'd been betrayed by the woman she loved. *Who claimed she loved me.*

What would Marguerite say about this sorry state of affairs? The story Marguerite had told about getting her job on the streetcars came back to Maddie.

I had to fight for that job like my mama told me to. I went there every day for two weeks and sat in their damn waiting room and put up with the glances, the whispers, and the outright insults from the secretaries. I wasn't going to leave until I got what I wanted. I wasn't about to let them stop me and it worked out. In the end, they hired me.

Was this the same type of situation as Marguerite's MTA job? No, it wasn't. Maddie thought she knew what she saw when she ran into Gerry with that other woman, whoever she was. But ought she at least talk to Gerry? It seemed fair. She had to know the truth anyway, whatever it was. Maybe what she saw was something else. Maybe it wasn't what it looked like. Gerry had never cheated on her, as far as she knew.

Maddie had stopped talking to Gerry because she didn't know what to say about having to move back to Arkansas. But that wasn't true anymore because she was staying in San Francisco. This thought lifted her, but she needed to talk to Gerry and tell her the news. She also needed to find out who the mysterious woman was, and why she was taking Gerry home that night.

CHAPTER SIXTEEN

December 1946

Gerry dressed in her nattiest clothes and styled her hair, carefully. She wanted to look her best.

The first piece of advice Pamela gave her was to approach the meeting as courtship. "Take flowers and/or candy."

She bought flowers but, not as Pamela advised, a showy bouquet of flowers like roses. She chose lilies. Maddie wasn't a fan of candy, so bringing that wasn't necessary.

On the bus over to Hunters Point, Gerry thought of another occasion she'd gone there—when Maddie had broken her arm. This time she was taking as big a risk as she had that time, maybe even bigger.

She had no idea if Maddie would even talk to her, but she surely hoped she would. She wanted to at least get Maddie to be open-minded, and if she was successful, then she wanted Maddie to talk to Pamela. Gerry thought vaguely that Pamela's crisp British accent would win Maddie over and convince her that they were friends but nothing more.

Gerry had spent some more time with Pamela, who fascinated her, but not in a romantic way. She seemed exotic but, in some ways, completely familiar. Pamela sounded like she was from the upper crust, but she was in fact from a middle-class family in the London suburbs who had to work for a living like anyone else. Mostly she seemed to take the fact that Maddie was a Negro in stride and never mentioned it. After listening to Jimmy and Woody's irritating opinions, that was a relief.

Gerry was preoccupied with her thoughts and had a roaring

case of nerves, so it was only by accident she caught a whisper from somewhere behind her on the bus.

"Boy or girl. I don't know what. Do you?" A volley of giggles followed, and her ears burned.

This wasn't usual. Typically, Gerry walked to school since it wasn't far away. When she went out at night, she stayed in her neighborhood, and there she didn't seem to draw any notice unless it was by a tourist once in a while at Mona's, which was sort of a joke anyhow and didn't bother her. The memory of the night at the police station was painful, as was her interrogation by the navy investigators. She shoved those away as fast as they surfaced. The gigglers finally got off the bus.

She willfully shut off her attention to her surroundings to think about Maddie. She closed her eyes to focus on how she looked and, in her mind, replayed how she spoke in her soft Southern accent. And inevitably, this led to thinking of being with her in bed. Every scenario caused its share of pain.

Gerry also wondered if Maddie's family would be there. It was likely they would be. How was that going to go? After their last deeply embarrassing encounter, she didn't fancy talking with Maddie under Wilma Grace's disapproving eye. Gerry gave herself an imaginary kick in the butt. Thinking about Wilma Grace was a distraction. *Ask Maddie if we can go somewhere private so we can talk.*

Wilma Grace asked Maddie, "Do you think we ought to look for a bigger house before Mama gets here?"

Maddie wasn't in the mood to discuss the practicalities of their housing at that moment. She hadn't been able to figure out how she wanted to approach Gerry. She could call, but she wasn't sure that was the best way. She was in a state of nervous exhaustion and didn't know what to do. She was in a whole new stew of uncertainty both over Gerry and over Mama moving out to San Francisco.

Someone knocked on the door, and Wilma Grace looked at her. "You expecting company?"

"No," Maddie said, shortly.

"I suppose I'll get it then. I'm not either."

Wilma Grace opened the front door to reveal Gerry on the doorstep holding a bouquet of flowers and looking fearful.

After a huge beat of silence, Wilma Grace said nonchalantly, "Oh, hey there."

Then she turned to Maddie and said, unnecessarily, "It's for you."

"Hi, Maddie." Gerry looked neither cheerful nor confident. She appeared to expect she would have the door slammed in her face.

"You know, I believe I have to get on down to the PX and buy some soap," Wilma Grace said.

They didn't need soap, but Maddie was again grateful for Wilma Grace's changed attitude.

"Hi," Gerry said with a weak smile. They stared at one another.

They waited until Wilma Grace had picked up her purse and her coat and left.

Maddie indicated a chair. "Have a seat."

"I brought you these," Gerry said and thrust the flowers at her.

"Thanks." Maddie did nothing but take the bouquet and drop it in the sink.

Gerry cleared her throat and said, "If I could have called you, I would have, but since I couldn't, I decided to show up here and hope for the best."

"It's fine," Maddie said neutrally. "I wanted to talk to you anyhow."

"You did?"

"Uh-huh. I got some news."

"You do?" Gerry's eyes widened.

"But before I go into all that, you need to talk. I see you brought me some flowers. Is that to apologize and, if so, for what, exactly?"

She didn't want her voice to sound so cold, but she couldn't help it. Instead of seeing the flowers as a tender gesture, she was thinking of them as some way to soothe her before Gerry gave her some fake apologies and vague explanations.

Gerry shuffled her feet a bit and swallowed. Her hands, clasped before her on the table, looked like they were trembling.

"I wanted to bring you something nice. I've never brought you flowers before. I don't want to apologize. I've done nothing I need to apologize *for*, as far as I can tell. What you saw the other night isn't what it might look like." Gerry's eyes drilled into her. Maddie stared right back at her. Gerry didn't look sorry for anything, but she did seem uncertain and like she was begging.

"Go ahead. Keep talking," Maddie said. "Who was that you were with? She looked pretty cozy. You both did."

"Her name is Pamela. She was helping me get home from Mona's because I drank too much. That's all."

Maddie didn't know what to say so she stayed quiet, jaw clenched, thinking. Gerry had been inconsiderate, but she'd never seemed to be unfaithful, though they'd been separated so much. Who knew what she'd really been up to? But those thoughts were uncalled for and unkind.

Into the silence, Gerry said, with a touch of anger, "I hadn't heard from you or seen you for weeks. I was in a bad way. I met Pamela, and we were drinking and talking. I told her all about you, including the fact that you might be leaving, probably forever. She was so nice to me. You know someone else could have tried to take advantage of me being so sad, but she didn't. She looked after me."

Her meaning was clear. Maddie *hadn't* looked after her. That, she supposed, was true. She'd been so guilty and so upset about leaving Gerry, she hadn't really had room in her heart or her mind to think of what Gerry might need. Instead, she'd disappeared, leaving a space for someone like Pamela to slide into. But had they slept together? Gerry said they hadn't. Maddie could choose to believe her.

Gerry hadn't budged from her position, and she was really still and quiet, waiting.

Maddie kept looking at her, but she didn't change her expression.

"I love you so much," Gerry said, softly. "I don't think it's possible for one woman to love someone as much as I love you. Are you going to leave me and leave San Francisco? Please just tell me. I need to know. I'm sorry I didn't say it like that before."

"No. I'm not going to leave. Mama's going to come live here."

Gerry slumped over and took a deep, relieved breath. "Thank God."

"She took some convincing, but she's moving here from Arkansas to live with us. Wilma Grace actually helped me talk her into it."

"I'll be darned."

"Yeah. She and Thom decided to stay in San Francisco, and she told Mama the whole family ought to be together. That was after I told Mama about you."

"You told her about me?" Gerry paled. "Why did you do that?"

"I had to give her a reason why I didn't want to come back to Sawyer. You're the reason."

"I am?"

"Yes, you silly thing. You are. I was coming over to your place to tell you I'm staying. But then I saw you with, eh, Pamela, and it completely threw me off."

"Wow. You don't think I cheated on you, do you? I could never do that."

Maddie made sure her expression was soft and loving. "No. I don't think that now. And I'm sorry I left you in the dark about what I wanted to do for so long. I didn't want to say anything in case I couldn't convince Mama that changing our plans was a good idea. I didn't want you to get your hopes up. And I didn't want to get *my* hopes up, in case. I'm so sorry."

"Well, I forgive you. Can we just leave this all behind us, please, and go forward?"

At that, all of Maddie's fear and distrust melted away. She reached across the table to take Gerry's hand. With their hands clasped, they stood at the same time and fell into each other's arms and kissed tenderly.

"Oh my God. I'm so relieved, and I'm so happy you're staying here."

Maddie kissed Gerry's cheeks and then her lips again. "Nothing and nobody's going to ever bust us up."

Gerry hugged her tighter. "Gosh, you feel so good." She ran her hands up and down Maddie's back.

There was a knock on the door, and they froze, then fell apart out of habit.

The door cracked. "Can I come in?" It was Wilma Grace.

"Sure," Maddie said.

She crossed the threshold and then stood still. "Hi, Gerry."

"Hi, Wilma Grace. How're you doing?" Gerry pitched her voice to be cheerful and even.

Considering what happened the last time Gerry encountered her, Wilma Grace was surprisingly unconcerned. "Fine and dandy. Yourself?"

This was like some kind of miracle from God. It gave Maddie hope that when Mama arrived, things might proceed smoothly, especially the part where Maddie would tell Mama she would be living with Gerry and not with the family. She was going to have to take it slow and careful. First thing would be for Mama to meet Gerry. Lord, she hoped Mama wouldn't have a fit because she was White, but she had no idea *what* would happen. She hoped Wilma Grace would be available for reinforcement.

"How about some tea?" Wilma Grace asked cheerfully.

"I could go for a cup." Gerry grinned, first at Maddie and then at Wilma Grace.

The three of the settled down at the kitchen table and had a regular old gabfest like normal folks, and Maddie thought she might expire from sheer happiness.

After they drank their tea, Gerry stretched and said, "I have to be going. Thanks for the tea. Maddie? Will I see you later?" She raised her eyebrows playfully.

"Yeah. I'll be along soon, and you better be at home." She raised her eyebrows and then mock-frowned.

"You bet, and you can call me when you're ready to leave so's I know when to expect you. I've got a phone now. Let me write the number down."

Maddie grinned and nodded. "See you soon." She fondly watched as Gerry put on her jacket.

"See ya, Wilma Grace." Gerry waved cheerfully as she walked out the door.

❖

Maddie couldn't stop kissing Gerry in happiness and in gratitude. They touched endlessly. Maddie was careful to not touch Gerry where she'd always said not to, though she wanted to so much, especially now.

As they lay together afterward, Maddie spoke up, no longer able to be silent. "Do you think when we live together, I could..." She was too shy to spell it out.

Gerry obviously knew what she meant because she sighed, deeply. "I can't, honey. I've told you."

Maddie propped herself up on her arm to look Gerry in the eye. "But you never said why."

Gerry shifted and sighed again. "Because it's not right."

"Who says?" Maddie made sure she didn't speak angrily, but she still thought it was a fair question.

"Everyone. I don't know. It's just how it is." She blew out a frustrated breath.

"But how come?"

"I don't know. Honey, I don't want to talk about it. Not now. We just got back together. I want to enjoy it."

Maddie rolled over on her back, hiding her frustration. It was infuriating. She wanted to touch Gerry so bad, it hurt. But she couldn't or, more exactly, she wasn't allowed to.

❖

Gerry sat across from Pamela in Mona's on an early Thursday evening a few days after getting back with Maddie. She raised her glass. "All's well. We made up, and she's staying in the City. Her mom's moving out here."

"That's that, then. Congratulations to you both."

Gerry gulped a huge mouthful of her vodka tonic. "I get out of school next month, and then I can get a real job. All these car dealerships are opening on Van Ness Avenue, and I want to work for one of them."

"Here's to you for finishing school then and best of luck for the future."

"Maddie's going to work for the government in the tax office."

"That's outstanding. As an employee of the British government, I can tell you those positions are secure and come with benefits. I assume the same is true of the US."

"Yeah. I think so." Gerry tapped her fingers on the table.

"You seem a little distracted, my friend. Just a moment ago you were all smiles."

Gerry sighed. "I know, I know. Things are looking up."

"But?" Pamela looked at her.

"For one thing, I may have to meet Maddie's mother. She's real close to her mom, and they haven't seen one other in years. I want her to move in with me, and I haven't asked her about that yet."

"One thing you do not want to do is get on the wrong side of anyone's mother. Especially not the mother of the love of your life. She's going to know about you, yes?"

Gerry frowned. "Yeah. She does know. Maddie had to tell her."

"Well, that's all to the good. You won't be a surprise. When you meet her, you will merely have to be your charming self, and I'm sure it will be fine."

"How do you know for sure?" Gerry was skeptical of Pamela's certainty.

"My dear friend, I may be unencumbered with a girlfriend at the moment, but this wasn't always so. Before I left London to take the position in the San Francisco consulate, I was involved with a girl, and her parents were aware of her, shall we say, interest. I went with her to family events. They never said a thing to me, and I'm not sure of what she told them, but I went along, chatted up the mum and dad and brother, and we all got along famously. It's not impossible."

"I guess," Gerry said, though she wasn't sure.

"Oh, cheer up, mate." Pamela signaled the bartender to bring them fresh drinks.

"I'll try." But she said no more.

"And what else is troubling you?" Pamela asked, severely. "My word, Americans are all overly optimistic and always in good moods until they are not, and then they act like it's the proverbial end of the world."

"God. Are you a mind reader? And how come you get to generalize about Americans?"

"I work with Americans at the consulate, and before I decided to try Mona's 440 Club, I went to a few other bars and talked to the girls. And no, I'm not a mind reader, but if you are not smiling and joking with me, something is the matter with you. I know you a bit, and I can see you're not in a good mood. If you don't wish to tell me what's bothering you, I understand. But please don't be a wet blanket. I won't abide that. We are here for enjoyment. Is it about Maddie?"

Gerry thought swiftly. It was embarrassing, but who else was she going to talk to? How was she going to solve her problem all by herself?

Gerry shifted in her chair uneasily. "Yeah, it's about Maddie. She, er, is not willing to go along completely with the, uh...Jesus, I may as well say it."

"Yes, please do." Pamela grinned. She was certainly not going to let her off the hook. She was a good person. Kind and compassionate and smart too. But no-nonsense.

"When we're intimate, I'm the one doing the work, if you know what I mean."

"Yes. You're the butch, and you know what's expected of you."

"Right. It's how I was taught. But Maddie wants, ahem, more of a part."

"I see. More of a part in *your* pleasure? And you aren't sure you want to go along with that?"

"I'm not. I don't think it will feel right."

"But you haven't tried it?"

Gerry looked away and then back at Pamela, "No. I haven't."

"Then how do you know?"

"I guess I don't." Gerry sagged.

"What am I? Butch or femme?" Pamela asked.

"Uh. I don't know, come to think of it."

Pamela was wearing tailored slacks and a blouse that seemed to be femme. Her light-reddish-brown hair was middle length and ended at her shoulders. It was well cut but not styled at all, merely parted in in the middle. Her air of brisk self-assurance seemed butch, but then again...Gerry really didn't know, and since she wasn't planning to date Pamela, it didn't seem to matter.

"That's right. I don't want to be one or the other. I've received a lot of questions and some pointed criticism of the 'you have to choose a side' variety, both back in London and here in the US, but I don't care."

She took a drag from her smoke and blew it out, smiling. Her hand was in her pocket, but she also held her cigarette in what Gerry considered a femme manner.

"I'm not either, darling, and I like it that way. I don't give a fig for what other girls think."

The way Pamela called her "darling" charmed Gerry, but not in a sexy way. She kept looking at Gerry in a matter-of-fact manner, seeming to invite more questions.

"So when it comes to the bedroom...you are...?" Gerry was too shy to say it out loud.

"I can be both, either. I'm what's called *comme ci, comme ça.* Sometimes with the same woman and on the same night." She laughed. "Like this or like that is what that translates to."

"Holy smoke," Gerry said finally, attempting to picture what that might be like if she did that herself. With Maddie. It seemed too fantastical. Also, the thought of not being in control terrified her.

"Maddie wants a more active role in bed, I expect."

"I take care of myself," Gerry said firmly. "That's what I'm supposed to do. I get my kicks from taking care of my girl."

"And who says it has to be that way?"

"Everybody," Gerry said automatically. "It's expected."

"Hmm. Well, I suspect neither of those things is totally true. Let me tell you a little about me."

Gerry nodded eagerly. Even if she found the topic embarrassing, she wanted to hear what Pamela would say. Her air of experience and the way she talked made it seem like she knew things. Gerry had to figure this dilemma out, or she was going either lose Maddie, or she would stay unhappy. She likely would never let the subject completely drop as well. Gerry wanted to give Maddie what she wanted, whatever that was.

"Well, I may go out on an evening dressed much like I am now. I look around, and I see who I fancy. It's somewhat of a sixth sense I have, but I can see a woman, and based on her behavior and not so much her clothes, I make a choice. Sometimes someone's clothes don't tell the story. I once bedded a butch who was so masculine, she could pass for a man anywhere. But once we were in bed, I took over, and she didn't make so much as a squeak of protest." Pamela took a sip of her drink and grinned, clearly remembering. "Her squeaks were of an entirely different nature, I assure you."

"Wow." Gerry couldn't think of much else to say. What would it be like? She couldn't picture it. Her teacher Pauline had never mentioned the possibility, and Woody had told her she was the butch and would be expected to be in charge because that was how it was done. Here was Pamela suggesting something completely different. Maybe Woody wasn't right about this. She'd gotten over thinking Woody was the source of all knowledge.

"How do you get off?" Pamela asked.

This question caught Gerry by surprise, but she took her time to come up with a good answer.

"When I'm doing it, her pleasure is mine."

"That's lovely, but that's not the only way."

"It's the way I am," Gerry said and crossed her arms.

"Of course, my friend, but there are other ways of doing it."

"For you maybe. But not me."

"Well, you may be destined for heartbreak if you won't bend a bit."

That could be true. It seemed like Maddie had made up her mind, and if so, she wasn't going to be talked out of what she wanted. But first things first. Maddie seemed poised to move in with her, and until that was done, she was happy to wait for any other major changes.

❖

Mama looked older than she had when Maddie and Thom had left Arkansas four years earlier. Her back was more bent, and she looked tired.

When they brought her back to the house in Hunters Point, it seemed like she didn't want to do anything but sleep. The train trip had been draining, she said.

Wilma Grace said, "She's left the only place she's ever known, and even if she's here with us, it's still got to be a shock. No wonder she's dog tired. Leave her be."

That was rich, Wilma Grace telling Maddie to leave something or someone be, but Maddie had to agree. As much as she wanted to fuss over Mama and ask her questions, she backed off. Of course, for the time being, she was content to set aside the whole problem of Gerry and who she was and what was going to happen if and when she and Mama met.

Because of the tiny house, Maddie had a good excuse to stay with Gerry so Mama could sleep in her room. But this arrangement could last only so long. Gerry wanted her to move in with her, and Wilma Grace and Thom were looking for a bigger home, one that would be comfortable for all of them. Maddie hadn't said anything about that one way or another, and she surely would have to at some point, because it was a question of what they could afford versus what amount of space they needed. But she wasn't ready to have the discussion with her family. It was a good bet that *someone* was going to end up sore, no matter what she decided.

"How you feeling, Mama?" Maddie asked her three days after her arrival. Mama had actually gotten up and had breakfast with them. Maddie was still at home all day since her new job wouldn't start until the next week. She was grateful to have the time to spend with her mama, even with the decision about where she was going to live hanging over her head.

"Oh, so-so, I guess. Three days on a train didn't do me no good. But it's wonderful to be here with y'all."

"We're so happy you're here."

"Where you staying at night, girl?" Mama asked all of a sudden.

"Uh, with my...friend Gerry. I told you about her." Maddie's throat closed.

"Yes, honey, you did." Mama's tone was neutral.

"You wouldn't have a bed to sleep in if I was here," Maddie reminded her.

"I see that. But you, Wilma Grace, and Thom, you're looking for a bigger house, he told me?"

"Yep. That's what we're doing." *I can't tell her yet that I might not live there with her. That would break her heart.*

"I miss you being close by when I'm here more than I missed you when I was back in Sawyer and you were out here."

"I know, Mama. It's hard on me too, but it's so you can be comfortable. We'll move as soon as we can."

"I know, honey. I'm impatient."

"When we have enough space, you and I have to start getting organized and set up for you to do your sewing and sell all your goods."

"I can't wait for that, Maddie. I been dreaming of that for the last three years."

"We're going to do it, Mama. I swear. I've got to go now. I'll be back tomorrow."

"But where are you going?" Mama asked, obviously dismayed.

"To see a friend. I'll be back tomorrow," Maddie said a little desperately.

"The one you talked about? Gerry?"

"Yes. That's the one." Maddie put on a bright, unconcerned smile.

"If you have to, I suppose that's okay, but I just got here."

Maddie hugged her mama and repeated, "I know, but I'll be back tomorrow. Wilma Grace and Thom'll be home soon. You won't be alone."

"I was alone for years, and I did just fine. It won't kill me," Mama said acidly.

"Bye, Mama." Maddie kissed her cheek and raced out the door so she wouldn't miss the bus or have to look at Mama's sad face longer than she needed to.

During the bus ride, Maddie brooded. She'd thought that once she and Gerry had made up, all would be well. She also figured it would be great once Mama arrived in San Francisco. And it was. It was such a joy to see her and be able to hug her and talk to her again. But Maddie hadn't reckoned that she would still be peeved at Gerry's stubbornness regarding their sex life. And it hadn't occurred to her that once Mama was actually in her life once again, she'd be in an emotional tug of war between Mama and Gerry, who were two competing but equally vital forces.

Ironically enough, she and Gerry were able to spend more time together since they were both about to start brand-new jobs but had no work to have to show up to at that moment. Well, Maddie also wanted to be with Mama. She'd decided that a discussion with Gerry, probably while they were in bed, was the right way to approach the dilemma. Gerry had to understand that Maddie was trying to balance her and Mama.

She ran up the stairs to Gerry's flat, and when Gerry answered her knock, they flung their arms around one another and then kissed passionately.

"I'm so happy you're here. This is like a dream. You can stay all night."

"We're not going to the bar tonight, are we?" Maddie asked suspiciously.

"No. We're going out to eat, but otherwise we'll stay here. Come in, come in." They were at the threshold, and Gerry had said she didn't want any of the neighbors spying on them.

Gerry picked up Maddie's overnight bag and took it to the bedroom. "Sit down, love, and get comfortable. How about an iced tea? I made some this morning."

Maddie settled on the couch and took a breath.

Gerry came back with her tea and flopped down on the couch, put her arm around Maddie, and pulled her close, kissing her head. "How are you doing? How's Mama?"

"Mama's good." Maddie stroked Gerry's linen-trousered leg. "Are these new?"

Gerry turned Maddie's head toward her and kissed her mouth. "Yeah. I bought 'em last week. Hmm. You smell good. You feel good. I missed you so much."

Maddie kissed her back, feeling guilty. She'd been so focused on Mama's arrival and making sure she was okay, she hadn't thought as much as usual about Gerry and what she might be doing. Or thinking. Or feeling. And at that moment, the last conversation with her mama and Mama's expression when Maddie said she was leaving floated through her mind.

"I missed you too, but I was just gone a few hours." It was only partially a lie.

Gerry kissed her again and touched her cheek. "We wouldn't miss each other if we were together all the time."

"When we're working again, we won't be together all the time either."

Gerry kissed her even more insistently. "But it'll be different. We can come home and be together. Do you know when you can move in with me?"

Maddie felt worse than ever and jumped up off the couch and went to the window. She felt Gerry behind her and then Gerry's hands on her shoulders.

"I don't want to upset you. I'm just telling the truth. You said you'd move in with me."

Maddie took a breath to try to calm herself, but it didn't work very well. "I did say that. But I can't think about it right now. Mama got here only a couple of days ago, and I can't tell her I'm leaving right away. She was sad when I left this afternoon to come over here."

Gerry took her hands away, and as Maddie turned around, she walked to the kitchen and began to wipe down the counter absentmindedly.

"Ger, honey. Don't be mad. I'll move in. Soon. I have to talk to Mama, get her used to you and…us. I got to spend some more time with her."

"You want me to meet her?"

That idea sent a stab of fear through Maddie. "Maybe, but not yet. I have to…prepare her."

"All right." Gerry didn't seem to agree with her. She only sounded resigned.

When they were in bed later, Maddie remembered her *other* dilemma with Gerry. It didn't seem like the time to try to do anything about it. Not until the Mama situation was fixed.

She didn't know how long that would take or if it could be fixed. In the meantime, how would she handle Gerry and Mama?

❖

When Maddie showed up to work at City Hall in downtown San Francisco, it was a relief in more ways than one. It let her stop thinking about Mama and Gerry for almost eight hours because she had to concentrate to learn her new work. She was thankful it was indoors and had nothing physical about it. It was a question of reading and sorting tax forms and checking them for completeness. If they were incomplete, and many were, she had to call the taxpayer or write them to request the missing information.

A number of Colored girls worked in the tax office, and seemingly many in other government departments as well. Maddie was grateful because she didn't have to worry so much about not fitting in. She just wished that was the only thing she had to worry about.

Mama was restless, even though she didn't have anything to be concerned about. Thom and Wilma Grace were still searching for a new house, looking at two- and three-bedroom places. Maddie said she wasn't sure if she was going to live with them, and Maddie and her mama had begun to plan their new sewing business. One of their biggest dilemmas was where Mama could work. She wanted to quilt as well as make garments, and that required space, which the house-hunting had to take into account. They were faced with a million other details, but all Mama wanted to talk about was Maddie and what her plans were. What Mama wanted to get at, without actually coming right out and saying so, was Maddie's relationship with Gerry and whether or not Maddie was going to live with the family or with Gerry.

Maddie couldn't make up her mind, so she avoided talking about it. Mama sensed her reluctance, and every time Maddie spent the night with Gerry, Mama had something to say.

"You off again? Child, I don't see why you can't spend time with your family when you're not at work."

Maddie told Mama, "I promised Gerry we'd have supper together. She has to work during the day too, so we can't see each other very much." She tried to keep from sounding angry or pleading, but it was almost impossible.

"Well, go have supper. Then you can come home," Mama said firmly. She definitely didn't want to bring up the fact that Maddie was spending the night at Gerry's flat, because that would make the nature of their relationship too obvious. Mama had settled uneasily into an opinion that Maddie and Gerry were friends of a sort. She didn't even lobby Maddie to bring Gerry around to meet her and join them for a meal at home, something she would have insisted on if Maddie was seeing a young man. Maddie sighed silently every time Mama brought up the subject of her time and who she spent it with.

Maddie told Gerry, "I have to stick around home this week. Mama has been buying up some fabric and other stuff she wants to show me and talk about what she's going to do."

Whenever Maddie said she had to spend time with her mama, Gerry's face would cloud. Maddie could see the obvious struggle she was going through to not get angry, not insist on Maddie doing what *she* wanted her to.

"I'm trying to be patient, sweetie pie, but it's not easy. I feel like we're stuck in limbo and nothing's going to change."

"Just hang on, Gerry, honey. It'll be better once Wilma Grace and Thom find a place to move and we can get Mama settled."

What Maddie didn't tell Gerry was that she kept making noncommittal answers to Mama's regular questions about her plans. She wasn't about to tell Mama she was moving in with Gerry, at least not until she had to, whenever that moment finally arrived. And she was going to put it off as long as she possibly could.

CHAPTER SEVENTEEN

January 1947

Wilma Grace said, "Can you eat supper with us tonight? I want to talk about the house hunting."

Maddie said, "Sure. I can be here."

That night they sat down to a supper of gumbo and cornbread.

"What's the news?" Mama asked as soon as they'd said grace.

"Well. It's like this. We can't afford no three-bedroom place unless Maddie comes along."

Maddie wanted to sink into the floor right then. Wilma Grace's tendency to just jump right in was going to cause a huge problem once again.

"What do you mean, Wilma Grace? Maddie's moving along with the rest of us," Mama said in her familiar "it's decided" tone.

Maddie wilted under Mama's stern expression. Wilma Grace raised her eyebrows and kept silent to let Maddie explain.

"I'm going to stay with Gerry," Maddie said, knowing she couldn't say it any other way to make it any easier.

"Lord, honey. Why would you do that? I came all the way out here to be with y'all, but now you're saying you're going to be somewhere else."

"I won't be far away, Mama. I'll be downtown. I'll see you all the time." That likely wasn't true, but Maddie had to think of something to reassure her.

Mama wasn't having it. She was usually calm, but she was clearly very upset this time. *I should have told her in private I was moving in with Gerry before now, but I didn't because I'm such a coward.*

"You let me think everything was going to go one way, and now you tell me it's another." With that, she stood up, threw her napkin on the table, and, leaving her largely untouched supper, stalked up the stairs and slammed the bedroom door shut.

"Thanks a lot," Maddie said, unreasonably angry with Wilma Grace. Of course, Thom didn't say anything but kept right on eating his gumbo as though nothing unusual had happened.

Wilma Grace said, calmly, "Hey, don't be blaming me. It was up to you to tell your mama what you were going to do, but you didn't."

"Okay, okay. I'll go talk to her."

She knocked on the bedroom door. *Her* bedroom, she noted. Not hearing anything, she went in.

Mama lay face down on the bed, crying softly, which made Maddie feel horrible.

"I'm sorry, Mama." She sat down on the edge of the bed.

"Sorry isn't good enough, Maddie."

"No. I know it's not. Mama, can you look at me while we talk?"

Mama turned a tear-stained face toward her.

Maddie took her hand between hers and took a deep breath. "You know I love you, don't you?" She rubbed Mama's hand as she talked. "I told you over the phone about Gerry. I didn't do a good job explaining, and I'm going to try again so maybe you can understand a little better."

Mama just stared at her without saying anything.

"When I met Gerry, I didn't understand her. I got to know her over time, and I realized I'd never felt like this about anyone. I really love her, and she loves me. I can't say it any plainer than that. I want to live with her. She wants me to live with her too."

"She's a woman."

Maddie smiled. "That's true. But she's a good person."

"But I'm your mama."

"That's true too." Maddie smiled. "You always will be. Nothing will ever change that. But I have someone I love, and I want to be with her." She squeezed Mama's hand again.

Mama sighed and looked at the ceiling, perhaps thinking God would write her a message there. "I suppose it's the same as if you was to marry."

"Pretty close."

"Well. I reckon you're gonna do what you're going to do. I always raised you to be independent and think for yourself."

"Well, I'd like to have your blessing, but if not that, your acceptance."

Mama was silent for a long time.

Finally, she said, "I can't deny you nothing, girl. I let you go far away from me 'cause I knew it would be good for you. I guess I have to believe this is good for you too."

"I think it is. I think you'll like her. Thom and Wilma Grace like her." This was true even if it was a little more complicated than Maddie let on. *What's Mama going to say when she finds out Gerry is White?*

"Hmph. Thom don't care about nothing but peace and quiet in his home and three squares. But Wilma Grace? Hmm. That's a surprise."

Maddie laughed. "Wilma Grace is a might pickier about things." It was good to share a little private joke about Wilma Grace with her mama.

Mama snickered. "Lord, yes, but she seems different, just like you seem different. I have to get used to the both of you. *I* know this isn't Sawyer, and we don't have that old Jim Crow nonsense hanging over us anymore. I'm grateful for that."

"I think it was Wilma Grace having to be at the shipyard with all sorts of folks and all the newness here on the West Coast and all that. She's had to grow up some. We all have."

"I can see that."

"So you all right now, Mama?" Maddie rubbed her shoulder.

"I suppose. San Fran isn't Sawyer, and I guess I can cope with the fact that you're not going to get married and give me grandchildren. I'll have to speak to Thom and Wilma Grace about that."

Maddie laughed. "Mama, some things here are almost the same as in Sawyer. Good things. There's the church and the social clubs. You'll see. We can have a good time like we did back home with all of us together. Folks still help each other. You can make your nice clothes and maybe quilts, and people will buy them. I know they will. You'll like it here, Mama."

Mama said, "I expect I will eventually. I can already tell the air here's lighter."

Maddie laughed. Mama wasn't only talking about the absence of heat and humidity.

❖

The day Maddie brought over her things to Gerry's flat, Gerry had never looked so proud and happy. On her first official day there, Maddie cooked them a dinner of pork chops and macaroni and cheese, and Gerry couldn't stop praising it.

"You're exaggerating a mite. I'm not that good a cook."

"But you are, sweetheart. I've never tasted anything like this macaroni and cheese."

Maddie giggled and finally said, "It's probably because you been eating diner food so much. Anything home-cooked tastes so much better."

"I guess that's true. But can't I still say you're a great cook?"

"Yes. You can." Maddie moved out of her chair to sit on Gerry's lap, and Gerry forked a chunk of pork chop and fed her.

"Hmm. That's good. If I do say so myself," Maddie said.

"You can say it." Gerry kissed her neck and held her tighter.

"You want to go over to Mona's later?" Her words were muffled in Maddie's neck.

Maddie stiffened and Gerry asked, "What's wrong?"

Maddie couldn't help squirming a little. "Can we go on special occasions but not all the time?"

"What else do you want to do?"

"Go to the movies? Listen to the radio?"

"I like to see my friends," Gerry said, and she sounded a little put out.

"That's just it. They're *your* friends. Not my friends."

Gerry's roving hands had stopped, though she still held Maddie in a loose embrace.

"They could be your friends too, honey."

"I know but…I'm not sure of how to put this. I don't feel like I'm one of the gang."

"'Cause you're Colored?" Gerry asked, and Maddie was impressed that Gerry understood that point and upset that it confirmed her fears.

"Uh, yeah."

"No one's been mean to you that I know of," Gerry said. "If they were, I'd tell 'em a thing or two." Gerry being tough was usually very cute, but not this time.

"It's not that anyone's mean. They kind of don't see me. It's like I'm invisible."

"What about you and Trixie and Sandy after you had to come bail us out of jail?"

This time, Maddie was squirming on Gerry's lap because *she* didn't know what to say.

"Uh. They're okay."

"But you haven't really given them a chance, have you?"

"No," Maddie admitted finally.

"What about Pamela?"

"Well, I'm not sure about her because, you know, she and you, y'all are kind of..."

"All she did was take care of me when I drank too much. I really like her 'cause she's smart, and she's nothing like anyone I ever met. I bet if you gave her a chance, you and her could be friends."

Maddie jumped off Gerry's lap and took their plates to the sink so she could have a minute to think. Gerry was right that she had to give Pamela a chance. She was mainly irked that Pamela had taken care of Gerry instead of her, even though she hadn't been anywhere around. It would be different now that they lived together. It was true that they ought to have friends. Maddie was suspicious of the bar and its customers. It didn't seem right. Where she came from, socializing meant going to people's homes or a church event. Come to think of it, she had to find a way to keep a connection to the Hunters Point community. She figured it would be via Mama, Thom, and Wilma Grace. Gerry probably wouldn't want any part of it and would stick out like a sore thumb there anyhow. She was going to have a strict separation between the two parts of her life. And there was still the matter of Gerry and Mama meeting.

"I'll give them a chance like you're asking me to. I'm not too optimistic though. I don't think any of them have ever met any Colored people." Their shared adventure when Gerry, Woody, and Jake had been arrested seemed like it would have made the other femmes a little less strange, but Maddie didn't feel like it had. Of course, she hadn't been around the bar much to merely sit and converse and socialize, so that didn't help. When she was out with Gerry, her shyness didn't make things any easier.

"Maybe not. Probably not. But now they're meeting you, so it's a start," Gerry said reasonably. "What do you say? We'll just have a couple drinks and then come back here and..."

She raised her eyebrows mischievously. Maddie understood what she meant, but she had misgivings about trying once again to change Gerry's mind, even though last time, Gerry seemed like she might be ready to try something new. Maybe. Maddie didn't want anything to spoil their first actual night living together. She sighed but kissed Gerry's cheek and said, "I'll do the dishes, and then we'll get ready and go out for a bit. And how about you invite Pamela over, and I'll cook us dinner, and we can sit and eat together like normal people, and Pamela and I can get to know each other."

Gerry's eyes widened and she beamed. "Honey, that's a great idea."

Maddie kissed her, then paused. "I want you to meet my mama."

Gerry stiffened. "Are you ready for that?"

"I don't know if I am or not, but it's got to happen. Don't be scared. You said you wanted to," Maddie said with more assurance than she felt.

Gerry squeezed her tight. "Okay."

As Gerry combed and Brylcreemed her hair, she secretly looked at Maddie, speculating and thinking about what Pamela had said. It wasn't as though anyone needed to know about their private life. Therefore, without knowing, no one could make a comment, especially Woody, the original source of her "education." She hadn't seen Woody for some time, so maybe it was all beside the point. What was important was for Maddie to be happy. She took a final look at her hair and straightened her collar just so over the lapels of her jacket.

Maddie wore a simple sheath dress, bright-red lipstick, and flat shoes. She'd curled her hair in a neat pageboy, and they were ready to go.

Inside the door of Mona's was a new doorman.

"Hi, Jimmy. What are you doing here? How the hell are ya? You remember Maddie?"

He took their cover charge, shook hands with Gerry, and kissed Maddie on the cheek, causing her to blush.

"I sure do. You look like a dish of chocolate ice cream, Miss Maddie. I needed a job because George was tired of supporting me. With my scintillating personality, this one is a breeze. Mona hired me right away after her other guy decamped to LA. Have a good time, girls. I'll come say hi on my break." He turned away and asked, "Who's next?"

Maddie hooked her hand under Gerry's arm, and they strode into the main bar. Howie the bartender waved, and right off, Gerry spied

Pamela at a table near the center of the room with Woody, Sandy, Jake, and Trixie. Pamela waved them over.

"Hello, you two. You look swell. I'm picking up American slang. What do you think?" Pamela waved her cigarette.

Gerry laughed. "You're never going to sound American. But that doesn't matter. You sound good when you talk British. Sophisticated. What do you think, Maddie? About Pam's accent?"

Maddie looked taken aback by Gerry's question, but she grinned gamely. "I like it. Sounds fancy."

"La-ti-da," Sandy said, like it was a joke or maybe not. Jake and Trixie snickered. Pamela ignored them and focused on Gerry and Maddie.

"So you're flatmates now?" Pamela asked.

"Yep." Gerry put an arm around Maddie proudly.

"Well done. Here's to your happiness." She raised her glass and gave Gerry a secret little knowing smile that Gerry understood, but no one else would.

Gerry turned and looked fondly at Maddie. "It's a dream come true. I've got everything I ever wanted. I'm working at the Cadillac dealership, and I'm with the best girl in the world."

"Hear, hear," Woody said. "That's all any of us ever need. That and good pals to share a laugh and a drink." All seven of them raised their glasses and murmured their agreement.

"After what happened to you three, I imagine this feels like the peak of joy," Pamela said, drily. Gerry had told her the story of their arrest when they'd first met.

Woody shook her head. "Man, I don't ever want to think about all that again. What about you, Ger?"

"I try not to," Gerry said, not adding that flashes of memory tended to pop up at odd times and catch her unawares. The same thing happened with the memories of her questioning by the navy investigators. She wanted all these memories to go away because they were too painful.

There was an awkward break in the conversation.

"Did anyone ever think that none of what happened to Gerry and Woody is right? I mean, we're human beings, aren't we? We're as good as anyone else." All eyes swiveled to focus on Maddie, and she seemed to shrink a bit under the scrutiny.

Gerry looked at her with new interest and thought about some of the things Maddie said in private to her. "Go ahead, honey. Tell them some more."

"Well. Like Colored folks get treated bad, especially where I came from. Why? 'Cause we're Colored is all." The group, except for Pamela, looked uneasy and stayed silent.

Pamela said, "Yes. It's a shameful way to treat people. And only because they're dark-skinned. Really. It's ridiculous."

Maddie spoke just above a whisper. "It's much more than that. It's cruel. I got an idea how much it mattered when I went to work on the ships. I coulda never got a job like that in Arkansas, but we worked alongside everyone else because of the war because President Roosevelt said so. We did the work, same as everybody, and we helped the war effort just like everybody else."

Gerry squeezed Maddie's shoulders to encourage her.

"Quite so," Pamela said, nodding. "Your government had to use everyone it could. It couldn't afford to turn down help."

"That's right," Gerry said. "I did my part. I was proud to be in the navy. I gave it everything I had."

Jake said, "Ha! And look how they thanked you. By booting you and trying to take away what they owed you."

"Yeah." Gerry remembered once more how that felt. "But at least I got 'em to change their minds."

"What if more people did what you did?" Pamela asked.

"Jimmy Price did it. He's the one who gave me the idea," Gerry said.

"Yes, but if enough of you made a stink about it, the navy might have to change its mind."

"They might, but it would take a lot to make them do that. They're…well, they're the navy. They have their rules. They love all their rules." Gerry shrugged. "I got lucky."

"Like the police have their rules, the ones that let them treat women awful just 'cause they're in a gay bar," Trixie said. She didn't ever say much when they were out, so it was a surprise that she spoke up. Jake didn't look especially pleased Trixie had said something.

"Yes. That's right," Pamela said. "More completely arbitrary rules. Who says gay people have to be mistreated as a matter of course? It's barbaric." She took a big gulp of her drink.

"Well, we're not normal, and that scares people," Jake said.

"Darling, we may not be normal, but we're not animals. We're humans," Pamela said, icily.

"Don't get cheesed off at me," Jake said. "I didn't make the rules."

"Pardon. I didn't mean any of it was your fault. I was merely making the point that it's not fair we're mistreated because we're different. I think it would be dandy if we were merely let alone to live our lives as we see fit."

Trixie said, "Right. We're not hurting anyone."

Gerry followed the back-and-forth. She remembered all the lessons she had from Woody and Jimmy about how to get by in the navy and how to *not* get in trouble. She'd ended up in trouble anyhow.

"Yet," Pamela said. "We have our own club here, and still we are subject to the whims of the powers that be in San Francisco. Any moment, constables can burst through that door and scoop up all and sundry and put them in the pokey. And worse." She looked right at Gerry.

Woody asked, "What are constables?"

"Officers of the law."

Jake rolled her eyes and shrugged. "Oh, well, that's how it goes. Bad luck, off night. You name it. We can't do anything about it."

Trixie said, "But honey, how come we don't get to just go to a club and enjoy ourselves. Like everyone else?"

"Because that's how it is, that's why, and you don't know what you're talking about."

"Don't you talk to me like that. I've got a right to have my opinion." Trixie was good and mad now. Gerry had always felt like Jake tended to be more dictatorial than she ought to be. If Gerry ever talked like that to Maddie, she'd get a tongue-lashing she'd feel for days. Being the butch didn't mean thinking you were better than your girlfriend.

Pamela rapped on the table, and that stopped the argument abruptly. "Fighting amongst ourselves will guarantee we never get anywhere. We have so little to begin with. We best concentrate on making the most of what we have. Gerry here got an unfair discharge, but she was able to change that. How? She found someone to help, and she didn't get discouraged. It was important for her to try because her life depended on it. We can't ever think we are helpless. We're not. End of lecture."

Trixie gave Jake a meaningful stare, but Jake looked away.

❖

"What do you think about what Pamela said?" Gerry asked as they relaxed, close to sleep.

"She's probably right. No one gets anywhere saying or doing nothing. That means nothing will change."

"Seems like asking for a whole lot of trouble. What if we'd tried to complain about the cops after we were arrested? Where would that get us?"

"Probably arrested again." Maddie snuggled in closer, tired of talking. She'd once again chickened out on trying to make love to Gerry. They were living together now, so she wondered what would give her the jolt she needed and if, as before, she would be rejected.

❖

Maddie reckoned her mama's curiosity about Gerry would overcome her misgivings, and she was right. She decided to keep it simple and get Mama away from the house and Thom and Wilma Grace's hovering. They went to the social club at Hunters Point. It was never made clear that there was one for Colored employees and one for White, but everyone knew which one was which. It was just as well, since she didn't want Mama to be more uncomfortable than she was already going to be when she met Gerry. She prayed that Gerry's uncomplicated good nature would win out. It had worked with Thom and Wilma Grace.

They went through all the motions of finding a seat, and Maddie left Gerry and Mama alone together while she went to fetch their coffee. Gerry seemed to be unconcerned that she was the only White person in the club.

She returned to the table. They were, at least, talking. Better than if they sat in stony silence.

"Gerry was telling me about being in the navy," Mama said a bit over-brightly, betraying her nerves.

"Yes. She was out in the bay on Treasure Island."

"I think being by the ocean is grand," Mama said.

"So do I. I grew up a ways from here, in the Central Valley. No ocean."

"What did your people do?" Mama asked.

"We have a farm," Gerry said and described it. This had worked so well with Thom and Wilma Grace, Maddie had coached Gerry to talk about it with her mama.

The meeting seemed to go just fine. Mama wasn't as talkative as she normally would be, but Maddie wasn't disturbed. They'd met and gotten over that hump. She hoped, with time, it would feel less awkward with her mama and her girlfriend in the same room.

❖

Maddie dashed back and forth in their tiny kitchen as Gerry half watched her and half made efforts to tidy up. They'd invited Pamela over for supper, and Maddie was concerned the visit go well. Gerry seemed thrilled that finally someone she knew had made such a favorable impression on Maddie.

"Don't worry. I think Pamela will love anything you cook. *I* sure do."

"That's great, Gerry, but Pamela is different from your other friends." Gerry winced but didn't say anything.

"She sure is, but she's not snooty in spite of the way she talks."

"I know, but I still want this to turn out good."

"And it will. Oh, there she is."

When Gerry went downstairs to let her in, Maddie's mind raced both around the cooking of their supper and her plot to get a few minutes of private conversation with Pamela without Gerry being there to hear it.

Pamela appeared at the front door, closely followed by Gerry. She carried a bouquet of daisies.

"For the chef," she said and handed them to Maddie.

"Thank you. I see where Gerry got her idea to bring me flowers," she said with a grin.

"Ah, yes. Flowers are quite versatile in their uses."

"Gerry, honey. I just realized I forgot to buy a bottle of wine. Will you go down to the corner store and buy one?"

"Wine?" Gerry asked, clearly confused. They didn't drink when they had supper.

"I think it's a white wine. Is that right, Pamela?" Maddie asked.

"If we are having chicken or fish."

"Yes. Roast chicken."

"Then a dry white wine will be nice."

"Dry white," Gerry repeated. "I'll try to find that."

Once she left, without preamble, Maddie said, "I wanted to ask you something."

"My dear, I'm at your service." She sat at the kitchen table, lit a cigarette, and crossed her legs.

Maddie sensed Pamela would be the only one of their acquaintances who could best offer her advice without either laughing at her or spilling her secret to Gerry. Gerry had talked about how worldly Pamela was but also how compassionate. And Gerry had told her Pamela's stories about sexual encounters where she was sometimes the butch and sometimes not. Also, Gerry told those stories with approval.

Maddie had to fight her usual shyness and distrust but thought that if she couldn't change herself, she'd never change Gerry. She needed someone to at least give her a little advice. Pamela was her only hope.

"I need some help and thought you might be able to help me," Maddie said. She had had the help of a second cocktail to bolster her courage.

"If I'm able, I'd be happy to help you, but you'll have to make yourself plain." Pamela didn't say this at all unkindly, but she looked at Maddie shrewdly, her eyelids lowered.

"When Gerry and I, uh you know…" she said, cringing a little.

"I *do* know, I believe, what you are referring to." Pamela gave a small grin, but Maddie didn't take at as laughing at her. "Pray go on."

"Well. Sometimes, I, er, would like, um, to be the active partner. But Gerry, you know her, she's the sort to, eh, sort of want to always be in control."

"She's mentioned this subject to me, but I told her life is not always so black and white and that she was missing out on an experience I'm certain she'd enjoy."

"I think so too, but I have to find a way to start."

"To be sure." Pamela smiled kindly, but her eyes glittered with amusement. "Well, you know how she goes about the business. You can do the same. You aren't without agency."

"What do you mean?"

"I mean you are an individual who can act as she chooses. I say you ought to take Gerry in hand and begin by kissing her soundly and touching her the way you like to be touched. She may put up some resistance at first, but it will fall by the wayside. She will soon be enraptured and turn into putty in your hands. Have a little patience, and by all means don't allow yourself to be stopped. She's told me she's not averse to this." Pamela smoked some more, narrowing her eyes.

"Uh. Okay. I know what *I* like, so will she be the same?"

"You may have to experiment a bit, but she'll let you know. I recommend nothing too aggressive but do *not* hesitate. She who hesitates will be lost. You must establish yourself as the leader. When you do, Gerry will follow."

"Thanks, Pamela. I appreciate your help."

"It's nothing." She waved her cigarette. "You know what to do. I believe you just need encouragement."

At that precise moment, Gerry returned and held up the bottle of wine in triumph.

"What do you think?"

Pamela read the label. "This will do admirably. I'll open it so we may let it breathe. Do you have a corkscrew?"

Gerry and Maddie looked at each other. "We don't."

"Gerry, darling, I'm certain you have a pocketknife. Maddie, the chicken smells divine."

After Pamela had left with big kisses for each of them, almost a blessing of sorts, Maddie had said, "Leave the dishes. I want to go to bed. Now."

It felt odd, at first, but the longer it went on, the more she relaxed. It was Maddie, it was what Maddie wanted, and Gerry wanted Maddie to have what she wanted. They'd had enough white wine to be loose but not too drunk.

Stay calm. It'll be fine. Gerry coached herself silently in much the same way she had when faced with a challenge at work, such as a new repair she had to execute with her male classmates and her instructor looking on. She was able to stop thinking about it and allow it to happen. And to her surprise, the feeling in her body was remarkable. She had only experienced pleasure before in a shadowy or echoing way, first with Pauline, and then with Maddie. This was not the same. It was physical and intense. That was one thing. The other thing was the expression in Maddie's eyes and on her face. Gerry had never seen it before. Triumph. That was it. She was like an explorer who'd come upon, finally, the looked-for, longed-for country.

Maddie rolled away from her, and neither said anything for several moments.

Gerry tapped her on the shoulder, and she turned. Gerry scooped her up in her arms and kissed her head and sighed. "I was scared," she whispered. "I didn't know how I would feel."

"How *do* you feel?" Maddie asked, an undertone of laughter in her voice.

"Good."

"Is that all you can say? *Good?*"

"Okay, okay, better than good. Great." The feeling, though centered between her legs, rolled through her entire body. Making love to Maddie had always resulted in a deep emotional satisfaction, along with whispers and twinges in her body. Nothing like this. "Mostly," Gerry whispered, "I know how *you* feel. Because I've felt that way too. Like I'm God or something."

"Don't take the name of the Lord in vain," Maddie said, though she was laughing. "But I know what you mean."

❖

It turned out a few of the Mona's regulars they knew had actually switched over to going to Tadich Grill, a restaurant. It was the tourists that finally got to them, Pamela said.

"Mona's is a bore. Actually, if there isn't a singer onstage, the tourists become bored and turn to the gay girls for amusement. I, for one, have had enough of it. At least at Tadich, we aren't treated like creatures in a zoo."

They went out earlier and came home earlier since their evenings now consisted of supper, followed by a few drinks, rather than a hasty supper at home, followed by too much drinking later. Gerry was thrilled to get home earlier and into bed faster with Maddie. She would never admit it except to Pamela, but it was a relief and a thrill to let Maddie take the upper hand.

I didn't know what I was missing. The memories of their nights that kept streaming through her head gave her such jolts of pleasure she could scarcely concentrate when it came time to do an oil change or a brake job at the garage. Cadillac was beginning to have their buyers return whenever their cars needed service, so Gerry was busier at work than ever. She found, as well, that her happiness spurred her to a greater commitment to do an outstanding job at the dealership. She hadn't felt such joy in work since her pre-discharge navy days.

❖

"The rent's outrageous, but it's a good neighborhood," Wilma Grace told Maddie. The family was going to move over to Pierce Street to a Victorian duplex.

She added, "The rooms are so big, I feel like a kid again, but the neighborhood feels homey."

Knowing Wilma Grace meant that Colored people were there, Maddie smiled and asked, "Does Mama have the room she needs?"

"It's got a huge dining room. We'll eat in the kitchen, I guess."

"Well, how's she settling in?"

"You know she talks about you *all* the time."

"Does she ever mention Gerry?"

"No, baby sister. She don't."

Maddie nodded. *Well, it could be worse. Like if she stopped talking about me or speaking to me.*

Her mama accepted reality very well. They all did, because Sawyer's Southern culture required it. San Francisco had a new reality, and they would ease into it over time. Maddie made sure to spend as much time as she could with Mama. And it turned out Gerry was agreeable to a lot more change than Maddie had ever thought possible.

May 1947

They met Pamela, Woody, Sandy, Jake, and Trixie for dinner at the Tadich Grill.

"I want the steak," Gerry announced and slapped her menu on the table and smirked. Maddie gave her a small, sidelong smile as she looked at her menu. It was great to see her in such a good mood and even better to be the one responsible for it. Gerry's long resistance to her was forgotten; they were equals in pleasure.

It makes no never mind to me if you want to be the butch when we're in public. I'm fine. Just as long as you let me have my way when we're by ourselves.

"Sure thing, baby." Post-orgasm, Gerry was the picture of satisfaction. She grinned and stretched luxuriously.

Their food arrived, and they attacked it vigorously, chattering about a new movie—*Crossfire.*

Jake and Trixie had seen it. "It's a mystery, and the guy who was murdered was Jewish, and that's why he was killed," Trixie said.

"Thanks for giving away the movie plot. Now I don't have to see it," Woody said.

Trixie was unrepentant. She said, "I *did* not give away the plot.

There was a whole lot more to it than that." She crossed her arms, and Jake patted her shoulder.

"Sweetie, it's fine." She addressed the rest of the friends. "I didn't get what the big deal was. So he was a Jew and someone didn't like that?"

Pamela tapped her fingers on the table and tilted her head. "We just fought an entire world war about that very thing. In case you forgot."

Jake looked confused. "Hey, whattaya mean? We had to stop Nazis from taking over the world."

Pamela raised an eyebrow. "The Nazis murdered Jewish people in concentration camps, millions of them. Entire families. Just for being Jewish. Remind you of anything?"

"I didn't know why you're looking at me like that. I don't know any Jews anyhow. What's your point?"

Maddie knew what Pamela was getting at, and so did Gerry. Jake could be a bit dense and prickly if she didn't understand something. They glanced at one another but kept quiet.

Pamela narrowed her eyes. "*We* may not be murdered, but we're not welcome in so-called polite society. Neither are Maddie's people. I see a sort of pattern here, don't you? Jews, Negroes, gay people?"

Maddie decided to keep her mouth shut. She didn't exactly dislike Jake, but she got the feeling that the only reason Jake tolerated her was because of Gerry. Jake was plain ignorant a lot of the time. Trixie was good people, though. Also, she didn't *need* to say anything because Pamela was making her point pretty good.

"I don't know what the hell you're talking about. I got nothing in common with Jews or n—" Jake stopped short and threw Maddie a glance. Jake said, "Negroes," exaggerating the vowels.

You sure don't, sister.

"You have something in common with gays. *You* are one."

Jake shifted in her chair. "It's not the same. Except for that, I'm a regular person."

"Exactly my point," Pamela said, crisply. "We're all just 'regular people.'" She glared at Jake, who looked away and drew a savage drag on her cigarette without saying anything further.

"Never mind. I wanted to show you all what someone gave me over at Mona's the other night. I was most impressed with it. I'd love to know who wrote it. All the woman who gave it to me said was she got it from someone who got it from someone else in a bar in Los Angeles."

"Can I see it?" Maddie asked.

Pamela handed the carbon-copied pages to her.

Maddie read the title: *Vice Versa—America's Gayest Magazine.* That was certainly catchy. Gerry leaned over her shoulder to read it with her.

Pamela kept right on talking. "I couldn't believe I was reading something like this. Someone had the balls to put it in print. I think it's a gay girl, but I'm not sure."

"Look." Gerry pointed to the title. 'Here to Stay.'"

They all leaned in to read the article.

"Look at this." Maddie pointed to another line a few paragraphs down, in which the author predicted a future where society accepted gay people.

Maddie and Gerry looked at each other, wide-eyed. *What a thought.*

"Pamela, did you read this? All of it?" Gerry asked.

"I did. All of it." She nodded, smoking serenely.

Gerry read aloud the two lines that had jumped out to her for their sheer breathtaking boldness.

Pamela continued to smoke and nodded once or twice more. "That's why I wanted you all to see it."

Maddie asked, "Do you think she's right?" It must have taken Jake a few moments to absorb what she heard, because before Pamela could respond to Maddie's question, she sputtered and stated flatly, "That's plain stupid. Never going to happen."

Maddie watched Pamela's face. Pamela smiled her knowing smile, and Maddie got the impression it was because of what Jake had said.

"Well, predicting the future is fun, but no one knows for sure. Including you." She drilled a meaningful look into Jake, who snorted and looked away.

"But what do *you* think?" Gerry asked Pamela. Gerry, Maddie knew, was not inclined to take Jake too seriously about anything. On the other hand, her admiration of Pamela bordered on hero worship, especially since the recent change in their sex life. Though Maddie said it was her idea, it was Pamela who finally gave her the courage to go ahead.

Pamela stubbed out her smoke and paused. "I'd like to think what the author says will come true. I'm an optimist though, unlike some." She smiled cheerily at Jake. Trixie, Maddie noticed, was gazing thoughtfully at Pamela but for once was keeping her opinion to herself.

"Maybe someday," Gerry said, finally, and grinned at Maddie, who grinned back.

"Yeah, maybe." They looked at each other lovingly.

Pamela said, "And with that, I think I'd like a piece of apple pie for dessert. What do you say, girls?"

And they all started to talk at once.

Author's Note

The street car conductor Maddie meets, Marguerite, is Maya Angelou, age eighteen. She related the story of her time in San Francisco to Oprah Winfrey a few years back, and it's part of SF history that Maya Angelou was the first African American woman to work on Muni in the forties. Maddie's encounter with her is invented, but I think the advice that Marguerite gives to Maddie is true to what Maya Angelou would have said.

The newsletter the gang reads at the end of the book was real and created by a Los Angeles lesbian whose pseudonym was Lisa Ben. She wrote and published it herself anonymously, and it was passed around the lesbian bars of LA and San Francisco in the forties.

About the Author

Kathleen Knowles grew up in Pittsburgh, Pennsylvania, but has lived in San Francisco for more than thirty years. She finds the city's combination of history, natural beauty, and multicultural diversity inspiring and endlessly fascinating.

Other than writing, she loves music of all kinds, walking, bicycling, and stamp collecting. LGBT history and politics have compelled her attention for many years, starting with her first Pride march in Cleveland, Ohio, in 1978. She and her partner were married in July 2008 and live atop one of San Francisco's many hills with their pets. She retired in 2018 after working for twenty years as a health and safety specialist at the University of California, San Francisco.

She has written short stories, essays, and fan fiction. She is the author of nine novels.

Books Available From Bold Strokes Books

A Fairer Tomorrow by Kathleen Knowles. For Maddie Weeks and Gerry Stern, the Second World War brought them together, but the end of the war might rip them apart. (978-1-63555-874-6)

Changing Majors by Ana Hartnett Reichardt. Beyond a love, beyond a coming-out, Bailey Sullivan discovers what lies beyond the shame and self-doubt imposed on her by traditional Southern ideals. (978-1-63679-081-7)

Highland Whirl by Anna Larner. Opposites attract in the Scottish Highlands, when feisty Alice Campbell falls for city girl about town Roxanne Barns. (978-1-63555-892-0)

Holiday Hearts by Diana Day-Admire and Lyn Cole. Opposites attract during Christmastime chaos in Kansas City. (978-1-63679-128-9)

Humbug by Amanda Radley. With the corporate Christmas party in jeopardy, CEO Rosalind Caldwell hires Christmas Girl Ellie Pearce as her personal assistant. The only problem is, Ellie isn't a PA, has never planned a party, and develops a ridiculous crush on her totally intimidating new boss. (978-1-63555-965-1)

On the Rocks by Georgia Beers. Schoolteacher Vanessa Martini makes no apologies for her dating checklist, and newly single mom Grace Chapman ticks all Vanessa's Do Not Date boxes. Of course, they're never going to fall in love. (978-1-63555-989-7)

Song of Serenity by Brey Willows. Arguing with the Muse of music and justice is complicated, falling in love with her even more so. (978-1-63679-015-2)

The Christmas Proposal by Lisa Moreau. Stranded together in a Christmas village on a snowy mountain, Grace and Bridget face their past and question their dreams for the future. (978-1-63555-648-3)

Wisdom by Jesse J. Thoma. When Sophia and Reggie are chosen for the governor's new community design team and tasked with tackling substance abuse and mental health issues, battle lines are drawn even as sparks fly. (978-1-63555-886-9)

The Infinite Summer by Morgan Lee Miller. While spending the summer with her dad in a small beach town, Remi Brenner falls for Harper Hebert and accidentally finds herself tangled up in an intense restaurant rivalry between her famous stepmom and her first love. (978-1-63555-969-9)

A Convenient Arrangement by Aurora Rey and Jaime Clevenger. Cuffing season has come for lesbians, and for Jess Archer and Cody Dawson, their convenient arrangement becomes anything but. (978-1-63555-818-0)

An Alaskan Wedding by Nance Sparks. The last thing either Andrea or Riley expects is to bump into the one who broke her heart fifteen years ago, but when they meet at the welcome party, their feelings come rushing back. (978-1-63679-053-4)

Beulah Lodge by Cathy Dunnell. It's 1874, and newly betrothed Ruth Mallowes is set on marriage and life as a missionary…until she falls in love with the housemaid at Beulah Lodge. (978-1-63679-007-7)

Gia's Gems by Toni Logan. When Lindsey Speyer discovers that popular travel columnist Gia Williams is a complete fake and threatens to expose her, blackmail has never been so sexy. (978-1-63555-917-0)

Holiday Wishes & Mistletoe Kisses by M. Ullrich. Four holidays, four couples, four chances to make their wishes come true. (978-1-63555-760-2)

Love By Proxy by Dena Blake. Tess has a secret crush on her best friend, Sophie, so the last thing she wants is to help Sophie fall in love with someone else, but how can she stand in the way of her happiness? (978-1-63555-973-6)

Marry Me by Melissa Brayden. Allison Hale attempts to plan the wedding of the century to a man who could save her family's business, if only she wasn't falling for her wedding planner, Megan Kinkaid. (978-1-63555-932-3)

Pathway to Love by Radclyffe. Courtney Valentine is looking for a woman exactly like Ben—smart, sexy, and not in the market for anything serious. All she has to do is convince Ben that sex-without-strings is the perfect pathway to pleasure. (978-1-63679-110-4)

Sweet Surprise by Jenny Frame. Flora and Mac never thought they'd ever see each other again, but when Mac opens up her barber shop right next to Flora's sweet shop, their connection comes roaring back. (978-1-63679-001-5)

The Edge of Yesterday by CJ Birch. Easton Gray is sent from the future to save humanity from technological disaster. When she's forced to target the woman she's falling in love with, can Easton do what's needed to save humanity? (978-1-63679-025-1)

The Scout and the Scoundrel by Barbara Ann Wright. With unexpected danger surrounding them, Zara and Roni are stuck between duty and survival, with little room for exploring their feelings, especially love. (978-1-63555-978-1)

Can't Leave Love by Kimberly Cooper Griffin. Sophia and Pru have no intention of falling in love, but sometimes love happens when and where you least expect it. (978-1-636790041-1)

Free Fall at Angel Creek by Julie Tizard. Detective Dee Rawlings and aircraft accident investigator Dr. River Dawson use conflicting methods to find answers when a plane goes missing, while overcoming surprising threats and discovering an unlikely chance at love. (978-1-63555-884-5)

Love's Compromise by Cass Sellars. For Piper Holthaus and Brook Myers, will professional dreams and past baggage stop two hearts from realizing they are meant for each other? (978-1-63555-942-2)

Not All a Dream by Sophia Kell Hagin. Hester has lost the woman she loved, and the world has descended into relentless dark and cold. But giving up will have to wait when she stumbles upon people who help her survive. (978-1-63679-067-1)

The Secrets of Willowra by Kadyan. A family saga of three women, their homestead called Willowra in the Australian outback, and the secrets that link them all. (978-1-63679-064-0)

Turbulent Waves by Ali Vali. Kai Merlin and Vivien Palmer plan their future together as hostile forces make their own plans to destroy what they have, as well as all those they love. (978-1-63679-011-4)

Protecting the Lady by Amanda Radley. If Eve Webb had known she'd be protecting royalty, she'd never have taken the job as bodyguard, but as the threat to Lady Katherine's life draws closer, she'll do whatever it takes to save her, and may just lose her heart in the process. (978-1-63679-003-9)

Trial by Fire by Carsen Taite. When prosecutor Lennox Roy and public defender Wren Bishop become fierce adversaries in a headline-grabbing arson case, their attraction ignites a passion that leads them both to question their assumptions about the law, the truth, and each other. (978-1-63555-860-9)

Unbreakable by Cari Hunter. When Dr. Grace Kendal is forced at gunpoint to help an injured woman, she is dragged into a nightmare where nothing is quite as it seems, and their lives aren't the only ones on the line. (978-1-63555-961-3)

Veterinary Surgeon by Nancy Wheelton. When dangerous drugs are stolen from the veterinary clinic, Mitch investigates and Kay becomes a suspect. As pride and professions clash, love seems impossible. (978-1-63679-043-5)(978-1-63679-051-0)

All That Remains by Sheri Lewis Wohl. Johnnie and Shantel might have to risk their lives—and their love—to stop a werewolf intent on killing. (978-1-63555-949-1)

Beginner's Bet by Fiona Riley. Phenom luxury Realtor Ellison Gamble has everything, except a family to share it with, so when a mix-up brings youthful Katie Crawford into her life, she bets the house on love. (978-1-63555-733-6)

Dangerous Without You by Lexus Grey. Throughout their senior year in high school, Aspen, Remington, Denna, and Raleigh face challenges in life and romance that they never expect. (978-1-63555-947-7)

Desiring More by Raven Sky. In this collection of steamy stories, a rich variety of lovers find themselves desiring more: more from a lover, more from themselves, and more from life. (978-1-63679-037-4)